66°NORTH

MICHAEL RIDPATH
66°NORTH

CORVUS

First published in Great Britain in 2011
by Corvus, an imprint of Atlantic Books Ltd.

9 8 7 6 5 4 3 2 1

A CIP catalogue record for this book is available from
the British Library.

ISBN: 978-1-84887-400-8 (hardback)
ISBN: 978-1-84887-401-5 (trade paperback)

Printed in Great Britain by the MPG Books Group

Corvus
An imprint of Atlantic Books Ltd
Ormond House
26-27 Boswell Street
London WC1N 3JZ

www.corvus-books.co.uk

for Julia, Laura and Nicholas

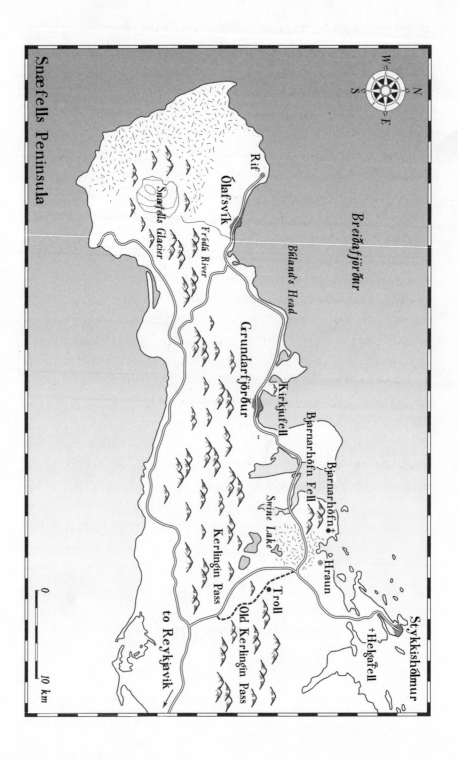

CHAPTER ONE

January 2009

ICELAND WAS ANGRY. As angry as it had ever been since the first Vikings stepped ashore in Reykjavík's smoky bay one thousand years before.

And Harpa, Harpa was angrier still.

She stood with four thousand other Icelanders in the square outside the Parliament building shouting, chanting, banging. She had brought a saucepan and a lid, which she beat together. Others had all kinds of kitchen implements, as well as tambourines, drums, whistles, a trawler's foghorn, anything that could make a noise. A tiny old lady next to her stood straight and defiant, banging her Zimmer frame against the ground, yelling, her eyes alight with fury.

The din was chaotic. The earlier rhythm of the crowd had deteriorated into a cacophony of anger, disjointed chants of 'Ólafur out!', 'Rotten Government!' and the simple 'Resign!'. It was the middle of January and it was cold – there was a dusting of snow on the ground. Making noise kept Harpa warm. But the shouting and banging also gave vent to the anger and the hatred that had been boiling inside her for months, like volcanic steam spitting out into the cold air from the country's geothermal depths.

It was getting dark. The flares and the torches that many had brought with them glowed brighter in the failing light. Lights blazed inside the Parliament, a small building of blackened basalt.

The people had gathered, just as they had gathered every Saturday for the previous seventeen weeks, to tell the politicians to do something about the mess that they had got Iceland into. Except this was a Tuesday, the first day of the Parliamentary session. The protests were becoming more insistent, the noise of the people was building up to a crescendo, the Prime Minister and the government had to resign and call elections. Ólafur Tómasson, the former Governor of the Central Bank and now Prime Minister, who had privatized the banks and then connived at them borrowing more – much more – than they could ever repay, he had to resign too.

This was the first time Harpa had been to one of these demonstrations. At first she hadn't approved of them, thought violence and conflict was not the Icelandic way, that the demonstrators didn't understand the complexities of the situation. But, along with thousands of other Icelanders, she had lost her job. She could do the sums, she knew that the debt the Icelandic banks had run up would take the nation decades to pay off. Markús, her son, was only three. He would still be bailing them out when he was forty.

It was wrong! It was so wrong.

Ólafur Tómasson was to blame. The other politicians were to blame. The bankers were to blame. And Gabríel Örn was to blame.

Of course she had played her own part. That had kept her away from the earlier demonstrations. But now as she banged and shouted, the guilt just added to her fury.

Proceedings had started in an orderly way, with rousing speeches by a writer, a musician and an eight-year-old girl. Icelandic flags had been waved, protest banners fluttered, the atmosphere was more carnival than riot.

But people were angry and getting angrier.

The police in their black uniforms and helmets formed a line in front of the parliament building, ushering in the politicians through the mob. They carried batons, shields and red canisters of pepper spray. Some squared up to the crowd, broad and tall. Some bit their lips.

Eggs and pots of *skyr*, Icelandic yoghurt, flew through the air. Protesters dressed in black, their faces covered in balaclavas or scarves, ran at the police line. The crowd surged. Some people, many people, shouted for the protesters to leave the police alone. Others cheered them on. The police lines buckled. Now it wasn't just yoghurt being thrown, it was flagstones as well. A police-woman fell to the ground, blood running down her face.

Whistles blew. The black uniforms raised their canisters and squirted pepper spray into the throng.

The crowd recoiled. Harpa was sent reeling backwards and tripped over the man behind her. For a moment she thought she was going to be trampled. A boot crunched her leg. She lay on her back and raised the saucepan in an attempt to protect her face. Anger turned to fear.

Powerful arms lifted her to her feet and pulled her back from the crowd.

'Are you all right? I'm sorry, I didn't mean to knock you over.'

The man was lean and strong, with thick dark eyebrows and deep blue eyes. Harpa felt a jolt as she looked up at him. She couldn't speak.

'Here, let's get back out of this.'

She nodded and followed the man as he pushed back through the mob towards the edge of the square, where the crowd was more sparse. The hand on her arm was broad and callused, a fisherman's hand, her father's hand.

'Thank you,' Harpa said, bending to rub her shin where the boot had dug into it.

'Are you hurt?' He smiled. A stiff, reserved smile, but betraying concern.

'I'll be OK.'

A kid barged past them, spluttering as he ripped off his balaclava and rubbed his eyes. He couldn't have been more than fourteen. Another protester tipped back the boy's head and poured milk into his eyes to soothe them.

'Idiot,' Harpa said. 'All this isn't the police's fault.'

3

'Perhaps not,' said the man. 'But we need the politicians to take notice. Maybe this is what it will take.'

'Bah, it's pathetic!' A deep voice rumbled from just behind them. Harpa and her rescuer turned to see a broad-shouldered middle-aged man with puffy eyes, a scrappy grey beard and ponytail, frowning down on them. His stomach hung out over his jeans and he was wearing a broad-brimmed leather hat. Harpa thought she recognized him from somewhere, but she wasn't sure.

'What do you mean?' said Harpa.

'Icelanders are pathetic. This is the time for a real revolution. We can't just sit around and talk politely about change and bang our pots and pans. The people need to take control. Now.'

Harpa's eyes widened as she listened. With the fisherman next to her, her fear was diminishing and the anger reappearing. He was right, damn it. He was right.

'Aren't you Sindri?' the fisherman asked. 'Sindri Pálsson?'

The man nodded.

'I've read your book. *Capital Rape.*'

'And?' The big man raised his eyebrows.

'I thought it was a bit extreme. Now I am not so sure.'

The big man laughed.

Now Harpa knew where she had seen his face. He had been a punk rocker in the early eighties, a one-hit wonder and had re-emerged two decades later as an Icelandic anarchist writer.

'My name is Björn,' the fisherman said and held out his hand. Sindri shook it.

'And you?' Sindri asked Harpa. She could smell alcohol on his breath and she recognized the look of interest in his eyes as he examined her. She might be an unemployed single mother in her late thirties, but men still liked what they saw, especially older men.

'Harpa,' she said, glancing quickly at the man named Björn as she did so. He smiled. God, he was attractive. There was something about him, or maybe it was just something about her, the afterglow of letting out all that anger.

He was certainly more attractive than Gabríel Örn. Pity he was a fisherman. Rule one ever since she had been a teenager was don't date fishermen.

'Ólafur out!' Sindri roared suddenly, punching a fist in the air.

The big man was a magnificent sight, bellowing his lungs out, his ponytail bobbing.

Harpa glanced at Björn. 'Ólafur out!' she shouted.

Night fell. The protest intensified. The older protesters left: the proportion of demonstrators with their hoods up and faces covered increased. The Christmas tree in the middle of the square toppled: in a moment it was on fire. Drums beat, people danced. Harpa and Björn stuck to Sindri, who moved through the throng chatting to all and sundry between bellows. Following him, Harpa felt part of the crowd, and her anger flared again.

Finally, the police had had enough. 'Gas! Gas!' the crowd shouted.

A moment later something stung Harpa's eyes. She bent over and Björn pulled her away. Something tickled her throat. They ran back out of the square, surrounded by hundreds of people, escaping before all but a particle or two of the gas reached their lungs. They lost Sindri for a moment, and then found him talking to a young man with his shirt off plunging his face into a bucket of water. The boy had spiky red hair and his torso glowed pink in the cold and the light of the flares. Sindri seemed to be congratulating him and slapping him on his back. The boy was shivering, but he was angry and the anger was keeping him warm.

They were standing a couple of hundred metres away from the square, right next to the impressive statue of Ingólfur Arnarson, who was that first Viking settler to step ashore in Reykjavík's smoky bay.

'At least the gas doesn't bother him,' said Sindri. 'If the country was still run by people like him they'd know exactly what to do with the bankers and the politicians.'

Harpa admired the statue's strong muscles. 'I wonder if he really looked like that,' she said.

'He always seemed a bit camp to me,' said Sindri. 'The way he's leaning on his shield, sticking his hip out.'

'Oh, no,' said Harpa. 'He's all man.'

'He was probably short and fat with a double chin,' said Björn. The three of them laughed.

'Come back to my place for a drink,' Sindri said to Harpa and Björn. 'It's just around the corner.' They exchanged glances: if you will, so will I.

'OK,' said Harpa. So they followed Sindri, together with the boy who was still bare chested, waving his shirt in the air in disgust.

'Another one, Harpa?'

Harpa nodded as Sindri refilled her glass from the brandy bottle. Her head was pleasantly fuzzy, the alcohol adding to the chemicals released by her own body during the glorious turmoil of the demonstration. It was weeks since she had had a proper drink. She had always been suspicious of people who drank in the middle of the week, but this was no ordinary Tuesday.

They were in Sindri's small flat, the five of them: Sindri, Harpa, Björn, the red-haired boy and a short, neatly dressed man, young enough to be a student, who had latched on to them somewhere along the way. The boy's name was Frikki, and the student's Ísak.

Sindri was enjoying himself, playing to the small crowd, and in particular playing to her. He had seated her next to him on a tatty sofa, Björn and Ísak the student sat on old armchairs facing them, and Frikki was slumped on the floor. The flat was a dump: small, cracked ceiling, scratched wooden floor, books, newspapers, magazines and ashtrays filled with cigarette stubs everywhere. There was washing-up in the sink in the alcove of the room that acted as a kitchen. The only things brightening up the place were three or four landscapes dotted around the walls, the biggest of which portrayed a farmer carrying an unconscious girl over the moors.

They had finished a bottle of red wine and were on to the brandy.

Harpa played up to Sindri; she was flattered by the attention and what he said was interesting. But it was Björn she was most aware of. He sat coolly listening to Sindri, calm, composed and furious. He wasn't trying any of the classic male competition for her attention, but she did catch him shooting the occasional glance at her.

She was enjoying herself. For a moment she felt guilty about leaving Markús, but her mother would be very happy looking after him. She was always telling Harpa to stop moping around, to get out more and meet a man. She was right. Since Gabríel Örn had betrayed her, Harpa had spent nearly all her time cooped up in her little house in Seltjarnarnes.

'I know I don't look like it,' Sindri was saying, 'but I am a farmer. Or at least my family are farmers. Until the bank forces them to sell up, that is.'

'What happened?' Harpa asked.

'Everyone's getting squeezed,' Sindri said. 'Even the farmers. My brother, who runs the farm now, can't make his payments. So it's *finito*.' Sindri made a throat-cutting sign with his forefinger. 'Just like that. A farm that has been around for generations, that was mentioned in the Book of Settlements, is destroyed. It breaks my heart.'

It was Harpa's understanding that farms were one of the few sectors of the economy actually doing well with the fall of the króna, but she didn't want to contradict Sindri in full flow.

He turned to her. 'It is the farmers who are the real soul of Iceland. Like Bjartur there.' He pointed to the painting of the peasant carrying the girl. 'I did that, you know.'

'It's good,' said Harpa. And it was. You could tell the brushstrokes were by an amateur, but the painting managed to portray nobility in a harsh but beautiful landscape.

'The farmers and the fishermen,' Sindri went on, taking the compliment in his stride. 'Men who will work hard in tough conditions, who save, who fight to earn a living on the fells or on the waves. And not just men, women. We have the toughest, most independent women in the world. We have needed them to survive. And now these bankers, these lawyers, these politicians, all they know how to do is spend and borrow, spend and borrow. The kids of today don't know how to do real work, what it's like to tramp over the fells in a howling gale looking for lost sheep.'

'Some of us do,' said Frikki. 'Until two weeks ago I spent all my waking life in a hellhole of a kitchen producing food for these guys to eat. And the prices they would pay! Ten thousand krónur for some swordfish flown in from the Pacific when we have perfectly good fish of our own all around us.'

'Sorry, Frikki,' Sindri said. 'You are right, not everyone has forgotten. There are many of us perfectly good Icelanders still willing and able to do real jobs. We have always been here. It's just no one has listened to us.'

Harpa wondered whether Sindri had ever done a 'real job' since he had left the farm. But he had a point. He was just the kind of guy she would have dismissed with contempt as an ignorant idealist a couple of months before, but now she thought he had a point.

'What chance have I of finding a real job?' Frikki asked. 'There's nothing out there.'

'What about you, Björn?' Sindri asked.

'I'm a fisherman,' Björn said. 'From Grundarfjördur. I rode down here on my motorbike this morning for the demonstration. And I agree with you, Sindri. I go out as often as my quota will allow, and I still can't earn enough to pay off my debts. There are many like me. The banks told us to borrow in foreign currencies because the interest rates were lower. And now they say that not only have my own debts doubled because of the collapse of the króna, but I have to pay off all the money the banks borrowed from the British and the Dutch to lend to me too. It's absurd. Mad.'

Harpa felt distinctly uncomfortable with the way the conversation was going.

Someone else had noticed her discomfort. 'What about you, Harpa?' It was Ísak, the student. He was watching her closely. She could tell he had somehow guessed what she was, or what she used to be, despite the months of unemployment. Was it the way she spoke, her clothes, something about her attitude? Harpa didn't like him. There was something creepy about his cool detachment, something at odds with the outrage of the rest of them. But she had to answer his question.

'Like Frikki I have lost my job.'

'Jesus!' Sindri snorted. 'Another one!'

'And what job was that?' Ísak asked quietly.

Harpa could feel herself blushing. Embarrassment. Shame. Guilt. They all washed over her. She felt they were all looking at her, but she avoided them, staring down into her glass of brandy, letting her dark curly hair flop down to hide her eyes.

There was silence. Björn coughed. She looked up to meet his eyes.

She had to accept who she was. What she and people like her had done. How she had been used as well.

'I was a banker. I worked for Óðinsbanki until two months ago when I was fired by my boyfriend. Somehow I never quite managed to get hold of all the cash everyone else had. And what cash I did have was tied up in Óðinsbanki shares which are now worthless.'

'Didn't you see it coming?' asked Ísak.

'No. No, I didn't,' said Harpa. 'I believed it all. The story that we were all financial geniuses, younger and quicker and smarter than the others. That we were the Viking Raiders of the twenty-first century. That we took calculated risks and won. That the wealth was here to stay. That this was just the beginning of the prosperity, not the end.' She shook her head. 'I was wrong. Sorry.'

There was silence for a moment.

'Capitalism carries the seeds of its own destruction,' said Ísak. 'It's as true now as it was a hundred and fifty years ago when Marx first said it. You wrote about that, Sindri.'

Sindri nodded, clearly pleased at the reference to his book. 'At least we have heard an apology,' he said.

'We're all screwed,' Björn said. 'All of us.'

'Can't we do something?' said Frikki. 'Sometimes I'd just like to beat the shit out of these guys.'

'I know what you mean,' said Björn. 'The politicians aren't going to do anything, are they? Is Ólafur Tómasson really going to lock up all his best friends? They appoint these special prosecutors, but they'll never get hold of the bankers. They all disappeared to London or New York. And they want our money to clean up their mess.'

'It's true,' said Harpa. 'Óskar Gunnarsson is the chairman of my bank. He's been skulking in London the whole time. He hasn't been seen in Reykjavík for the last three months. But some of the others are still here. I know they still have money stashed away.'

'Like who?' said Ísak.

'Like Gabríel Örn Bergsson, my former boss. When he was encouraging me to take out a loan from Óðinsbanki to buy shares in it to prop up the stock price, he was selling those very same shares himself. When he made bad loans to companies in the UK, it was me who took the blame, even though I had told him not to do the deals. And when the bank was nationalized and they brought back the old rule that two people in a relationship couldn't work together, it was me who was fired.'

'Sounds like a nice guy,' said Björn.

Harpa shook her head. 'You know, he never was a nice guy, really. He was funny. He was successful. But he was always a bastard.'

'So where is he right now?' asked Ísak.

'You mean at this minute?' said Harpa.

Ísak nodded.

'I've no idea,' Harpa said. 'It's a Tuesday night. He must be at home – I'm quite sure he wasn't at the demo. He lives in one of those apartments in the Shadow District, just around the corner.'

'Do you think he knows where the money is?'

'Maybe,' said Harpa. 'Yeah, maybe.'

'Why don't we ask him?' said Ísak.

Sindri smiled, the puffy skin under his eyes rumpling. 'Yeah. Get him over here. Let him tell us where those thieving bastards have hidden the money. And he can try to defend how he treated you. How he treated all of us.'

'Yeah. And I'll smash his face in,' Frikki slurred.

Harpa's immediate reaction was to refuse. It wasn't as if Gabríel would ever tell a bunch of drunk strangers the details of the complicated network of inter-company loans that Óðinsbanki had set up. They wouldn't understand him even if he did. But on the other hand... On the other hand why shouldn't Gabríel meet the people he had screwed? Own up to who he was as she had just done? Why the hell shouldn't he? The bastard deserved it, boy did he deserve it. Revenge feels good when you have had a couple of brandies.

'All right,' she said. 'But it will be difficult. I'm not sure how I can get him to come here.'

'Couldn't you say you had something you needed to discuss with him?' Sindri said.

'At a bar, maybe. Or at his house. But not with a bunch of strangers.'

'Get him to meet you at a bar in town and we'll stop him on the way,' said Ísak. 'Bring him back here.'

Harpa considered Ísak's suggestion. 'OK,' she said. 'I'll give it a go.'

It was nearly midnight. The bars in Reykjavík would still be open, but it would be hard to force Gabríel out.

She pulled out her mobile phone and selected his number. She was surprised she hadn't deleted him from her address book. He should have been deleted totally from her life.

'Yes?' he answered with little more than a croak.

'It's me. I need to see you. Tonight.'

'Uh. What time is it? I've just gone to sleep. This is ridiculous.'

'It's important.'

'Can't it wait?'

'No. It's got to be right now.'

'Harpa, are you drunk? You're drunk, aren't you?'

'Of course I'm not drunk!' Harpa protested. 'I'm tired and I'm upset and I need to see you.'

'What is it? Why can't you tell me over the phone?'

Harpa's brain was fuzzy, but an idea was emerging. 'It's not the kind of thing you can discuss over the phone.'

'Oh, my God, Harpa, you're not pregnant are you?'

Gabríel had obviously stumbled on the same idea.

'I said not over the phone. But meet me at B5. In fifteen minutes.'

'All right,' said Gabríel and hung up.

Harpa rang off. 'Done,' she said. B5 was a bar on Bankastraeti, a street that rose eastwards up a gentle hill from Austurvöllur, the square outside the Parliament building, to Laugavegur, the main shopping street. She and Gabríel Örn used to go there with their friends on Friday nights. 'I know the way he will take, we can cut him off.'

'Let's go,' said Frikki.

Sindri's flat was on Hverfisgata, a scruffy street that ran parallel to Bankastraeti and Laugavegur, between those roads and the bay. As they spilled out into the open air, Harpa felt exhilarated. The frustration and misery of the last few months were pouring out. Sure, the bankers and the politicians were to blame, but one man was most to blame for ruining Harpa's life.

Gabríel Örn.

And in a moment he would come face-to-face with the ordinary decent people whom men like him held in such contempt. He would try and weasel out of it, but she wouldn't let him. She would *force* him to stand in front of them and apologize and explain what a shit he was.

The cold didn't sober Harpa up, but it energized her. She led the way, hurrying the others on. The Skuggahverfi or Shadow District was a new development of high-rise luxury apartments that lined the shore of the bay. Only a few had actually been finished before the developers had run out of money; they looked down on their half-completed brethren, and the condemned buildings surrounding them, like Sindri's place, yet to be demolished. She was only about a hundred metres from the spot where Gabríel Örn would cross Hverfisgata on his way to B5.

A couple of snowflakes fell. It was late, but there were still people on the street, jazzed up by the demonstrations. Down at the bottom of the hill towards the square outside Parliament, flames rose out of a wheelie bin, illuminating hooded shadows flitting around it, and two firecrackers went off.

Harpa led them down one of the little side streets off Hverfisgata, on the route she knew Gabríel would take. Sure enough, there he was, head down against the snow.

She stopped in front of him. 'Gabríel Örn.'

He looked up in surprise. 'Harpa? I thought we were going to meet at the bar?'

Harpa felt a surge of revulsion as she saw his face. He was a couple of years younger than her, a little flabby around the jowls and neck, fair hair thinning. What had she ever seen in him?

'No, I want you to come with us.'

Gabríel Örn glanced behind her.

'Who are these people?'

'They are my friends, Gabríel Örn, my friends. I want you to talk to my friends. That's why you have to come back with me.'

'You *are* drunk, Harpa!'

'I don't care. Now come with us.'

Harpa reached out to grab Gabríel on the sleeve. Roughly he shook her off. Frikki growled and strode up to him. The boy wasn't wearing a coat, only his Chelsea football shirt, but he was too drunk to care.

'You heard her,' he said, stopping centimetres away from Gabríel. 'You're coming with us.' He reached out to grab the lapel of Gabríel's coat. Gabríel pushed him back. Frikki swung at him, a long wide arc that someone as sober as Gabríel had no trouble avoiding. Gabríel was a good fifteen centimetres shorter than Frikki, but with one hard jab upwards, he caught Frikki on the chin and felled him.

As Frikki sat on the ground, rubbing his jaw, Harpa was surprised. She had never expected Gabríel to be capable of such physical prowess.

Gabríel turned to go.

The anger exploded in Harpa's head, a red curtain of fury. He was *not* going to walk away from them, he was *not*.

'Gabríel! Stop.' She reached out to grab him, but he pushed her back. She lurched into a low wall surrounding a small car park. On the wall was an empty Thule beer bottle. She picked it up, took three steps forward and, aiming for the bald spot on the back of Gabríel Örn's head, brought it crashing down.

He staggered, swayed to the right and fell, his head bouncing off an iron bollard at the entrance of the little car park with a sickening crack.

He lay still.

Harpa dropped the bottle, her hand flying to her mouth. 'Oh, God!'

Frikki roared and ran at the prone body of Gabríel Örn, launching a kick hard into his ribs. He kicked him twice in the chest and once in the head before Björn grabbed him around the waist and flung him to the ground.

In a moment, Björn was on his knees examining Gabríel Örn.

The banker was motionless. His eyes were closed. His already pale face had taken on a waxy sheen. A snowflake landed on his cheek. Blood seeped out of his skull beneath his short thin hair.

'He's not breathing,' Harpa whispered.

Then she screamed. 'He's not breathing!'

CHAPTER TWO

August 1934

'A AAGH!'
Hallgrímur swung his axe as they came at him. Eight of them. In a frenzy, he chopped off the leg of the first warrior, and the head of the second. His axe split the third's shield. The fourth he hit in the face with his own shield. Swish! Swish! Two more down. The last two ran away, and who could blame them?

Hallgrímur flopped back against the stone cairn, panting, the fury leaving him drained. 'I got eight of them, Benni,' he said.

'Yes, and you got me too,' said his friend, rubbing his mouth. 'It's bleeding. One of my teeth is loose.'

'It's just a baby tooth,' said Hallgrímur. 'It was coming out anyway.'

He relaxed and let the weak sun stroke his face. He loved the feeling right after he had gone berserk. He really felt that there was so much repressed anger in him, so much aggression, that he was a modern berserker.

And this was his favourite spot. Right in the middle of the twisted waves of congealed stone that was Berserkjahraun, or Berserkers' Lava Field. It was a beautiful, eerie, magical place of little towers, folds and wrinkles of stone, speckled with lime green moss, darker green heather, and the deep red leaves of bog bilberries.

The lava field was named after the two warriors who had been brought over to Iceland as servants from Sweden a thousand years before by Vermundur the Lean, the man who owned Hallgrímur's family's farm, Bjarnarhöfn. The Swedes had the ability to make themselves go berserk in battle, when with superhuman strength they could smite all before them. They proved a handful for the farmer of Bjarnarhöfn, who passed them on to his brother Styr at Hraun, Benedikt's farm on the other side of the lava field.

There had been trouble between Styr and his new servants, and the berserkers had ended up buried under the cairn of lava stone and moss, right where Hallgrímur was leaning.

Of course Hallgrímur had grown up knowing the story of the two berserkers, but his friend Benedikt had just started reading the *Saga of the People of Eyri*, and had come up with all sorts of new details, the best of which was that one of the berserkers had the same name as him, Halli. At eight, Benedikt was two years younger than Hallgrímur, but he was a brilliant reader for his age. Their favourite game had become to stalk the lava field pretending to be the berserkers. It worked quite well, Hallgrímur thought. Benedikt came up with the stories, but Hallgrímur was much better at going berserk. And that was, after all, the point.

'What shall we do now?' he asked Benedikt. It was more of a command for Benedikt to come up with another game than a question.

'Any sign of your parents?' Benedikt asked.

'Father won't be back for ages. He's gone to look for a ewe on the fell. I'll just check for Mother.'

The cairn was in a depression, out of sight of grown-ups, which made it such a good playing place. Hallgrímur climbed the ancient footpath between the two farms, which had been hewn out of the lava a millennium before by the berserkers themselves, and looked west towards Bjarnarhöfn. It was a prosperous farm, nestling beneath a waterfall which tumbled down the side of Bjarnarhöfn Fell. It was surrounded by a large home field, bright green against the brown of the surrounding heath. A tiny wooden church, little more than a black hut, lay between the farm and the grey flatness of Breidafjördur, the broad fjord dotted with low islands. Just up from the shoreline were wooden racks on which lines of salted fish hung out to dry. Hallgrímur could see no sign of life. His mother had said she was going to clean the church, something she did obsessively. This seemed a pointless activity to Hallgrímur, since the pastor only held services there once a month.

But there was no reasoning with his mother.

He was supposed to be in the room he shared with his brother, doing arithmetic problems. But he had sneaked out to play with Benedikt.

'All right,' said Benedikt. 'I have heard that Arnkell's men have stolen some of our horses. We must find them and free the horses. But we must take them by surprise.'

'That's a good idea,' said Hallgrímur. He wasn't entirely sure who Arnkell was, he was probably a chieftain from the saga. Benedikt would know the details.

They crept southwards through the lava field. It had spewed out of the big mountains to the south several thousand years ago, ending up in the fjord just between the two farms at a place called Hraunsvík, or Lava Bay. For several kilometres it flowed in a tumult of stone and moss, twenty or thirty metres above the surrounding plain. It was possible to crawl along the wrinkles of the lava, to slither through cracks, to lurk behind the extraordinary shapes that reared upwards. There was one spot where the lava seemed to form the silhouettes of two horses standing together, when viewed from a certain angle. That was where they were heading.

They had been crawling and sliding for five minutes when Hallgrímur suddenly heard a grunt ahead of them.

'What was that?' Hallgrímur turned to Benedikt.

'I don't know,' Benedikt squeaked. A look of terror on his face. 'It sounds like some kind of animal.'

'Perhaps it's the Kerlingin troll come down from the Pass.'

'Don't be silly,' said Hallgrímur. But he swallowed. The grunting was getting louder. It sounded like a man.

Then there was a short, high pitched squeal.

'That's Mother!' Hallgrímur wriggled forward, ignoring Benedikt's whispered pleas to come away. His heart was beating. He had no idea what he would see. Could it really be his mother, and if so was she in some kind of danger?

Perhaps the berserkers were walking through the lava field again.

He hesitated as the fear almost overcame him, but Hallgrímur was brave. He swallowed and wriggled on.

There, on a cushion of moss in a hollow, he saw a man's bare bottom pumping up and down over a woman, half dressed, her face, surrounded by a pillow of golden hair, tilted directly towards him. She didn't see him; her eyes were shut and little mewling sounds came from her parted lips.

Mother.

Mother seemed to be in a good mood at dinner that evening. Father had returned from the fell having found the ewe stuck in a gully.

His mother was very fond of her children, or most of them. She was proud of Hallgrímur's obedient little brother, and of his three sisters, whom she was raising to be hard working, honest and capable women about the farm.

But Hallgrímur. She just didn't like Hallgrímur.

'Halli! How did you scratch your knees?' she demanded.

'I didn't scratch them,' Hallgrímur said. He always denied everything stubbornly. It never worked.

'Yes you did. That's blood. And they are dirty.'

Hallgrímur looked down. It was true. 'Er, I fell coming up the stairs.'

'You were playing in the lava field, weren't you? When I specifically told you to do your schoolwork.'

'No, I swear I wasn't. I was here all the time.'

'Do you take me for an idiot?' His mother raised her voice. 'Gunnar, will you control your son? Stop him lying to his mother.'

His father didn't seem to like Hallgrímur much either. But he liked his wife even less, despite her beauty.

'Leave the boy alone,' he said.

His mother's good mood was long gone. 'To your room, Halli! Right now! And don't come down until you have finished your homework. Your brother can eat your *skyr*.'

Hallgrímur stood up and looked mournfully at the dish of *skyr* and berries he was abandoning. He sauntered towards the hallway and the stairs.

He paused at the door.

'You are right, Mother. I did go to play in the lava field with Benni.'

He was pleased to see his mother's cheeks flush.

'I saw you and Benni's father,' he went on. 'What were you doing?'

'Out!' his mother cried. 'To your room!'

That night, after all the children were in bed with the lamps snuffed out, Hallgrímur heard his father shouting and his mother sobbing.

The little boy fell asleep with a smile on his face.

CHAPTER THREE

Wednesday, 16 September 2009

SERGEANT DETECTIVE MAGNUS Jonson of the Boston Police Department closed his eyes as he slipped into the deliciously warm water. His body tingled after the thirty lengths he had done and the shock of warm water after cold air. It was six degrees Celsius in the outside air, but forty degrees in the geothermally heated tub. Steam hovered a couple of feet above the Olympic sized pool, which was crowded with serious swimmers. It was six o'clock, rush hour in the open-air Laugardalur Baths, as Reykjavík's men and women gathered after work for a swim and a chat. The fact that they were outside and nearly naked on a cold grey September evening didn't bother any of them.

'Ooh, that feels good,' said the tall, skinny man who slid in beside Magnus. 'You're a fast swimmer.'

'I've got to get rid of the energy somehow, Árni,' Magnus said. 'And the aggression.'

'Aggression?'

'Yeah. I'm not used to sitting around in a classroom all day.'

'What you mean is you would rather be running around the streets of Boston blasting punks with your three fifty-seven Magnum?'

Magnus glanced at his companion. Despite living in Reykjavík for four months, Magnus was never entirely sure when Icelanders were being serious. It was a particular problem with Árni Holm. He was good at the deadpan irony. On the other hand he occasionally said the most spectacularly stupid things. 'Something like that, Árni.'

'I hear your course is pretty good. There's a waiting list of people to sign up for it. Did you know that?'

'You should come.'

'I'm on the list.'

Magnus was teaching a course at the National Police College on urban crime in the United States. He enjoyed being an instructor; it was something he had never done before and it turned out he was good at it.

He had been seconded to the Icelandic police at the request of the National Police Commissioner who was worried about big-city crime hitting his small country. Not that crime was unknown in Iceland. There were drugs aplenty and Friday and Saturday nights brought a regular haul of drunks into the cells at police head-quarters. And of course there had been the winter demonstrations outside the Parliament that had culminated in the 'pots-and-pans' revolution which overthrew the government and stretched police resources to their limits.

But the Commissioner feared that it was only a matter of time before the kind of crimes that occurred in Amsterdam or Copenhagen or even Boston arrived in Reykjavík. Foreign drug gangs. Knives. Maybe even guns. And he wanted his men to be ready for it. Hence his request for an American police detective with practical experience who spoke Icelandic.

There weren't a whole lot of those among America's big-city police forces. Magnus, who had left Iceland for the States at the age of twelve with his father, fitted the bill, and when he had been shot at as a witness in a police corruption scandal he had been sent to Reykjavík as much for his own safety as for what he could do for the Icelanders.

'Anything going on at CID?' he asked Árni.

'We have a bird thief.'

'A bird thief?'

'Someone has been stealing exotic birds. Parrots mostly, and budgerigars. There are scarcely any left in Reykjavík now. It's a big problem. This man, and we think it is a man not a woman, is very clever.'

'I thought you just did violent crimes?'

'You go wherever they need you. Burglaries have doubled in the last six months and they have had to lay off twenty uniforms. The *kreppa*. You know what I'm talking about, you've seen the cost-cutting at the police college.' *Kreppa* was the Icelandic term for the financial crisis, and Icelanders' current favourite topic of conversation.

'Got any leads?'

'Some. Not enough. I'm confident we will crack the case by the end of the week. When will you be joining us? I'm sure we could use your expertise.'

'Two more months, I think,' Magnus sighed. The Commissioner had insisted that Magnus do six months of the one-year basic-training course at the police college before he was given a badge. Magnus had grudgingly accepted. It was hard to argue with the Commissioner's point that it was impossible to uphold the law if you didn't know what it was.

So he had spent most of the previous four months as a student and part of it teaching. He preferred the teaching.

The water jets began to bubble and Árni closed his eyes and leaned back. Magnus took the opportunity to examine the scar on Árni's chest. The surgeon at the National Hospital had done a good job of patching him up. Magnus had seen many plugged bullet holes that looked a lot worse.

Magnus had worked with Árni on a case immediately after his own arrival from Boston four months before. Árni was not known as Reykjavík's best detective, some said that he only had the job because his uncle, Chief Superintendent Thorkell Hólm, was head of CID. At times he had frustrated the hell out of Magnus, but Magnus liked him and admired his loyalty.

And he would never forget that Árni had taken a bullet for him.

They pulled themselves out of the hot tub, and went for a cold shower followed by a warm one.

As they were getting dressed in the changing room Árni checked his phone. 'A call from Baldur,' he said, examining the display. He pressed a couple of buttons and put the phone to his ear.

Inspector Baldur Jakobsson was the head of the Violent Crimes Unit. A good, traditional Icelandic cop, he was suspicious of Magnus and his big-city methods. Magnus understood, but he still thought he was a pain in the ass.

It looked to Magnus like a big breakthrough with the macaw. Árni's eyebrows shot up as he listened, and his Adam's apple started bobbing wildly. His cheeks flushed with excitement.

'Yes,' he said. 'Yes… Yes. Yes, right away.'

Magnus's interest was piqued.

'What was that?' Magnus said, as soon as Árni hung up.

'I've got to get back to headquarters,' Árni said. 'You know Óskar Gunnarsson?'

'I think so,' Magnus said. 'Isn't he a banker?' That was Magnus's problem. Although he had done a good job of brushing up on his language so he was fluent with barely an accent, Reykjavík was a small town where everyone knew everyone else. Apart from Magnus who had never heard of anyone.

Árni hurried to pull on his clothes. 'Ex-CEO of Ódinsbanki. He was fired a year ago. He's under investigation by Financial Crimes and the Special Prosecutor. Anyway, he was shot dead in London last night.'

'Is there an Icelandic angle?'

'The British cops haven't found one yet, but Baldur wants us all out checking.'

'I bet he does.'

'You should get yourself involved,' Árni said, as he pulled on his jacket. 'With the foreign angle.'

'Baldur won't like it,' Magnus said.

'Since when has that stopped you?' said Árni, as he grabbed his bag and hurried out of the changing room.

*

Magnus unlocked the front door of the little house in 101, the postcode for the centre of Reykjavík. The outside walls were cream concrete, and like most Icelandic houses the roof was brightly painted corrugated metal, in this case lime green. The house actually belonged to Árni and his sister, although only his sister Katrín lived there. Magnus paid her a very reasonable rent.

Magnus climbed the stairs to his room. He pulled a Viking beer out of the refrigerator, flopped into a chair and opened it. Icelanders might not drink during the week, saving their efforts for heroic binges at the weekend, but Magnus was enough of an American cop to need a beer when his shift ended.

His body tingled after the swim. The room was small, but it was enough for Magnus. He didn't have much stuff. Before coming to Iceland he had shared a place with his former girlfriend, Colby, but he had always felt a guest, his possessions overwhelmed by hers. He did have books, though, which spilled out from the bookshelf along one wall on to the floor. In the middle of this chaos stood in a neat row his beloved sagas, in Icelandic, many of them bought by his father many years ago, their pages ragged with use.

Outside his window, a couple of blocks up the hill, the Hallgrímskirkja lurked, its sweeping spire clad in scaffolding like a spaceship ready for launch, surrounded by gantries.

Magnus sighed as he sipped the cold fizzy liquid. That was good.

In Boston, a shift would frequently include a dead body. Solving the crime didn't usually involve random shooting of bad guys, as Árni had suggested, but it did take a whole lot of talking to people: people whose lives had just been destroyed by the loss of someone they loved, people whose lives were already destroyed by the hell that was their everyday existence, witnesses who wanted to talk, witnesses who didn't. Most of the time was spent on making sure the prosecution case went smoothly, the witness statements were typed up accurately and the forensic evidence was all in the proper place with the chain of evidence intact.

It was long hours, painstaking, frustrating, depressing, but

Magnus could never get enough of it. Every victim had a family, *someone* who cared that they had died, and Magnus would do his best for that someone.

Of course he knew that he was doing it for himself as well. His own father had been murdered in a small town just outside Boston when Magnus was twenty and a student at college. The local police had got nowhere in solving the crime, and neither had Magnus, despite spending the best part of a year trying. In fact, he was still trying; he had never given up. That was why Magnus had joined the Boston Police Department. That was why he always had the energy for another dead body.

And now here he was, in Iceland. On his arrival in the spring he had been thrown into a case, a very interesting case, but since then there had been nothing but teaching and studying. The orange Penal Code lay on his desk by the window. He knew probably three-quarters of it by now.

It wasn't as if the boys in the Violent Crimes Unit downtown had had much to do. In June a man had been found stabbed to death in the street at four on a Sunday morning. The first cops to the scene had solved the crime, figuring that the eighteen-year-old kid out of his skull on speed, waving a knife soaked in blood around his head and shouting how he would kill anyone else who came near him was a likely suspect.

Magnus had given his word to Snorri Gudmundsson, the National Police Commissioner, that he would stay for two years. He owed it to him for providing him with refuge when the Dominican gang from back home were after him, and to Árni for taking a bullet when the hit man they sent to Reykjavík had caught up with him.

Of course the Dominicans knew where he was now. Their boss might be in Cedar Junction jail back in Massachusetts, put there with the help of Magnus's testimony, but there were plenty of gang members still at large. Magnus hoped that now that he had done his stint as a witness he was no longer a target, but he couldn't be sure. He could never be sure.

But it was going to be hard to stick it out in Reykjavík. Four months and he was already climbing the walls.

Árni was right though. He should make a call. Try to get assigned on to this Óskar Gunnarsson case. You never knew, there might be something in it. It would make a change. And it might be interesting to deal with the British police.

But who to call? Baldur would just say no, that was for sure. Magnus knew the Commissioner would take his call, but he wanted to save that access for when he really needed it. Thorkell Holm, head of CID, was his best bet. It would piss Baldur off, but that was just tough.

He took out his phone, called the police switchboard and asked to be put through.

Then he heard a giggle.

He looked up.

There was a naked woman lying on his bed.

'Ingileif! What the hell are you doing here?'

She threw off the covers and bounded over to him in the chair. 'You didn't see me, did you? What kind of cop are you when you can't even spot a woman lying under your bed covers, desperate for sex?'

'You were hiding!' Magnus protested.

'Pathetic.'

She straddled him. Her familiar, delightful breasts shook inches away from his face as she laughed, her blonde hair falling loose over her face.

'How did you get a key?'

'Oh, do be quiet, Magnús. I've been waiting here half an hour for you. And you have far too many clothes on.'

'But—'

She kissed him. Deeply. He raised his hands to her bare hips. He didn't care how she had got in. He wanted her. Now.

A muffled crackling came from his phone, which had dropped to the floor. Ingileif broke away and picked it up.

'Yes?'

'Give it to me!' Magnus cried, reaching for the phone.

Ingileif turned away. 'I am sorry, Sergeant Magnús is busy right now. He'll be with you as soon as he has finished. He probably won't be more than a couple of minutes. Doesn't usually take him longer than that.'

'Ingileif!' Magnus pushed her off his lap and on to the floor. Ingileif triumphantly hit the red disconnect button just before Magnus could grab the phone.

'That was a Chief Superintendent someone or other,' Ingileif said. 'Don't worry, he said he quite understood.'

Magnus picked her up off the floor and threw her down on to the bed.

It is extremely difficult to make love to a woman who won't stop laughing.

'Can I watch *LazyTown* now?'

Harpa glanced at her son's plate, which was empty.

'Did you watch TV at Granny's house?'

'No.' Markús shook his curly head and looked straight at her with his big clear brown eyes. Harpa knew that small children often lied, but not Markús. He never lied, at least not to her. Where did he get that honesty from? Not from his father, that was for sure.

And not from her.

'All right, off you go.'

Harpa followed her child as he scampered into the living room and she slotted the DVD into the player.

She went back into the kitchen and stacked their dishes in the dishwasher. She liked to eat with her son, even though it was early.

From out of the kitchen window she looked out over Faxaflói Bay. To the right, behind the oil storage tanks, was the city of Reykjavík, a jumble of brightly coloured houses overlooked by the Hallgrímskirkja, its majestic sweeping spire boxed in by scaffolding. Straight across the bay squatted Mount Esja, a horizontal rampart of granite, still free of snow at this time of year. And to the left lay the small town of Akranes, stuck on the end of a peninsula, a thin trail of smoke emerging from its tall cement-works chimney.

Her little house was right on Nordurströnd, the road that ran along the north-eastern edge of the prosperous suburb of Seltjarnarnes, which was perched on its own promontory sticking out into the bay. The house had been expensive because of the view, but Harpa had been able to take out a big mortgage to cover the cost, a mortgage that she had been easily able to service with her banker's salary. She should have taken a straightforward repayment mortgage, but like many other Icelanders she had chosen a loan where the principal was linked to inflation. The advantage was that the monthly payments were lower.

The disadvantage was that when inflation was high, for example after a massive devaluation of the currency, the value of the loan soon overtook the value of the house.

She had no banker's salary any more so she couldn't afford the payments. The house was now worth less than the mortgage. She was going to lose it, that was inevitable. The only reason she hadn't lost it already was the government's temporary edict that the banks had to delay foreclosures until November.

What would happen then? Perhaps the bank would be lenient. Or perhaps she and Markús would end up living with her parents like some teenage mother just out of high school.

If her parents could keep their own house, that is. She knew they had financial difficulties – she was after all responsible for them – she just didn't know how bad they were. And she was too afraid to ask.

Why had she taken out that stupid mortgage? She had an MBA from Reykjavík University. She knew there was a theoretical risk. She had just been sucked up in the mindless optimism of jam today, jam tomorrow that had swept Iceland.

She switched on the news. Something about ministers threatening to resign over the agreement the government had made to repay the four billion euros it had borrowed from the British government to bail out depositors in Icesave, the London Internet operation of one of the Icelandic banks.

Then she heard a name that was all too familiar.

'The Icelandic banker, Óskar Gunnarsson, former chairman of Óðinsbanki, has been murdered in his house in London. He was shot.'

Harpa froze, the hot water running over the dish she was rinsing.

'Óskar Gunnarsson was under investigation by the authorities in Iceland over alleged fraud at Óðinsbanki prior to its national-ization nearly a year ago. It is not clear yet whether his murder had anything to do with the alleged fraud.'

Harpa grabbed her laptop and opened it up, looking for more information. As she waited for the computer to boot up, she thought of the charismatic banker. But she also thought of Gabríel Örn. One murdered banker. Another murdered banker.

Would there ever be a time when she *didn't* think of Gabríel Örn?

She checked the BBC website. There were a couple more details. The house was in Onslow Gardens in Kensington. Harpa remem-bered Óskar buying it just before she finished her two-year stint in London in 2006. At that time he was based in Reykjavík, but spent a lot of time in Britain. Someone had entered the house the night before and shot him. His girlfriend was in the house at the time, but was unharmed.

'Hello?' Her front door opened with a clatter. 'Harpa?'

'I'm in the kitchen, Dad!'

A moment later her father came in. There was a scampering of feet as Markús rushed into the room and leaped at his grandfather. '*Afi!*'

Einar Bjarnason swung the boy around like a feather, laughing as he did so. 'Hey, Markús! How are you? Pleased to see your old grandfather?'

'I'm watching *LazyTown*, *Afi*, do you want to come see it with me?'

'In a moment, Markús, in a moment.'

The hard weather-beaten face crinkled in a smile. Einar was a fisherman, and when he was still taking his boat out to sea he had had the reputation as one of the toughest captains in the fleet. But not where his grandson was concerned. Or his daughter.

He opened his arms to hug her. With difficulty she pulled herself away from the computer and went over to him. They were the same height, but he was broad and strong, and it was comforting to feel his big meaty hands on her back.

He had always been tender towards her, but he never used to hug her as much as he had over the last few months.

He knew she needed it.

To her surprise, safe in his arms, Harpa began to cry.

Einar broke away to look at her. 'What is it? What's happened?'

'The boss of Ódinsbanki has been murdered. Óskar Gunnarsson.'

'He probably deserved it.'

'Dad!' Harpa knew that her father disliked bankers with a passion, especially those who had fired his beloved daughter, but that was a bit callous, even for him.

'I'm sorry, love, did you know him?'

'No, not really,' Harpa said. 'A bit.'

Einar was looking straight at her, his blue eyes seeing right into her soul. He knows I'm lying, Harpa thought in panic. Just like he knew I was lying when I talked to the police about Gabríel Örn. She felt herself blush.

She stepped back and collapsed on a kitchen chair and started to sob.

Einar poured a cup of coffee for both of them and sat down opposite her. 'Do you want to talk about it?'

Harpa shook her head. She tried, and succeeded, to control her tears. Her father waited. 'How was the fishing?' she asked him.

She meant the fly-fishing. Einar had had to give up sea-fishing fifteen years before when a wave had broken over the *Helgi* and flung him against a winch, breaking his knee. He had spent a few years managing the boat from land before selling it and his quota for hundreds of millions of krónur. Since then he had been a wealthy retired fisherman. Until he had listened to his daughter, that is.

At first, he had invested the money in high-interest accounts at Óðinsbanki, which gave him plenty of income to live on. But some of his mates were making a fortune speculating on currencies or investing in the booming Icelandic stock market. He had asked his clever daughter who worked for a bank for advice.

She had told him to steer clear of the currency speculation and of investing in the racier new shares on the stock exchange. But bank stocks, they were safe. And she could recommend Óðinsbanki. It was the smartest of all the Icelandic banks.

And so Einar had put all his savings in Óðinsbanki shares. Shares which were all but worthless when the government nation-alized the banks the previous autumn.

Harpa wondered how he could still afford to go fly-fishing.

'I didn't catch much. And it rained most of the time. But I'm going again over the weekend. Maybe my luck will change.' He put his arm around his daughter. 'Are you sure there is nothing you want to tell me?'

For a moment Harpa considered it. Telling him everything. His love for her was unconditional, wasn't it? He would stand by her whatever she had done. Wouldn't he?

But what she had done was awful. Unforgivable. She had certainly never forgiven herself, could never possibly forgive herself in the future. He was a good man. How could he forgive her?

She couldn't bear it if he didn't.

So Harpa shook her head. 'No, Dad. There's nothing.'

CHAPTER FOUR

October 1934

BENEDIKT HAD A really good idea for a game.

He had just finished the *Saga of the People of Eyri* and he had read that there was a chieftain called Björn from Breidavík on the other side of the Snaefells Peninsula, across the mountains from Hraun and Bjarnarhöfn, who had travelled all the way to a land far overseas that Benedikt guessed was America. Björn had become a chief there amongst the natives. What if Hallgrímur and Benedikt discovered America?

Hallgrímur wanted the berserkers to go too. They could fight the Skraelings, the name the Vikings had given to the Native Americans. Benedikt said that was all right.

But they would need to go on a long journey of exploration. Hallgrímur suggested that they go to Swine Lake, a lake formed by the congealed lava several kilometres to the south. Although Benedikt's mother was happy for him to be out playing for long periods, Hallgrímur's was much stricter. So he waited until his father had ridden off for the day to Stykkishólmur, the nearest town, and his mother had gone to visit the wife at a neighbouring farm.

It was hard slow going over the lava field, especially since the boys were careful to keep out of view. There was some sunshine, but it was cold, with a stiff breeze blowing in from the north-east. Snow had fallen on the mountains to the south the week before, and there was a dusting on the top of Bjarnarhöfn Fell. They paused to watch a motor car in the distance clatter down from the Kerlingin Pass on the high road from Borgarnes to Stykkishólmur. A horse neighed in fright.

'A Buick,' Benedikt said. He was knowledgeable about motor cars, or claimed to be, although Hallgrímur had his doubts. Every car seemed to be a Buick.

A pair of eider ducks flew low overhead, on their way back to the dwarf willows by the stream at Bjarnarhöfn.

They pressed on. Benedikt was getting tired, as was Hallgrímur. Perhaps this wasn't such a good idea after all. But then the Vikings who discovered America had put up with much worse conditions than this. And Hallgrímur was a berserker. He certainly couldn't give up.

'Halli, let's go back!'

'Don't whine, Benni.'

'But I'm tired!'

Hallgrímur sighed. 'All right. We'll rest for a couple of minutes. But then we have to get on to America!'

They found a comfortable hollow and sat down. The lava protected them from the wind, and the sun warmed their cheeks. Hallgrímur looked up at the savage profile of the Kerlingin Pass, with its outlandish shapes along the ridge. From here he could just make out the silhouette of the Kerlingin troll herself, a giant woman walking along with a bag over her shoulder. The bag was full of naughty children from Stykkishólmur. The troll had been caught by the rising sun just before she had returned to her cave and was frozen there, on top of the pass, for evermore.

Could the berserkers beat the troll in a fair fight? Hallgrímur wondered. It would be tough. Maybe both of them together could.

He turned to ask Benedikt for his opinion when he heard voices, angry voices.

'Do you think they will ever find him?' It was Hallgrímur's mother, and she was sobbing.

33

'No chance.' His father. They were coming closer. 'He's at the bottom of the lake and he will stay there. The fish will eat him. It's what he deserves.'

'You are a horrible vile man! I'm not going back with you!'

'Do you want to join him, you whore? Well, do you?'

Hallgrímur heard his mother sobbing.

'I thought not. I left the horse by the road. Now, come on!'

They were really close now. Hallgrímur and Benedikt could not risk being seen; Hallgrímur could only guess at how angry his parents would be if they discovered him. The boys pressed themselves tight against the ground, their faces buried in the moss. It was only after Hallgrímur was sure that his parents were long gone that he raised his head.

'Benni? What were they talking about? What's a whore?'

His friend didn't answer. He was staring over the lava field towards Swine Lake, tears streaming down his face.

Thursday, 17 September 2009

It was still dark when Harpa walked along the Nordurströnd to the bakery. She had had the job for a couple of months. During the summer she had enjoyed the walk, with the lights of Reykjavík blinking sleepily as the town woke up in front of her, and the sun rising over the mountains to the east, beating a golden path towards her over the bay. But that morning the dawn was just a band of steel blue under the clouds on the horizon. A cold breeze clipped in from the sea. She looked forward to the warm comforting smell of bread from the bakery's ovens.

When she had first been fired from Ódinsbanki, she had spent a couple of months in shock, cocooned in her house with her son. But eventually she realized she would have to get a job. She considered the bakery that she stopped in every day on her way to work. They liked her, she was sure they would be bound to hire her, but she could do better, she thought.

Well, it turned out that she couldn't. So after a couple of months of fruitless search she presented herself to Dísa, the woman who ran the bakery. Dísa was kind but firm. There were no vacancies. It was only then that the truth hit Harpa. In the *kreppa* there were no jobs for someone like Harpa. None.

She tried everywhere; it was only at the end of June that Dísa eventually called her and said that a vacancy was opening up and Harpa could work for them. It was a good job: the people were friendly and it provided some flexibility for her to spend time with Markús. Her parents looked after their grandson in the early morning, and took him to the nursery. And she earned some money.

Not nearly enough to make the mortgage payments though.

She thought again about Óskar's death. And Gabríel Örn. The familiar anxiety wriggled in her stomach. She stopped. Faced the breeze coming in from the sea. Took some deep breaths. And wept.

Björn. She needed to see Björn. He was always up early, looking for work on a fishing boat. She pulled out her phone and dialled his number.

He answered quickly. 'Hi, Harpa, how are you?'

'Not good.' She could hear the sound of engines and waves in the background. Sometimes he could get reception on his mobile when he was out at sea. 'Are you fishing?'

'Just on our way out. What's up?'

'Did you see the news. About Óskar Gunnarsson?'

'The banker? Yes. Did you know him?'

'A bit.'

'Wasn't he one of the bastards who fired you?'

'I suppose so, yes. But...'

'But what?'

Harpa gulped. 'But it just brings the whole Gabríel Örn thing back.'

'Yeah.' Björn's voice was sympathetic. 'Yeah. I can see that.'

'Björn? I hate to ask you this, but can you come down to Reykjavík?'

'That's going to be a bit difficult. We'll be back in harbour tonight, but I'm going out again for a couple of days tomorrow afternoon. Maybe on Sunday?'

'Any chance you could come late tonight? I really need to see you.' It was two and a half hours from Grundarfjördur, although Björn could do it considerably faster on his motorbike. Seltjarnarnes was still a long drive after a full day's fishing.

'Yes,' Björn said. 'Yes. I'll be there. Late. But I'll be there.'

'Thank you, Björn.' She could feel the tears coming again. 'I really need you. You are the only one I can speak to about this.'

'Hey, Harpa, I understand. Believe me, I understand. I'll see you tonight. I'll give you a call when I'm on my way.'

'I love you,' said Harpa.

'I love you too.'

CHAPTER FIVE

'**G**OOD MORNING, MAGNÚS.'

Baldur's tone was icy as he welcomed Magnus into his office. Two other detectives, Árni and Vigdís Audarsdóttir were already waiting.

It had proved remarkably easy for Magnus to get assigned to the case. The biggest problem had been summoning up the courage to call Chief Superintendent Thorkell back.

Thorkell had been businesslike on the phone, although he did start off the conversation with a dig. 'Ah, Magnús, you took longer than I had been led to believe.'

'Look, I'm sorry, Chief Superintendent,' Magnus began. 'You see I dropped the phone and—'

'I want you on the Óskar Gunnarsson case,' Thorkell interrupted.

'Good,' said Magnus.

'That was what you were calling about, wasn't it?'

'Er, yes. Yes.'

'OK. Be in Baldur's office downtown at eight o'clock tomorrow morning. He will be expecting you. I'll square it with the police college director.'

'Very good. Thank you.'

Thorkell hung up, but Magnus heard the beginnings of a guffaw just before the line went dead. Somehow Magnus thought that Thorkell would not keep his earlier eavesdropping confidential.

Oh, well. Magnus glanced at Árni. No smirk yet: he hadn't heard. Vigdís, the other detective, was much too professional to betray gossip. And he would soon find out whether Baldur knew.

'A little tired this morning, are we?' Baldur said with the tiniest of smiles. He knew. It wasn't really a smile, more of a twitch on one side of his thin mouth. Baldur had a long lugubrious face and a high dome of a forehead. Not one of the Metropolitan Police's greatest jokers.

'Fully refreshed,' said Magnus, trying not to think too much about Ingileif still curled up in his bed, and more about the task at hand.

'I spoke to an officer from the British police in London yesterday,' Baldur said. 'Her name was,' he paused as he examined his notes, 'Detective Sergeant Sharon Piper. At this stage she has no reason to think that there is an Icelandic connection. Which is surprising when you think that the British believe we are all a bunch of terrorists.'

Baldur was referring to the British invocation of anti-terrorist legislation the previous October to seize the London assets of one of the Icelandic banks. It still rankled, a year later, especially with the controversy over the Icesave repayment negotiations.

'Did she give you any details of what happened?' Magnus asked.

'Not much, it is still very early in the investigation.' Baldur's English wasn't very good. Magnus wondered whether he had understood all of what Piper was saying. 'You should call her this morning, see if she has turned up anything new.'

He dictated a phone number which Magnus wrote down.

'Árni, Vigdís, what did you find out last night?'

'Óskar has no criminal record,' Árni said. 'I did check with the Financial Crimes Unit and he is under investigation by the Special Prosecutor.'

'What for?'

'Market manipulation and securities fraud,' Árni said, confidently.

'And what does that mean?' Baldur asked.

'I'm not sure,' Árni admitted. 'Something about lending money to people who bought their shares. Or sold their shares. Or something.'

Baldur shook his head in despair. 'Vigdís?'

Vigdís was a conscientious detective of about thirty. She was wearing a white Keflavík basketball sweatshirt, and her disconcertingly long legs were clad in jeans. 'Óskar is thirty-nine. Until last October he was chairman of Óðinsbanki. He is also a major shareholder, through the family holding company OBG Investments, which is registered in Tortola, in the British Virgin Islands. As you know, he was one of the most successful of the Viking Raiders, the businessmen who built up big foreign operations for their companies.'

'And dumped us all into this shit,' Baldur muttered.

'He was well respected amongst his fellow bankers, at least until the *kreppa* broke last year. Since then he has spent most of his time in London. He was forced to resign as chairman of Óðinsbanki last November.'

Magnus noticed that Vigdís had a photograph in the file in front of her.

'Can I take a look?' he asked. She slid the print over to him.

A good-looking man with dark floppy hair stared confidently into the camera. He had large brown eyes and a square, cleft chin. He looked successful but approachable.

'Is he married?' Baldur asked. 'Sharon Piper mentioned a girlfriend was with him when he died.'

'Married Kamilla Símonardóttir in 1999, divorced 2004, two children. He did have a Russian girlfriend, Tanya Prokhorova. Was it her?'

'She didn't give me a name,' said Baldur. 'Good work so far. I don't think we need go overboard on helping the British on this, but I do want to make it clear that there is no Icelandic involvement. Of course, if you do turn up anything, let me know.' He said this in a tone that made clear he was sure they wouldn't.

They left Baldur's office. Magnus commandeered an empty desk in the Violent Crimes Unit. He felt invigorated: it was good to be involved in a real investigation, even if he was only on the periphery of the inquiry and a thousand miles from the body. Vigdís and Árni joined him as Magnus made the call to London.

'DS Piper.'

'Hi, there. This is Magnus Jonson. I'm with the Reykjavík Metropolitan Police.'

Magnus realized he had introduced himself using his American name. He had two identities. In Iceland he had been christened Magnús, pronounced 'Magnoos'. His father was Ragnar, and his grandfather Jón, so his father was Ragnar Jónsson and he was Magnús Ragnarsson. So far so simple. Except that when he arrived in the States at the age of twelve the bureaucracy couldn't cope with the fact that he had a different surname to both his father and his mother, whose name was Margrét Hallgrímsdóttir, and like so many immigrants before him he had changed his name to something easier on the American ear. He became Magnus Jonson. On returning to Iceland he had reverted to Ragnarsson, but that sounded strange when he was speaking English.

'I'm glad you called,' said Piper.

'Do you mind if I put you on the speaker?' said Magnus. 'I'm here with two detectives, Árni and Vigdís.'

'No, that's fine.'

Magnus clicked the button on his phone and put down the receiver. 'Inspector Baldur gave us some background on the homicide, but maybe you can tell us some more?'

'You speak very good English,' said Piper. 'Better than your inspector. I wasn't sure how much he understood.'

Magnus looked over his shoulder at Baldur's closed office door. 'Thank you,' he said, resisting the smart-ass comment. 'And so do you.' Piper's British accent was a local London one, as far as he could tell.

'Right,' Piper began. 'Gunnarsson was killed at twelve forty-five on Wednesday morning. Shot in the chest in the hallway of his house with three rounds from a SIG Sauer P226. He died before the ambulance got there.'

'Any witnesses?' Magnus asked.

'His girlfriend was in bed. She said the bell rang, Gunnarsson answered the door, she heard him talking to someone. The front door shut. A few seconds later there were the three shots and the front door banged again. Then she heard a motorbike start up and roar off.'

'The neighbours hear it?'

'Yes. Three of them. They heard the shots. They heard the girl-friend's screams. And they heard the motorbike, although one of them said it could have been a scooter. Small engine. We've got CCTV pictures of several motorbikes at about that time on the Old Brompton Road and the Fulham Road which are the two main streets at either side of Onslow Gardens. We're trying to trace them all now.'

'Any Icelandic connection?'

'Nothing firm. The girlfriend said that she heard Gunnarsson talking with the visitor in a foreign language. It could have been Icelandic. Or Russian. Or anything else that wasn't English or Spanish for that matter. The girlfriend is Venezuelan, by the way.'

'Russian? Why do you say Russian?'

'We found a little yellow Post-It note with Gunnarsson's address written in Russian letters. What do you call it? Cyrillic. It was screwed up in a ball by the gate to the front garden.'

'That's a rookie mistake for a hit man to make,' Magnus said.

'Yes,' Piper agreed. 'But it might not have been the killer who dropped it. The killer may well have been someone Gunnarsson knew. He did let him in, after all.'

'In which case the killer could have been an Icelander,' said Magnus. 'Is there much of a Russian connection? Óskar had a Russian girlfriend, right, before the Venezuelan?' Magnus checked his notes. 'Tanya Prokhorova.'

'We've interviewed her. She claims she dumped him two months ago. She's a model, skinny, legs up to her armpits, but she's switched on, all right. Degree in accounting – she claims she real-ized that Gunnarsson was actually skint which is more or less why she got rid of him.'

'Does she have Russian friends?'

'She does. She's right in with the billionaires' circle in London. And some of those are pretty dodgy. What about you? Have you turned up a Russian connection in Reykjavík?'

'Not yet,' said Magnus. 'But we will ask around. Óskar was under investigation here for securities fraud and market manipulation.'

'There are rumours in the City that some of the Icelandic banks got their money from the Russian mafia,' Piper said.

Magnus raised his eyebrows and looked at his colleagues. Árni looked baffled. Vigdís shook her head. 'We'll check that out too,' Magnus said, aware of his own ignorance. 'We'll call you at the end of the day with an update.'

'Great. Cheers, Magnus.'

Magnus turned to his colleagues. 'Did you get all that?' he asked in Icelandic.

He knew Árni would. Árni had studied Criminology at a small college in Indiana, and his English was very good. But Vigdís claimed she didn't speak it, a claim Magnus didn't believe. All Icelanders under the age of thirty-five spoke some English, and he didn't see why she shouldn't just because of her colour.

For Vigdís had the distinction of being the only black police officer in the Reykjavík Metropolitan Police. She was fed up with Icelanders and foreigners treating her as if she wasn't an Icelander herself. As she had explained to Magnus, even though her father had been an American serviceman at the US air base in Keflavík, she had never met him, had no desire to meet him, and thought herself as Icelandic as Björk.

Magnus liked her. She was a conscientious police officer, and there was something comforting and familiar for an American cop working with a black face among so many pale ones.

Árni nodded, but Vigdís didn't respond.

'I'll take that as a yes,' said Magnus. 'OK. Let's figure out who is going to do what.'

*

The Ódinsbanki headquarters was on Borgartún, a boulevard that ran along the bay, lined with expensively designed glass- and marble-clad buildings. It was not the dense thicket of skyscrapers that you would find in a US city's financial district, it was more sedate than that and more soulless.

Árni and Magnus pulled up into a car park behind one of the most lavish offices. They walked through revolving doors under the words 'New Ódinsbanki'. The lobby echoed with the sound of rushing water from the various waterfalls, fountains and streams that flowed around the glass atrium.

They were met by the Chief Executive's assistant, who took them up in the elevator to the top floor. She led them through a dealing room big enough to seat forty. It was eerily quiet, the screens blank, the chairs empty, apart from a group of a dozen or so men and women lined along the far wall. Behind these survivors was a wonderful view across the bay to Mount Esja, at that moment squatting under a grey cloud.

'It's quiet today,' the assistant said. And then, with a wry smile: 'It's quiet every day.'

Eventually, after a couple of twists and turns, they came to the Chief Executive's office and met the man himself. He was tall, about sixty, with a strong square face, thick grey hair and an ingrained frown. His name was Gudmundur Rasmussen and he had been turfed out of retirement to take over the running of the bank a year ago. His office was ostentatiously plain: simple desk, functional chairs and conference table. A couple of packing cases were stacked in the corner. It reminded Magnus a little of the police headquarters he had just left.

'Terrible news about Óskar, terrible,' Gudmundur said. 'I didn't really know him well. He was from a younger generation, we did things very differently in my day.' He shook his head and tutted. 'Very differently. Of course, I have spent most of the last year trying to clear up the mess that Óskar and his cronies left.'

'Was he popular within the bank?' Magnus asked.

'Yes,' Gudmundur said. 'Yes he was. Even after all the mistakes he made came to light. He had charisma, people liked working for him.' The frown deepened. 'It has made my job difficult competing with that. The staff all seem to hark back to the good old days when Óskar was in charge. They don't seem to realize that they weren't good, they were disastrous. Things have to change. Now the bank is owned by the government we must behave cautiously. Not do anything rash.'

There was a knock at the door, and a man in his late twenties entered. He was self-assured with slicked-back hair and an expensive suit. A hint of cologne entered the office with him. He proffered his boss a single sheet of paper. 'Can you sign off on this, Gudmundur?'

Gudmundur grabbed the paper and scanned it. 'But these people are brokers, aren't they?'

'Yes. We do a lot of business with them.'

'No. The bank's not paying for this. I've told you before, if it's not a client, you pay for your own lunch.'

He stared at the young banker as he returned the paper into his hands, unsigned.

'But—'

'I've been very clear,' Gudmundur said.

The banker took back the paper and left the office without another word.

Gudmundur shook his head. 'Some of these people don't realize the world has changed. Now. Where were we?'

'You were saying Óskar was popular. He didn't have any enemies in the bank?' Magnus asked.

'Not that I am aware of. He may well have outside. I mean he is one of the gang of young bankers that has ruined the country, and people blame him for that, along with the others.' Gudmundur shook his head. 'They just didn't have the *experience* to run a bank. It was irresponsible to let them do it.'

Magnus detected as much pleasure as pain in Gudmundur's reaction to the comeuppance of the whippersnappers. 'We understand that Óskar was under investigation by the Special Prosecutor for market manipulation. What was that about?'

'Lending money to clients and friends to buy shares in the bank, and doing it secretly. At least that is what the allegation is.'

'Were any of these clients Russians?'

Gudmundur's frown deepened. 'I don't *think* so, but I can't be absolutely sure. There is a web of holding companies and subsidiaries in places like Tortola and Liechtenstein and it's a nightmare trying to figure out who the real owners are. But the bank has very few Russian clients.' He paused. 'In fact, none that I can think of.'

'Presumably some of these offshore companies were owned indirectly by Óskar?'

'Yes. The main holding company is OBG Investments. As well as Óðinsbanki it has holdings in a major chain of hotels and some retailers in Germany and Britain. And that's just what is public knowledge. The company is run by Emilía Gunnarsdóttir, Óskar's sister. Their offices are right here on Borgartún.'

Magnus asked some more questions about the bank and Óskar, and Árni took copious notes, although Magnus got the impression that he wasn't really following what was going on.

Just as they were about to leave, Árni asked his own question. 'Didn't Gabríel Örn Bergsson work here?'

'Yes he did,' Gudmundur replied. 'That was another sad case. It is unfortunate that two senior members of staff died in such awful circumstances, no matter how much damage they did to the bank.'

'Did Gabríel Örn do much damage?'

'Yes,' Gudmundur sighed. 'Most of the bad loans the bank made were in his department.'

'What about Harpa Einarsdóttir?' Árni asked.

'I didn't know her well; she left the bank just after I arrived,' Gudmundur replied. 'She worked with Gabríel Örn. I think she was his girlfriend. She had a good reputation within the firm, but she was too young. Too optimistic. No sense of what might go wrong.'

'Was there any connection between them and Óskar?' Árni asked.

'Well, yes, obviously. Gabríel Örn was in charge of the lever-aged lending group which was an important department. I'm sure that he and Óskar knew each other well. I have no idea about the relationship between Harpa and Óskar, but once again she was a fairly senior executive. And Óskar used to socialize with his staff. You must have read all about the parties in the newspapers.'

Even Magnus was aware that the Icelandic press had had a great time describing the excesses of the bankers, Óskar prominent among them: the parties, the private jets, the apartments in New York and London. To Magnus's jaundiced eye it seemed nothing beyond the regular corporate excesses which you would expect in the boardrooms of America. It might not be in the Icelandic tradi-tion, but it was certainly in the tradition of Wall Street.

'What was all that about?' Magnus asked Árni once they had left the CEO's office. 'Who the hell is Gabríel Örn?'

'A banker who killed himself in January, a few months before you arrived in Iceland. Harpa was his ex-girlfriend who used to work for him. I interviewed her afterwards.'

'Why did he kill himself?'

'We're not absolutely sure. He only left a brief text message as a suicide note. But he was responsible for bankrupting a bank. A few bad days at work, to put it mildly.'

'And do you think there is a connection with Óskar's murder?'

'Um, no.'

'Are you sure?'

Árni waited for the lift doors to close behind them as they headed down to the lobby.

'Yes, I'm sure,' he said.

Magnus looked at him closely. He didn't believe him.

CHAPTER SIX

EMILÍA GUNNARSDÓTTIR HAD poise. She was in her mid-thirties, slim, with her dark hair tied back. She was wearing an elegant black trouser suit and expensive but discreet gold adorned her ears and neck.

The offices of OBG Investments took up one floor of a five-storey building a hundred metres along Borgartún from the Ódinsbanki headquarters. Magnus saw from the directory in the lobby that the other occupants were firms of lawyers and accountants, plus the odd enigmatic financial company, like OBG itself. It was obvious when they had reached OBG's floor: the reception area was dominated by a life-size sculpture in bronze of a Viking in full warrior gear riding a Harley Davidson.

Emilía led Magnus and Árni through to her office: thick white carpet, black leather armchairs and sofa, a broad black desk, uncluttered with papers, but bearing a sleek computer screen. The contrast with Gudmundur's office was stark. 'I am very sorry about your brother,' Magnus began.

For a moment, a second or so, the poise cracked. But then with a purse of the lips it was back. 'Thank you,' was all Emilía said. 'Sit down. I hope you don't mind waiting a couple of minutes. I've asked my lawyer to be present. She works in this building so she won't be long.'

Magnus was surprised. 'I don't think there's a need for a lawyer, Emilía. You are not a suspect.' Or not yet, he thought. Asking for a lawyer this early in proceedings certainly raised alarm bells.

'Not for this crime, perhaps. But don't forget that our company is under investigation.'

'I'm not interested in the Special Prosecutor's case,' Magnus said. 'I just want to find out more about your brother.'

'Which I will tell you once my lawyer is here. Would you like some coffee?'

Just then the door opened and a woman came in.

A woman whom Magnus recognized. He couldn't keep the shock from registering on his face. The woman seemed just as surprised herself.

'This is Sigurbjörg Vilhjálmsdóttir, my lawyer,' Emilía said. 'But it seems that you know each other already.'

There was a brief pause as both Magnus and the lawyer struggled for something to say. 'Yes,' Magnus said, eventually, clearing his throat. 'We do know each other. Sigurbjörg is my cousin.' He hesitated and then stepped forward to kiss her on the cheek.

'Oh, I see,' Emilía said, unsurprised at the connection. This was Reykjavík, after all. But she could tell there was something strained between them, although she could not possibly know what. 'Is there any reason why you shouldn't advise me on this matter, Sigurbjörg?'

'No,' said Sigurbjörg. 'No, there will be no problem.'

'We aren't close,' said Magnus, and then regretted it. While true, it sounded unnecessarily rude.

'OK,' said Emilía. 'Well. Let's begin, shall we?'

'Can you tell me a bit about Óskar?' Magnus asked. Árni pulled out his notebook, a look of intense concentration on his face as he prepared himself for more financial gobbledygook.

'He was a very special person.' Emilía hesitated. It was as if the simple question threatened to unleash emotion, which had been Magnus's intention. But once again she was back in complete control in an instant. 'Very bright. Energetic. Funny. People liked him. People loved him. Especially the people who worked for him.'

'What about his enemies?'

'He didn't have any enemies.'

'Oh, come on, Emilía. How could someone like him not have enemies?'

Irritation flared in Emilía's eyes. She didn't like being contradicted.

'Well, there were business rivals, I suppose. But they didn't *hate* him. The press loved to gossip about him, but they needed him for their copy. During the demonstrations some of the speakers were asking for his head, but they didn't really know him.'

'Clients of the bank? Depositors? Shareholders? A lot of people must have lost money when Ódinsbanki was nationalized.'

'Yes, that's true. But I don't think most people blamed my brother. All the Icelandic banks collapsed: Ódinsbanki was probably the best run of all of them.'

'What about his personal life? His wife? Or rather ex-wife?'

'Kamilla? She was devastated when they broke up. He was having an affair and she found out about it. But that was five years ago. More. They've got along fairly well since then. He sees the children regularly, or did until this year when he was holed up in London.'

'He had a Russian girlfriend? Tanya Prokhorova, a Russian model.'

Emilía shuddered. 'She may have been a model but she certainly wasn't dumb. Óskar was besotted with her. She was cool and beautiful and played him along. I never liked her. And then of course she dumped him when she realized that he wasn't quite as rich as she thought he was. He was much better off with Claudia.'

'The Venezuelan?'

'Yes. She is much more like him. She has money from her own divorce. She's actually a year older than him, although she wouldn't want anyone else to know that. Óskar was much more relaxed around her. I only met her twice, in London, but she was good for him.'

'Did he know many Russians? Apart from Tanya?'

'I'm not sure,' Emilía said. 'He probably met friends of hers socially.'

'What about clients of the bank?'

Sigurbjörg, the lawyer, coughed.

Emilía glanced at her. 'I'm afraid I can't comment on clients of the bank.'

'Were there any Russian clients that Óskar dealt with personally?'

Emilía didn't answer.

Magnus persisted. 'Any money laundering? Russian businessmen who lost money dealing with Ódinsbanki?'

Sigurbjörg interrupted. 'These are sensitive issues. The Special Prosecutor is examining the files of all the bank's customers. Emilía doesn't want to prejudice that examination.'

Magnus ignored her. 'Your brother is dead, Emilía. Someone killed him. I want to help the British police find out who that person was. We need to know if there was a Russian connection, especially one via Iceland.'

'Don't worry, Sigurbjörg,' Emilía said. 'There were no Russian clients. Maybe one or two small ones, but nothing major. Óskar didn't trust them, it was as simple as that. It was a bank rule: no Russian exposure.'

'Could Tanya have introduced him to some dodgy businessmen looking for places to park money?'

'Possibly. Not that I know of. And I would rather doubt it. Those are exactly the kind of people that Óskar would have avoided. I said he was besotted with Tanya, but he never really trusted her.'

'OK.' Magnus was half convinced. 'And your family? Any tensions there?'

'Oh, Óskar was the golden boy as far as our parents were concerned.' Emilía said this without rancour or jealousy.

'Even after the *kreppa* struck?'

'Even then. I have another brother and a sister. My brother is pretty tense about suddenly realizing that he isn't as rich as he thought he was. But he basically idolizes Óskar.' She swallowed, realizing her mistake. 'I mean idolized.'

She closed her eyes. A tear ran down her cheek. The cool façade crumbled in front of Magnus. She sniffed. 'I'm sorry,' she said. 'Is that everything?'

Suddenly an image of Latasha, a sixteen-year-old girl from the projects in Mattapan came into Magnus's mind. Her fifteen-year-old brother had been shot in the face on the street just behind their building a few hours before Magnus interviewed her. She was proud, she wasn't going to help no cops. She was brave. She was cool. Her mother was off her head on crack in the bedroom, her sister needed her diaper changing. It was only when Magnus was about to leave the apartment that a tear ran down Latasha's cheek and she asked Magnus to find whoever had killed her little brother.

It didn't take Magnus long: it was her brother's fourteen-year-old best friend. An argument over a stolen iPod.

Whether it was a kid from the projects, or a cool Icelandic businesswoman, Magnus sympathized with the victims' relatives. Always.

'Thank you, Emilía,' he said. 'We might come back and ask some more questions later.'

Emilía nodded, tears leaking from both eyes now, and Magnus and Árni left.

Sigurbjörg caught up with Magnus by the lifts. She was several years older than him, about forty, with short red hair and a broad face. Although the hair was a different colour, she reminded him a little of what he remembered of his mother, but she looked older. His mother had only been thirty-five when she had died.

'Is he your client too, Sibba?' Magnus asked, nodding at the Viking on the Harley. 'At least *he* doesn't say much.'

'I'm sorry about my intervention in there,' Sigurbjörg said in English. She had been brought up in Canada, and like Magnus had returned to the land of her parents when she was an adult. 'The Special Prosecutor's investigation into Ódinsbanki is crucially important to OBG.'

Magnus shrugged. 'You were only doing your job.' That's what lawyers did, impeded police investigations. That was the way the system worked and Magnus had given up railing against it long ago.

'Look, here's my card,' Sigurbjörg said. 'I know I kind of ran off last time we met. But give me a call, eh? Come and have dinner at my house. I would love to introduce you to my husband.'

Magnus took the card and stared at it. The law firm he recognized, and the address was the building they were in, of course. 'OK,' he said. 'I will.'

He didn't mean it. He wanted to keep that part of his life safely locked away in its box. Sigurbjörg could tell he didn't mean it. She looked disappointed.

She took the first lift heading up.

'Family feud?' Árni asked, as he and Magnus entered the next one going down.

'I don't know,' Magnus replied, frowning. 'You could say that.'

CHAPTER SEVEN

'HERE THEY COME!'

Sindri looked up at the mountainside and saw a stream of white burst over the ridge, as first a few dozen, then a hundred, and then more than a thousand sheep hurried down the slopes towards the pens. On either side of the flow were the black shapes of the dogs darting, crouching and running to keep control. In a moment a horseman appeared, and then another, and then some more.

It was a magnificent sight.

The crowd, mostly made up of the families of farmers in the dale, pointed and waved. The drovers had been away for three days scouring the highlands for sheep who had spent the summer roaming wild over the fells, gorging themselves on sweet grass. It was the annual *réttir*, or sheep drive, one of the biggest events in the farming calendar. It was the first time Sindri had attended since he had left the farm at sixteen, but the memories came flooding back.

He himself had been a drover three times from the age of fourteen. The first couple of times he had been filled with excitement as he had followed his father and his neighbours on horseback over the fells, looking for the ewes and lambs. The third time had been a disaster. The weather was bad, he had got horribly drunk in the rest hut on the last night, and his father had shouted at him for not pulling his weight on the drive.

Two weeks later he had left home to go to Reykjavík. Music, drugs and alcohol, and later London and more drugs and alcohol. His father's disappointment in him was deep and unyielding.

Which wasn't quite fair. At twenty, Sindri had been the charismatic lead singer of the band Devastation, whose jumbled anarchic screams had reached number two in the UK charts. He was a sensation in his home country and in Europe.

But it lasted less than a year. The money meant the drugs were endlessly on tap. The songs lost any semblance of tune, and Sindri returned to Reykjavík.

He lost a decade of his life. Eventually he managed to pull himself together and got a steady job in a fish factory. He channelled the urge to rebel, tamed it and gave it focus. He joined environmental groups in Iceland opposed to the exploitation of the Icelandic landscape for economic gain. He wrote a book, *Capital Rape*, which contrasted the simple hard-working life of the Icelandic farmer who nurtured his resources and lived with nature, with the exploitation by the desk-bound urban capitalists who extracted resources and destroyed nature. Capital raped the world around it.

The book was big in Germany, and Sindri earned a bit more money. His father disapproved and Sindri very rarely came home. The truth was that Sindri was as distant from the farm of his childhood as the urban capitalists he ranted against.

Sindri scanned the familiar hills, resplendent in their golds and browns glistening in the September sunshine. The sky was a soft pale blue, dotted with jaunty puffs of white. Horses and dogs were fanning out around the giant flock of sheep, channelling them towards the communal pens. He saw his youngest niece, ten-year-old Frída, jumping up and down in anticipation of seeing her own pet lamb again.

It was nice to see the little girl so happy. She had had a tough year.

Sindri sighed. Frída might not be reunited with her pet lamb for very long.

It turned out that the financial difficulties that his younger brother was suffering over Christmas were not the result of a banker-induced squeeze on agricultural incomes as Sindri had supposed. It was worse than that, although it was still the fault of the bankers. Matti had taken over the family farm when their father had died. For three years, he had been investing in the stock market. With astonishing success, at least initially. He had trebled his money. It was easy.

He had borrowed from the bank against the farm and invested more. And doubled his money. He had bought a new Land Cruiser and taken the whole family on safari to Africa. And invested more. With his new-found expertise, Matti had identified Óðinsbanki as the most promising of the banks. He had first invested two years before. As prices had dipped Matti had recognized a buying opportunity, and ploughed all his profits into the bank stock.

Then of course, it all went horribly wrong.

Matti had never told his wife, Freyja. Oh, she knew that he had invested some of their savings in the stock market, and she knew he was worried about how tight money was, but she had no idea how dire the situation had really become, until one morning in March she had woken up early to find the other side of her bed empty. She was unable to get to sleep herself, and had gone looking for her husband. She had found the back door open and footprints in the snow.

She pulled on boots and a coat and followed the footprints out into the darkness, until she found her husband at his favourite spot at the bottom of the slope down from the home meadow where the brook tumbled over the rocks into a pool.

She hadn't heard the shot. Or maybe she had. Maybe that was what had woken her up.

She was devastated. But she was a strong woman, a farmer's daughter from a neighbouring dale, and determined not to let Matti down, despite what he had done to her. Blow after blow fell on the family. The bank threatened foreclosure unless its loans were repaid. The kids were a mess. And there was still a farm to run.

Sindri had felt terrible. He liked Freyja, a blonde woman now in her forties with a strong jaw and a bright eye. He had been fond of his little brother Matti, who had done his duty and taken over the farm from their parents. Matti was the strong, hard-working, slightly unimaginative farmer that over the years Sindri had begun to idolize as the real hero of Iceland.

But perhaps it was Freyja who was the real hero.

As he watched the sheep squeeze into the network of communal pens on the valley floor, Sindri thought again of Bjartur. The man was never far from his thoughts. He had always admired Bjartur, but over the last twelve months the tough crofter had become an obsession.

Bjartur wasn't real: he was a fictional character, the hero of Nobel Prize winning writer Halldór Laxness's book *Independent People* written in 1935. But he *was* real to Sindri, what he stood for was real, what he represented. Bjartur was a farm labourer who had saved enough to buy his own property, a croft called Summerhouses. He was strong, resilient, proud and above all independent. Through the years in which the book unfolded, he put up with appalling hardship, the death of his wives and children, the ruining of the harvest and consequent shortage of hay for his sheep, the patronizing of his more prosperous neighbours, the curses of the local ghosts.

But Bjartur of Summerhouses never gave up. The First World War came, the 'Blessed War' that brought high prices and prosperity to Iceland's sheep farmers. Improvements were made, the old turf-walled crofts gave way to modern concrete farmhouses.

At first Bjartur resisted, but eventually he too took out a loan from the local Cooperative Society run by Ingólfur Arnarson, a neighbour's son named after the famous first settler of Iceland, and built himself a house.

The bust followed the boom, as night follows day. Money was scarce. Farmers defaulted. Ingólfur Arnarson left the area for Reykjavík where he soon became Governor of the National Bank and later Prime Minister. Bjartur's new concrete house was cold, draughty and almost uninhabitable. In the end, he couldn't keep up with the payments either. The house and the land at

Summerhouses was sold off at auction, and Bjartur trudged off over the heath to start all over again, carrying his sick daughter in his arms.

But even at the end, when he had not a króna to his name, he still had his pride, his independence.

In the aftermath of the *kreppa*, Iceland needed to remember Bjartur.

Unfortunately, it had turned out that Matti wasn't Bjartur. Matti had succumbed to the bankers, the borrowing, the easy money. Like the rest of Icelandic society, they had destroyed him.

'Sindri! Will you give us a hand sorting the sheep?' Freyja was walking rapidly towards him. 'If you remember how.'

'I'll remember,' said Sindri, and followed her towards the pen.

Once the sheep had been corralled into the communal pens, each farmer's family went in to sort out their own animals. They were clearly identified by tags, but of course the farmers recognized many of their own animals and had given them names. Frída soon found her Hyrna, much bigger and stronger after the summer in the hills. Sindri was amazed how they could do it; he could dimly remember in his youth that one sheep looked very different from another, but now they all looked pretty much the same. Apart from the odd black one, of course. Sindri had always preferred the black ones.

'Come on!' Freyja called to him. Sindri entered the fray. He got butted a couple of times early on, but the technique of straddling the sheep, avoiding their horns, and dragging them off to the correct pen soon came back to him. It was hard work, but there was an air of exhilaration among the farmers of the dale. They were happy to have their sheep back. The animals would graze the home meadows for a month or so, before many of them would go off to slaughter. The rest would spend the winter indoors, pampered by their masters.

After two hours it was all done.

'Thanks, Sindri,' said Freyja. 'That was a great help. The *réttarkaffi* is at Gunni's house. Are you coming?'

'No,' said Sindri, wiping his brow. 'I need to get back to Reykjavík.'

'Why don't you stay the night with us?' Freyja asked.

Sindri smiled. 'I'd like to. But I have some things I have to do tomorrow.'

Freyja looked at him oddly. She clearly didn't believe that Sindri ever had anything to do that was genuinely important. Which, until recently, was probably true.

'Well, it was nice to see you. Thank you for your help. And if you ever do have some time and want to stay with us, we could use the extra hands. We couldn't pay you, but we can feed you well.'

'Maybe I will,' said Sindri. 'Do you know yet when you will have to sell the farm?'

'The bank are holding off for the time being. But there's no chance I can ever meet the payments. Why they lent Matti so much money, I will never understand.'

'I'm sorry about that,' said Sindri. 'About what he did.'

Freyja shrugged.

'What will you do?' Sindri asked.

'I'd like to carry on farming if I can, for the girls to have the same upbringing I had. But I don't know how. My brother works in Reykjavík, he runs a small software company. He thinks he might be able to get me a job. I don't want to move to Reykjavík, but perhaps we will have to.'

'Well, let me know what happens,' Sindri said. 'Good luck, Freyja.' He kissed her on the cheek.

As he walked back to his car and the long drive back to Reykjavík he thought that perhaps Bjartur did live on after all.

He felt sick with shame. It was urban dwellers like him who had shafted the farmers; not just the bankers and the politicians like Ólafur Tómasson, but the shoppers in the boutiques on Laugavegur, the easy spenders, the borrowers, the speculators. It was true Sindri had always protested about the capitalist system, but he had abandoned the countryside himself. His brother had succumbed to the allure of easy money.

He liked to blame others for what had happened to Iceland, but the truth was he felt as guilty as the rest of them.

He owed Freyja. And Frída. And he would do something about it.

Back at the station, Magnus phoned Detective Sergeant Piper, with Árni and Vigdís listening in. After seeing Emilía, Magnus and Árni had interviewed Óskar's younger brother at his house in the Laugardalur district of Reykjavík. He was clearly put out that the family fortune had disappeared, but he was more inclined to praise Óskar for making the money than blame him for losing it.

Vigdís had visited the distraught parents, and searched Óskar's empty house in Thingholt. Nothing. The banker hadn't lived there for nine months. The only visitors had been a cleaner every fortnight and a secretary from OBG Investments checking for mail.

Magnus relayed the information, or rather lack of it, to Piper. 'So no real signs of an Icelandic connection from this end,' he said. 'Nor Russian. How about you? Any luck with the motorbikes?'

'Some. One of the owners is a small-time drug dealer to the wealthy in Kensington. He claims he has never heard of Gunnarsson. We are inclined to believe him. Besides, his bike was a nine-hundred-cc Kawasaki, and one of the witnesses said he thought the killer's sounded smaller than that.'

Didn't seem like much of a suspect to Magnus. He was wary of the tendency for policemen the world over to fall upon the nearest small-time dealer and try to pin big crimes on him. At least the British police were resisting the temptation. 'Anything on any of the others?'

'Yeah. One of the bikes was nicked last week in Hounslow. A Suzuki one-two-five. We are trying to trace it. Might be something there.'

'What about the Russian girl?'

'We pulled her in again. Nothing. She's cool as a cucumber, though: she could be hiding something. But we have turned up one lead.'

'What's that?'

'A neighbour said a bloke came round a few days ago with a package for Gunnarsson. Didn't have the right number house. She didn't know where Gunnarsson lived, but when we asked the other neighbours, one of them remembered pointing him to the right address.'

'Interesting. Did you get a description?'

'Yes. Young guy, early twenties, short fair hair. Five-eight or five-nine.' Magnus was pleased to hear the familiar feet and inches. He still found heights in metres difficult to translate. 'Broad face, slight dimple on his chin, blue eyes. Black leather jacket, jeans and checked shirt, but neat. Very neat. Too neat for a genuine courier, the neighbour thought. Foreign accent.'

'What kind of foreign accent?'

'Ah, that's the question. The witness is French herself, although she speaks good English. Virginie Rogeon. And she remembered him well. Fancied him, we think, said he was good-looking. She thought the accent might be Polish, but she didn't know. Northern or Eastern European rather than Italian or Spanish.'

'Could it be Icelandic?'

'Is an Icelandic accent distinctive?'

Magnus thought about it. 'Yes. Yes, I guess it is. You could get some Icelanders to speak to the witness, see if it sounds familiar.'

'Good thought. We could try the embassy. Or some of Gunnarsson's friends in London.'

'So apart from that, no real leads then?'

'No. It's early days, but we are struggling a bit. The guv'nor wants me to go to Iceland, if that's OK with you guys.'

'Sure,' said Magnus. 'Glad to have you. When are you coming?'

'Probably tomorrow. I'll let you know when I've booked my flight.'

'Do that. I'll meet you at the airport.'

'I've never been to Iceland before,' Piper said. 'A bit parky is it?'

'Parky?'

'You know. Cold. Chilly.'

'There's no snow on the ground yet, but the latitude is sixty-six degrees north. You can safely leave the sunscreen at home.'

'Baldur's going to love that,' said Árni when Magnus had hung up. 'A British bobby on his patch.'

'I'll look after her,' said Magnus. It did seem a bit of a waste of time, but it would be nice to have a native English speaker around.

'So what now?' said Vigdís.

Magnus leaned back in his chair and thought. It was quite likely that there was indeed no Icelandic connection, but they had to keep an open mind; more than that, they should operate on the basis that there *was* a link, otherwise they would definitely miss one if it did exist.

There were still people to talk to, files to read. But he asked himself the key question: from what he had learned so far, what felt wrong?

'Árni?'

'Yes?'

'Tell me more about Gabríel Örn's death.'

'I'm sure that doesn't have any relevance.'

'Tell me.'

'OK,' said Árni. 'It was last January, right at the peak of the demonstrations. The department was stretched to the limit. We were all out there on the lines, even the detectives, we were working round the clock. We were knackered.

'Anyway, a body washed up on the shore at Straumsvík by the aluminium smelter. It was naked. The clothes were found ten kilometres up the coast, just by the City Airfield, next to that bike path that runs along the shore. It was Gabríel Örn Bergsson. It turned out he had sent two suicide texts before he went for a swim, one to his mother who raised the alarm, and another to his ex-girlfriend, Harpa Einarsdóttir, who didn't, or not until the following morning.

'I went to interview Harpa. She had some story about how she was supposed to meet him at a bar, but he never showed up.'

'And you didn't believe her?'

'She had an alibi. She was seen at the bar, waiting. In fact she got in some kind of argument there. But no, it didn't seem quite right.'

'Why not?'

Árni scrunched up his face, frowning deeply, painfully. 'I don't know. Nothing I can put my finger on. That's why I said it was irrelevant.'

'Were they sure it was suicide?'

'The pathologist had some slight doubts, I think. As did Baldur. But they were pretty much squashed from on high.'

'Why?'

'There was a revolution going on,' said Vigdís. 'And up till then it was peaceful. If Gabríel Örn had been murdered on the night of those demos, it would have put an entirely different flavour on the whole situation. The politicians, the Commissioner, everyone was shit scared that things would turn seriously violent. We all were.'

'Árni, let me tell you something,' Magnus said. 'If your gut tells you something, listen to it. It may turn out to be wrong, it often will, but every so often it will be the best evidence you've got.'

Árni sighed. 'All right.'

'Where does this Harpa woman live?'

'Seltjarnarnes. I can call her to see if she's in?'

'No, Árni. We are going to surprise her.'

CHAPTER EIGHT

HARPA LIVED IN one of a row of identical white houses facing the bay. Small, but expensive enough in the boom times, Magnus thought. Not now though.

When she answered the door Magnus got the firm impression that she had been expecting to hear from the police. For a second she looked panicked, before badly feigned surprise kicked in.

She was in her late thirties, with pale skin, pale blue eyes and dark curly hair reaching down to her shoulders. She had been pretty once, and no doubt could be pretty again, but at that moment she looked tense and worn out. Two deep creases lined her face either side of her mouth, and two smaller notches like deep cuts separated her eyebrows. At first Magnus thought she was wearing make-up, until he realized that the smudges around her eyes were fatigue.

Árni introduced himself and Magnus. They took off their shoes and went through to the kitchen.

A grey-haired man was kneeling on the floor with a curly-haired little boy. They were playing with toy cars and a garish plastic multi-storey car park.

The man pulled himself to his feet, wincing as he did so. He was short, with a broad, hard face criss-crossed with wrinkles. He appeared to be in his late sixties. 'What's this about?' he asked in a gruff voice, squaring his shoulders as he faced up to the detectives.

'We are investigating the death of Óskar Gunnarsson,' Árni said.

'Oh yes?'

'This is my father, Einar,' said Harpa.

Magnus addressed him directly. 'It's your daughter we would like to speak to, Einar. We would prefer to talk to her alone.'

'I'll stay,' said the man.

'She is over eighteen,' said Magnus. 'She doesn't need a parent present.'

He could feel Harpa tense next to him.

'She became quite upset the last time you lot interviewed her,' Einar said. 'I don't want that to happen again.'

'Don't worry, Dad,' said Harpa. 'I'll be much better this time. Why don't you take Markús down to the harbour?'

The small boy's face broke into a wide beam and he started jumping up and down. 'Harbour! Harbour!'

Despite himself, Einar's eyes softened as he struggled to repress a smile.

'Are you sure, my love?'

'Yes, Dad, I'll be fine.'

'OK, come along then, Markús.'

The old man held out his big meaty hand, and it enveloped the little fist of the boy. Magnus, Árni and Harpa waited awkwardly while they put on their shoes and coats and went outside.

'Sorry about that,' said Harpa. 'My father is a bit overprotective.'

'Nice kid,' said Magnus.

'Yes. And his grandfather dotes on him as you can see. He'll be telling him all kinds of stories about his fishing days once they get down to the harbour. Markús loves it although I'm sure he doesn't understand what Dad is saying: he just likes the rumble of his voice.'

Magnus and Árni sat at the kitchen table as Harpa poured them some coffee and sat opposite them.

'You heard Óskar was shot in London?' Árni asked.

'Yes,' Harpa said, tensing. 'Yes, I heard it on the radio. It was quite a shock.'

'Did you know him?'

'Yes, I did. He was my boss, or rather my boss's boss. Oh, I didn't know him well. But I have had plenty of meetings with him over the years.'

'Did you know him socially?'

'No,' Harpa said firmly. Too firmly. 'Absolutely not.'

The denial piqued Magnus's interest. Already he could sense that things were not quite right with Harpa. 'So you were never invited to any of his parties?'

'Um. Yes, yes, I was,' Harpa said. 'I suppose I did see him socially at business gatherings within the company. He was good with all his staff. But I wouldn't call him a friend. And we never met outside work.'

'When was the last time you saw him?'

Harpa blew air out of her cheeks. 'I suppose it was the goodbye speech he gave to all the staff the day he left.' She smiled. 'Gudmundur Rasmussen, the idiot they brought in to take over when the bank was nationalized, insisted Óskar leave around the back. So Óskar calmly walked around the building and through the front entrance. He'd planned it all before, a bunch of us were waiting for him in the atrium.' She smiled. 'It was a good speech.'

'But you haven't seen him since then?' Magnus asked.

'No. From what I have read he went straight to London and pretty much stayed there. I don't think he ever came back to Iceland.'

Magnus nodded. Harpa was becoming more convincing.

'I'd like to ask you about the death of Gabríel Örn Bergsson,' Magnus said.

Immediately Harpa tensed again. 'Why? That was suicide. What connection can there be with Óskar?'

'That's a good question,' said Magnus. 'Do you know of a possible connection?'

Harpa's face betrayed a mixture of confusion and panic. She tilted her head forward to let her curly hair hang over her eyes, and then tossed it irritably out of the way. Playing for time. 'No. No.

There can't be one. I know they both worked for the same bank, but one man killed himself and the other was murdered.'

'Do you know why Gabríel Örn killed himself?' Magnus asked.

'I don't. But he was responsible for a lot of bad loans,' said Harpa. 'Big losses for Óðinsbanki.'

'But there were plenty of other bankers responsible for losing money last year. They haven't committed suicide. Why was Gabríel Örn so sensitive?'

'I don't know.'

'You knew him intimately. Did it surprise you that he drowned himself?'

Harpa sighed. 'Yes. Yes, it did,' she said quietly. 'He was usually pretty confident about his talents. Maybe he finally realized what a bastard he was. Maybe he couldn't look at himself in the mirror.'

'He treated you badly?'

'You could say that. He took all the credit for the good work I did, he was the one who got the big bonuses while I got diddly-squat. He blamed me for the bad deals he did. That infuriated me. I argued against doing all of the three big deals that eventually went wrong, but Gabríel overruled me, said I wasn't smart enough to see the opportunity. I wasn't smart enough to stop listening to him, that was the problem.

'Then one day, as a special reward for my achievement at the bank, he told me I had become one of the golden circle of privileged employees who would be allowed to buy stock in the Óðinsbanki on special terms. The bank would lend me the money to do it, at low rates. I knew that it was how he had made tens of millions of krónur over the previous few years and I thought it was my big chance, so I went for it.'

She shook her head. 'Six months later the shit hit the fan, the stock price fell to zero practically, and the bank was nationalized. But somehow the loan I had taken out was still there.'

'Presumably everyone else suffered too?'

Harpa's laugh had no humour and a tinge of hysteria. 'A lot of us did. But not the true "golden circle". While we were buying, they were selling. Gabríel sold three-quarters of his shares and had paid down all his loan.'

'So you dumped him?' Magnus asked.

'I didn't know anything about that at that stage.' Harpa sighed. 'He dumped me. There used to be a rule in all the banks that staff in a relationship couldn't work together. After Gudmundur arrived, that rule was reinstated. Guess who had to go?'

'Tough,' Magnus said.

'Yes. Though once I had left, my friends told me Gabríel was having an affair with a twenty-three-year-old trainee anyway. It was very convenient for him.'

Harpa's bitterness had overwhelmed her initial confusion.

'Can you tell me what happened the night he died?'

'Killed himself, you mean?'

'Died.' Magnus repeated himself firmly.

'But I told your colleague in January.'

'Tell us again,' said Magnus. He had pulled out his notebook. Árni's notes from that first interview, which Magnus had skimmed on the way to Seltjarnarnes, were very sketchy.

Harpa hesitated, as if looking for a way out. There wasn't one.

'I went to the demonstration that afternoon in the Austurvöllur square outside the Parliament building. I met a man there, Björn Helgason. After the tear gas broke up the protest, I went back to his place.'

'Where was that?' Magnus asked.

'Up the hill by the Catholic Cathedral. Actually it was his brother's flat. Björn lives in Grundarfjördur; he was staying with his brother so he could attend the demo.'

'Was Björn's brother there?'

'No, he was out somewhere or other.'

'Then what happened?'

'We had a drink. We talked. We got to the point where I thought something might happen. But then... then I guess I got cold feet. I felt bad about Gabríel. I needed to see him. So I called him and told him to meet me at B5 on Bankastraeti.'

'What did Björn think about that?'

'He seemed disappointed, but he was a gentleman about it. He insisted on giving me his number.'

'So then what happened?'

'So I walked over to Bankastraeti. Got into B5 and waited. Gabríel never came. By this stage I was a bit drunk. Some student began to annoy me. I slapped him. He slapped me. A couple of guys stepped in to protect me. The barman threw the student out.'

'What was the student's name?' Magnus asked, knowing the answer from Árni's notes.

'Ísak, I think,' Harpa said. 'I can't remember.'

'And then?'

'I got a text from Gabríel. It said something like "Gone swimming. Sorry. Goodbye." I didn't really understand this, but I was pretty drunk at the time. I think I assumed it was a typical smart-arse Gabríel remark meaning he was standing me up. So I called Björn and asked him to pick me up.'

'What time was all this?' Magnus asked.

'I don't know. Midnight? One? Two? I told your colleague at the time.'

And my colleague didn't write it down, Magnus thought.

'OK. And where did you go with Björn?'

'Back to his brother's place,' said Harpa. 'And what happened then you can guess.'

'Did you see the brother?'

'I did, but not till the following morning. I saw him on my way out.'

'And what time was that?'

'No idea. Can't remember. But as I was walking home – I walked the whole way, I do remember that – I started thinking about the text Gabríel sent me. It worried me. I dithered a bit, but once I got home I rang the police.'

The story was possible, unlikely, but possible. But there was one thing that made no sense to Magnus. 'Why did you suddenly call

Gabríel Örn? You just told me why you hated him, for what seem to me to be perfectly good reasons.'

'Er...' Magnus waited, as Harpa struggled. It seemed to him that she was trying to remember something, rather than figure something out, as if the key thing for her was to repeat what she had said before rather than to come out with the truth.

'I suppose I still loved him,' she said.

'Oh, come on!' said Magnus. 'He'd behaved appallingly to you.'

'Yes,' Harpa said. 'But I was a bit drunk, I had never been with a man since Gabríel Örn, I was nervous, scared even. I felt guilty.'

Magnus shook his head. 'I don't believe any of this.'

'I don't care what you believe!' Harpa cried. 'I don't know what I believe, now. After Gabríel's death everything changed. I can't remember why I loved him, I can't remember how I felt towards him then. The man I loved killed himself! Yes, I hate him. Yes, sometimes I love him. And sometimes I feel guilty. I don't know why, but I do.' She fought to control herself. 'Now I have no idea why I called him. I was a different person then.'

That, Magnus could believe. It was difficult to imagine how a normal woman would feel if her former boyfriend killed himself, no matter how horrible he had been to her. He knew it wouldn't be logical; it wouldn't be consistent.

But everyone was making an assumption here, an assumption that Magnus was not entirely happy with.

'Harpa,' Magnus leaned forward, facing her over the kitchen table, 'do you think there is a chance that Gabríel Örn's death wasn't suicide?'

'No,' said Harpa. 'No chance at all. It was suicide. It must have been. You investigated it.'

'Did Gabríel Örn have any enemies?' Magnus asked. 'Apart from you, that is?'

'What are you insinuating?'

'I'm just asking a question.'

'A lot of people didn't like Gabríel Örn. He was scum, basically.'

'And the world's better off without him?'

'No!' said Harpa, looking close to tears now. 'No! Not at all! You are twisting my words. His death was dreadful, as was Óskar's. Now why don't you go out and find out who killed them?'

'Them?' said Magnus with half a smile.

'Him, damn you! Óskar! And don't try to trick me, it doesn't prove anything. Now please go.'

'Your instincts were right, Árni,' Magnus said as they drove back downtown. 'No wonder she didn't want her father to stay. She's not telling us the truth.'

'I thought so. Do you think we should have kept him there?'

'No, she would just have clammed up completely,' Magnus said. 'Árni, you must take more detailed notes. What you've got on that interview in January is useless. You *must* write down the specifics. That's how you catch people out, when they get the details wrong.'

'It didn't seem important at the time,' said Árni. 'We were just going through the motions. The Big Salmon was clear that this was suicide and nothing more.' The Big Salmon was Snorri Gudmundsson, the National Police Commissioner. 'Also, I was tired. I was in that demo too, you know, but I was the one having *skyr* thrown at me. They pulled in everyone, including the guys from CID, we did sixteen-hour shifts protecting the Parliament building. I think I had just done twelve hours straight before I was told to investigate this case.'

Magnus grunted as he skimmed Árni's notes on the interview with Björn Helgason. That too was brief.

'Did Björn corroborate what Harpa said?'

'Yes,' said Árni. 'And he was much more convincing. You are not suggesting we should go and see him in Grundarfjördur, are you? That's at least two hours away. It would take a whole day to get there and back.'

Magnus knew that they should. There was a hole in Harpa's story and Björn was a natural place to start looking for it. But

Grundarfjördur was a fair distance away, on the Snaefells Peninsula on the west coast of Iceland. He had his own reasons for not wanting to go anywhere near that area if he could avoid it.

'Maybe later,' he said.

The *Kría* was heading home. It had been a rotten day and tempers were frayed. The crew couldn't wait to get back to harbour and unload what little there was of the day's catch, a couple of disappointing hauls of small haddock.

It was dark. To the right, Búland's Head rose in massive blackness against the lighter darkness of the cloud-torn sky. Ahead was Krossnes light, the rhythm of its winking so familiar. The crew stood in silence. Gústi, the skipper, had screwed up. He had misjudged the effect of the tide on the seine net and it had drifted on to a known wreck on their third haul of the day, snagging. When Björn had seen where they were fishing, he had suggested they were too close, but Gústi had ignored him. Then they had spent the whole of the rest of the day trying to free the net, before eventually kissing goodbye to two hundred thousand krónur's worth of equipment. Björn had suggested cutting it after an hour or so, at least then they could have used the spare net to salvage something of the day.

It was difficult being the skipper of a fishing boat. You had to be able to find the fish. And you constantly had to weigh up the risks of different courses of action. Björn had a knack for it. Gústi didn't. And it was almost as if Gústi was determined not to take Björn's advice.

Björn was as much a threat as a help to Gústi. Since Björn had lost his own boat he went out with any of the skippers he could either from Grundarfjördur or one of the little ports that lined the north coast of Snaefells Peninsula: Rif, Ólafsvík, Stykkishólmur. The *Kría* didn't belong to Gústi, but to a fishing company, and although Björn was ten years younger than the skipper, everyone in Grundarfjördur knew what a good fisherman he was. Gústi was afraid for his job. Björn had to be careful or there was a good chance that Gústi wouldn't take him on as crew again.

Still, the small catch meant it wouldn't take long to unload the boat and clean up. Then he could be on the road down to Reykjavík to see Harpa.

She was getting to him in a way that no woman had ever got to him before. She wasn't his type at all, and he was beginning to realize that that was the reason why she had such an effect on him. He liked self-assured women; women who knew what they wanted and what they wanted was sex with him. He was happy to oblige, and when things got a little complicated, a little heavy, a little emotional, as they inevitably did, he moved on. Some were upset: most had always known that was the deal. He had lived with a woman for two years once, Katla, but that had only worked because they had managed to keep their emotional distance despite sharing the same bed and roof. As soon as the relationship had developed into something more, it finished.

But Harpa was different. She was smart – he actually liked talking to her. Like him, she had been screwed by the *kreppa*, even if in an entirely different way. She was vulnerable and there was something about the vulnerability of such a capable woman that Björn found appealing. She needed him in a way that no woman had needed him before, and rather than running a mile, he responded to it.

He didn't have to ride the best part of two hundred kilometres to see her that night, but he was happy to do it. It was worth it.

She was worth it.

CHAPTER NINE

MAGNUS WAS IN a good mood as he parked the Game Over on Njálsgata, opposite his house, or rather Katrín's house. 'Game Overs' were what they were calling Range Rovers these days: Magnus had bought his at a knockdown price from a bankrupt lawyer who owned two, but couldn't really afford one. It was a gas guzzler, but once you got outside Reykjavík a good four-wheel-drive was a must.

The quick couple of beers he had had at the Grand Rokk were partly responsible for his mood. The Grand Rokk was a bar just off Hverfisgata. Warm, scruffy, populated during the week by men and women who liked to drink, it reminded Magnus of the places he and his buddies would unwind after a shift in Boston. That kind of thing was much less common in Reykjavík, except on the weekends when everyone went crazy. In fact, weekday drinking was frowned upon. Which kind of added to the allure of the Grand.

On occasion when he had first arrived in Iceland a couple of beers had turned into many more, plus uncounted chasers, which had got him into trouble. But these days he had things under control.

It wasn't just the beer, though. It felt good to be doing straight-forward police work again. And the case was piquing his interest. He wasn't sure whether they would find an Icelandic link to Óskar's death, but if they did he was willing to bet that it would be through Harpa. It was to be expected that she should be upset after her ex-boyfriend topped himself. But Harpa's agitation was more complicated than that: she was hiding something.

And Gabríel Örn's suicide didn't make sense. So far they had found no signs of suicidal thoughts or actions, or of extreme depression. And if he did want to commit suicide, walking three miles to the sea and jumping in seemed a very strange way to do it, especially on a cold night. Why not drive? Take a taxi? Or just stay at home and take some pills?

It may be that further investigation would reveal a suicidal side to Gabríel Örn that would make sense of it all.

But Magnus wouldn't be surprised if it didn't.

As he took out his house keys, the door opened and his landlady appeared, in full regalia.

Katrín was tall with short dyed-black hair, white make-up, and metal sprouting from her face and ears. She was wearing black jeans, T-shirt and coat. She looked a little like her brother Árni, but where Árni's features were weak, hers were strong. Under her arm was a tiny bird of a girl with short blonde hair.

'Hi, Magnus,' Katrín said in English. She had spent some time in England and liked to speak to him in that language. 'We're just going out. This is Tinna, by the way.'

'Hello, Tinna,' said Magnus. 'How you doin'?'

Tinna nodded, smiled, and leaned into her taller companion's side.

Magnus wasn't yet familiar enough with the conventions of female friendship in Iceland to be sure of what exactly he was witnessing.

Katrín noticed his confusion. 'I've gone off men, Magnus. They smell and they lie. Don't you think so?'

'Well...' Magnus said.

'Tinna is much nicer,' Katrín said, squeezing the small blonde.

Tinna smiled up at her friend and they kissed each other quickly on the lips.

'Oh, don't tell Árni, will you, Magnus? I wouldn't mind, but it will only upset him.'

'I won't,' said Magnus. One of the reasons Árni had installed Magnus with his sister was so that Magnus could spy on her. This was something Magnus was not prepared to do. He liked Katrín, she made a good house mate, even if they didn't see very much of each other. Perhaps *because* they didn't see very much of each other.

As he entered the hallway, he smelled cooking. He checked the kitchen, wondering if Katrín had left something on the stove. There was Ingileif, pushing some scallops around a frying pan with a wooden spoon.

'Hi,' she said, leaving the stove and coming towards him. She gave him a long, lingering kiss.

'Hi,' said Magnus, smiling. 'This is a bit of a surprise.'

'You've been to the Grand Rokk, haven't you? I can smell it on your breath.'

'Does it bother you?' said Magnus.

'No, of course not. I think that dive suits you perfectly. Just don't try and drag me in there. Do you like scallops?'

'I do.'

'That's lucky.'

'Um. How did you get in here, Ingileif?'

'Katrín let me in. Oh, by the way, did you meet Tinna? Cute, isn't she?'

'Um. Possibly,' said Magnus. He wasn't quite sure what he thought about Ingileif talking herself into his house without asking him.

'I've been invited to a party on Friday night. Jakob and Selma. Do you want to come?'

'Is he the little guy with the big nose?'

'More of a big guy with a little nose. You have met him. They are two of my best clients.'

Ingileif ran a fashionable gallery. Ran it very well. Her clients were some of the wealthiest citizens of Reykjavík, beautiful people, who owned beautiful art and dressed beautifully. They were all perfectly friendly to Magnus, but he didn't fit. For a start he didn't have the right clothes, there was not a designer T-shirt or a designer suit in his wardrobe. His two favourite shirts were by LL

Bean, but he didn't think that counted, and neither did his suit from Macy's. The main thing, though, was that all these people had known each other since they were kids.

'I don't know,' said Magnus. 'I expect I'll have work to do on the Óskar Gunnarsson case.'

'OK,' Ingileif said. She didn't seem bothered. She never seemed bothered that she went out without him.

He never quite knew where he stood with her. But it was kinda nice when she showed up in his home, right in the middle of his life, unannounced, uninvited.

She glanced at him. 'You know, these scallops can wait.'

Magnus smiled as he looked down at Ingileif. She was snuggled under his arm, her head resting on his chest, her blonde hair bunched up under his chin. Her eyes were closed, but she wasn't asleep. He noticed the familiar little nick above one of her eyebrows. There was a small smile on her own lips.

'I fit very nicely in here,' she said. 'Am I just the right size, or are you?'

'I guess we both are,' said Magnus. 'We fit.'

'We do.'

It was true, Ingileif was one of the good things about Iceland, a reason to stay. Magnus had had a girlfriend in the States for several years, a lawyer named Colby. She was smart, she was attractive and she knew what she wanted. And what she wanted was for Magnus to quit the police force, go to law school, get a decent job and marry her. That wasn't what Magnus wanted, which is why they had broken up.

That and the fact that Colby didn't like being shot at by hoodlums with semi-automatic rifles on the streets of Boston.

Ingileif seemed to have no intention of marrying him, or changing him. They had met in his first week in Iceland, she had been a witness and then a suspect in the murder case he had worked on. They had gone through a lot together. Like Magnus, her father had been killed when she was a child. Magnus had discovered how that had happened, a discovery that had been very difficult for Ingileif to take.

He had supported her, talked to her, understood her pain, helped her come to terms with it, or at least accept that she could never completely come to terms with it. It was a bond between them.

She shifted in his arms. 'So, have you solved Óskar's murder yet?'

'Not yet,' said Magnus.

'That's pathetic. You've had all day.'

'It might take me more than a day,' Magnus said.

'Even for CSI Magnús?'

'I think you mean CSI Boston?'

'Do I? I never watch those programmes. But I bet I can solve your crime.' Ingileif disentangled herself from Magnus and sat up in bed. 'Give me your clues.'

'It doesn't really work like that,' said Magnus. 'We haven't found an Icelandic connection. The murderer probably lives in London. That was where Óskar was killed, after all.'

'Huh. Well, have you sorted out Óskar's sex life?'

'Do *you* know about Óskar's sex life?'

'Not personally, you idiot. But I have come across him. Kamilla, his wife, or rather his ex-wife, was one of my clients. Nice woman. Pretty. A bit dull.'

'Vigdís interviewed her,' Magnus said. 'She didn't think there was much animosity there now.'

'Probably not,' said Ingileif. 'But there was for a bit. Especially when María was involved.'

'María?'

'Yes. She's an old friend of mine. And she was Óskar's girlfriend for a couple of years. She was the reason he got divorced. She's married now, to someone else, but she can tell you all about him.'

'Hmm.' Sexual jealousy as a motive for murder was one of the old favourites. Ingileif was right, they should probably find out more about Óskar's lovers, at least the ones who lived in Iceland.

'I'll call her now,' Ingileif said. 'We can meet up.'

'Vigdís can interview her tomorrow.'

'What do you mean? She's my witness,' said Ingileif, rolling out of bed to dig out her mobile phone. 'Isn't that the technical expression?'

'Not exactly.'

Ingileif held up her finger to shush him. 'María? Hi, it's Ingileif. Hey, I wanted to talk to you about Óskar. It must be terrible for you.'

Five minutes later Ingileif had fixed up for Magnus to go to María's house to interview her the following morning. Ingileif was pleased with herself. 'We'll have this solved in no time,' she said. 'So who did you see today?'

'My cousin, Sibba,' Magnus answered.

'Is she a witness?'

'No. But she was acting as a lawyer for Óskar's sister.'

'Wait. You mentioned her before. She's the cousin on your mother's side, isn't she?'

'Yes. Yes, that's right.'

'The one who told you about your father screwing your mother's best friend?'

'Yes.' Magnus's voice was hoarse. 'Do you mind if we don't talk about it? I shouldn't have mentioned it. I don't want to think about it.'

'OK,' said Ingileif, and squeezed his hand.

But Magnus *was* thinking about it. Until the age of eight Magnus had had an idyllic childhood. His mother taught at school, his father at the university and he and his brother Óli played in the garden of their little house with its bright blue corrugated metal roof, only a short distance from where Magnus was living now in Thingholt.

But then things had changed, changed horribly. His father had announced he was leaving to go to a university in America. His mother, alone in charge of the boys, began to drink. The two boys were sent to stay with their grandparents on their farm at

Bjarnarhöfn on the Snaefells Peninsula. That period of his life Magnus had blanked from his memory, but he knew that the scars were still there, buried deep under his skin.

The scars were more obvious in the case of Óli. He had never really recovered from his time at the farm.

Then one day their mother killed herself in a car crash. She was drunk. Finally, the two boys' father, Ragnar, came over from America to rescue them and take them back with him to Boston. Magnus was twelve, Óli ten.

As Magnus had grown up and begun to understand more about alcoholism, he had developed his own way of making sense of his parents' lives. His mother, his alcoholic mother, not the beautiful woman he dimly remembered from his childhood, was the villain, his father the hero.

That was until he had bumped into Sigurbjörg in the street four months before. She had shattered Magnus's idea of history by telling him that his father had had an affair with his mother's best friend. That's what had driven her to drink. That's what had caused him to run away to America. That's what, ultimately, had led to her death.

It was this knowledge that Magnus had tried to cram back into its box.

'You're still thinking about Sibba, aren't you?' Ingileif said. 'I can feel it.'

Magnus sighed. 'Yes.'

'You know you should face up to it. See her. Find out what really happened between your father and your mother's friend.'

'I said I didn't want to talk about it.'

Ingileif ignored him. 'I remember when you decided that you were going to stay on in Iceland. One of the reasons was that you thought there might be an Icelandic link to your father's death.'

Magnus shook his head. 'Ingileif...'

'No, listen to me. You've obsessed about how your father was murdered and who by all your adult life. That's why you do what you do, it's who you are. Isn't it?'

Reluctantly Magnus nodded. It was why he had joined the police, why he had become a homicide detective, why he was so relentless in tracking down the killer of every victim he came across.

'OK. So you are all excited about spending time trying to find the Icelandic angle to Óskar's death, which you admit is very unlikely, yet you won't find out more about an Icelandic angle to your own father's murder. That doesn't make sense.'

'It's different,' Magnus protested.

'Why?'

'Because.' He struggled to conjure up a plausible reason, but then settled on the truth. 'Because it's personal.'

'Of course, it's personal!' Ingileif said. 'And that's exactly why you have to deal with it. Just like I had to find out how my own father died even though the answer was so painful to me. And don't tell me that that wasn't personal!'

Magnus stroked her hair. 'No. No, I won't tell you that.' Ingileif's pain had been real, was real. She was right. It had been important for her to find out the truth. So why wasn't it important for him?

'You're scared, Magnús. Admit it, you are scared of what you might find out.'

Magnus closed his eyes. He hated being called a coward. It was not his self-image at all. Since his youth he had been an avid reader of the Icelandic sagas, the tales of medieval revenge and daring. There were heroes and cowards in those stories, seekers of justice and hiders from it, and Magnus saw himself as one of those heroes. He smiled to himself. There were also women urging their men-folk to get off their asses and go avenge the family honour. Women like Ingileif.

'You are right,' he said. 'I am scared. But... Well...'

'Well, what?'

'You know I told you I spent four years at my grandfather's farm when my father left us?'

'Yes.'

Magnus swallowed. 'Those are four years I don't want to remember.'

'What happened?' Ingileif asked, touching his chest. 'What happened, Magnús?'

Magnus exhaled. 'That's something I really don't want to tell you. That memory has to stay in its box.'

Harpa stared out of her window at the blinking lights of Reykjavík across the bay, waiting for Björn to come. He had a big powerful motorbike, and she knew she could trust him to get down to her as fast as he could. It was a hundred and eighty kilometres, but the road was good all the way and, with the exception of the last stretch through the Reykjavík suburbs, empty.

She had been agitated since the interview with the two detectives. The big one with the red hair and the slight American accent had got under her skin. He was smarter than the skinny one she had spoken to in January. There was something about his eyes, blue, steady, understanding, that seemed to miss nothing, to see through all her protests and posturing. He knew she wasn't telling the truth. They had no link between Gabríel Örn's death and Óskar's, the Gabríel Örn case was firmly closed by the authorities, but that detective knew there was something wrong.

He would be back.

Harpa had been mean to Markús, snapping at him for not tidying up his trucks. Later, when they were reading one of the poems in *Vísnabókin*, favourites from her own childhood, Markús had had to point out that she had read the same verse twice.

After he was in bed she had paced around the house, desperate to go for a walk on the beach at Grótta at the end of the Seltjarnarnes promontory, but unwilling to leave Markús alone in the house. She thought of calling her mother to babysit, but she couldn't face the explanations, the small lies hiding the much bigger lie.

So in the end she had poured herself a cup of coffee and sat at the kitchen table staring out of the window, watching night settle over Faxaflói Bay, forcing herself to remain still. She was in a kind of a trance. Inside she was screaming. Outside she was motionless, frozen.

Gabríel's death would never leave her. In some strange way, his death, or her part in it, had lodged itself somewhere inside her. It had bided its time for a few months, but now it was growing like some ghastly tropical parasite, eating her up from the inside.

That evening, she had been unable to look Markús directly in the eye. Those big, trusting, honest brown eyes. How could she tell him that his mother was a liar? Worse than that, a murderer?

How could she live her life never being able to look her son in the eye?

She wanted to throw back the kitchen chair and scream. But she didn't move. Didn't move a muscle. Didn't even raise the cup of cold coffee in front of her to her lips.

Where the hell was Björn?

She stared out into the gathering darkness, at Gabríel Örn lying there on the ground in the car park just off Hverfisgata, blood from his skull mingling with dirt in the slush.

She heard her own screams.

'Shush, Harpa, shush.' Björn's voice was calm, and authoritative. Harpa stopped screaming. She sobbed instead.

He crouched down beside Gabríel. 'Is he dead?' Harpa whispered.

Björn frowned. By the way he moved his fingers around Gabríel's throat, pressing on one spot and then another, Harpa could tell that he couldn't find a pulse.

Harpa pulled out her phone. 'I'll call an ambulance.'

'No!' Björn instructed her, his voice firm. 'No. He's dead. There's no point in calling an ambulance for a dead person. We'll all end up in jail.'

'Let's get out of here,' said Frikki.

'No. Wait! Let me think,' Björn said. 'We need a story.'

'No one will know it was us,' said Sindri. 'Let's just go.'

'They'll know Harpa called him just before he came out,' Björn said. 'Phone records. The police will interview her. Perhaps someone was with him, someone who knows he was going to meet her.'

'Don't tell them anything, Harpa,' Frikki said.

'Oh, God,' said Harpa. She knew she would tell the police everything.

'Quiet!' Björn urged. 'Let's calm down. We need a story. An alibi for everyone. First let's get him out of the way. And try not to get his blood on your clothes.'

Sindri, Frikki and Björn dragged Gabríel into the small car park and laid him between two parked cars.

'Harpa needs to go to B5,' Ísak said. The others looked at him. 'She needs to go to B5 right away. She needs to make a fuss about something so they remember that she is there. Start an argument with someone. Me perhaps. There is no connection between us, the police won't suspect anything.'

'But where was she before?' Sindri asked.

'With me,' Björn said. 'We met at the demonstration. She came back with me to my brother's place. Things went wrong: she called her old boyfriend, wanted to see him.'

'She waited at the bar for him and he never came,' Ísak said.

'What are we going to do with the body?' Sindri asked.

'I can move it somewhere,' said Björn.

'Fake a suicide,' said Ísak. 'I don't know, a fall? Hang him some-where?'

'That's horrible,' Harpa said. 'I think I am going to be sick.'

'I'll take him down to the sea for a swim,' said Björn. 'Sindri, you can help me. OK, give me your phone number, Harpa. You go to B5 with Ísak, but make sure you arrive separately. Make a fuss, but try not to get thrown out; we need you there as long as possible. I'll get rid of the body now and call you in an hour or two. Then you can come back to my brother's place with me. We can go through the details of your story then.'

Harpa nodded. She pulled herself together and set off for Bankastraeti and the bar, Ísak following by a different route.

Even though the plan was made up on the spot and there were plenty of holes in it, it worked. Harpa could never have thought of it. It took Ísak's brains and Björn's calm.

She had coped with the police questioning well. If it hadn't been for Björn she would have cracked. He gave her the strength and determination to stick with her story. And now she was going to have to go through it all again, but this time she wasn't sure she would be able to do as good a job.

She heard a motorbike approaching fast along Nordurströnd. She heard it come to a stop outside the house.

Her heart leapt. She ran out of the house and threw herself into the arms of the driver even before he had a chance to take his helmet off.

'Oh, Björn, I'm so glad you are here.' She began to sob.

He slipped off the helmet and stroked her hair. 'There, there, Harpa. It's all going to be OK.'

She pulled back. 'It's not going to be OK, Björn. I killed someone. I'm going to hell. I'm *in* hell.'

'There is no hell,' Björn said. 'You feel guilty, but you shouldn't. Of course killing people is wrong, but you didn't mean to kill him, did you? It was an accident. People die in accidents.'

'It wasn't an accident,' said Harpa. 'I attacked him.'

'The whole thing happened because Sindri and that kid egged you on. They were the ones who made you call him up and get him to come out and meet you. What we both did wrong was to go along with them. Look at me, Harpa. You're not a bad person.'

But Harpa didn't look at him. She pressed herself into Björn's leather-clad chest. She wanted to believe him. She wanted so desperately to believe him.

CHAPTER TEN

November 1934

HALLGRÍMUR LOOKED OUT over the snow as he made his way to the barn where the sheep were huddled together for the winter. He had to check on the hay.

It was ten o'clock and just getting light. The snow, which had fallen a few days before, glowed a luminescent blue, except at the top of the far mountains where the rising sun painted it red. He could still see the dark shapes of the twisted rocky waves of the Berserkjahraun. The warmth of the lava stone meant that the snow always melted there first.

A cold wind whipped in from the fjord. Hallgrímur saw a small figure tramping his way across the snow towards the little church. Benni.

Hallgrímur hadn't seen much of his friend over the past few weeks, but he felt sorry for him. Benedikt's father's disappearance had taken everyone by surprise. His mother had not the faintest clue where her husband might have gone. Search parties went out everywhere: over the Bjarnarhöfn Fell in case he had been looking for a lost sheep, along the shore in case he had fallen into the sea, over the Berserkjahraun, into the towns of Stykkishólmur and Grundarfjördur. When nothing turned up, the search went further afield: over the mountains to the south and the Kerlingin Pass, along the coast to Ólafsvík, the sheriff down in Borgarnes was informed.

There was no sign of him anywhere.

Hallgrímur had joined in the search parties, sticking closely to his father wherever he went. He was amazed and impressed by his father's determination to help, the long hours he spent on the fells looking for a body he knew lay at the bottom of a lake only a few kilometres away.

The atmosphere at Bjarnarhöfn was awful. His father and mother didn't talk. The hatred was palpable. Hallgrímur's brother and sisters assumed it was grief and shock. Only Hallgrímur knew the real reason.

The boy hated his mother for what she had done with Benni's father. And, although he knew it was wrong, he couldn't help admiring his father for doing something about it.

Of course things were much worse at Hraun. Benni's mother had been demented with worry, but she was a strong woman and she didn't let the farm slip. Neighbours were eager to help.

Where had Benedikt's father gone? The theories became more and more wild. The two wildest were that he had emigrated to America with a woman, and that the Kerlingin troll had got him.

More sober heads assumed he had somehow fallen into Breidafjördur and been swept away into the ocean.

Hallgrímur walked over the snow-covered home meadow down to the church. It was little more than a hut, with black painted wooden walls and a red metal roof. There was no spire, just a white cross above the entrance. It was surrounded by a low wall of stone and turf, and a graveyard of a mixture of old grey headstones and newer white wooden crosses. Hallgrímur's ancestors lay there. One day, in the far off future, perhaps in the twenty-first century if he was lucky, Hallgrímur would join them.

There was no pastor of Bjarnarhöfn. The pastor at Helgafell, the small bump in the distance near the town of Stykkishólmur, held services there once a month.

Hallgrímur opened the door. Benni was sitting in the front pew, staring at the altar. He had a book on his lap. Hallgrímur recognized it, it was Benedikt's copy of the *Saga of the People of Eyri*.

'Hello,' said Hallgrímur, joining him. 'What are you doing?'

'I am trying to pray,' said Benedikt.

'What for?' said Hallgrímur. 'They won't find him.'

'For his soul.'

'Ah,' said Hallgrímur. He had never quite got to grips with the concept of soul. 'Are you all right, Benni?'

'No. I feel so bad for my mother. She has no idea what happened to Dad and she will never find out. Unless I tell her.'

'You can't do that,' said Hallgrímur.

'Why not?' said Benedikt. 'I think about it all the time.'

'It will get us into trouble.'

'Not very much trouble,' said Benedikt. 'We didn't kill him.'

Hallgrímur frowned. 'It would get my father into a lot of trouble.'

'Perhaps he deserves it.' Benedikt glared at Hallgrímur.

'And your father, too. I know he's dead, but everyone thinks he's a hero. They won't think that if they know what he did.'

'Maybe.'

The two boys stared at the altar and its simple cross.

'Benni?'

'Yes?'

'If you do tell anyone, I will kill you.' Hallgrímur didn't know why he made the threat: it just came out of nowhere. But he knew he meant it. And the fact that he had uttered it in the church gave it greater meaning.

Benedikt didn't answer.

'Tell me a story from in there, Benni,' Hallgrímur said, tapping the book on Benedikt's lap.

'All right,' said Benedikt. He was still staring ahead at the altar, not looking at Hallgrímur. 'Do you remember Björn of Breidavík?' Benedikt didn't need to open the book: he knew all the stories.

'The one who went to America and became a chieftain?'

'Yes. Do you want to know why he went there?'

'Why?'

'There was a beautiful woman called Thurídur who lived at Fródá. It's near Ólafsvík.'

'I know.'

'Even though she was someone else's wife, Björn kept on going to see her. He loved her.'

'Oh.' Hallgrímur wasn't sure he liked the sound of this story.

'Thurídur's brother was a great chieftain called Snorri who lived at Helgafell.'

'Yes, you have told me about him.'

'Well, Snorri was angry with Björn and had him outlawed so he had to leave Iceland.'

'That was then,' Hallgrímur said. 'My father couldn't have got your father outlawed. That doesn't happen any more.'

Benedikt ignored him. 'A few years later Björn returned to Breidavík and went back to seeing Thurídur. This time Snorri sent a slave to kill Björn, but Björn caught the slave and had him killed instead. There was a big battle between the families of Björn and Snorri on the ice below Helgafell. In the end Björn left Iceland of his own accord. He ended up in America with the Skraelings.'

'Perhaps your father should have gone to America,' said Hallgrímur.

Benedikt turned away from the altar to look straight at Hallgrímur. 'Perhaps Björn should have killed Snorri.'

Friday, 18 September 2009

Magnus carried the two cups of coffee from the counter and sat down opposite Sigurbjörg. They were in a café on Borgartún. He had called her early, catching her just as she arrived in her office, and she had agreed to see him for a few minutes before the working day began in earnest.

He had woken up at four-thirty thinking about what Sigurbjörg had told him back in April, and had been unable to get back to sleep. Denial wasn't going to work. He had heard what he had heard and he was going to have to make sense of it. The sooner the better.

The café was busy with office workers loading up on caffeine, mostly to go, so there were a few seats available.

'I'm glad you called,' said Sibba in English. 'I didn't think you would.'

'Neither did I,' said Magnus. 'It was kinda weird seeing you yesterday.'

'OBG is a good client of our firm's, as you can imagine. Do you want to ask me about Óskar Gunnarsson? That might be tricky.'

'No, no.' Magnus took a deep breath. 'I wanted to talk about our family.'

'I wondered,' said Sibba. 'Have you seen any of them since you've been here?'

'Only you that once.'

'I can understand why you would want to avoid them, especially after the way Grandpa treated you last time you were here.'

Magnus had summoned up the courage to travel back to Iceland when he was twenty, just after his father died. He had hoped to achieve some kind of reconciliation with his mother's family. It hadn't worked: the trip was as painful as he had feared.

'Have you been up to Bjarnarhöfn recently?' Magnus asked.

'Yes. I took my husband and the kids to stay in Stykkishólmur for a few days in July with Uncle Ingvar. He's a doctor at the hospital there. But we visited Grandpa and Grandma a few times.'

'How are they?'

'Very good, considering their age. They both still have all their marbles. And Grandpa still potters about on the farm.'

'But Uncle Kolbeinn does most of the work?'

'Oh, yes. And he lives in the farmhouse. Grandpa and Grandma have moved into one of the smaller houses.'

Bjarnarhöfn was made up of a number of buildings: barns, three houses and of course the little church down towards the fjord.

'Has he changed much?'

'No. He's pretty much set in his ways.'

'The old bastard,' Magnus muttered.

Sibba looked sympathetic. 'You didn't enjoy your time at Bjarnarhöfn, eh?'

'No. You were lucky growing up in Canada, away from them.'

'I remember visiting when I was a child,' Sibba said. 'In fact, I remember staying at Bjarnarhöfn when you and Óli were there. You were both very quiet. Like you were scared of Grandpa.'

'We were. Especially Óli.' Magnus winced. 'It's still difficult to think about it now. You know Óli and I never talked about it after we went to America? It's like the whole four-year period was blanked out of our minds.'

'Until I came along?' Sibba said. 'I'm sorry. I should never have told you about your father and the other woman. It just didn't occur to me that you wouldn't know, it's all that the rest of the family ever talked about. But of course I was older than you: you and Óli were just little kids.'

'I'm glad you did, Sibba. In fact, that's what I want to ask you about.'

'Are you sure?' Sibba said.

'Yes.' Magnus nodded. 'I need to find out what happened in my parents' lives. It's been nagging at me ever since Dad was murdered.'

Sibba's eyebrows rose in surprise. 'This doesn't have anything to do with *that*, does it?'

'I doubt it. But I'm a cop, I like to ask questions until I get answers. You are the only member of the family I think I could talk to. Grandpa has turned the others pretty much against me.'

Hallgrímur, Magnus's grandfather, had three sons and a daughter: Vilhjálmur the eldest, who had emigrated to Canada in his twenties, Kolbeinn, Ingvar and Margrét, Magnus's mother. Sibba was Vilhjálmur's daughter who had grown up and been educated in Canada, but had moved to Iceland after university, gone to law school and then on to a career as a lawyer in Reykjavík. Magnus had always liked her the most of his mother's family.

She looked at Magnus closely. 'So, fire away. I'm not sure how much I can help you.'

Magnus sipped his coffee. 'Do you know who the other woman was?'

'I did, but... no... I forget her name,' Sibba winced, struggling to remember. She shook her head. 'No. It will come to me. She was Aunt Margrét's best friend from school. She lived in Stykkishólmur. They both went to teacher training school in Reykjavík.'

'Was she teaching at the same school as Mom?'

'No idea.'

'Did you ever meet her?'

'No. But I heard about her. I could ask my father, if you like?'

'That would be great. But do me a favour. Don't tell him that it was me asking.'

'OK,' said Sibba, reluctantly. She checked her watch. 'I've got to go. I've got a meeting in five minutes.'

She stood up and kissed Magnus on the cheek. It was a nice gesture. Magnus was short of family in Iceland: there were none left on his father's side. This was the closest he got.

'Are you *sure* you want to know all this?' she asked.

Magnus nodded. Ingileif was right. 'I'm sure.'

Björn rode his bike the short distance from Seltjarnarnes down to the harbour. Harpa had left early for the bakery, dropping Markús off with her mother on the way. Björn had told Harpa he was going back to Grundarfjördur to join a trawler that was going out for a couple of days. He had an hour or two to kill, so he went down to his favourite place in Reykjavík.

He parked his bike and strolled along the quayside. There were not many boats around: a large Russian trawler, and a couple from the Westman Islands, plus a few much smaller vessels. The Old Harbour in Reykjavík was of course much larger than Grundarfjördur, but these days it seemed quieter. The concentration of fishing quotas in fewer and fewer hands over the previous twenty-five years meant that there were fewer boats, and those boats that were around spent more time at sea. It was all much more efficient, and Iceland was one of the very few countries in the world whose fishermen made money rather than consuming government subsidies. But this profitability had come at a cost: boats scrapped, fishermen losing their jobs, sometimes whole communities shut down.

Until the *kreppa*, Björn had been a beneficiary of all this. His uncle in Grundarfjördur had been one of the original recipients of a quota, which had been granted to those men who were fishing between the years 1980 and 1983. The quota represented the right to fish a certain proportion of a total amount of catch set each year by the Marine Research Institute and the Ministry of Fisheries, depending on the level of fish stocks. The fortunate 'quota kings' as they soon became known, had either continued to fish, or sold out to larger companies for millions, or sometimes hundreds of millions of krónur. Einar, Harpa's father, had done just that. Björn's uncle had sold his quota and his boat, *Lundi*, to Björn at a low price, but even so, Björn had had to borrow heavily from the bank.

Björn had been fishing with his uncle since the age of thirteen. He was a natural, they said he could think like a cod, and he was also quick to understand and make the most of the new technology that was becoming available for mapping the sea bed and locating shoals of fish. Soon he had paid down most of his debt. Then he borrowed more to buy the quota of another small fisherman in Grundarfjördur. The quota applied to the proportion of a catch and not to a particular boat, so the secret to profitability was to own as high a level of quota as one boat could sustain. Then, in 2007, he took down another loan to buy a third small quota and some state-of-the-art electronics for *Lundi*.

His old school friend from Grundarfjördur, Símon, who had become a banker rather than a fisherman, and who had just left one of the Icelandic banks to join a hedge fund in London, advised him. The thing to do was borrow in a mixture of Swiss francs and yen, because the interest rates were low and the Icelandic króna would stay strong. It was what Símon was doing on a major scale at his hedge fund, and he was making a fortune.

Björn took his friend's advice and for a while things worked out fine. Then the króna began to depreciate, and although the interest rate was still low, the size of his loan in krónur was growing fast. The *kreppa* came in earnest, the Icelandic banks went bust, the króna collapsed and Björn's loans ballooned way above any amount he could ever possibly repay.

He received a good offer for his quota and his boat from a large company in Akureyri in the north. He took it, and paid down the bank as much as he could. And now he was begging for work from anyone who would take him on. He had an excellent reputation as a fisherman, but he found it difficult to shut up and take orders when he had his own views on where the fish were and how to catch them, so some of the captains, like Gústi, saw him as a threat. But Björn could still just about make a living and he could still go out to sea.

He had lost his boat and his dreams. All he had wanted since he was a boy was to own a fishing boat and hunt the fish. And now it was denied him.

When he had seen Símon one Friday night in Reykjavík a month after the banks collapsed, his friend was surprised at Björn's misfortune. Símon had unwound that trade the previous spring and gone the other way. His fund had made millions.

Bastard.

Björn hadn't seen Símon since then.

Now the politicians were talking about joining the European Union. They promised that Icelandic fish would be kept safe for Icelandic fisherman, but Björn knew that within a decade the Spanish, the French and the British would have helped themselves to his country's carefully husbanded stocks, leaving nothing for the Icelanders.

And all this had been caused by a bunch of speculators sitting on their fat arses in overheated offices borrowing money they didn't have to buy stuff they didn't understand.

Bastards.

Björn's father, a postman and a lifelong communist, was right after all. They were all bastards.

The wind was picking up. Small clouds skipped across the blue sky above, and even in the sheltered harbour the little fishing boats bobbed, creaked and rattled. Björn walked back down the quay to Kaffivagninn, the café used by the fisherman. It was almost empty. He glanced around, looking for Einar who often hung around there, eager to share a yarn with anyone who would listen, but he couldn't see him. He bought himself a coffee and *kleina*, sat at a table by the window and thought of Harpa.

He was glad he had come down the night before. There was no doubt she needed him. He treated her well. Unlike Gabríel Örn. Harpa spoke about him sometimes in the middle of the night. That man was scum. He had taken her for granted, mistreated her, in a way that Björn would never have done.

Björn was worried about how Harpa would handle further police questions. It would put a lot of pressure on her, especially since they both had thought that they had got away with it in January. They had made some mistakes when they had covered up Gabríel Örn's death. Sending the suicide text message from Gabríel Örn's phone was one: Björn had regretted it as soon as he had pressed send. It drew unnecessary attention to Harpa.

He had done all he could to bolster her courage, make her believe in herself. He blamed the others: Sindri, the student, the kid. They were the ones who wanted to attack Gabríel Örn. They had used her, manipulated her to reel in a banker for them to abuse. It wasn't her fault.

Their stories had hung together under the initial police investigation: there was no reason why they shouldn't now. All they needed was their luck to hold and Harpa's courage not to fail her.

Magnus, Vigdís and Árni were in the small conference room in the Violent Crimes Unit, the papers from the Gabríel Örn Bergsson file spread out on the table in front of them. Árni had been involved in the initial investigation, but Vigdís hadn't, and Magnus appreciated her independent point of view.

'So, what do you think?' Magnus asked her.

'I don't like the bed,' Vigdís said. 'It was unmade when we checked Gabríel Örn's flat the next day. He had already been sleeping in it when Harpa called. She woke him up, he got dressed, and went out to meet her.'

'Except he didn't go to meet her,' Magnus said. 'He went off to the sea two kilometres away and drowned himself.'

'And why would he do that?' Vigdís asked. 'It seems to me one of two things happened. Either Harpa told him something on the phone that so upset him that he felt an immediate desire to drown himself, or he didn't kill himself at all. Someone else put him in the water.'

'The pathologist's report is inconclusive,' Magnus said. 'He wasn't shot and he wasn't stabbed and it didn't look like he was strangled. But he could have been struck somewhere – the body was so battered by its time in the sea that the pathologist couldn't tell.'

'The report doesn't say whether Gabríel Örn was breathing when he went in the water,' Vigdís said.

'To be fair, that's a hard one to figure out,' Magnus said. 'You get water in the lungs either way.'

'What if Harpa had told Gabríel Örn something about Óðinsbanki?' Árni said. 'Maybe she was going to cooperate with the authorities. Put him in jail. Maybe he couldn't face that?'

Magnus glanced at Vigdís. She was frowning. So was he.

'There's nothing from his parents or his new girlfriend that suggests that he was any more worried about what was going on at Óðinsbanki than anyone else. He hasn't been implicated in anything apart from a few bad loans. No fraud. No gambling debts. Some drugs use, but nothing out of control. Why him? Why not any of the other bankers in this town?'

Árni shrugged.

'And let's say he suddenly decides at midnight to kill himself. There are many quicker and easier ways of doing it.'

'Perhaps he went for a walk,' Árni said. 'Got more and more miserable the further he went. Found himself near the sea. Decided to end it there and then.'

'Possible,' said Vigdís.

'But unlikely,' said Magnus.

'The witnesses' stories stack up,' said Árni. 'Ísak Samúelsson, the kid who had the fight with Harpa. And Björn Helgason, the fisherman.'

'Who has a criminal record.'

'Two assaults when he was nineteen and twenty,' Vigdís said. 'On a night out in Reykjavík both times. There is nothing unusual about a fisherman getting drunk and into a fight.'

'What about this motorcycle gang he's a member of. The Snails?' Magnus smiled. 'Is that the Icelandic for Hell's Angels?'

Vigdís shook her head. 'Some of them would like to be, but they are much tamer than that. A lot of them are fishermen, but they have all kinds of people as members, even some lawyers and bankers. They just get dressed up in leathers and ride around the country together.'

'And his brother? Who he was supposed to be staying with?'

'He's credible,' Árni said. 'His name is Gulli: he runs a small decorator's business. He was out all night. Came home in the morning, saw Harpa as she was going out. He said Björn stays with him regularly when he comes down to Reykjavík for the weekend, but they often go out separately. '

'That leaves us with Harpa,' Magnus said. 'The weak link.'

Baldur stuck his head into the conference room. 'What time does the British policewoman arrive?'

'Her flight gets in at one-thirty,' Magnus said. 'I'm going to meet her at the airport.'

'I'd like to see her when she gets here,' said Baldur. 'And so would Thorkell.'

'I'll bring her in.'

'Good.' Baldur picked up a report on the conference table and examined it. 'What's this?' he said. 'The Gabríel Örn investigation from January?'

'That's right,' said Magnus.

'What has this to do with Óskar Gunnarsson?'

'They were both senior executives at the same bank.'

'And you think Óskar's murder had something to do with Gabríel Örn's suicide? How can that be?'

Magnus took a deep breath. 'We don't think Gabríel Örn killed himself.'

Baldur frowned. 'That's absurd.'

'Is it?'

'Of course it is. There was an investigation. We examined all the evidence. Case closed.'

'Do *you* think it was suicide?'

Baldur pursed his lips. 'I said, case closed.'

Magnus examined Baldur closely. There was anger in his eyes. Despite their disagreements, Magnus didn't underestimate Baldur. He was a smart enough cop to know that suicide didn't stack up. So why did he want to sit on the case? Magnus needed to find out.

'I think we should reopen it,' Magnus said. 'It smells. Harpa Einarsdóttir, Gabríel Örn's former girlfriend who was supposed to meet him that weekend, was lying.'

'Have you proof of that?' Baldur said.

'Not yet.'

'Or any hard connection to Óskar, beyond them all working in the same bank?'

'No.'

'Then drop it.'

'Why?' Magnus said.

'Because I tell you to.' Baldur stared at him. Vigdís and Árni sat motionless.

'I need to have a better reason than that to drop a case that is crying out to be reopened,' Magnus said carefully. 'Especially if it involves murder.'

'Are you suggesting something?' Baldur asked in little more than a whisper.

Magnus folded his arms. 'I guess I am. This looks like a cover-up to me. Where I come from, cover-ups happen from time to time. I guess I just didn't expect to see them in Iceland.'

'You don't understand the first thing about this country, do you?' said Baldur, his voice oozing contempt.

'I think I do,' said Magnus, but he couldn't hide his uncertainty.

'Have you any idea what it was like here last January?'

'I guess it was pretty hairy.'

'Pretty hairy?' Baldur almost shouted. 'You don't have a clue.' He shook his head and sat down opposite Magnus, leaning forward towards him. The muscles in his long face were tight, anger seeping out of every pore. 'Well, let me explain.'

'OK,' Magnus said, taken aback by the emotion in Baldur's normally dry voice, but trying not to show it.

'In January the Metropolitan Police faced the biggest test of its history. By far. We were all working double shifts, every man and woman we could get our hands on was wearing riot gear, we were defending our parliament, our democracy.

'And we were angry too.' He glanced at Vigdís. 'We are citizens and taxpayers. We don't get paid very much and we never made out during the boom years apart from some of us who spent too much, took on too much debt. Many of us sympathized with the demonstrators. But we had a job to do and we did it as well as we could.'

Magnus listened.

'We used the most conciliatory tactics we could. We didn't hit people. We didn't corral them and beat them up like the British police did a few months later in their anti-capitalist demonstration in London. No one was killed. Then one day it all looked like it was going wrong: the anarchists got the upper hand and started attacking us. They threatened us, they threatened our families. And then do you know what happened?'

Magnus shook his head.

'They formed a line. The people formed a line to protect the police from the anarchists. You don't see that in any other country but Iceland. A few days later the government resigned: it all happened without violence.

'And it was all down to the way we policed the demonstrations. I'm proud of that. The Prime Minister wrote a personal letter of thanks to every police officer who played their part.'

Magnus was impressed. Policing riots was notoriously difficult; it was so easy for one officer to go too far, to make a bad judgement call in the heat of the moment, to panic. He had never faced a riot; he wasn't at all sure how he would cope with angry protesters throwing stuff at him. He would probably hit them back.

'You see, if right in the middle of all that a young banker had been murdered, it might have been just the spark that could have set this country on fire.'

Magnus hesitated. He could see Baldur's point of view. But on the other hand... 'We don't know yet whether Gabríel Örn was murdered,' he said. 'But it looks very much like he might have been. His family, his parents, his sister, have a right to know. We have a duty to tell them.'

'Don't lecture me on what my duty is,' Baldur growled. 'You don't live here, this isn't your country. I decide what our duty is. And I am telling you to drop Gabríel Örn. Forget about him. And above all don't mention him to the British police. Do you understand?'

Baldur's words were like a slap in the face to Magnus. Iceland *was* his country, dammit. That was a thought, a belief he had clung to through all his years in America. And yet. And yet he hadn't been in Iceland in January. He hadn't taken part in the pots-and-pans revolution, either as a participant, or as a policeman or even as an observer. In fact he had scarcely noticed what had been going on – he was deeply involved in a police corruption investigation back in Boston at the time. And what the Icelandic people had achieved, the overthrow of a government through entirely peaceful protest, *was* impressive, in a typically Icelandic way.

What right had he to mess all that up?

He nodded. 'I understand.'

CHAPTER ELEVEN

MARÍA HALLDÓRSDÓTTIR LIVED in a quiet street in Thingholt, on the other side of the hill from Magnus's place, facing the City airport. The houses were bigger here, grander by Icelandic standards. The little street was full of Mercedes and BMW SUVs, Land Rover Discoveries and outside María's house, a white Porsche Cayenne. Magnus's Range Rover looked quite at home.

The wind had picked up, and Magnus and Vigdís had to lean into it on the short walk from the car to the front door. Magnus rang the bell and María answered in just a few seconds. She was tall, slim, with long dark hair and long legs clad in tight jeans and tan boots.

'Come in,' she said. 'Ingileif is here.'

'Ingileif?' Magnus said, surprised.

'Hi, Magnús.' Ingileif appeared from a sitting room and kissed him. 'Oh, hello, Vigdís. You don't mind me being here, do you, Magnús? María is my friend.'

'Well, it would probably be more appropriate if you weren't present while I spoke with María.'

'More appropriate? I remember how you ended up interviewing me. I wouldn't want you to use the same techniques on María.' She exchanged a glance with María, and burst out laughing.

Magnus, as usual, was wrong-footed. Although the first time he had interviewed Ingileif things had been very professional, and in fact Vigdís had been with him at the time, it was true that later he had been friendlier with a witness than he should have been.

He glanced at Vigdís. She was trying not to laugh.

'OK,' Magnus said. 'But don't interrupt.' As soon as he had said it he knew how pointless it was.

María showed them into the living room. It was large, elegant in an Icelandic minimalist way, with white walls, blonde polished wood floors and furniture that was made as much of glass as wood. Smooth abstract sculptures twisted and turned as they posed for visitors. The art on the walls was bright, eye-catching and original. Tropical flowers in ones and twos stood proudly out of their vases.

A good client for Ingileif, no doubt.

Magnus quickly took in the family photographs. There were a couple of María with a gaunt man with greying temples, wearing a well-cut suit. Husband. And successful, given the price of the house.

Magnus, Ingileif and Vigdís sat down while María poured coffee. There was a catalogue on the coffee table, open at nursery furniture. María and Ingileif had obviously been looking at it. Magnus surreptitiously checked for a bulge above María's jeans, but couldn't see one.

'Don't worry,' said Ingileif, nodding towards the catalogue. 'It's not for us, Magnús.'

'I didn't think it was,' said Magnus.

'Yes you did,' said Ingileif, with an amused smile.

'It's me,' said María. 'I'm three months pregnant.'

'Congratulations,' said Magnus. He cleared his throat in an attempt to gain some control over proceedings. 'So, María, tell me how you knew Óskar?'

María took a deep breath. 'Óskar. He was quite a few years older than me. I'm not sure where we met, but I remember first getting interested in him at a dinner at a friend's house – Birta, you know her, Ingileif?'

Ingileif nodded.

'It was 2003, six years ago. We all went out later as a group, we danced: I could tell he liked me.'

'He was still married at the time?'

'Oh, yes,' María said. 'But it was never going to work.'

Magnus raised his eyebrows.

'Óskar and Kamilla had been going out since high school,' Ingileif said. 'Those marriages never last. It's just a matter of time.'

Magnus threw a glance of disapproval at Ingileif.

'Sorry,' she said.

'Ingileif is right,' María said. 'He was on the lookout, I could tell. We ended up sleeping together. It went on a couple of years.'

'Did his wife know?'

'I don't *think* so. Óskar didn't think she did, at any rate.'

'So your relationship was serious?'

'Yes, it was.' María faltered for the first time. 'I really liked him. He was an attractive guy. And he was funny, lively. He had that air of success about him, you know? Everything he touched turned to gold.' She smiled.

'I remember he took me to the South of France for a weekend. We stayed in this wonderful hotel high up on the Corniche, with an amazing view of the Mediterranean. We went gambling in one of the casinos in Monte Carlo. I had been making small bets on red and losing mostly. He split my stake into three and slid a third on to number fourteen, my birthday. He lost. So then he pushed the second third on that number and lost again. He raised his eyebrows at me for permission to place the last third and I nodded. I trusted him. And he won! Over a thousand euros. That would *never* happen to me, but it seemed kind of inevitable with him. He was a winner, you know?'

'Quite a catch.'

'I thought so,' said María. 'I guess I fell for that classic mistress mistake. I hoped he would leave his wife and marry me.' She sighed. 'Then I heard that he had gone off with some slut from his bank's London office at a party there. I confronted him, he said it would never happen again, but of course it did.'

'With the same woman?'

'No, a different woman. I think the first one was genuinely a one-night stand. This other one was in London too. This was before he bought his house in Kensington, but he used to travel there a lot. I realized that that was where he messed around. With two women to hide from in Reykjavík, his wife *and* his mistress, I guess it made some sense.'

'When was all this?'

'About four years ago.'

'So you dumped him?'

'I did. And then six months later I met Hinrik.' She glanced at a photograph of the gaunt man behind her shoulder.

'Who was a *much* better bet,' said Ingileif.

'Since then you haven't seen Óskar?'

'No. I mean I've bumped into him at one or two social occasions, but never alone.' Her lower lip began to quiver. 'He was a good man. I don't know whether he committed any technical financial crimes, but I am quite sure he did nothing wrong. He was honest, you know, you could trust him.' She stared at Magnus, daring him to contradict her. It struck Magnus that a man who could be unfaithful to his wife and then his mistress and still give the impression of being trustworthy, must have had some charisma.

It was strange with murder victims. You never got to meet them, obviously, but you came to know them better and better as the case went on. Óskar was more intriguing the more Magnus found out about him. Was he really the evil banker that the press made out?

Whoever he was, he hadn't deserved to die.

Vigdís had been taking notes. 'Do you know the name of this woman?'

'No, I don't. He never told me.'

'Was she Russian?' Vigdís asked.

'No. No, she was English. A lawyer, I think.'

'I see. And the first one? The one-night stand?'

'The slut? Oh, she was Icelandic all right. She was an employee of Óðinsbanki in London. She's back in Reykjavík now.'

'And do you know her name?' asked Magnus.

'Yes. Harpa. Harpa Einarsdóttir.'

Frikki stood in the arrivals hall at Keflavík Airport staring at the screen, shifting from foot to foot in impatience. Where the hell was she? The plane from Warsaw had arrived twenty minutes ago. It couldn't take her that long to pick up her bags and go through customs, could it? Frikki had never flown before, in fact this was his first time at the airport, so he had no idea what happened on the other side of the double swing doors. Perhaps Customs had stopped her? Oh, God! Perhaps Immigration hadn't let her in to the country?

He couldn't bear that thought. He bit his thumbnail. Where the hell was she?

He had been overjoyed when Magda had messaged him on Facebook that she had bought a cheap ticket to come and see him. She had been a chambermaid at the Hotel 101 where he had been an assistant chef. He had been distraught when, like him, she had lost her job, because in her case it meant she had to go back to Poland. That had been in early January, just after New Year. Since then they had managed to keep their relationship going, through the wonders of Skype and Facebook. She was a year older than him, and much more sensible. He was a different person when he was with her, calmer, happier. Better.

And in a few minutes he would see her again. If the immigration people didn't stop her.

At the same time, he was nervous. Since he had lost his job he had let things slip, and she would pick up on that. He had always been a bit of a wild kid, getting himself into all kinds of trouble, until he had gone on that cooking course. He was a natural. More than that, cooking calmed him down, channelled his energy away from getting drunk and causing trouble. He had been so proud to get his job at 101, the trendiest hotel in Reykjavík. And he had done well there. He was a good-looking kid and had no trouble pulling girls, but he was aware that it was his new self-confidence that had attracted Magda.

It was an inevitable result of the *kreppa* that one of the hottest places to hang out in the good times would slow down. It wasn't their fault that he and Magda were sacked, he knew that.

Life since then had been difficult. He lived with his mother, an office cleaner, in Breidholt, a mostly poor suburb of Reykjavík. His existence had become desperately boring. He had started doing drugs again. He had gone back to stealing. It had started when his laptop had suddenly died on him. With that went his means of communicating with Magda. Try as he might, he hadn't been able to fix it. So then he had nicked another one some idiot had left lying around on a car seat.

And then, unbidden, memories of that dreadful night in January forced themselves to the front of his brain. Yet again.

That was something he absolutely mustn't tell Magda. She would never understand.

'Frikki!'

He looked around and there she was! How could he possibly have missed her?

'Oh Frikki!' She rushed up to him, flung her arms around him, kissed him, and hugged him tight.

All thoughts of that January night melted away.

Magnus brushed past the two kids embracing in the Arrivals Hall and looked out for someone who might be Detective Sergeant Piper. He had no idea what she looked like and he hadn't brought a sign with her name on it. But he should be able to recognize a cop, even a British one.

His phone rang. It was his cousin Sibba.

'I called Uncle Ingvar. I've found out who the "other woman" was.'

Magnus took a deep breath. 'Tell me.' But he still wasn't sure he wanted to know.

'Unnur. Unnur Ágústsdóttir. As I thought, she was a friend of Margrét's from school. They went off together to do teacher training in Reykjavík and then both got jobs in the city.'

The name was familiar. Magnus could remember a presence from his early childhood, a friendly blonde woman who used to come to their house sometimes. She was called Unnur, wasn't she?

'So Dad met her through Mom?'

'I guess so.'

'Did Uncle Ingvar tell you where she is now?'

'Apparently she moved back to Stykkishólmur about ten years ago. She's teaching at the school there. Her husband is one of his colleagues at the hospital.'

'Thank you, Sibba. Thank you very much.'

'Are you going to see her? It might not be such a good idea.'

'I don't know. I just don't know.'

The box was opening. The box where he had crammed all the unpleasant stuff. The four years in Bjarnarhöfn. His father's infidelity. It was all oozing out.

He couldn't shut that box.

For most of his adult life Magnus had been obsessed with later events, events from several years after he had settled in America. His father, Ragnar, had been murdered when Magnus was twenty, at a house that Ragnar was renting from a fellow MIT professor for the summer. The house was in Duxbury, a small town on the shore to the south of Boston. Ragnar's new wife, Kathleen, was out, ostensibly checking on a plumbing problem at their own house back in town. Ollie, as Magnus's brother called himself in the States, was at the beach with his girlfriend, and Magnus himself was waiting tables in a restaurant in Providence over the college vacation.

Someone had walked into the house through the unlocked front door, stabbed Ragnar in the back, and finished him off with a couple of thrusts to the chest.

The police had struggled to find a killer. The only forensic evidence was a single strand of sandy-coloured hair from which it had been possible to recover a partial DNA sequence. Magnus had been convinced that his stepmother was responsible, but she had turned out to be in bed with a local air-conditioning engineer at the time. After the police had given up, Magnus himself had spent long hours trying to solve the crime. He had eventually managed to locate a mysterious bearded birdwatcher who had been seen poking around near the house. But the new potential witness hadn't seen or heard anything, nor did he have any conceivable link to Ragnar.

Another blind alley.

Magnus had never really given up. But he had always focused on America, where Ragnar seemed to have no real enemies.

But his father *did* have enemies in Iceland. If Hallgrímur held Ragnar responsible for his daughter's alcoholism, for her eventual death, then he would certainly count as an enemy.

Which was why Magnus would have to go and speak to Unnur Ágústsdóttir, and open the lid of that box just a little wider.

'Magnus?'

'That's me.' He looked down at a short woman with blonde hair, a worn face but a friendly smile.

'Sharon Piper.' She held out her hand and he shook it.

'Flight OK?'

'Bumpy landing in all that wind. Do you have any trees on this island? I thought we were coming down on to the moon.'

'They used to tell the GIs before their posting here that there was a blonde Viking virgin tied to every tree.'

'Is that what persuaded you to come?'

'I am actually Icelandic,' Magnus said. 'I've lived in the States since I was twelve. But even for me it takes some getting used to. Are you OK to go straight to police headquarters or do you want to go to your hotel first?'

'Let's get down to work.'

As Magnus drove Piper along the thirty kilometre stretch of straight road from the airport at Keflavík to Reykjavík he kept two hands firmly on the steering wheel as gusts of wind buffeted the Range Rover.

'Is the whole country like this?' asked Piper, staring out of the window at the brown volcanic rubble.

'Not all of it,' said Magnus. 'There was a big eruption around here a few thousand years ago. You can see where the moss is beginning to eat away at the lava. Eventually, in a few more thousand years, it will become soil and grass will grow.'

'Do you really think the human race won't have permanently screwed up the earth in the next few thousand years?'

'Er, no,' said Magnus. An environmental cop. That was a new animal for him, although he suspected there were quite a few in Iceland.

'You say the eruption was that long ago? It looks more like ten years. Or last year. How can people live here?'

'They're a tough lot, the Icelanders. There was a time in the eighteenth century when one of the volcanoes erupted and the whole country was covered in a haze for several years. Crops died, animals died, the population got down to less than thirty thousand. They thought about quitting then, but they stayed.'

'They?' Piper said. 'You said "they".'

Magnus smiled. 'You're right. I guess I meant "we". I feel a bit like a foreigner in my own country.'

'Where are you from in the States?'

'Boston. I worked as a detective in the Homicide Unit. Same kind of thing you do. More guns, I guess.'

'Probably,' said Piper. 'Although there are a hell of a lot of guns in London these days.'

'Do you feel vulnerable not carrying?' Magnus asked. It was something he had always wondered about the British police.

'Most of the time, no,' Piper said. 'We do have more and more officers who are firearms trained. I haven't been threatened with a gun yet. Have you?'

'A few times,' said Magnus. 'That's one of the things I find difficult here. Cops don't carry guns.'

'Do the criminals? That's the key question, I suppose.'

'Not until I showed up,' Magnus said. That was not one of his proudest moments, luring a Dominican hit man from Boston to Reykjavík with a gun that he had managed to plug Árni with. The real problem with guns was when you ended up shooting the bad guys. Magnus had done that twice, once at the start of his career when he was a uniformed officer on patrol, and once earlier on that year when a couple of guys were trying to kill him.

He still had the dreams. A bald fat guy on the street in Roxbury telling him he had some information about a homicide Magnus was investigating. Stupidly following the guy down the alleyway. Too late realizing that the kid on the corner had an out-of-neighbourhood gang tattoo. Diving, turning, shooting. The kid falling. Spinning around, plugging the fat guy on the crown of his bald head. And then doing it all again and again all night.

But Magnus still felt naked without a weapon.

The truck in front wobbled as a gust of wind tried to sweep it off the road.

'Jesus.' Piper tensed and reached out for the dashboard in front of her.

Magnus gripped the Range Rover's steering wheel harder. White spray whipped off the top of the waves skimming the ocean to their left.

'Any news on the investigation?' Magnus asked.

'No real breakthroughs,' said Piper. 'We are still pursuing the Russian angle, although that's looking less likely. A handwriting expert took a look at the script on the Post-It note we found outside Óskar Gunnarsson's house. He reckons that whoever wrote it wasn't a native Russian speaker, or should I say, writer.'

'You mean it was a decoy?'

'Looks like it.'

'Did you try out an Icelandic accent on your witness?'

'Yes. We took her to the Icelandic Embassy and she listened to some of the people there. She thinks the courier she saw could have had an Icelandic accent. But he spoke very good English.'

'Interesting.'

'Yeah. Of course he could have been a genuine courier from one of Gunnarsson's Icelandic contacts in London, but we haven't discovered anyone who was trying to deliver anything to him at home.'

'What about the killer himself? Was he speaking Icelandic?'

'We did try the girlfriend with the Icelanders from the embassy. She thought the language she heard might have been Icelandic, but she was stretching it. She didn't really know.'

'And the motorbikes?'

'Nothing. But we traced the gun: it was used in a gang shooting in Lewisham two months ago – that's in south London. No one was killed or even injured. But that probably just means the gun was second hand. I've brought a list of Icelandic citizens we know that Gunnarsson was in contact with in London. Can we go through that?'

'Sure. And I have fixed up an appointment with the Special Prosecutor into financial crimes. That might give you an idea of where Óskar and Ódinsbanki fit into the inquiries into the banking crisis last year.'

'Good. Thank you. Have you turned up anything?'

'Nothing on a Russian angle,' Magnus said. He considered telling Piper about Harpa, but Baldur had been quite explicit. The fact that Harpa had once had sex with Óskar about four years ago was not yet a conclusive link. Reykjavík was a small place, and although that didn't quite mean that everyone had slept with everyone else, that kind of coincidence could not be ruled out.

Four years? Harpa had a three-year old son. Hmm.

'Magnus?'

Magnus shook his head. 'Sorry. It's nothing.'

CHAPTER TWELVE

'WELCOME TO ICELAND, Sharon,' said the chief superintendent. 'My name is Thorkell. And this is Inspector Baldur who is in charge of the investigation from our end.'

Thorkell was beaming at Piper, who fell under his charm instantly. They were in the chief's office on the top floor of the building, with a view of the windswept bay and Mount Esja, standing strong and immobile against the gale. Thorkell's round face was all pink-cheeked smiles. Baldur eyed Piper suspiciously.

'Thank you,' she said.

'How long are you planning to be with us?' Thorkell asked.

'I've left it open,' Piper said. 'Probably just a day or so, but I can stay longer if necessary.'

'I doubt it will be,' said Thorkell. 'We haven't found any Icelandic link at our end have we, Magnus?'

Magnus recognized a question requiring the answer no when he heard one. 'No,' he said.

'Any breakthroughs at your end?'

'Not yet,' said Piper. 'But we can't rule out that Gunnarsson was murdered by an Icelander.'

'Mr Julian Lister is incorrect. We are not all terrorists,' said Baldur in halting English. Julian Lister was the British Chancellor of the Exchequer.

'I didn't know there were any terrorists in Iceland,' said Piper. 'We have no idea what the motive for Óskar Gunnarsson's murder was, but there are no signs of terrorism.'

'Good, good,' said Thorkell. 'Sharon, I would like you to come with me to meet Óskar Gunnarsson's family. He was an important man here in Iceland, and it would be good for them to see what is being done to find his killer.'

'I would be happy to,' said Piper.

'What was all that terrorism crap?' Piper said as they left Thorkell's office.

'Yeah, you'll find the Icelanders are a bit sensitive about that these days,' Magnus said. 'When all the banks blew up last year, the Brits seized the UK assets of one of them under anti-terrorist legislation. Some people here think that that caused the two biggest banks to go bust. The British government put out a black-list of terrorist organizations with the Icelandic banks appearing just beneath Al-Qaeda, the Taliban and North Korea. A lot of Icelanders were very upset. They set up a petition on the web with pictures of ordinary people saying they weren't terrorists. There's still a whole lot of anger at your Prime Minister and Julian Lister.'

'Can't say I blame them,' said Piper. 'Lister got the elbow over the summer, but the Prime Minister is still there.'

'Anyway, let's take a look at your list.'

Back in the Violent Crimes unit, Magnus introduced Piper to Árni and Vigdís. Vigdís deigned to say 'good afternoon' in English.

'So, Sharon, how do you like Iceland?' Árni asked her, a look of eager anticipation on his face.

'Er, windy,' said Piper. 'I haven't really seen very much of it yet. I'd like to see a tree.'

Vigdís rolled her eyes. There was a famous moment in Icelandic folklore when an over-eager reporter had asked Ringo Starr that very question as he was getting out of his aeroplane at the Reykjavík City Airport.

Árni could have been that reporter.

'I don't think we'll have time to find you a tree,' said Árni. 'Sorry.'

'Let's see that list of names,' Magnus said.

They spent a couple of hours at it. Magnus's team didn't cover themselves with glory. He himself had barely heard of any of them. Árni insisted on making bold statements and wild guesses about them that turned out to be wrong. And Vigdís, who knew her way around the police files and seemed to recognize most of them, insisted on having everything translated into Icelandic.

Magnus had called her on it, he still could not believe that she only spoke Icelandic, to which she simply replied: *'Jeg taler dansk.'*

But nothing leapt out at them beyond the fact that Óskar knew all the most important people in Iceland's business world, which wasn't exactly surprising. Piper was clearly disappointed.

'We'll take the list to the Special Prosecutor's office,' Magnus said. 'See if they can come up with something.'

The Special Prosecutor into Financial Crimes had an office around the corner from police headquarters. He was a burly, fresh-faced man in his forties with an air of solidity about him. Magnus had read about him. He was the former chief of police of a small town outside Reykjavík. None of the more obvious candidates among the many lawyers in the capital itself could take the job since they were either married or related to the suspects, so the government had looked outside to fill the role. The man they had chosen had zero experience of international fraud, but he did have a good reputation for hard work and integrity.

He was reading from one of a pile of files on his desk. There were several piles more behind him. Electric cables ran between the papers over the floor, connecting up to a mess of computer equipment. The office had a feel of haphazard industry to it.

They spoke in English.

'Can you tell us something about your investigations into Óskar Gunnarsson?' Magnus began.

'Certainly,' said the Prosecutor. 'We haven't narrowed down our focus on to him specifically yet, but we are looking closely at Ódinsbanki, as we are all the other banks.'

'Fraud?' Magnus said. 'Money laundering?'

'Nothing that straightforward, I'm afraid. It's more market manipulation: lending money to related companies and individuals to buy shares in the bank.'

'Is that illegal?' Piper asked.

The Prosecutor shrugged. 'That is the big question. It's certainly wrong, and in many countries it would definitely be against the law. But Iceland doesn't have very sophisticated securities legislation. It partly depends how many of these transactions were publicly disclosed.'

The Prosecutor picked up a pencil and drummed it on his desk. 'It's also how the Icelandic banks managed to grow so big so fast. One investment company borrowed money to invest in another, which borrowed yet more money to invest in a third, which borrowed money to invest in the banks that were lending them the money in the first place. Before you know it a hundred million krónur has become ten billion.'

'Sounds complicated,' said Piper.

'It is. Especially when it's all done through a web of holding companies in the Virgin Islands. It's going to take us years to unravel it all.'

'Years? So it wasn't the case that Óskar Gunnarsson was just about to be prosecuted for something?' Piper asked.

'No. Certainly not yet. Perhaps down the line. We are not going to be rushed. The public may want blood, but if we do bring a prosecution, I want it done properly.'

Although he was wearing a dark suit, the Special Prosecutor looked uncomfortable in it. It didn't fit quite right. Magnus thought of Colby's investment banking and hot-shot lawyer friends back in Boston. They would run rings around this guy. But he knew better than to underestimate the value of patient, dogged police work. It would be interesting to see what happened. And he admired the Icelanders for going outside the establishment for their prosecutor.

'We have put together a list of Icelanders who we believe

Gunnarsson saw in the last few months in London.' Piper handed the Prosecutor the list. 'Do you recognize any of the names?'

The Special Prosecutor peered at the names through his glasses. 'Yes, I recognize nearly all of them. Businessmen, bankers, lawyers. It's Iceland's business elite.'

'How do they operate, this business elite?' Piper asked. 'Do they all gang up together to protect their own, or are there rivalries?'

The Prosecutor laughed. 'Rivalries would be putting it mildly. Some of these guys bear grudges going back decades. Look, I'm not part of this world, which is why I have this job, but I am beginning to understand it.

'There are the old establishment families, sometimes known as "The Octopus" for the tentacles they wrapped around Icelandic businesses throughout the twentieth century. They owned the shipping companies and the importers and distributors. They are powerful, but low key. Then there are the new guys, the young Viking Raiders who built up the big network of companies over the last decade. They are the guys who bought all those businesses in your country: Hamleys, House of Fraser, Mothercare, the supermarket chain Iceland, Moss Bros, even West Ham United. There are three groups of them and they ended up owning stakes in three of the big banks. And then there is our former Prime Minister, Ólafur Tómasson. Some of these businessmen were his friends, some his enemies, he held serious grudges against some of them, gave others preferential treatment in privatizations.'

'And how does Óskar Gunnarsson fit into all of this?' Magnus asked.

'He did a good job of being friends with just about everyone. Ódinsbanki wasn't allied with one group or the other, it did deals with all of them.'

'So he didn't have any specific enemies?'

The Prosecutor shook his head. 'You know, people sometimes talk about the Icelandic mafia. And it's true that all the big families here in Iceland know each other. But there is absolutely no violence. We are not talking about the Italian mafia here, or the

Russian. I suppose it's always possible that an individual could be violent or a murderer, that's possible in any society. But as a group, these guys don't kill people.'

'And what about the Russians? There are rumours in London that the Icelanders were using Russian money.'

The Prosecutor shook his head. 'A couple of these Viking Raiders made their money from a bottling plant in St Petersburg in the nineties. That's perhaps how those rumours started. They probably still have Russian contacts. But the rest, no.'

Piper sighed. 'Thank you very much. Let us know if you turn up anything on any of those names.'

'We'll keep a close eye on Ódinsbanki,' the Prosecutor said. 'And if anything like a motive for Óskar's murder emerges, I'll let you know. But there is nothing there at the moment.'

'One last question,' said Magnus.

The Prosecutor raised his eyebrows.

'Was Óskar a crook?'

The Prosecutor sighed. 'He didn't steal from anyone. He didn't hurt anyone physically, at least not that I'm aware of. But if he and his friends did set up a web of offshore companies to invest in each other's companies secretly, he broke the rules. And that is more than just a technicality, it matters. It means the whole edifice of Iceland's boom was built on deceit.'

He gave a rueful smile. 'But you can't just blame the bankers. All of us Icelanders have to ask ourselves what we were doing borrowing money we could never repay. And we're just going to have to pay it all back.'

Magnus leaned back away from the animated chatter around the table. He felt pleasantly drunk. They had all been drinking for hours. They had started off with a couple of bottles of wine at Ingileif's place before going out to dinner, and then on to a bar on Laugavegur. The evening would cost him a small fortune, but it seemed like the right thing to take the visiting cop out, especially on a Friday night. In the current atmosphere of cost cutting there was no way he could ask the department to spring for it.

That afternoon, together with Thorkell, Sharon Piper and he had visited Óskar's parents at their house in Gardabaer. He was struck by how ordinary they were. Whereas Emilía had looked like a wealthy sister of a Viking Raider, their parents were a respectable, unassuming couple. Óskar's father was still working as a civil engineer for a government department, his mother had retired as an administrator in the tax office. They were both devastated. It was clear that their son had meant everything to them, that they had worshipped him ever since he had been a small boy, given him the self-confidence to succeed.

They were glad of the visit by the police officer from London. Sharon had done a good job of assuring them that the British police were putting everything into the investigation. She also managed to throw in some of her own questions about any personal problems that Óskar might have had, any enemies, but nothing new had emerged. The parents had met both girlfriends: they were overawed by the Russian, and thought the Venezuelan incredibly exotic. They were clearly proud, but a little anxious about their son's jet-setting lifestyle. The anxiety had turned to guilt: if they had somehow kept their beloved Óskar in Iceland, he would still be alive.

It was frustrating. Magnus could feel himself being drawn into the investigation. He wanted to find Óskar's killer, the person who had taken their son from them. He'd love to fly back to London with Sharon to see the investigation through at first hand, but he knew that Thorkell and the Commissioner would never authorize it. Why should they?

He wanted there to be an Icelandic link so that he could get properly involved. Perhaps Harpa was that link. His intuition told him that there was more than a common employer and a four-year-old night of passion connecting Harpa, Gabríel Örn and Óskar. But maybe that was just what he wanted to believe.

It was a shame he couldn't talk to Sharon about it.

There were five of them at the table in the crowded bar: Magnus, Sharon Piper, Ingileif, Árni and Vigdís. Ingileif had abandoned her party with her fashionable clients to join them, which Magnus appreciated, although he suspected it was curiosity that had drawn her.

As usual, the Icelanders were much better dressed than the foreigners, and when it came to dress sense Magnus was definitely a foreigner. Árni looked cool in a gangly kind of way in a black sweater under a linen jacket. Both Vigdís and Ingileif were wearing jeans, but both looked stunning, with subtle make-up and jewellery, whereas Sharon was wearing the grey pants and pink blouse she had had on all day, and Magnus a checked shirt over a T-shirt and old jeans.

The conversation was animated but slurred. Árni and Magnus had moved on to whisky, but the women had been drinking wine all night. How many bottles, Magnus had long lost count. Vigdís was quizzing Sharon about what it was like to be a woman in the Metropolitan police, with Árni translating frantically and inaccurately.

'It's nice to get away for a night or two,' Sharon said.

'Have you got kids?' Ingileif asked.

'A couple. My daughter's at uni, and my son has just left school. No job – says he can't get one with the recession, which might be true. But he's been getting into all kinds of trouble recently. He expects me to get him out of it, but I've had enough. I don't know what I did wrong. He was a good kid until three years ago.'

'And your husband?'

'Oh, he can't control him. He just sits at home now, watching golf on tellie all day.'

'Is he retired?' Vigdís asked.

'He used to work in a bank, in the back office. He never got paid very much, and they made him redundant in March. He's tried to get another job, but he's too old, they say. Fifty-one. So it's all down...' She blinked and swayed alarmingly. 'It's all down to me.'

'Are the police losing their jobs?' asked Vigdís, in English. 'They are in Reykjavík.'

Árni translated into slurred Icelandic.

'No,' Sharon said. 'But they are going to screw us on our pensions, I'm sure of that.' She blinked. 'Hang on. You *do* speak English.'

Vigdís glanced at Magnus and Árni. She giggled. 'Only when I'm drunk.'

Árni translated into Icelandic faithfully. 'Wait a minute,' he said in English, looking perplexed.

'Why don't you speak English when you are sober?' Sharon asked.

'Because everyone expects me to speak English,' Vigdís said in a strong Icelandic accent. 'Because I am black nobody believes I am an Icelander.'

'I had noticed you look a little different from all these others,' said Sharon. 'But I didn't want to say anything.'

Vigdís smiled. 'Foreigners are OK. It is the Icelanders that are a problem. Some of them think that it doesn't matter where you were born, what language you speak, unless your ancestors, *all* your ancestors, arrived here in a longship a thousand years ago, then you are a foreigner.'

'Let me guess,' said Sharon. 'One of yours didn't.'

'My father was an American soldier of some kind at Keflavík air base. I never met him. My mother never talks about him. But because of him people don't believe that I am who I am.'

'I believe you are an Icelander, Vigdís,' Sharon said. 'A very nice Icelander. And a good copper. That's important, you know.'

'Have you ever been to America?' Ingileif asked. They were all speaking English now.

'Not yet.' Vigdís tried and failed to suppress a smile.

Ingileif noticed. 'But?'

'I'm going next week. Tuesday. To *Nýja Jórvík*. New York.'

'What are you going to see?' Árni asked.

'*Who* are you going to see?' Ingileif corrected him.

'A guy,' Vigdís admitted.

'Not an American, surely?' said Magnus.

'No, an Icelander,' said Vigdís. Her smile broadened. 'He's the brother of an old friend from Keflavík. He works for a TV company. I met him when he was visiting his family here over the summer.'

'Sounds good,' said Piper.

'How are you going to deal with the language issues?' Magnus asked.

'She'll be OK,' said Árni. 'As long as she stays drunk all the time, she can speak English.'

'I'll have to think about that,' said Vigdís. 'You're right, it's an important point of principle.'

A phone chirped from somewhere. Everyone glanced at each other, then Sharon reached into her bag. 'Hello.'

She listened and straightened up. 'This is DS Piper,' she said, carefully. Magnus felt sorry for her. It was always tough getting a call from the station when you had had a few.

'Yes, Charlie is my son... You are holding him for what?... Tooting police station?... He did what to an officer?... Did you call my husband?... The problem is I'm not in the country at the moment, I'm in Iceland... If I were you I would lock him up and throw away the key.' She hung up.

'Trouble at home?' asked Ingileif.

'Charlie is in trouble again. He thinks he can rely on me to bail him out, literally. But not this time. This time he's going to get what's coming to him.' She leaned back into the bench and closed her eyes.

Her phone rang again. She ignored it. 'Is she asleep?' said Ingileif. Magnus picked up the phone. 'Hello?'

'Can I speak to my mum?' It was a young male voice.

'She's kinda busy right now,' said Magnus, glancing at the woman lolling opposite him.

'Who the fuck are you?' the voice shouted. 'Are you shagging my mum? I want to speak to her!'

'One moment.' He put his hand over his phone. 'Sharon? It's your son.'

Sharon opened her eyes. 'You know what? Tell him I'll talk to him in the morning.' She closed her eyes again.

'Night, night, Charlie,' Magnus said. 'Sleep well.'

CHAPTER THIRTEEN

May 1940

THE SUN WAS shining over Ólafsvík as Benedikt rode Skjona out of the town back towards Hraun. He had been representing his family at his cousin Thorgils's confirmation – his mother couldn't afford to spend the time away from the farm.

The talk in Ólafsvík had been all about the invasion of Iceland the previous week by the British. Opinion was divided. Some people thought it was better to be invaded by the British than the Germans. Others saw no reason why Iceland couldn't be left alone, they had no part in a war fought on a continent a thousand kilometres away. But everyone was hoping for a boom to match that of the Kaiser's war. Fish, wool and lamb prices were already rising, and people thought that with the British around, Icelandic exports would be protected.

Of course no one had actually seen a British soldier. They were all two hundred kilometres away in Reykjavík. Benedikt smiled to himself. He could imagine Hallgrímur preparing himself to fight off any British invaders that tried to cross the lava field to Bjarnarhöfn.

Hallgrímur and Benedikt, now aged sixteen and fourteen, barely spoke any more. They were polite to each other, especially in front of others from their respective families, but they had stopped playing together that winter. Gunnar, Hallgrímur's father, was a frequent visitor to Hraun. He was a good neighbour to Benedikt's mother, in particular helping fix things around the farm. He was careful to teach Benedikt while he worked. Benedikt hated these times. He knew that there were a lot of important skills he could learn from Gunnar, but he could not bear to treat his neighbour like a helpful uncle.

He preferred talking to Hallgrímur's mother, but she was much less often seen at Hraun.

Benedikt rode Skjona down to the beach, and set off at a gallop. Horse and rider thrilled as they splashed through the surf and the black sand. A few kilometres in front of them rose Búland's Head, a massive shoulder of rock and grass that jutted out into the sea. A broad cloud draped the top of the mountain, and seemed to be slipping down towards the water.

Benedikt rode back to the road and the bridge over the River Fróðá. This was where Thurídur had lived, the beautiful woman whom Björn of Breidavík had wooed a thousand years before. The same Björn who had defied the great chieftain Snorri, and who had ended up in America amongst the Skraelings.

But Benedikt's father hadn't escaped. He was still lying at the bottom of Swine Lake, or at least his bones were.

And neither Benedikt nor Hallgrímur had told anyone what they had heard that day.

Benedikt knew that his father had been wrong to betray his mother, but he didn't hold that against him. His mother had been robbed of her husband, which was much worse. She was a tough woman, and she had coped well. Widowhood was common in Iceland, many husbands lost their lives at sea, a few on the fells. There were four children and Benedikt and Hildur, his elder sister, had done all they could to help her. But Benedikt was not a natural farmer like Hallgrímur, or like his father.

It was all Gunnar's fault.

It was funny, for the couple of days that he had been staying with his aunt and uncle in Ólafsvík, he had forgotten about Gunnar. The rage, which constantly seemed to be churning within his breast, had disappeared.

But now, seeing the River Fróðá, the scene of that other seduction so many centuries ago, it had returned.

He felt apprehensive as he began to climb the path up the edge of Búland's Head. The sunshine was behind him now, and the base of the cloud only a few metres above.

He remembered the first time he had ridden that path around Búland's Head. It had been with his father, the summer before he died, and they had been visiting his aunt's family in Ólafsvík. Benedikt had been scared to death. There were all kinds of stories that drifted around Búland's Head. Trolls who threw travellers into the sea. Criminals who were hanged there, witches who were stoned. But what was really scary wasn't the stories, but the path itself, an impossibly narrow ledge cut into the side of the mountain, hundreds of metres above the sea.

There was a story about a father and son, who lived on either side of the head, who had argued and become bitter enemies. One day they both met while riding around the headland. Neither gave way and each passed the other at a trot; miraculously neither one slipped. Afterwards, they discovered that the silver buttons that each wore at the side of their trousers had been torn off.

There was a stone on the other side that Benedikt had tapped for luck on his way out. He wished there was one on this side that he could tap on the way back.

The path wound higher and higher. Mist swirled all around them, pressing in on horse and boy in a clammy, silent grip. He was now so high up that he could no longer hear the surf on the rocks below. Just the clopping of hoofs on stone, and the trickle of water on rock all around him. He hoped to God he didn't come across someone approaching from the other direction.

There was nothing much he could do, apart from concentrating on keeping his balance. It was all up to Skjona, and she had picked her way over this route several times before.

The path rose inexorably. They came to a section where it had completely worn away. Skjona's hoof loosened a stone that clattered down to the sea below. The mare paused, snorting, planning her route.

And then Benedikt heard a sound. Hoofs. A boulder jutted out about ten metres ahead and in a moment a horse and rider appeared.

'Hello, there!' the rider called.

Benedikt recognized the voice. Gunnar.

'Is that Benni?'

'Yes, it is.'

Gunnar kicked on his horse who picked his way through what remained of the path and paused a couple of metres in front of Skjona.

'What are you doing here?' Gunnar asked, his voice friendly.

'I've just been to my cousin's confirmation in Ólafsvík.'

'Ah, yes, your mother told me about that. Thorgils, isn't it?'

'That's right.'

'All right, son,' Gunnar said. 'This is going to be a bit tricky.'

Benedikt winced. He *hated* it when Gunnar called him 'son'. Fear fed his anger.

'Get Skjona to go backwards. It's not far. Just a few metres and we will be able to pass.'

'But she won't be able to see,' Benedikt protested. 'She'll fall.'

'No she won't. She'll be fine. Just take it slowly. Don't scare her.'

But Benedikt was paralysed with fear. 'I can't. You'll have to go back yourself.'

'That won't work,' said Gunnar. 'I have much further to go than you. Come on. It's only five metres. If we try to pass right here, one of us will fall.'

Suddenly, Benedikt knew what he had to do. He summoned up his courage and tugged gently at the reins. Skjona pinned back her ears, but shuffled backwards. Another stone rattled loose down the cliff until it was lost in the cloud.

'That's it,' said Gunnar, his voice calm, encouraging. 'That's it, Benni. She's doing fine. You're nearly there.'

And indeed Skjona and Benedikt were back on the path proper. It was just wide enough for two horses to pass.

'All right, hold still,' said Gunnar. Gently he urged his own horse on. Slowly he passed Benedikt on the outside.

For a moment Benedikt hesitated. He knew what he did or didn't do in the next two or three seconds would change his life.

He freed his left foot from his stirrup. Placed it gently on the flank of Gunnar's horse.

And pushed.

Saturday, 19 September 2009

He parked the vehicle at the foot of the hill, lifted the shapeless canvas bag off the front seat next to him, and set off up the side of the fell along a sheep track.

He was three kilometres from the nearest minor road, four kilometres from the nearest farm, neither of which he could see. He was a long way from any human being, out of sight, out of earshot.

He looked up the lush green flank of the fell. It was still dark, but the edges of the clouds gathering around its upper slopes were tinged with a bluish shade of grey. There was a breeze, but it wasn't as strong as the day before. He hoped it would be calmer where he was going, and that he would be able to see.

Ten minutes later he was in the cloud. A further twenty minutes and he was out of it again. He was scrambling downhill into a valley, with steep sides but a flat strip of marsh grass running along next to a stream. Isolated. Quiet. And sheltered from the wind. Perfect.

It was definitely dawn now, although the sun was hidden by layers of roiling cloud. He paused and slid the bag off his shoulder. An unseen golden plover emitted a series of peeps nearby.

He unzipped the bag and lifted out the rifle, a bolt-action Remington 700. It was three years since he had fired it, and he was out of practice. He spotted a patch of dryish grass next to a stone, and laid the rifle to rest there. Then he took the empty petrol container out of the bag and paced out one hundred and twenty-five metres along the side of the stream. The elevation had dropped a few metres that far downstream, so he looked for a likely boulder on which to place the container so that it would be at about the same height as the stone. Then he returned to the rifle.

Tomorrow, he would only get one chance. He would be using a similar rifle, the same model, but not the same weapon. The ammunition was the same, he had checked that, 7 mm Remington. They had examined Google Earth to estimate the range, somewhere between one hundred and one hundred and fifty metres. At two hundred metres the bullet should go pretty much where he aimed it. At one hundred and twenty-five, there would be about a six centimetre rise, meaning he would have to aim a little low, only a little. Six centimetres was not much when compared to the size of a man's chest.

Since he would be firing an unfamiliar rifle with no time to check that it was zeroed in correctly, he had decided not to use a scope. Plus a scope could get banged about and knocked off zero while the weapon was being concealed. So, open sights. Keep it simple, fewer things to go wrong.

It had been easy with the handgun, even though he had never fired one before that evening. At two metres he couldn't miss the banker. Everything had been prepared perfectly then: the plan, the weapon, the motorbike. He hoped the preparation would work out as well this time. There was no reason to believe it shouldn't.

He lay down on the grass, rested the rifle on the stone, and aimed at the petrol container. Then he lowered the barrel a touch to allow for the rise, and gently squeezed the trigger. He felt the familiar kick in his shoulder, heard the shot echo around the little valley, but saw rock splinter just below the container. A pair of golden plovers took to the air, complaining loudly.

He cursed. He had overcompensated for the rise. He operated the bolt mechanism. Aimed. Fired again. This time the container leapt backwards off the boulder on to the ground beneath. He aimed, fired again. Again the container jumped. And again. And again.

He smiled. He could do this.

'That was quite a night,' said Sharon. Magnus and she were sitting in the conference room nursing cups of strong black coffee. She looked like death. 'It's a while since I've had a night like that.'

'Traditional Icelandic Friday night,' Magnus said. 'Or at least half of one.'

'Half of one?'

'Yeah. We went home at about one, I think. A lot of people don't finish until four or five.'

'Young people,' Sharon said. 'Oh, hi, Vigdís. You don't look too bad.'

'*Góðan daginn*,' said Vigdís with a smile. She was carrying her own cup and took a seat with them. '*Og takk fyrir síðast*.'

Sharon laughed. 'Oh, I get it. It's like last night never happened, is it?'

Vigdís glanced at Magnus. '*Já*.'

'That means "yes",' said Magnus. 'Where's Árni?'

'He's got the weekend off,' Vigdís said.

'Was it my imagination, or was my son arrested last night?' Sharon asked.

'I think he was,' said Magnus.

Sharon winced. 'Can you remember what police station he was at? Did I say?'

Magnus shook his head.

'Toot,' said Vigdís.

'Tooting? What the hell was he doing in Tooting?'

Baldur appeared at the door. 'Sergeant Sharon? Magnús? Come to my office.'

Baldur was insistent that Sharon had uncovered all she was going to in Iceland, and Sharon herself couldn't really argue. So Magnus agreed to give her a lift back to her hotel, and pick her up in a couple of hours to take her out to the airport.

Baldur pulled Magnus aside and told him that he should go back to the police college on Monday morning unless anything new cropped up from London. Vigdís could do the remaining work on Sharon Piper's list of Óskar's contacts. Magnus protested, but he got nowhere.

It wasn't far at all from police headquarters to the Hotel Reykjavík, Sharon could easily have walked it. As Magnus pulled up outside he took a decision.

'Sharon, pack your bag and bring it down here. I think we should leave early for the airport. There's someone I want you to see.'

'OK,' said Sharon, her curiosity aroused. 'I'll be ten minutes. I need to ring my husband to make sure Charlie is all right.'

A quarter of an hour later, Magnus was driving along the ring road that skirted the city centre towards Seltjarnarnes. He told Sharon all about Harpa and Gabríel Örn and his suspicions about Gabríel Örn's death. He also told her about Harpa's dalliance with Óskar in London.

'Why didn't you mention any of this before?' said Sharon. She sounded offended that Magnus hadn't trusted her.

'Baldur didn't want me to,' Magnus said. 'He figures there's no connection. He wants to make sure there is no connection. And Gabríel Örn Bergsson's death is firmly filed under suicide. It's politics. Even in this country politics intrudes in police work.'

He explained the background, the pots-and-pans revolution, the fear of violence, the sense of relief that there hadn't been any, the unwillingness to rewrite history and admit that there had.

'I get it,' said Sharon. 'So then I suppose the question becomes why *are* you telling me all this?'

'It may be nothing,' Magnus said. 'In which case you can just forget it. But if there is a real link it's important that you know about it in case you come across something in London that fits. I want to nail whoever it was who killed Óskar.'

'OK,' Sharon said. 'Let's meet Harpa.'

The bakery where Harpa worked was on the corner of Nordurströnd, the road that ran along the shore. The wind had died down from the previous day, but there was a chill in the air, and the warmth of the bakery was welcoming. Harpa was one of two women behind the counter, both wearing red aprons and with their hair tied up under white hats.

She tensed when Magnus walked in.

'Do you have a moment, Harpa?' Magnus asked.

'I'm busy,' said Harpa, glancing at the woman next to her. 'Can't you see I'm working?'

'Would you like me to talk to your boss?' Magnus said.

Harpa turned to the woman. 'Dísa? Do you mind if I speak to these two people for a minute? It won't take long.' She glanced at Magnus as she said these words.

Magnus nodded.

'Go ahead,' said the woman named Dísa, her curiosity aroused.

Harpa led Magnus and Sharon to a table in the far corner of the bakery.

'Do you mind if we speak English?' said Magnus. 'This is Detective Sergeant Piper of Scotland Yard.' He didn't think that Sharon actually worked out of Scotland Yard, but it sounded good.

'That's fine,' said Harpa. Magnus was surprised to note a slight relaxing of the tension in Harpa's shoulders. 'I've told you I know nothing about Óskar's murder.' Her English accent was good: British English.

'Yes, you have told me that,' said Magnus. 'Thing is, we know you and Óskar met at a party in London four years ago.'

'Oh,' said Harpa. 'Well, yes, of course we did. I was working in the London office then. The head of the office used to have quite a few parties. I am sure that Óskar will have come to one or two.'

'I've spoken with María Halldórsdóttir,' Magnus said. 'She figures you and Óskar got along very well at one of these parties.'

'That was just a rumour,' said Harpa. 'There was nothing in it. María was jealous, that's all. She's imagining it.'

Magnus didn't say anything.

'What?' said Harpa. 'What is it? Don't you believe me? I wouldn't be so stupid as to have an affair with the boss.'

Magnus relaxed and smiled. 'No, of course not. You got a picture of your son, by the way?'

'Yes,' said Harpa. 'On my phone.' She pulled out her phone and began searching for the photo. Then she stopped suddenly, and made to put the phone away. 'I'm not sure,' she said. 'I made a mistake. I don't have a picture of him.'

'Come on, Harpa,' said Magnus. 'You can't hide what he looks like from us. Markús is his name, right? Just show us.'

Harpa fiddled with the buttons on her phone and passed across a picture of a little boy smiling next to a football on a beach of black sand.

Magnus took a photograph out of his pocket and laid it next to the phone. Despite the differences in age, it was quite clear that Óskar Gunnarsson and Markús Hörpuson were related. The same cleft chin. The same big brown eyes.

Harpa's shoulders sagged.

'Did Óskar know?' Magnus asked.

Harpa shook her head. 'I never told him. I made sure he never met Markús. I didn't want him to know.'

'Why not?'

'It really was only one night. I was drunk. So was he. I'm not trying to say he forced himself on me or anything, but it was a mistake. We never mentioned it again. The first couple of times we met in a business situation, it was awkward, but then we both succeeded in ignoring what had happened and so things became easier. Until I realized I was pregnant, of course.'

'Did he suspect he was the father?'

'He might have done; we never spoke about it. We really didn't know each other that well, he had no idea what my sex life was like. In fact it wasn't that exciting, but he didn't know that.'

'But when you lost your job, you weren't tempted to ask Óskar for money?' Magnus asked.

'No,' said Harpa. 'I didn't want Markús to have Óskar for a father, however rich he was. We had no connection. And I suppose I didn't want to share my son with a man I barely knew.' She leaned forward. 'Please don't tell anyone about this. I don't want Óskar's parents to know they are grandparents. It may sound awful, but I don't want to introduce people I don't know into Markús's life.'

'I won't tell them for now,' Magnus said. 'I can't make any promises about later. That will depend on what this investigation turns up.'

'It won't turn up anything,' said Harpa, defiantly.

'In that case you have nothing to worry about,' said Magnus.

'You were fired from Óðinsbanki, weren't you?' asked Sharon.

'Yes,' said Harpa.

'Did you hold Óskar responsible?'

'No. Not directly.'

'What do you mean, not directly?'

'Well, it was him who led the expansion of the bank. He grew it too fast, borrowed too much money from the bond markets. That's why it went bust eventually, and why I lost my job.'

'So who did you hold directly responsible?' Magnus asked.

Harpa's eyes held his. She then closed her own. 'Oh, God, here we go.'

'Gabríel Örn?'

Harpa nodded. 'I've told you that.'

Magnus glanced at Sharon. It was too early to do a full-blown interview with Harpa. Apart from anything else, such interviews had to be in Icelandic if they were going to provide admissible evidence. Also Baldur would disapprove. But there was one last question he had to ask. 'Harpa, where were you on the night Óskar was killed?'

Harpa flinched. 'He was killed in London, wasn't he?'

Magnus nodded.

'Well, I was in Iceland.'

'Can you prove it?'

'Yes, of course. Um, I came in to work here early the following morning. You can check with Dísa if you want.'

Three-quarters of an hour later, Magnus pulled up outside the airport terminal.

'Thank you for introducing me to Harpa,' Sharon said. 'I appreciate the difficulty.'

'Her alibi was good for that night,' said Magnus. 'But I do think there is some link. I just thought you should know what her story is. In case something turns up your end.'

'Óskar was an interesting man,' Sharon said.

'The press here hate him,' Magnus said. 'And his banker buddies.'

'I can understand that,' said Sharon. 'But the people who actually knew him seemed in awe of him.'

'I guess that's how he got people to follow him,' Magnus said. 'He had success written all over him. But I can't help getting the feeling that's why he died.'

'Are you suggesting he deserved to die?'

'No, not at all. That's not for us to judge, is it? And I've investigated the murders of far more unpleasant people than Óskar; I'm sure you have too. He hasn't actually killed anyone himself, has he?'

'No, but he bankrupted a whole country. Him and his mates.'

'Yeah,' said Magnus. Of course Óskar and his buddies hadn't destroyed the economy on purpose. It wasn't what you'd call premeditated, more accidental. Manslaughter rather than homicide. But people went to jail for manslaughter.

'What are you going to do now?' Sharon asked. 'Drop the investigation?'

'Baldur wants me to. But Gabríel Örn's suicide just doesn't sound right to me. I'm off duty this weekend. I think I'll nose around, maybe speak again with some of the people we interviewed after his death.'

'Keep in touch,' Sharon said.

'I will,' said Magnus. 'And good luck with Charlie.'

CHAPTER FOURTEEN

HAFNARFJÖRDUR WAS A fishing port on the edge of the lava field just outside Reykjavík, on the way back from the airport. Magnus drove past the enormous aluminium smelter at Straumsvík, where Gabríel Örn's body had washed ashore back in January. A golf course ran alongside the road, winding higgledy-piggledy through the lava, each green like a vivid crater. Magnus turned off the highway.

The harbour was surrounded by a ring of low hills. The town had become a popular location for Iceland's wealthier middle classes, and some of the houses had exchanged hands at sky-high prices a couple of years before. But not any more, of course.

Magnus drove along the ridge until he came across a development still under construction. There was even a crane standing motionless over a half-finished house. Somehow Magnus didn't think anyone was going to finish the house in a hurry.

Some of the dwellings at the far end of the development were occupied, and it was outside one of these that Magnus checked the copy of the interview with Ísak Samúelsson that Árni had conducted after Gabríel Örn's death. Once again, Árni's notes were sketchy. They stated Ísak was a student, although Árni hadn't recorded where, and that he lived with his parents, one of whom, Samúel Davídsson, was a government minister, or had been in January when the interview had been conducted. Presumably not any longer, since the pots-and-pans revolution.

Magnus got out of his car and walked up to the white single-storey detached house. It was well designed, with a great view of the harbour, and would have been an attractive place to live, had it not been for the construction site a hundred metres away.

He rang the bell. No reply. He waited a minute and tried again.

The door was opened by a thin woman wearing a headscarf. At first Magnus thought she was an old lady, but as he looked closer he realized she was probably not much older than fifty.

She smiled, a brief flicker of life in a weary face.

Cancer.

'My name is Magnus, I am with the Metropolitan Police,' Magnus said, fudging his official status a bit. Fortunately the Icelandic police were less scrupulous about introducing themselves and flashing badges than their American counterparts. 'Can I speak to Ísak?'

'Oh, he's not here,' the woman said. 'He's at university.'

'On a Saturday?' Magnus asked. 'Is he in a library?' Magnus hoped he was: it would be easy enough to track him down.

'Oh, no.' The woman smiled again. Magnus warmed to that smile. He hoped that her condition was a result of chemotherapy rather than the cancer itself. Of course there was no way of knowing and he couldn't ask. 'He's in London.'

'London? He's at university in London?'

'Yes. At the London School of Economics. He has just started his final year.'

Magnus inwardly cursed Árni. He wondered whether Reykjavík's finest detective had never found out where Ísak went to university, or had found out but decided that it wasn't important enough to make a note of. Either eventuality was pretty bad. Moron.

'I assume you are his mother?'

The woman nodded.

'Do you mind if I ask you a couple of questions? It's in relation to the death of Gabríel Örn Bergsson back in January.'

'Of course, come in,' the woman said. 'My name is Aníta. Let me get you some coffee.'

'Please don't bother,' said Magnus.

'Nonsense. It's one of the few things I can still do. My husband is playing golf: he won't be back for hours.'

Magnus took off his shoes and followed Aníta into the kitchen where a pot of coffee was waiting. Agonizingly slowly she poured a cup for him. They sat at the kitchen table.

The woman seemed to be tired out already. Magnus resolved to get through his questions as fast as possible. 'So Ísak was a student in London last year?'

'Yes. He came back home for Christmas. And he was very interested in the demonstrations. Although term had started at the LSE he came back just for the opening of Parliament. He said it was a historic moment and he wanted to be there. I suppose he was right.'

'So he went to the demonstration the day Gabríel Örn was killed?'

'Yes. His father was furious, of course. He lost his job as a result of the protests.' Aníta hesitated. 'You said "was killed". Didn't the poor man commit suicide?'

'Er, that's what we thought,' said Magnus. 'So your son and your husband disagree politically?'

'You can say that again. Samúel has been a member of the Independence Party since he was eighteen, and Ísak is a committed socialist. They disagree on everything: climate change, the aluminium smelters, Europe, you name it. It's ironic, really, since they are both so fascinated by politics.'

'How radical is Ísak?' Magnus asked.

Aníta paused. 'That's an interesting question,' she said. 'By today's standards, I suppose he is radical. I mean most of his friends want to go off and become bankers or go to law school. Or at least wanted to until this year. But Ísak still reads Marx and Lenin, although I don't think he's a communist or anything. Compared to my generation he's just mildly to the left. Iceland has changed, hasn't it?'

'It certainly has,' said Magnus.

'Perhaps it will change back,' Aníta said. 'To the way it was. I hope it does before...'

Magnus was about to say 'before what?' when he realized the woman was referring to her cancer. She was growing greyer by the minute in front of him. He would be quick.

'Did Ísak know a woman by the name of Harpa Einarsdóttir? She used to work at Óðinsbanki?'

'No, I don't think so. I suppose he might do, but most of his friends are still at university. Was she the woman he had a fight with in the bar?'

Magnus nodded.

'No. That was the first time he met her.' She frowned. 'I don't know what he was doing. He had never done anything like that before. He drinks sometimes when he's out with his friends at weekends, but he never gets into fights. It must have been the excitement of the demonstration.'

'What about Björn Helgason, a fisherman from Grundarfjördur?'

'I very much doubt it,' Aníta said. 'One or two of his friends from school might have become fishermen, but he never mentioned anyone going to Grundarfjördur.'

And Björn Helgason was probably ten years older than Ísak, Magnus thought. 'Or Óskar Gunnarsson? The former chairman of Óðinsbanki. He has lived in London for the past year.'

'The banker who was murdered this week?'

Magnus nodded.

'But I thought you were asking about the other banker's suicide? You don't think Ísak had anything to do with that man's murder, do you?'

The distress came through strongly in her voice.

'No,' said Magnus. 'No, not at all. I'm just trying to establish connections, that's all.'

'Well, the answer to your question is "no". My son has never mentioned Óskar Gunnarsson.'

Magnus decided it was time to wrap things up. As he was leaving, Aníta, who had been frowning deeply, suddenly brightened. 'Oh, there is one thing. Ísak was here this week. He came home on Monday and flew back to London yesterday. Óskar Gunnarsson was killed at the beginning of the week, wasn't he?'

'That's right. Tuesday night.'

'So that means Ísak couldn't have been involved.'

'I never suggested he was,' said Magnus, apologetically.

'Maybe not. But you were thinking it, weren't you?'

As Magnus left Hafnarfjördur he thought about Ísak. It was a bit of a coincidence that he was a student in London. Magnus believed that Ísak's mother really had no idea of a connection between Ísak and Óskar, and he was pretty sure that her son was indeed in Iceland when Óskar had been shot. But she was wrong when she said that didn't mean he was *involved*. Maybe he hadn't pulled the trigger, but it was quite possible that he had had something to do with the person who had.

Harpa was definitely linked to the two dead bankers. In Ísak's case, the connections were much more tenuous, but still enough to alert Magnus's interest. The next person to check out was Björn Helgason.

Magnus had the report of Árni's interview with him in the car. It was probably three hours from Hafnarfjördur to Grundarfjördur, but it was a Saturday and he didn't have anything else to do. But first he decided to drop in on Björn's brother Gulli, with whom Harpa and Björn had stayed the night of Gabríel Örn's death.

Once again checking Árni's scanty notes, Magnus drove to the address in Vesturbaer, just behind the Catholic Cathedral. He parked outside a square grey three-storey building, and rang the bell marked *Gulli*. No reply.

He had just tried again, when a young woman in tracksuit bottoms and a hoodie took out a key to the building.

Magnus stopped her and introduced himself. 'Do you know Gulli Helgason who lives in Flat Three?' he asked.

'Oh, yes I know Gulli,' she said. 'What's he done?'

'Nothing,' said Magnus, his suspicions aroused. 'Does he often get visits from the police?'

'Oh, no,' said the woman, looking confused. 'No, not at all. He's a nice guy, actually. Good at fixing things. Helps out the neighbours, especially the old lady on the ground floor.'

'Do you have any idea when he's likely to be back?' Magnus asked.

'No. I'm pretty sure he's away on holiday. I haven't seen him for a few days and his van has been parked there for a while. Hasn't moved.'

She nodded towards a blue VW Transporter, with Gulli Helgason's name and phone number painted on the side panel.

'He's a decorator, isn't he?'

'Yes. He used to be very busy, but not any more. With the *kreppa*.'

'No, of course,' said Magnus. Painters and decorators would have been hit hard, he supposed. 'Thanks for your help.'

According to his notes, Árni's interview with Gulli back in January had confirmed that Björn had been staying with him, and that Gulli had seen Harpa at the flat the morning after Gabríel Örn's death. It was unlikely that a further interview would reveal more, but you never knew. Magnus would be back.

After jotting down Gulli's phone number, Magnus returned to his car and the long drive to Grundarfjördur.

Harpa walked rapidly along the edge of the bay, head down. The sun was out and the clouds had lifted off Mount Esja, but she scarcely noticed. She had been shaken by the return of the detective Magnús with the policewoman from Scotland Yard. Now the police knew about Óskar and about Markús, they wouldn't leave her alone.

She had been distracted all morning, and eventually Dísa had given her an hour off. Harpa had explained that the police were asking about Gabríel Örn's suicide, and that she was the banker's former girlfriend. Dísa listened with sympathy, but Harpa could detect a hint of suspicion. Dísa was clearly wondering why in that case the police had asked her where Harpa was on Tuesday and Wednesday.

It was bad enough having to lie to Dísa, or at least to conceal the truth. But it was Markús that Harpa was having real problems with. She couldn't look him in the eye. She couldn't look her own son in the eye!

He had begun to realize something was wrong. Usually so well behaved, he had started to act up. That would only get worse.

And now that the police knew that Óskar was his father, it would be impossible for Harpa to keep that quiet. Markús would find out in the end, as would Óskar's family. Maybe even the press. And then, eventually, he would discover that his mother was a murderer.

Harpa had a strong bond with her son. The fear that that might be shattered terrified her.

She was desperate to call Björn. But he was out in the middle of the Atlantic somewhere.

She couldn't go on like this. She should put an end to it all. Go to the police station and confess everything. Face up to what she had done. She hadn't meant to kill Gabríel, the judge would understand that. Perhaps she would be found guilty of manslaughter instead of murder. She would go to jail, but not for the rest of her life. This was Iceland after all, with its famously lenient legal system.

But they would arrest Björn as well. He would probably be locked up as an accessory or conspirator or whatever they called it, as would the others who had helped her, even that student, Ísak, who had been suspicious of her at first. They had done so much for her, she couldn't betray them now.

And what about Markús? Sure, her mother would look after him, look after him very well, but Harpa couldn't bear the thought of missing him grow up.

She took a deep breath. Somehow she would have to get through this, stick to her story, keep her wits about her, keep herself out of jail. Somehow she would have to find the strength to do that.

She sniffed. The moisture on her cheeks cooled in the crisp air. She hadn't even realized she was weeping. She was falling apart.

It was strange. She used to think of herself as a tough woman, smart and tough. You had to be to get on in Óðinsbanki. Although there were women in all jobs in Iceland, the banks had a macho culture. Work hard, play hard. They won deals because they were quicker than everyone else and they were ready to take risks that other banks wouldn't. Óskar had insisted that they all read his favourite book, *Blink* by Malcolm Gladwell, with its thesis that the best decisions were those taken by instinct in seconds. Harpa had kept up, helped, she had to admit, by Gabríel Örn. They were a team: Harpa was his analytical muscle, he had the aggression and ruthlessness to close the deals.

And they had been fun, those glory days, she couldn't pretend they hadn't been. The trips to the Monaco Grand Prix, the yachts in the Mediterranean, the birthday parties in Barbados, following Manchester United Football club to exotic cities around Europe. It was only after going out with Gabríel for three months that Harpa realized he had supported Liverpool all his life, at least until he joined Óðinsbanki and discovered that Óskar followed Manchester United.

But she wasn't much better. She hated football. She just didn't let anyone at work know that.

Then there were the salmon fishing trips back in Iceland. That was corporate entertaining on a spectacular scale. Fly the clients to Reykjavík by private jet, and then from the City Airport to the river by helicopter. Each client had his own gillie, and even the most cack-handed could land a salmon. Her father had been so jealous. And proud.

She smiled.

But it was never going to last. In her heart of hearts she had known that. She had argued furiously with Gabríel over the car dealership deal, and the chain of shoe shops, both in Britain, both now bankrupt. And there were several others that she had serious doubts over. They would do fine while the economy was growing, but come a recession and they wouldn't be able to meet their interest payments. That was a feature of nearly every deal Óðinsbanki did.

They were winging it. And when the recession did come, everything crashed at once.

She *knew* that would happen. While the others had such boundless optimism, such faith in their own abilities that they thought they had defied the laws of boom and bust, she never really believed it. Yet she had still followed them blindly.

Something else to feel guilty about.

She approached the harbour. She saw Kaffivagninn and smiled. She had had a part-time job there as a waitress for a few years when she was at school. She used to love to hang around the harbour. Her favourite job was cleaning out the *Helgi*, her father's boat. Sometimes she would find coins and she would be allowed to keep them. It was ironic, at school people saw her as a 'quota princess', but in reality her father made her earn all her money.

Of course, that was the real reason she had liked to hang around the harbour, to be near him. She didn't see him for days at a time. He would often arrive home after she had gone to bed, and be off again before she had woken up. But he loved her. His love for her was always unquestioning. It was to please him that she had worked so hard at school, that she had got a job in a bank, that she had earned so much money.

She was amazed that he had forgiven her for losing him all his savings. He had a hot temper and bore grudges, and his money was extremely important to him. She had been terrified that he would never forgive her.

But he had. Over time she realized that he had decided that she had been duped as well, that in his eyes she was just as much a victim as him. While this wasn't true, Harpa was extremely grateful.

She looked at her watch. Only ten minutes until she was due back at the bakery. She didn't want to abuse Dísa's kindness, so she hurried to the bus stop and caught a number 13 back to Seltjarnarnes.

CHAPTER FIFTEEN

MAGNUS'S SPIRITS ROSE as he drove north from Reykjavík. The clouds were blown away and the sun shone out of a pale blue sky. It felt good to fly along the open road, away from the people and the bustle of the city, the grey sea shimmering to his left, the mountains looming on his right.

The road plunged deep under Hvalfjördur, Whale Fjord, one of the deepest fjords in Iceland, swung through a valley between two fells and then crossed Borgarfjördur, its surface creased by strong currents. Just beyond the little town of Borgarnes, the road forked to the left. A couple of kilometres outside the town was the church of Borg, where Egill had lived, the hero of one of Magnus's favourite sagas.

The sagas were like the great architectural monuments of other countries. In a land with no great settlements and precious few sizeable buildings, Icelanders looked to their literature for a sense of their identity, of their past. During his adolescence in America, and then later into adulthood, Magnus had read and reread these medieval tales obsessively, conjuring in his mind's eye the heaths and fjords of Iceland in the tenth century.

They had become a refuge for a lone Icelandic kid who found himself overwhelmed by his big American Middle School. Egill was one of the most extraordinary characters from the sagas: a brave and cruel warrior, who fought against great odds in Norway and England, before returning to his farm at Borg. But he was also a poet, whose elegy to his drowned son Magnus knew by heart. It was kind of cool to be driving past his farm now.

It was a good road, almost empty of traffic. The flanks of the fells glowed orange and gold in the low autumn sun, and the sheep were rounded balls of wool, ready for the oncoming winter. Soon the Snaefells Peninsula approached, a backbone of ragged mountains with the Snaefells glacier itself a white dome at the western end capping a slumbering volcano. The entrance to the Centre of the Earth in Jules Verne's book. Magnus took the turning at Vegamót up the pass and into the mountains. The road wound upwards, until he cleared the pass and Breidafjördur opened out before him.

He pulled over.

Beneath him was the Berserkjahraun, a frozen stream of rock spilling down towards the sea in dramatic folds of grey and green. In the foreground Swine Lake twisted around the edge of the lava, its water level low at this time of year. Then down by the seashore was the farm of Hraun, and on the other side of the little cove, nestling under its own huge fell, Bjarnarhöfn.

Magnus's good spirits evaporated as he felt icy fingers clutch at his chest. The fears of childhood never left you. Just over the mountain to his right was the parallel pass where the Kerlingin troll stood, the stone sack of babies over her shoulder. Down in the lava field, the murdered Swedish berserkers roamed. On the heath over to the east strode the ghost of Thórólfur Lame Foot, killed by his neighbour Arnkell a thousand years before.

And in that farm down there, right now in the twenty-first century, lived Hallgrímur, Magnus's grandfather.

Magnus shook his head. How could he, a fit thirty-three-year-old who had got through many a tough situation, be afraid of an old man in his eighties?

But it wasn't just the man. It was the memories.

Magnus looked over to the right, beyond the mole that was Helgafell, to Stykkishólmur, a white splatter of dots by the sea. Among those dots somewhere was Unnur Ágústsdóttir with answers to other questions.

But in the meantime, he had to find Björn.

Grundarfjördur was twenty kilometres further west along the coast from the Berserkjahraun. It was a compact fishing village of white houses, a church and large sheds dedicated to processing fish, squeezing around a crescent-shaped harbour. Behind it a heath of browned grass and waterfalls led up to mountains. To one side, thrusting out of the sea, was a tower of green-and-grey hooped rock known as Kirkjufell or Church Fell.

Björn's house was a small one-storey affair on the western edge of town, right by the shore, in the shadow of the rock.

No one was at home. His neighbour said that she hadn't seen Björn for a couple of days.

Magnus drove back to the harbourmaster's office. The harbourmaster, a tall man with thinning sandy hair and glasses, knew Björn Helgason well. Over a cup of coffee he explained that Björn had sold his boat a few months before to pay off his loans, and now crewed for other captains either in Grundarfjördur, Stykkishólmur or some of the other ports along the north coast of the peninsula. There were three fishing companies in town that Magnus should try.

This he did, without success. As far as they knew, Björn was on none of their boats.

Damn! It was a risk of course, it was always a risk to interview a suspect without calling ahead first to ensure they were there, but it was a risk Magnus often took. He liked to catch them by surprise. You could tell a lot from the look on a guilty man's face when he answered the door to the police when he hadn't been expecting them.

Magnus dropped in on the local police station, a brown wooden building just behind the harbour. There he met an affable constable in his forties with a full moustache, named Páll. Another cup of coffee. It was clear that Páll was excited by a visit from the Reykjavík Violent Crimes Unit, although he pretended not to show it. He knew Björn well, of course. Although not from

146

Grundarfjördur originally, Páll had been stationed there for ten years and he liked the place.

Times were tough, though, for the fishermen, both the independent operators and the fishing companies with their fish factories in town. Too much borrowing. Even here, two hundred kilometres from Reykjavík, people had borrowed too much. It was those damn bankers and that arrogant son-of-a-bitch Ólafur Tómasson.

Magnus humoured the constable as he went through the traditional *kreppa* litany, and asked him to keep an eye out for Björn over the next few days. He left Páll his number, and told him that he wanted to see Björn in connection with Óskar Gunnarsson's murder.

Then, after stopping at a café in town for a late lunch, Magnus decided to take a slight detour to Stykkishólmur. Perhaps Björn was working on a boat out of there. And if he wasn't? Well, Magnus might drop in on Unnur.

Magnus sped through the Berserkjahraun without glancing left towards his grandfather's farm. A little further on a sea eagle heaved itself into the air, its distinctive white tail fanned out behind it, and beat a path towards a knoll. This little hill, a familiar sight from the farm at Bjarnarhöfn, was only two hundred feet high and was known as Helgafell, or Holy Mountain. One of the first settlers in those parts, Thórólfur Moster-beard, had decided that this little mountain was in fact holy and that he and his kinsmen would be swallowed up by it when they died. To preserve the sanctity of the place he insisted that no man should do their 'elf-frighteners' on the hill, on pain of death. Of course his neighbours did just that, defecating in full view of Thórólfur's men, and started the first of countless feuds.

And in the church under the hill, Magnus remembered, was the grave of Gudrún Ósvifsdóttir, the heroine of another great saga, the *Laxdaela*.

This landscape, that had changed so little over the last thousand years, brought those sagas that Magnus had read and reread two thousand miles away to life. Each of the farms mentioned in the sagas was still there, still farmed. Bjarnarhöfn, his grandfather's farm, was named after Björn the Easterner, Styr had lived at Hraun, Snorri the Chieftain at Helgafell, Arnkell at Bolstad just over the mountain. The farms then would have housed more people than they did now. Most of the time, just as now, they would have taken their sheep up to the fells, tended to their horses, cultivated hay in the home meadow. Except in those days every now and then the Norse farmers would stomp back and forth across the lava plain clutching swords and battleaxes to beat the shit out of each other. Magnus's grandparents had told Óli and him some of these stories. But they had added a veneer of darkness to them that had at first thrilled and then terrified the boys.

Magnus drove into Stykkishólmur, past his old school and on to the harbour, surrounded by a jumble of multicoloured houses clad in corrugated iron, some of them quite old. At first glance the town hadn't changed much. The large white hospital and a Franciscan convent dominated one side of the harbour. It had been strange to see the nuns, many of them from southern European countries, around town. Iceland was emphatically not a Catholic country, so the nuns and their unfamiliar ways had seemed exotic to the local kids.

The hospital was called St Francis's, and Magnus's Uncle Ingvar was a doctor there. It brought back memories too. Visiting Óli. Magnus's own brief stay for an arm broken, ostensibly while falling off a haystack. The lies. The nurse who didn't believe him. The fear of being found out.

Forcing himself back to the present, Magnus asked around at the offices of the local fishing companies. They knew Björn Helgason, but hadn't seen him for a couple of weeks. They were pretty sure that he wasn't on a Stykkishólmur boat.

As he walked out along the quay, Magnus considered what to do next. He could drive back westwards along the peninsula to Ólafsvík and Rif to ask around for Björn. Or he could drive back home. Or...

Or he could see Unnur.

He knew deep down he had already taken the decision. That was one reason why he had driven all the way up here to look for Björn. That was why he had checked Stykkishólmur rather than Ólafsvík. Who was he kidding? He was here to see his father's mistress.

Tracing someone in a small Icelandic town is not difficult. He returned to the fishing office, borrowed a phone directory, and looked under 'U' for Unnur – the Icelanders listed people under their first names.

She lived in a neat white house on top of a cliff overlooking the harbour. It was just beside Stykkishólmur's modern church, which was an extraordinary edifice: a cross between a white Mexican adobe church and a space ship. It had been under construction the whole time Magnus lived around there. It was a different kind of interplanetary rocket to the Hallgrímskirkja in Reykjavík, but it made Magnus wonder if there was some kind of strange inter-galactic theology behind Icelandic church design.

Weird.

Magnus sat outside the house for a couple of minutes. Perhaps, finally, he was getting close to understanding why his parents had split up. And maybe, just maybe, why his father had been murdered. He took a deep breath, got out of the car and rang the doorbell.

It was answered by a grey-haired woman with blue eyes, fine cheekbones and pale, translucent skin. Magnus had calculated that if she was the same age as his mother Unnur would be fifty-eight. She looked about that age, but she had a graceful beauty about her. Magnus couldn't reconcile her with the woman he dimly remembered from his childhood. She must have been a stunner in her time. In Magnus's father's time.

'Yes?' She smiled hesitantly.

'Unnur?'

'That's me.'

'Do you mind if I speak with you for a few minutes? My name is Magnús Ragnarsson.' Magnus waited a beat for the name to register. 'I am Ragnar Jónsson's son.'

For a moment, Unnur seemed confused. Then her lips pursed.

'Yes, I do mind,' she said. 'I don't want to talk to you.'

'I want to speak with you about my father.'

'And I don't want to talk to you about him. That was a long time ago and it has nothing to do with you.'

'Of course it has something to do with me,' Magnus said. 'I have only just found out about the affair. It explains things about my childhood, about my mother and my father. But there is still a lot I don't understand.'

The woman hesitated.

'I know it will be painful for you, and for me too. But you are the only person who can help me. I don't talk to my mother's family any more, or rather they won't talk to me.'

Unnur nodded. 'That doesn't surprise me.' She took a deep breath. 'All right. But my husband is due back soon. He works at the hospital. When he returns, we change the subject, OK?'

'OK,' said Magnus.

Unnur led him into the living room, and disappeared to get some coffee. Despite her initial hostility, she couldn't skip on this basic prerequisite of Icelandic hospitality. Magnus scanned the room. It was comfortable and, like every Icelandic living room, it had the full complement of family photographs. One wall was lined with books in Icelandic, Danish and English. Through a big picture window there was a magnificent view over the grey waters of Breidafjördur, dotted with flat islands, and the silhouettes of the mountains of the West Fjords on the far side.

Unnur moved a pile of exercise books off the sofa to make room for Magnus. 'Sorry. Marking.'

He sat down.

'I think I could just about recognize you,' Unnur said. 'Your hair's a bit darker, it used to be really red. You must have been seven or eight then.'

'I don't really remember you,' said Magnus. 'I wish I recalled more of that time in Reykjavík.'

'Before everything went wrong?' Unnur said.

Magnus nodded.

'So, what can I tell you?' she asked as she poured Magnus some coffee. Her face was hard and firm, almost defiant.

'Can you tell me something about my mother?' Magnus said. 'What she was really like? I have two different memories of her. I remember warmth and laughter and happiness in our house in Reykjavík. Then distance – we didn't see her very much, my brother and I stayed up here with my grandfather and she was in Reykjavík a lot of the time. At the time I thought she was always tired; now I am pretty sure she was drunk.'

Unnur smiled. 'She was good fun. Really good fun. We were at school together, here in Stykkishólmur.'

'I went to school here as well,' Magnus said.

'It was a good school,' Unnur said. 'It still is. I teach there now – English and Danish. Anyway we became best friends when we were about thirteen, I suppose. Margrét was smart. She loved to read, as did I. And the boys liked her. We both spent a summer together in Denmark at a language school, which was fun. And we decided we wanted to go to Reykjavík and become teachers.'

Unnur was warming up. 'We had a blast. We shared a flat together in 101; we had a great time. We both qualified and started teaching in schools in Reykjavík, different schools. Margrét met your father, they fell in love, got married, and I moved out to make room for him. We got along very well, the three of us. We were all good friends.'

Unnur paused. 'Are you sure to want to hear this?' she asked Magnus.

'Yes. And please tell me the truth, however unpleasant it is. Now I am here I want to know.'

'All right. That was when your mother started to drink. I mean we all drank, although in those days it was mostly spirits, it still wasn't legal to sell beer in Iceland and wine was almost unheard of. But Margrét began to drink more than us. At the time, I didn't know why. She wasn't unhappy with her life, and up till then she didn't seem to be unhappy with Ragnar.'

'At the time?'

'Yes. I've thought about it a lot since then, and perhaps I do know the reason.' Unnur took a deep breath. 'Her father was a brute. I was scared of him at school, I've always been scared of him. And he had a weird relationship with Margrét. He was fond of her, doted on her, yet he was very strict. He had a strong psychological hold over her: that was why she wanted to move away to Reykjavík, I am sure. He messed with her head.'

That didn't surprise Magnus.

Unnur took a sip of coffee. 'Anyway, then you and Óli showed up. Your mother was fine most of the time, but then she would get depressed about something, drink a lot and give Ragnar a hard time. A very hard time.'

She bit her lip. 'And now we come to the difficult bit. Ragnar used to confide in me about her. One time, they had been having a massive fight about him going to America. He had done a fellowship at MIT for a couple of years, before he met your mother, and they wanted him back to teach. It was some strange branch of mathematics, topology or something?'

'Riemann surfaces.'

'She changed her mind and didn't want to go. They had a major row about it. He and I had a drink together, and then, well...' She hesitated. 'Well. I had always fancied him ever since I had first seen him. I always wished he had chosen me. I was wrong, very wrong. So was he. We have no excuses.' She looked straight at Magnus. 'I'm not going to make excuses to you, of all people.'

'Thanks for telling me about it,' said Magnus. His mind was a turmoil of confused judgements, against his father, against his mother, against the woman sitting opposite him. But he wanted to find out the truth, so he suppressed them, at least for now.

'Then Margrét began to suspect something. Your father thought the best thing to do was to be honest, admit everything. I thought that was a really bad idea, but he didn't listen to me.' Unnur shook her head. 'So he told her. It tipped her over the edge as far as drinking was concerned. She kicked Ragnar out. Ragnar dumped me. He went to America by himself. The whole thing was horrible.'

'I can imagine.'

'Margrét wouldn't speak to me, unsurprisingly. I never saw her after that. Of course I heard about her, the drinking, her parents looking after you and Óli, and then her death.'

Magnus swallowed. He knew his mother had drunk half a bottle of vodka and driven into a rock. 'Was that suicide, do you think?' It was a question he had asked himself countless times.

'I *think* so,' said Unnur. 'But I really don't know. That's no more than an opinion. Your grandparents swore that she didn't crash on purpose. The rumours around Stykkishólmur were that she did. But no one really knows. When someone is that drunk they don't know what they are doing anyway, do they?'

'No,' said Magnus. 'They don't.'

They sat in silence for a moment. 'What about my father?' he asked. 'What was he like?'

'He was a fine man,' said Unnur. 'Kind. Considerate. Very smart. Very good-looking.'

That was too much for Magnus. 'He can't have been that fine a man,' he said. 'Screwing his wife's best friend.'

Unnur tensed. 'No,' she said coldly. 'He can't have been.' She looked directly at Magnus. 'Perhaps you had better go now. You are right, this is painful for both of us.'

'I'm sorry,' said Magnus, fighting to control himself. 'The thing is, I thought he was a wonderful man too, and then I find out he did this to Mom. But I do appreciate you telling me.'

Unnur hesitated. 'It must be tough for you,' she said. 'And I suppose that wasn't such a wonderful thing that we did, was it?'

'What happened to you?'

'I met a doctor in Reykjavík. We got married, had children. I moved back here to teach, and he works in the hospital. I'm OK. No, better than OK, happy.'

'Unlike my parents.'

'Unlike your parents,' Unnur said. 'It's not really fair, is it? I mean, it was me who caused all this. I remember them both very fondly, before everything got messed up, before I messed everything up.'

Magnus remained silent. Despite his instincts, who was he to apportion blame? But Unnur's sense of guilt seemed justified. He wasn't going to absolve her either.

'I heard about Ragnar, of course,' Unnur said. 'Did they ever find out who did it?'

'No,' said Magnus. 'They think that a random stranger drove into town, stabbed my father, and then left leaving no trace.'

'I suppose that happens in America,' Unnur said.

'Not really,' said Magnus. 'I ended up becoming a homicide detective there. And usually there is a reason why one person kills another. It may be a stupid reason, but there is a reason.'

'Just not in this case.'

Suddenly the suspicions that had been bubbling deep under the surface of Magnus's consciousness ever since he had first heard of his father's infidelity forced themselves into the open. He couldn't ignore the connections his detective's brain was making, couldn't order it to stop doing what it had been trained to do.

But unlike the rush of excitement he usually experienced when things slipped into place, he now felt suddenly cold. His throat was dry, and when he spoke the sound that came out was little more than a croak.

'I wonder.'

Unnur noticed something was wrong; she was watching him closely. 'What do you wonder?'

'Whether Grandpa was in some way responsible.'

Unnur frowned for a moment and then smiled.

This irritated Magnus. 'What's so funny?'

'There is no chance of that,' Unnur said. 'I mean, he's a nasty old man, for sure, and he had a terrible hold over your mother. And he didn't like Ragnar at all. But that's the point. He was *glad* Ragnar went to the States and left Margrét here. In fact, that was what he wanted all along.'

'What do you mean?'

'Well, at first Margrét was very excited about MIT. She had always wanted to live abroad and this seemed like a great opportunity for both of them.'

'So she intended to go *with* Dad?'

'Absolutely. But when she told her parents, they went ballistic, both of them. I don't know why exactly, they got it all out of proportion. Hallgrímur demanded Margrét stay in Iceland, but she insisted on going with Ragnar. It became a trial of strength. Her parents used every psychological weapon at their disposal. Made her feel guilty, refused to speak to her, that kind of thing. They were difficult people to oppose.'

'I remember,' said Magnus.

'At first Margrét held out. But it was eating her up. She began to drink a lot. She fought with Ragnar, she was just totally unreasonable. And in the end she changed her mind. Said that Ragnar should go by himself, and that she would stay in Iceland with you and Óli.

'Ragnar was furious. That's when... well... it happened between me and him.'

Unnur paused. Sighing.

'So, when Margrét found out about the affair her parents were overjoyed. They had won, Ragnar lost, their daughter and grandchildren stayed in Iceland.'

'I see,' said Magnus. But the thought that his grandfather might have been responsible for his father's murder, once expressed, could not be easily abandoned. 'That's not quite the story that I heard from my cousin. She said that it was the affair that *caused* Margrét to drink. That led to her death.'

'That's not right,' said Unnur. 'Like I said, she had been drinking seriously for several months before then. I'm sure it's the story Hallgrímur made up. He was hardly likely to admit that he drove his own daughter to drink, was he?'

'No,' said Magnus. 'But do you not think that later, after my mother had died, and especially after my father took us away from them, my grandfather might have wanted revenge?'

MICHAEL RIDPATH

'Perhaps. I mean, as I said, he certainly didn't like your father. But I get the impression that there are many people whom your grandfather doesn't like. And I don't think he kills all of them.' She frowned, thinking. 'And anyway, why wait? I mean it was ten years after your mother died, wasn't it?'

'Eight,' said Magnus. 'And that is a good point. I don't know. But I can imagine him capable of it.'

'That's true.'

Unnur paused, as if considering whether to say more. Magnus recognized the signs. He waited. Eventually she spoke. 'Did you know Hallgrímur's father murdered someone?'

'What! I never heard anything about that.'

'Of course you didn't. It was his neighbour at Hraun. Jóhannes.'

'How do you know?'

Unnur stood up and searched her shelves. She handed Magnus an old paperback. *Moor and the Man* by Benedikt Jóhannesson.

'What's this?'

'Read chapter three.' They were interrupted by the sound of a car pulling up. 'You'd better go now, that's my husband.'

Still trying to make sense of all he had heard, Magnus stared dumbly at the book in his hands. *Another* murder in his family?

'Magnús?'

'All right, I'll go,' he said. 'Thanks for the coffee. And for speaking to me so honestly.'

'Not at all,' said Unnur. 'Keep the book. And read chapter three.'

156

CHAPTER SIXTEEN

AS FRIKKI DROVE along the busy Miklabraut his heart was singing. He and Magda had taken the bus back from the airport to Reykjavík, and another out to Breidholt, and then they had spent the afternoon in bed, screwing. Seeing the sun outside, Magda had said why don't they go down to the Grótta beach on Seltjarnarnes to walk and see the sunset? It was something they used to do after their shifts at the hotel. Frikki wasn't going to argue, and his mate Gunni had lent him his car.

Frikki glanced across at Magda. She was glowing. She always glowed. She always had this incredible goodness about her, like she was always looking on the bright side, everything was wonderful, everyone was a good person, he was a good person. And he could tell that today she was really happy. She had put on a little weight, she was always soft and round and cuddly and now she was softer and rounder, but he didn't care. She had got herself a job in a hotel in Warsaw. A bloody miracle when there were all those other Poles coming back from hotels all over Western Europe. Except it wasn't really a miracle. Any hotel manager would be able to tell what an amazing girl she was.

Frikki already felt a better person, and she had only been with him for a few hours. If only she could stay; her strength would rub off on him. He was a fucking good cook, none of his bosses could deny that, and with Magda around employers would give him the chance to prove it. But she was staying one week, that was all. He was determined to enjoy every second of it.

157

Magda smiled as she caught him glancing at her, and put her hand on his thigh as he was driving. 'Do you remember that bakery in Seltjarnarnes? The one with those delicious strawberry pastry things?'

'Yeah.'

'Can we stop there on the way? We might get there just before it closes.'

Once again, Frikki wasn't going to argue. Ten minutes later he pulled up on Nordurströnd, and they both went inside the warm shop. Magda let out a little squeal of delight when she spotted the only two strawberry delicacies still left, and Frikki asked the woman behind the counter how much they were.

Then he froze. As did the woman.

'Hello,' she said.

'Hello,' said Frikki.

'You remember me?'

'Yes.'

The woman smiled nervously. 'How are you doing?'

'All right,' said Frikki. 'Still haven't found a job.'

'As you can see, I have,' said the woman. 'Took a while though. Have you seen any of our friends?'

'No,' said Frikki. 'And you?'

'I see Björn every now and then. I've had people stop by asking me questions recently.'

'The police?' Frikki asked in a low voice and with a glance towards Magda, who seemed preoccupied with the cakes.

'Yes. Don't worry, I haven't told them anything. They don't know anything about you, do they?'

'No, I don't think so,' said Frikki. 'I've never spoken to them.'

'Good.' The woman smiled. 'Let's hope it stays that way. That will be four hundred and fifty krónur.'

Frikki handed her the money. 'Nice to see you,' he said.

'And you.'

'Who was that?' Magda asked as they left the bakery. Frikki and she spoke a mixture of English and Icelandic to each other, and

Magda could understand Icelandic reasonably well. 'You Icelanders never introduce people!'

'Sorry. It's a woman I met last winter during the protests. I haven't seen her since then. Her name is Harpa.'

'What was that about the police?' Magda asked.

'Nothing,' Frikki said.

'What do you mean, "nothing"?' Magda said. 'I could see it was something.'

Frikki hesitated. A dozen different stories flashed across his brain, but he didn't want to lie to Magda. Then again, he didn't want to tell her the truth either.

'There was some trouble after the demonstrations. The police asked some questions.'

'What kind of questions?'

'I don't want to talk about it, Magda,' Frikki said.

'OK,' Magda shrugged, although Frikki could tell she wasn't happy. They got into the car. 'Let's go. And I will try to save this pastry for when we get to the beach.'

On the long drive back to Reykjavík Magnus thought about what Unnur had said. She had been quite convincing that his grand-father was actually glad that Ragnar had been caught in an affair with her. Yet there was no doubt that Hallgrímur must have disliked Ragnar intensely.

Could his grandfather really be responsible for his father's death?

Hallgrímur would have been in his sixties when Ragnar was stabbed in Duxbury. Magnus knew he was still farming actively at that age, and he would have been fit and strong enough to stab Ragnar. Especially in the back. The medical examiner's report was etched on Magnus's brain. The first stab wound was probably taken in the back, with the two subsequent ones in the chest, after Ragnar had fallen. This, together with the lack of any sign of a break-in, suggested that Ragnar had not felt threatened by whoever had called on him that day. It also meant that the murderer did not have to be big and strong enough to overcome him.

Stabbed in the back. Yes, Magnus could imagine Hallgrímur stabbing someone in the back.

But was Hallgrímur in the United States at the time? Magnus had never checked on that specific point. His grandfather seemed embedded in Bjarnarhöfn, part of the soil. Magnus could scarcely imagine him travelling as far as Reykjavík, let alone Boston. When he had visited Iceland himself just after his father's death, there had been no mention of any travel to America. That was something he would have to check up on. Since 2001 he was sure US Immigration records would show everyone who had come into the country. But Ragnar was killed in 1996.

There should be a way of checking it out.

It didn't quite feel right, though. Magnus knew that Hallgrímur was a cruel and vindictive man. For that reason he could imagine the pleasure that the old man would have felt at the discovery of Ragnar's affair, even if it hurt his daughter. It was true that when his father had come back to Iceland to retrieve Magnus and Óli, the two men had had almighty rows; in the heat of the moment Magnus could just about imagine Hallgrímur killing his father then.

But eight years later? It didn't feel right.

The key thing would be to figure out whether Hallgrímur was in the States at the time. If he was, that would be pretty conclusive.

But Magnus had the strong feeling he was heading up yet another blind alley. A blind alley with his grandfather at the end of it.

His spirits lifted as he drove south. The sun was setting to the west, burnishing the endless silver flatness of the Atlantic. The hillsides glowed. As he emerged from the tunnel under the Hvalfjördur, with Mount Esja looming above him, his phone rang.

'Magnus?'

'Yes?'

'It's Sharon Piper.'

Magnus could detect the excitement in her voice.

'Hi, Sharon, did you get back OK?'

'I went straight into the station. I've been checking the interview notes. You remember Óskar had a Venezuelan girlfriend, Claudia Pamplona-Rodríguez?'

'Yes.'

'When she was interviewed, she mentioned a woman coming around to the house in Kensington once over the summer. She thinks some time in July. An Icelandic woman. She wanted to speak to Óskar in private, so they went into the living room with the door shut. It only took about a quarter of an hour. Afterwards the woman came out looking angry and left. Óskar didn't seem too bothered.'

'Let me guess. The woman was tall and thin with dark curly hair?'

'You've got it. In her thirties. Quite attractive. Or attractive enough for Claudia to be suspicious.'

'You don't have a photo of Harpa, do you?'

'No, but if you send me one I can get Claudia to ID her.'

CHAPTER SEVENTEEN

H ARPA LOOKED NERVOUS as she sat in the interview room. One
hand was tugging and twisting the curls in her hair.

Magnus had called Vigdís, who was still on duty, and asked her
to bring Harpa in and take her photograph. A copy had already
been sent by e-mail to Piper in London.

Magnus and Vigdís had hatched a plan for the interview.

'Hi, Harpa, thank you for coming in,' Magnus said. 'Have you
been offered some coffee?'

Harpa shook her head.

'Would you like some?'

'No thank you.' Harpa glanced at both detectives suspiciously.
'Why am I here?'

Magnus smiled. 'We've got a couple more little questions to ask
you. Things come out in an investigation like this, and we have to
go back and check them out with witnesses. Sorry, but that's just
the way it works.'

Harpa seemed to relax a bit. 'OK. What do you want to know?'

'Have you travelled abroad in the last few months?' Magnus
asked.

Harpa didn't answer right away. At that moment, Magnus was
sure that Harpa was the woman that Claudia had seen. Magnus
and Vigdís waited expectantly.

'Yes,' she said. 'I went to London in July. Just for a couple of
days.'

'Ah, I see. And why did you go?'

'Oh, you know, shopping.'

'Shopping?' Magnus raised his eyebrows. 'That might have made sense a year ago. But now? Everything is so expensive abroad now, isn't it? And you can't have very much money or you wouldn't be working in a bakery. In fact how many weeks' wages did the trip cost?'

'It's true. It was expensive,' Harpa said. 'But I needed a holiday really badly.'

'I'll bet,' said Magnus.

'What did you buy?' Vigdís asked.

'Oh, um, nothing in the end,' Harpa said, trying to sound casual. 'You are right. I hadn't realized how expensive things are there until I was actually in the shops.'

'Did you visit any friends?' Magnus asked.

'Er. No,' said Harpa.

'So you didn't see any other Icelanders?'

Harpa glanced at the two detectives. Magnus could see that she understood the trap. She didn't know how much they knew. How far she would have to tell the truth in order to avoid being caught out.

'I did see one Icelander,' she said, carefully.

'And who was that?' Magnus asked innocently.

'Óskar,' Harpa said. 'Óskar Gunnarsson.'

'Huh.' Magnus didn't mention the fact that Harpa had left that information out of their previous discussions. Not yet. 'And what did you talk with Óskar about?'

'Er, well, I don't remember. I suppose I was a bit lonely in London and I wanted to see an old friend.'

'And how long did you spend with him?'

'Twenty minutes. Half an hour. He was busy, he had somewhere to go.'

She must have figured out that Claudia had seen them together.

Magnus leaned forward. 'How much money did you ask him for?

'What? I, er, I didn't ask him for money.'

'Yes you did, Harpa. How much? A million krónur? Ten million? Perhaps something every month?'

'I don't know what you are talking about. Why would I ask him for money?'

'To pay for his son, Harpa. To pay for his son.'

'No, no that's not right,' Harpa said, her voice rising. 'He never knew Markús was his son. He never knew that. I *told* you that.'

'You told us a lot of things, Harpa, and frankly I don't believe many of them. Now, how much did you ask for?'

Harpa was breathing heavily. 'Am I under arrest?'

'Not yet,' said Magnus. 'But we can fix that if you like.'

'I won't say anything more unless I have spoken to a lawyer. I have a right to speak to a lawyer, don't I?'

'You do,' said Vigdís, nodding towards the tape recorder. Magnus understood. This all had to be done according to the book, if the evidence was going to be admissible. It was just a slightly different book than he was used to. 'Do you have one in mind, or would you like us to call one for you?'

'Um, I have a friend who is a lawyer. Can I call her?'

'Just wait a moment,' said Vigdís. She turned off the tape and indicated to Magnus that they should leave the room.

'So we get her a lawyer, right?' said Magnus, once they were outside.

'We speak to Baldur first,' said Vigdís.

'But you know what he'll say,' said Magnus in frustration. 'Let her go.'

'Actually, I don't,' said Vigdís. 'But I do know that if we take this interview any further without discussing it with him he will be seriously pissed off.'

'Well, let him be pissed off!' Magnus had trouble keeping his voice down. 'Someone's got to crack this case open, and if we don't do it, no one else will!'

'Magnús,' Vigdís said. She looked at him steadily.

'All right,' said Magnus, the frustration subsiding to a simmer. 'You're right. Let's go talk to him.'

Baldur was in his office. He listened closely to what Magnus and Vigdís had to report. He was a good detective. He spotted what had been going on at once.

'How did Sharon know that the dark-haired Icelandic woman who visited Óskar was important?'

Magnus could try bullshitting his boss, but that was never a good long-term strategy. 'I told her about Harpa. In fact she was with me when Harpa admitted that Óskar was the father of her child.'

Baldur glared at Magnus. 'I specifically told you to leave Harpa out of it.'

'I know. I kept it unofficial,' Magnus said. 'And Sharon didn't make a big deal of it at the British end. But she needed to know about Harpa just in case a link came up at her end. Which it did.'

Baldur ran his hand over his bare forehead where his hair had once grown many years before. 'OK. OK, I take your point. But we know Harpa didn't actually kill Óskar, right? She was in Iceland at the time.'

'Yes, it looks that way. Her boss says she came to work early the following morning. We can check out the alibi more thoroughly, but my guess is it will stand.'

'So what about the boyfriend?'

'We don't know where he was. I tried to see him today up in Grundarfjördur but he was out on a boat somewhere.'

'I didn't realize you were working today?'

Magnus shrugged.

'OK,' said Baldur. 'You need to check him out.'

'What about Harpa?' Vigdís asked.

'Let Harpa get her lawyer. And then ask her about Óskar and only Óskar. I don't want you linking this to Gabríel Örn's suicide, do you understand?'

'But what if there is a link?' Magnus protested.

'There isn't,' Baldur said. 'There is no firm evidence of one. And I don't want you conjuring evidence out of thin air. '

'But the lawyer will tell her to keep her mouth shut,' Magnus said.

'Quite possibly,' Baldur said. 'And in that case, you let her go.'

Frikki and Magda sat on a stone on Grótta beach and watched the sun set. Despite the recent wind, the sea was calm and quiet, lapping against the black gritty shore. Ducks patrolled the water a few metres out, while along the shoreline a busy little gathering of small grey and white birds scampered in and out in time with the gentle waves.

The sun, a milky yellow ball, was heading for the horizon straight ahead of them. Layer upon layer of creamy clouds reflected its light in orange and gold. Way out to sea, there was nothing. Just the Atlantic.

Frikki and Magda had talked incessantly as they had walked along the beach, with Frikki doing most of the talking. It was strange: before she had come he had decided he would hide the dullness and the misery of his life, the fact that he found it difficult to get up in the morning, the way his whole week was concerned with looking forward to getting smashed at the weekend. But actually he found he wanted to talk to her about it, and she listened.

He didn't tell her everything, of course. Nothing about the drugs. Or the petty burglary.

And now they sat in silence, watching the sun on its slow, inexorable descent towards the sea.

'I know you stole that laptop, Frikki,' said Magda.

'What!' Frikki was shocked out of his reverie. He turned to her in fake outrage. 'I bought it off Gunni. Cheap. I told you that.'

Magda looked at him steadily, her eyes warm, without judgement.

'Honest,' he said.

'OK,' she said at last, and turned back to the sea.

The sun slipped further. 'You're right,' said Frikki. 'I did steal it. Some idiot left it on the front seat of his car. Mine was bust and I *needed* a computer. I had to keep in touch with you. Do you understand?'

'I understand,' said Magda.

She didn't say: 'but it was still wrong'. She didn't have to.

'I'm sorry,' said Frikki. 'Can you forgive me?'

'Of course, I can forgive you,' said Magda. 'But what I really want to do is help you.'

'What do you mean?'

Magda took hold of his hand. 'I love you, Frikki. I'm sure this year has been hard for you. I know you've been trying to hide it, but I can see you are letting things go. Doing things you shouldn't do.'

'You're right,' said Frikki, giving her hand a quick squeeze. He took out a cigarette and lit it. Magda didn't smoke.

'What did the police want to see you about?'

'I don't want to say,' said Frikki.

'Was it stealing?'

Frikki didn't answer. Magda removed her hand. They sat in silence.

'It was worse than that,' said Frikki. 'A lot worse.'

'Tell me.'

Frikki took a deep breath. And told her.

Magnus went to Ingileif's apartment that evening. As she cooked supper she talked about her day in the gallery and quizzed him about the case. He told her about missing Björn at Grundarfjördur and about Harpa's visit to Óskar in London. He mentioned nothing about Unnur.

After dinner he called Sharon Piper in London to tell her about the interview with Harpa. Unsurprisingly, Harpa had said nothing once her lawyer had arrived, and following Baldur's instructions Magnus had let her go. Magnus also told Sharon about Ísak, the student at the London School of Economics who had had an argument with Harpa the night Gabríel Örn had died. Sharon agreed to talk to him.

When he had finished the call, Ingileif picked up her cello. She was still quite a serious player and practised almost every day. Magnus liked to listen to her, or to read while she was playing. She started on one of her favourites, a piece by Brahms. Magnus knew that whenever he heard that particular piece in future he would think of her.

It was all very domestic. And yet there were things that Magnus didn't understand about Ingileif. They were not 'in a relationship' in the American sense of the word. Ingileif came and went as she pleased, made her own plans. Magnus wasn't quite sure what his role in her life was. Should they spend time together at the weekend? Should he ask her what she was doing? What *was* she doing?

Sometimes Magnus wondered whether she was seeing other men. He had asked her once and she had denied it and got angry at him for even thinking it. But he was still suspicious. Perhaps that was because he was a cop, always suspicious.

He dispelled those uncomfortable thoughts from his mind and opened the novel Unnur had given him, *Moor and the Man*. He decided to read chapters one and two before getting on to chapter three.

It was about a family recently arrived in Reykjavík in 1944. The war and the British and American occupation of Iceland had brought wealth to the country. The man of the title was a young farm labourer named Arnór from an unspecified area of the countryside who had moved to Reykjavík looking for work. The book was well written and the story had gripped Magnus by the time he turned to chapter three, a flashback to Arnór's childhood.

It was spring, and Arnór and his best friend Jói from a neighbouring farm crept into the barn to play in the hay, something they were strictly forbidden from doing. They heard rustling and grunting. At first they thought that some large animal had found refuge there, or perhaps a tramp. As they crept nearer they recognized the sounds as human, and not just human, but coming from their parents. Arnór's father was making love to Jói's mother, the farmer's wife, right there in the hay.

The two boys ran away without being seen.

A month later, the boys were playing by a secluded lake some distance from the farm. They were on their way home when Arnór realized he had forgotten his knife and returned to the lake. He saw Jói's father the farmer rowing out from the shore of the tarn, a large sack visible at the bow of the boat. When he reached the middle he paused and shipped his oars. With a fair bit of heaving and cursing, he rolled the heavy sack out of the boat and into the water.

Arnór returned home. His father was late back from a trip to the local town. When he failed to return home that night, his mother raised the alarm. Arnór's father was never seen nor heard from again. The theory was that he had fled to America, but if he had, he never sent word back to Iceland. And Arnór never told anyone what he had seen.

Magnus closed the book. 'Jesus Christ,' he said in English.

Unnur had claimed that Hallgrímur's father had killed Benedikt's father, Jóhannes, who was the farmer at Hraun. If the episode in the novel was based on that, that would mean that Benedikt and Hallgrímur were the two small boys, and Jóhannes's body was in a nearby lake: either Swine Lake or perhaps the lake next to it, Hraunsfjardarvatn.

Magnus hadn't heard anything about a neighbour being murdered, or even disappearing. But if it had happened when his grandfather was a child, that would have been in the 1930s. Neither had he heard about a writer living nearby, there certainly wasn't one there during Magnus's four-year stay in the 1980s. But Benedikt could easily have moved away years before.

Ingileif paused in her playing. She had noticed the stunned expression on Magnus's face.

'What are you reading?' she asked.

Magnus held up the cover of his book.

'Oh, I've read that. It's not bad. I like him.'

'I've never read anything he wrote until now.'

'He's quite good. A bit like Steinbeck, but not *that* good. I've read most of his books, I think. Why the sudden interest? And why the "Jesus Christ"?'

Magnus told Ingileif about his visit to Unnur. He felt slightly guilty about not mentioning it to her before, but she seemed to understand, and she didn't dwell on what Unnur had said about her affair with his father, for which Magnus was grateful.

'I remember that chapter,' Ingileif said. 'So this woman thinks that the guy who killed Benedikt's father was your great-grandfather?'

'That's right. Gunnar was his name.'

'Do you remember him? Was he still alive when you were at Bjarnarhöfn?'

'No, he had been dead a long time. I don't know very much about him. Apart from how he died.'

'And how was that?'

'Have you heard of Búland's Head?'

'It's on the Snaefells Peninsula somewhere, isn't it? I've never been there.'

'That's right. It isn't too far from my grandfather's farm. It's one of those places that has a bunch of folk tales attached to it. The road from Grundarfjördur to Ólafsvík runs along its edge. It used to be very narrow, and it's still pretty scary, or it was in the nineteen eighties. Apparently my great-grandfather slipped and fell. He was riding his horse.'

'But no one told you about him being suspected of killing anyone?'

'No. But then my grandparents would be hardly likely to tell me. As you know, I lived with my father from the age of twelve and he never spoke about my mother's family. Do you know anything about this guy Benedikt Jóhannesson?'

'A bit. He wrote in the sixties and seventies. I think that might have been one of his last books.'

Magnus checked the front of the book. 'Copyright 1985.'

'There you are. Actually, he died about then. I think he might have been murdered. I'm sure he was. Hold on, let's google him.'

Ingileif grabbed her laptop and after a certain amount of fiddling about they were on the Icelandic Wikipedia entry for Benedikt Jóhannesson. Born 1926, died 1985. He was born and brought up on a farm on the Snaefells Peninsula. He studied Icelandic at the University of Iceland and lived in Reykjavík. He published a dozen novels, the last of which was *Moor and the Man*, and several collections of short stories.

'Those are quite good,' said Ingileif. 'I think I prefer them to the novels, although they are not as popular.'

They read on. 'Look at that!' exclaimed Ingileif, pointing to the section headed *Death*.

Magnus was a couple of lines behind her; he skipped a bit, and read the section. 'Jeez.'

In 1985 Benedikt Jóhannesson was found murdered at his home in Reykjavík. The crime was never solved, but the police assumed it was a burglar.

'There you are, Mr Detective,' said Ingileif. 'There's something to get your teeth into.'

CHAPTER EIGHTEEN

August 1942

HILDUR'S BACK ACHED as she raked up the hay. Her brother Benedikt was twenty metres away, laying low the tall lush grass with rhythmic sweeps of his scythe. Hildur glanced up towards Bjarnarhöfn Fell. A black cloud was gathering on the other side of the mountain, preparing to pounce. They had only harvested half of the home field, and time was running out if they were to get all of it in for the winter. Cutting the hay was the easy part. The difficulty was drying it and then keeping it dry. A row of haycocks behind her testified to their efforts so far.

She saw a figure on a horse picking its way along the Berserkjagata through the lava field. Hallgrímur. He was eighteen and although not tall, he was broadening out. Some of the younger girls in the region even found him attractive, much to Hildur's disgust. She was surprised to see him pause as he passed her younger brother. Usually the two of them ignored each other.

'Hello, Benni!'

Benedikt paused and straightened up. 'Hello, Halli.'

'What are you bothering to get the hay in for? I thought you'd sold the place?'

'The new owner will need to feed his sheep this winter just like we do.'

'Huh. He's from Laxárdalur, isn't he? Can't he bring his own hay?'

Benedikt shrugged at the stupidity of the remark and made as if to go back to work.

'I hear your mother has bought the clothes store in town?' Hallgrímur said.

'That's right.'

'So you will be selling ladies' underwear?'

'I'm going to school in Reykjavík. The Menntaskóli.'

'That's a bit of a waste of time, isn't it? But I suppose your mother won't need you at home any more once she sells the farm.'

'I suppose not.'

'Well,' Hallgrímur said. 'When you get to Reykjavík, remember what I told you.' He glanced at Hildur, who looked away. 'In the church, when we were kids. Do you remember?'

'I remember,' said Benedikt. 'I remember very well.'

'And you will keep your word?'

'I always keep my word.'

'Good,' said Hallgrímur. He kicked his horse on.

'Oh, Halli,' said Benedikt.

Hallgrímur paused. 'Yes?'

'Do you remember what *I* said in the church?'

Hallgrímur frowned. 'No. No, I don't.'

Benedikt smiled and went back to his scything.

Hallgrímur hesitated and then rode off. Hildur approached her brother. 'What was all that about?'

'Oh, nothing.'

'Was it something to do with Dad?'

'Really, Hildur, you don't want to know.'

Hildur did want to know, but she knew there was no point in pushing her brother. He was stubborn in his own way.

'I'm glad that boy won't be our neighbour any more,' she said.

'So am I,' said Benedikt. 'So am I.'

Sunday, 20 September 2009

Magnus put the cup of coffee down on the nightstand inches from Ingileif's head and climbed into bed beside her. As he sipped from his own mug, he studied her back. Her fair hair was spread over the pillow and her shoulders were moving up and down in a tiny shallow rhythm. She had a cluster of faded freckles above one shoulder blade that formed the shape of a crescent – he had never noticed them before. He felt an urge to lean over and run his hand down her spine, but he didn't want to disturb her.

He smiled. He was lucky to wake up next to someone like her.

As though she could feel his eyes upon her, Ingileif stiffened, grunted and rolled over, blinking.

'What time is it?' she said.

'Just after nine.'

'That's a bit early for a Sunday, isn't it?'

'I need to get going soon. I've got to go back up to Grundarfjördur.'

Ingileif sat up, her back against the pillow, and sipped her coffee. 'Again?'

'Now we know Harpa saw Óskar in London over the summer it's all the more important to check up on her boyfriend. If he's there. I'll call the police up there to make sure he's at home before I set off.'

'Can I come? We could go for a walk afterwards. I could see Bjarnarhöfn, if only from a distance. Or we could go talk to Unnur about Benedikt Jóhannesson. If you want to, of course.'

'I don't know,' said Magnus.

'Oh, come on. You supported me last spring when I was trying to come to terms with what I learned about my father's death. I'd like to do the same for you.'

The idea of going anywhere near Bjarnarhöfn again didn't thrill Magnus. Ingileif may be right, perhaps it would be more bearable if she accompanied him.

'You have to promise to leave me alone to interview Björn.'

'I promise.'

Magnus smiled. 'All right. Let me check with the Grundarfjördur police and then we'll go.'

The sun was shining out of a pale blue sky as they drove north.

Ingileif put a Beethoven symphony on the car's CD system, great music for driving through the Icelandic countryside, she said. She was right. Magnus had little knowledge of classical music, but Ingileif was a good guide.

Páll, the constable in Grundarfjördur, had confirmed that although there were no lights on in the house, Björn's motorbike was in his driveway as was his pickup truck. Magnus asked the constable to keep a discreet watch on the house until he got there. If Björn left home, Magnus wanted to know where he was going.

As they descended the north side of the mountain pass down towards Breidafjördur, Magnus pointed out the Berserkjahraun and Bjarnarhöfn.

'Is that a little church there, down by the sea?' Ingileif asked.

'Yes. It's tiny,' Magnus said. 'Not much more than a hut.'

'It's cute. And why is it called Bjarnarhöfn?'

'It's named for Björn the Easterner,' Magnus said. 'The son of Ketill Flat Nose, and the first settler in the area.'

'I remember,' said Ingileif. 'But it's a long time since I've read the *Saga of the People of Eyri*.'

Ingileif had studied Icelandic Literature at university, and knew the sagas almost as well as Magnus. 'And this is where the Swedish berserkers cut their path?'

'Yes. You can still see the cairn where they were buried.'

'Cool. Let's stop there on the way back.'

'Maybe,' said Magnus.

Ingileif detected the note of caution in his voice. 'Does your grandfather still live at the farm?'

'He does. My uncle Kolbeinn farms the place now, but my cousin said that Grandpa still lives there with Grandma.'

'And you don't want to bump into him?'

'No. I don't.'

They drove on to Grundarfjördur. Magnus pulled over on the shore of the sheltered fjord a kilometre outside town and called Constable Páll. The sun glimmered off the quiet grey waters of the sheltered fjord.

Páll answered on the first ring. Apparently Björn had driven his pickup truck down to the harbour, and was working on a boat down there. Magnus drove through town and pulled up outside the police station, which was only a few metres away from the harbour. Páll was waiting for him, in uniform.

Magnus introduced Ingileif. 'I'll just go for a walk around town,' she said. 'Give me a call when you've finished.'

Magnus was glad to have the constable with him. He was still in a legal limbo-land, since he hadn't yet graduated from the police college, and he wanted Páll to take notes. If Björn gave them any useful evidence, he didn't want it questioned by a defence lawyer.

Páll was very happy to oblige.

There were a few boats of various sizes in the harbour. For a small town it had some serious fishing industry – several large buildings for processing the fish, a market, storage sheds and numerous empty pallets guarded by fork-lift trucks.

And the whole thing was watched over by the tower of rock that was Kirkjufell. In Iceland it was difficult to believe that such features were just random movements of geology. Icelandic mountains had personality and purpose. This church of rock completely overshadowed the white building with the little cross on a hill above the town. It was as if it provided the town's inhabitants with not just physical shelter but spiritual strength as well.

Páll led Magnus towards a fishing boat tied up against the quay, *Bolli*. 'Hello, Siggi!' he shouted. 'May I come on board?'

Two men in thick sweaters poked their heads out of the cabin. One was an overweight balding forty-five, the other was lean and in his early thirties.

Björn, no doubt.

Páll greeted the older man and asked if they could have a word with Björn. Björn stepped off the boat and joined them on the quay. 'A new navigation system,' Björn said. 'I was just helping Siggi install it, but it keeps crashing. I swear these days you need to know as much about computers as about engines to keep a boat running.'

They sat on a wall, a short distance from the boat, the captain peering at them curiously from the cabin window. A couple of seagulls landed on the quay a few feet away, hoping for scraps.

'So what's this about?'

'We want to ask you some questions about Gabríel Örn Bergsson and Harpa Einarsdóttir.'

'Harpa told me you had been talking to her,' Björn said.

'Oh, have you seen her recently?'

'Yes. I went down to Reykjavík a couple of days ago. You left her quite upset.'

'It's unavoidable in these circumstances,' Magnus said. 'Are you and she together?'

'You could say that. I go down to see her whenever I can. She comes up here sometimes. I like her. I like her a lot.'

'Harpa didn't mention that you and she still had a relationship.'

Björn shrugged. 'It's not a secret. As I said, she was upset. You probably didn't ask her.'

'No, we didn't,' Magnus admitted. But he still had the impression Harpa had been trying to hide it. 'Had you two met before the night Gabríel Örn died?'

'No. We first met at the demo that afternoon. I had come down from Grundarfjördur for it specially. I had been to one of the Saturday protests before Christmas and, well, I thought it was important to be there. I wanted to be heard. I wanted the government to resign.'

'Tell me about that evening.'

Björn's story tallied pretty closely with Harpa's. He was vague on the details, arguing quite reasonably that the whole thing had happened nine months before. Magnus took him backwards and forwards over the same ground and tried to trip him up.

Nothing.

So Magnus changed the subject. 'Has Harpa told you about Óskar Gunnarsson?'

'Yes,' Björn said. 'She said you thought she was linked in some way to his murder.'

'We were just asking questions.'

'You should be careful how you ask them,' Björn said. 'Harpa has never got over Gabríel Örn's suicide. From what she tells me about him the man was a jerk, but I think in some ways that makes it worse for her. She feels guilty about going out with him, about breaking it off. She's a mess. Your questions don't help.'

'Do you think she had anything else to feel guilty about?'

'No,' said Björn calmly.

'Had you ever met Óskar?'

'No,' said Björn.

'Has Harpa told you anything about her relations with him?'

'No. I didn't think there were any.'

Magnus took out a photograph of Óskar. 'Do you know who this is?'

'That's him, isn't it? I've seen his picture in the paper.'

'That's right. Now, does he remind you of anyone?'

Björn studied the picture. 'Looks a bit like Hugh Grant perhaps. Darker hair.'

'No. Someone you know.'

Björn shook his head.

'Markús.'

Björn looked at Magnus in surprise. 'What? Harpa's Markús?' He studied the picture more closely. 'That's ridiculous.'

'No, it's not. Didn't you know?'

'What do you mean, didn't I know? Know what? What are you suggesting?'

'I'm suggesting that Óskar was Markús's father.'

'That *is* ridiculous.'

'Harpa confirmed it.'

'When?'

'Yesterday.'

Björn studied the photograph more carefully.

'She didn't tell you then?' Magnus said.

'I still don't believe you.'

'Did she say who the father was?'

'No. I asked her once, she didn't want to answer, and so I never asked her again. It was none of my business.' He handed the photograph back to Magnus. 'It's still none of my business.'

Magnus had to admire Björn's composure. A couple of fishermen strolled past, nodded at Björn and Páll, and stared at Magnus, the stranger from out of town, with undisguised curiosity.

'Did you know that Harpa travelled to London recently?' Magnus asked.

'Yes. A couple of months back. Just for a few days.'

'Do you know why?'

'She said she needed a break.'

'How could she afford it?'

Björn shrugged. 'I don't know. She used to be a banker. She's probably got savings. It's true she's usually careful with money, but she deserved a treat.'

'Did she tell you she saw Óskar?'

'No,' said Björn.

'Are you jealous?' Magnus asked.

'Of course I'm not jealous!' Björn said. 'Look. If there's one person in this world I trust, it's Harpa. Who she saw before she met me is none of my business. I had no idea that Óskar was Markús's father, and frankly I still don't believe you. But if he was, maybe Harpa went to see him, I don't know. And if she did, I'm not surprised she kept it a secret from me.'

'Does it make you angry that Harpa keeps secrets from you?'

Björn stared hard at Magnus. His blue eyes were remarkably bright. And angry. But Magnus got the impression it was with him, not with Harpa. 'No.'

'Björn. Where were you on Tuesday night?'

'Let me guess. Was that when Óskar was killed?'

'Just answer the question.'

'I was out at sea that day. Got back about seven. A good catch, lots of mackerel. Helped unload and clean up. Came home.'

'And Wednesday morning?'

'Went out again, early in the morning. Same boat. The *Kría*. She's out right now, but she'll be back later this afternoon. One of the regular crew had flu. Gústi is the skipper. Páll knows him.' He nodded to the constable. 'He can check with the crew. And actually on Tuesday night I went to the fishing company's office to pick up some pay they owed me. You can ask Sóley, she'll tell you. In fact they probably have it written down.'

He stared at Magnus. 'So I wasn't in London shooting bankers.'

'Did you get what you needed?'

Magnus and Páll were walking back along the quayside towards the police station.

'He's a cool customer,' Magnus said. 'It's hard to say whether he's telling the truth. If he wanted to lie, he could do it well, I'm sure.'

'I'll check out his alibi,' said Páll. 'But I bet it will stand up. Which means he can't have shot that banker.'

'You're probably right,' said Magnus. 'But be thorough. In a small town like this, people could easily cover for their friends.'

'Gústi is an honest man,' said Páll. 'In fact, I'd have to say that Björn has a very good reputation here.'

'Tell me,' Magnus said. 'Do you know him well?'

'Quite well. As you say, this is a small town. He had his own boat, the *Lundi*. Bought it off his uncle. He was very successful, bought up more quotas, worked long hours. But he did it all on borrowed money, and when the *kreppa* came he had to sell. Since then he's been crewing on other people's boats whenever he can.'

'Have you seen Harpa around?'

'I think so. Curly dark hair? About one eighty high?'

Magnus was only just getting used to thinking metric again. Heights still confused him, but that sounded about right. 'That's her.'

'She's been here a couple of times.'

'Does Björn ever get into trouble?'

'No. Not here at any rate. I think he used to go down to Reykjavík to party every now and then. He stays with his brother Gulli down there.'

They walked on.

'Magnús?'

'Yes?'

'I can't imagine Björn murdering anyone.'

Magnus paused and looked at the constable. He had a bit of a belly and an imposing moustache, but he had kind eyes. And they were troubled.

'Is Björn a friend of yours?' Magnus asked.

'No. Not exactly. But...'

'But what?'

'Did you have to tell him about his girlfriend's son? I mean that the father was a banker? What does that really have to do with the police? Isn't that a secret she has a right to keep from her boyfriend if she wants to?'

Magnus felt a flash of irritation. In a town like this, with a population of a thousand people, two thousand max, the loyalty of the local cop was more likely to be with his buddies than with a detective parachuted in from the big city.

But then Magnus needed Páll.

'Murder is always painful. To the victims, to their friends and family, obviously, to all kinds of other people. Murder investigations hurt witnesses. I know you like Björn, and I hear what you say about him being a good guy. But we've just got to ask the questions. Every now and then we piss people off, good people. Although, unlike you, I'm not convinced Björn fits into that category.'

Páll grunted.

They got to their vehicles, Magnus's Range Rover parked next to Páll's police car outside the wooden police station.

Ingileif was waiting. She had that air of barely suppressed excitement that Magnus knew well.

'Good interview?' she asked.

'OK, I guess,' said Magnus. 'What is it?'

'Páll, isn't it?' said Ingileif, giving the constable her best smile.

'That's right.'

'I assume the town library isn't open on Sundays?'

'No.'

'But you know the librarian?'

'Yes. She's my wife's cousin.'

'Is there any chance that you could get her to open it up for us?'

Páll glanced at Magnus. 'Why?'

Ingileif looked at Magnus, her eyes shining. 'When I was wandering around, I remembered something. A Benedikt Jóhannesson short story. I think it's called something like "The Slip". I need to show it to you.'

'Is this police business?' Páll asked Magnus.

'No,' Magnus said.

'Of course it is!' said Ingileif. 'It's about a murder. At Búland's Head, fifty years ago.'

Páll raised his eyebrows. 'I can't get the library open for you, but my wife is a keen reader of Benedikt's. She's from around here, and he used to live over by the Berserkjahraun. We'll see if she's got the book you want.'

The policeman's house was on the edge of town: it took all of five minutes to drive there. His wife's name was Sara, and she did indeed have a copy of Benedikt Jóhannesson's short stories. Eagerly, Ingileif found "The Slip". It was only five pages.

She skimmed it and then began to read out loud. A boy was riding a horse along a cliff. He met the man who had raped his sister riding the other way. They squeezed past each other and the boy gave the other man's horse a shove. Man and horse fell into the sea below.

'Well?' said Ingileif, her eyes shining.

'You think Benedikt pushed my great-grandfather into the sea at Búland's Head?'

'Don't you?'

Magnus glanced at Páll and his wife and their poorly concealed expressions of curiosity. He had blurted out his family's secrets in front of these strangers without thinking, but it would be useful to learn if there was any local gossip that might cast some more light on those events. So he explained how his great-grandfather had died, and also the chapter in *Moor and the Man* that suggested that Gunnar had killed Benedikt's father.

'I remember that,' said Sara. 'It caused a little local scandal when that book came out. I was about fifteen at the time, I remember my parents discussing it. The mysterious disappearance of the farmer at Hraun was still talked about around these parts, even though it had happened fifty years before. And Benedikt's book hinted at a solution, one that the locals noticed right away. He was murdered by his neighbour. And that was your great-grandfather?'

'Yes. He lived at Bjarnarhöfn. I hadn't heard anything about it until recently.'

'And then of course Benedikt himself was murdered soon afterwards. But that was down in Reykjavík. I don't think they ever caught whoever did it.'

'Were there any rumours of a local connection?'

'No, certainly not. That's the kind of thing that happens in the big city, isn't it? Nothing to do with people from around here.'

'And nothing about Gunnar's death on Búland's Head?'

'No. There were occasional accidents up there, especially in the old days before the road was improved. And of course there were lots of stories about trolls throwing people into the sea.'

'I bet,' said Magnus.

'Are you investigating all this?' Páll asked Magnus.

'Only in a personal capacity,' Magnus said. 'It's not official police business by any means. But thank you, Sara, for letting us look at your book. And please keep this to yourselves.'

Magnus knew he couldn't be a hundred per cent sure of their discretion, but Páll was a policeman and they seemed decent enough.

'No problem,' said Sara, with a smile. 'Although you can imagine how much the town would love this gossip. Stay and have some lunch with us. I've made some soup. I'm sure there is enough for two more.'

CHAPTER NINETEEN

THE SOUP WAS indeed tasty; lamb and vegetables. Páll and Sara had two noisy but good-humoured kids and both Magnus and Ingileif enjoyed the good-natured warmth. Páll had to take the boy to basketball practice, so they left soon after the meal was over.

'So, what do you think of that story?' Ingileif asked. 'Do you think your great-grandfather was pushed?'

Magnus smiled. 'It's the classic question, isn't it? Did he fall or was he pushed? In this case I suppose it's possible he was pushed. But who by?'

'It must have been Benedikt himself.'

'Or someone he knew well. A brother? I can't believe he would as much as admit to it in a story.'

'Perhaps he had to get it out of his system somehow,' Ingileif said. 'After all, that chapter in *Moor and the Man* is clearly about Gunnar.'

'It could all be a coincidence,' Magnus said.

'You're a cop. You don't believe in coincidences, surely?'

'Actually, I do,' said Magnus. 'In real life coincidences happen. You have to keep an open mind.'

'So are we going to see Unnur? Find out if she has read that short story?'

'I'll give her a call,' said Magnus.

Unnur agreed to meet them in an old restaurant in Stykkishólmur. It was a warm, cosy place, but empty apart from a Spaniard and an Icelander talking to each other about fish in English. There was a good view of the harbour, where a ferry was gathering speed as it headed off towards the West Fjords.

Unnur was waiting for them with a cup of coffee. Magnus introduced Ingileif.

'I didn't want to meet at the house this time,' Unnur said. 'My husband is at home, and I haven't told him about the stuff with your father. I'm not proud of it: I'd rather he didn't know.'

'I understand,' said Magnus. 'But don't worry. Like I said on the phone, we won't talk about that.'

'You read the chapter in *Moor and the Man?*' Unnur asked.

'I did,' Magnus said. 'You think that shows that Gunnar killed his neighbour?'

'Yes. I'm pretty sure. As you can imagine there was a lot of gossip around here when the book came out. It didn't take long for someone to spot the similarity. I was still working in Reykjavík at the time, but it was all the conversation of family visits.'

'Do you know what Benedikt said about it?'

'Oh, he denied it, but no one believed him. I think he was surprised that people had made the connection. And of course your grandfather said it was all nonsense. As you can imagine, he was angry about the whole thing. It was my aunt who convinced me that there was something in it.'

'Your aunt?'

'Yes. My uncle's wife. She was also Benedikt's older sister. She lived at Hraun at the time.'

'And she confirmed the story?'

'No,' said Unnur. 'She wouldn't say anything. She just gave this kind of knowing smile.'

'Did you know Benedikt?'

'Only vaguely. We met once or twice at some of the larger family gatherings. A nice guy, very clever, rather quiet. His mother had sold the farm at Hraun and moved into town here. She used to own a clothes shop. I can just about remember it. She died some time in the sixties. But you said you have found another story?'

'Yes. Ingileif remembered it. Do you own any of his short-story collections?'

'No,' Unnur said.

'Well, there's one called "The Slip",' Ingileif said. She summarized the story for Unnur, who listened closely.

'I see,' she said. 'I seem to remember that Gunnar fell off a cliff somewhere, didn't he?'

'Yes,' said Magnus. 'On Búland's Head. And he was riding a horse at the time. That was something my grandfather did tell me.'

'And you are suggesting that someone pushed him? Benedikt?'

'Possibly. In the book the boy is taking revenge for the rape of his sister. In this case it would be for the murder of his father.'

Unnur mulled it over. 'It is possible, I suppose. I can't imagine Benedikt killing anyone. It's all ancient history now, isn't it?'

'Perhaps not so ancient,' Magnus said. 'Remember Benedikt was murdered himself. In 1985.'

'But that was a burglar,' Unnur said.

The three of them sat in silence, thinking it all through.

Unnur shuddered. 'This is creepy. Three deaths. Over, what, fifty years? From the nineteen thirties to the nineteen eighties.'

'Is your aunt still alive?' Ingileif asked.

'Yes. But I doubt she would tell you anything.'

'You never know with old people,' Ingileif said. 'Sometimes they are happy to talk when the people they are talking about are no longer with us.'

'It's important,' said Magnus.

'Yes, I suppose it is,' said Unnur. 'Well, let's go and see her. She lives just around the corner.'

They left the restaurant and followed a small street that rose behind a fish factory. They came to a tiny house, that looked like an illustration out of a children's book. It was clad in corrugated iron, painted a bright green with a red roof. A series of elfish knick-knacks adorned the windows. Unnur rang the bell. Above the door was a white plaque upon which the year 1903 was carefully painted in black, with purple flowers winding around the numbers.

Unnur's aunt Hildur was a tiny woman with a crooked back, bright blue eyes and a sharp mind. Her face lit up when she saw her niece. She led them through to an over-heated and over-furnished sitting room, with landscapes on the walls, and little Icelandic flags sprouting up among various elves, seals, trolls and birds on every surface. Unnur was sent to the kitchen to fetch some coffee, there was some brewed.

Hildur picked up some knitting. 'It's for my great-grandson,' she said. 'He'll be two next week, and it's for his birthday, so please don't mind me if I keep working.'

She held up an almost completed tiny *lopi* sweater, with an intricate pattern of blue and white crossing chest and shoulders in concentric circles.

'That's beautiful,' said Ingileif with enthusiasm.

The old lady grunted, but she was clearly pleased.

Unnur returned with the coffee. 'This is Magnús Ragnarsson, aunt. Hallgrímur's grandson.'

Immediately Hildur's blue eyes fastened on Magnus, warmth replaced by suspicion.

'I lived with my grandparents at Bjarnarhöfn for four years when I was a boy,' Magnus said. 'It wasn't a happy time in my life.'

'I imagine it wasn't,' said the old woman.

'You know my grandfather, I take it?'

'Of course,' said Hildur. 'We were neighbours until I was about twenty. We lived at Hraun. I have tried to avoid him since then.'

'You don't like him?'

'No. I don't. Benni and he used to be great friends when they were little, but I thought he bossed Benni around a bit. They grew apart as they got older.'

'I don't like him either,' said Magnus. The old lady was shocked. Loyalty to grandparents was a given in Icelandic society.

'Do you remember my great-grandfather?' Magnus said. 'Gunnar.'

'Yes,' said Hildur.

'What was he like?'

188

Hildur didn't answer straight away. 'He was a bad man,' she said eventually.

'A very bad man,' Magnus said. 'He killed your father, didn't he?'

There was silence in the room, apart from the ticking of a clock, which seemed suddenly very loud. 'I believe he did,' said Hildur eventually. 'I had no idea when I was a child. He used to come over to our farm often after Father disappeared. He helped my mother out around the place, he was a good neighbour. But all the time he knew that he had killed her husband.' She shuddered.

'How did you find out? Did Benedikt tell you?' Magnus fought to keep the excitement out of his voice. He didn't want to spook her.

Hildur glanced at her audience. For a moment Magnus thought Ingileif might be right, that Hildur might decide that there was no point in keeping the secret any longer. But then she shook her head. 'I can't tell you. Some secrets go beyond the grave.'

'Have you read your brother's story "The Slip"?' Magnus asked.

The old lady smiled knowingly. 'Yes. Yes, I have.'

'Do you think that your brother might have pushed Gunnar over the edge at Búland's Head? In revenge for what Gunnar had done to your father?'

'Let's just say that on the day Gunnar fell into the sea, Benedikt was returning from Ólafsvík. He claimed he never saw Gunnar. Everyone believed him. Benedikt was an honest boy.' Her eyes twinkled. 'In fact he was an honest adult. He had to tell the truth somehow, in the end.'

'I understand,' said Magnus with a smile. 'And thank you.' He stood up to leave. 'I know it happened a long time ago, but I am very sorry about your father.'

A tear suddenly appeared in the old lady's eye. 'So am I.'

Ingileif got her way. Despite Magnus's reluctance, they stopped by the Berserkjahraun on the way back. They parked the Range Rover just below the farm of Hraun, on the eastern side of the lava field, the opposite side to Bjarnarhöfn.

Hraun was much as Magnus remembered it, with several large outbuildings, and a couple of small houses in addition to the main farmhouse. Circular bales of hay in white plastic lined the home meadow, on which round woollen balls of sheep grazed. Magnus and Ingileif headed into the lava field, and a few metres in they found the Berserkjagata, the 'Berserkers' Street'. It was a footpath cut into the rock, only a few inches wide.

'I thought it would be bigger than this,' said Ingileif.

'If you think it was made by two men cutting into solid rock, it's big enough,' Magnus said. 'And it made it much easier to walk to Bjarnarhöfn.'

'Show me the cairn.'

The path wound through the twisted rock, down into hollows and up again. Autumn in Iceland has its own beauty. Not as striking, perhaps, as the change of leaves in Massachusetts, but the heather and grasses turn to gold and orange, and the bilberry leaves to a deep red. Peaceful.

They caught glimpses of the little Hraunsvík, the 'Lava Bay' between the two farms, where the lava flow had spilled into the sea. Two eider drakes in their black and white finery patrolled the cove. Magnus wondered whether the inhabitants of Bjarnarhöfn still collected their mates' dun-coloured down every summer after the ducklings had left their nests. Beyond the bay, flat islands dotted Breidafjördur, familiar to Magnus from fishing trips in the farm's skiff.

'It's quite hard to take in,' said Magnus. 'Jóhannes. Gunnar.'

'Sounds like you've got yourself your very own family feud,' Ingileif said. 'It's fascinating really. Just like the old days. Arnkell and Thórólfur and Snorri and – who was the other one – Björn of Breidavík?'

'That's him,' said Magnus. 'It does sound a bit like that.'

'What do you think of Benedikt's murder? Do you think it is connected?'

'It must be a possibility,' Magnus said. 'Burglars don't usually murder people in Iceland, although of course it can happen. I'll pull out the police file next week and take a look.'

'At least your grandfather wasn't involved.'

'I don't know about that,' Magnus said. 'He would be right there for a family feud.'

'You mean he could have killed Benedikt?'

'Possibly. Once I take a look at the file it will be clearer.'

'You really don't like him, do you?'

Magnus didn't answer.

They reached the cairn nestling in a hollow, a flat mound of stone big enough to contain two large men.

'This is it?' Ingileif said. 'Wow. And do they really think the berserkers are inside?'

'They dug it up a hundred years ago,' Magnus said. 'There are two skeletons buried there. Apparently they are not particularly tall, but they were powerfully built.'

Ingileif stopped and looked around at the wondrous stone shapes. 'This must have been a great place to play as a kid.'

'Yes. Although Óli was scared of it. Grandpa told him the berserkers were still roaming around.'

'But not you?'

Magnus took a deep breath. 'I tried not to let my grandfather scare me. I didn't always succeed.'

Ingileif glanced at him. Magnus could tell she wanted to ask him more.

Suddenly he needed to leave. 'Let's go.'

'No. I'd like to walk a bit further.'

'Come on.' Magnus turned on his heel and strode rapidly along the path back to the car. He didn't look behind him until he reached it. Ingileif was struggling to catch up.

Wordlessly, Magnus started the engine and drove off.

They passed a spot where a road peeled off to the right. 'Is that the way to Bjarnarhöfn?' Ingileif asked.

Magnus didn't answer.

The track became narrow, with a ten foot drop on either side into the rocky waves. A car approached kicking up dust, an old station wagon. Magnus pulled over as close as he could to the side of the track, leaving enough room for the other car to pass.

The car stopped a few feet ahead. It flashed its lights and sounded the horn.

An old man was behind the wheel.

'Oh, Christ,' said Magnus in English.

There was really nowhere for Magnus to go, unless he tried to reverse the Range Rover a hundred yards back down the track.

'Come on, you old git,' Ingileif said good-naturedly. 'There's plenty of room.'

The 'old git' edged forward until he pulled parallel with Magnus. Magnus recognized the broad weather-beaten face, the angry blue eyes. The wrinkles were deeper, the grey wiry hair thinner, but it was the same man.

Magnus stared straight ahead.

The man lowered his window. 'Can't you pull over further, you selfish bastard!' he shouted. Then, 'Magnús?'

Magnus put the car into gear and accelerated along the track, almost driving the large vehicle over the edge.

'Jesus!' said Ingileif. 'Was that him?'

'Of course it was him,' said Magnus.

'And he recognized you?'

'You heard him say my name.'

The car lurched and skidded through the lava until it hit the main road. Magnus turned to the right up the pass over the mountains.

'Slow down, Magnús!' Ingileif said.

Magnus ignored her.

Ingileif stayed quiet as Magnus threw the car around the bends up the hill. But after they had crested the head of the pass, the road on the other side was straighter.

'What did he do to you, Magnús?' she asked.

'I don't want to talk about it.'

'But you have to.'

'No, I don't.'

'Yes, you do, Magnús!' Ingileif said. 'You have to face up to it some time. You can't just bury it.'

'Why not?' Magnus said. He could feel the anger in his voice. 'Why the fuck not?'

Ingileif's eyes widened at Magnus's tone. But she didn't back down. Ingileif didn't do backing down. 'Because otherwise it will eat away at you for the rest of your life. Just like it has for the last twenty years. You told me it was your father's murder that bothered you, but there's more to it than that, isn't there?'

Magnus didn't answer.

'Isn't there? Answer me, Magnús.'

'No.'

'Answer me.'

'Ingileif?'

'Yes?'

'Shut the fuck up.'

A hundred and seventy kilometres is a long way to drive in silence, even if you are going thirty kilometres an hour over the speed limit.

He turned his motorbike off the little road, on to an even smaller road, not much more than a track with a strip of tarmac at its centre, and stopped to examine his Michelin map. He couldn't believe how many trees there were in this country, specifically how many apple trees. They were unknown in Iceland. He would have plucked a fruit from the small orchard adjacent to the road, but that would mean taking off his helmet to eat it, and he didn't want to do that.

He knew exactly where he was. He had spent a couple of hours examining the map at home and checking it against Google Earth, until this small strip of Normandy was etched on his brain. Sure enough, beyond the orchard the road curved to the left. On one side were small fields of pasture, on the other, woodland.

He kicked the motorbike into life and drove it slowly and quietly along the lane. He couldn't see anyone. That was good.

The bike had Dutch number plates, which made him feel conspicuous here in France. They should have thought of that, but as long as no one saw him, it wouldn't matter.

He counted the telegraph poles running along the side of the road. At the seventh, he stopped and pushed the bike into the woods opposite. He spent a couple of minutes making sure that it was concealed from the road, yet ready for a quick getaway.

He made his way through the trees about twenty metres until he reached the other side. A group of cows were chewing their cud in a small field, their tails swishing away the flies. Beyond the field was the barn.

He moved through the edge of the wood just a few metres in from the field, until he found the tree he was looking for. It had been carved with a 'B' a metre above the ground. 'B' for Bjartur, although only he would know that; the French police would have no clue what it stood for when they discovered it. The patch of freshly dug ground was five metres to the west of the tree, partially hidden under a broken branch.

He slid the pack off his back, took out a trowel, and started to dig. The earth came away easily, and within a few minutes he had revealed a polythene bag containing rifle and ammunition.

A Remington 700. He grinned. He eased the rifle out of its bag and checked the mechanism. Everything worked perfectly.

Then he pulled out his binoculars and examined the barn. It was large and had been converted into a holiday home. Behind it was the farmhouse to which the barn must once have been attached. It was a sunny afternoon, and so there were no lights on in the building, but a door out to the garden was open. And in the garden were two chairs, a book resting open on the seat of one of them. There was a car parked on the patch of gravel in the front – only one car, which implied there were no bodyguards. Excellent. The car was an Audi estate: he could just make out the number plate – British, not French.

It was hard to estimate range with any precision, but he guessed a hundred and twenty-five metres was about right. The chair seemed to be about the same distance away from him as the petrol container had been back in the mountain valley the previous morning.

He found a good spot to lie, with the barrel resting on a log, and waited. It was a sunny day, the French September sun was much stronger than its Icelandic counterpart, and he felt uncomfortably warm in his motorcycle leathers. He would wait until nightfall if he had to, although having spotted the open book on the chair he was optimistic that that would be unnecessary.

He ran through the getaway in his mind. He would be sure to drive the bike at a steady speed so as not to attract attention. It was fifteen kilometres to the isolated water-filled quarry where he would chuck the polythene bag containing rifle, trowel, binoculars and bullet casings, and then twenty more kilometres before he hit the autoroute and the long ride back to Amsterdam.

Through the binoculars he could see movement in the house. He tensed. The target emerged.

He put down the binoculars and rested the rifle on his shoulder. The target was wearing a narrow-checked shirt and carrying a mug. Tea, no doubt – so English. The target walked across to the chair and bent to place the mug by its side. Stood up. Surveyed the landscape.

He pressed the trigger. Several things happened at once. The window behind the target exploded. The noise of the rifle shattered the rural quiet. Rooks further along the copse took to the air, yelling angrily.

The target turned towards the window and then back towards the wood, jaw open, reactions dulled by the surprise.

He had missed. Keep calm. He fired again. This time the target took a step back and raised a hand to his upper arm. A short, sharp cry of pain. One more shot. The target crumpled to the ground, just as a woman ran out of the door screaming.

Time to go.

CHAPTER TWENTY

FRIKKI SAT IN the back of the church as the priest droned on. Magda had forced him to come with her to the large concrete Catholic cathedral on the hill on the other side of the centre of town from the Hallgrímskirkja. She was sitting next to him now, struggling to make sense of the sermon the priest was giving. Frikki had given up after the first sentence.

She had wanted him to pray for forgiveness. He wasn't sure how to do that. He closed his eyes. 'Forgive me, God,' he muttered to himself. Was that enough? He wasn't sure. 'Forgive me, God,' he repeated. Why should God forgive him, a loser without a job, who stole, who never went to church? Who had killed someone.

The only good thing about Frikki's life was Magda. If God had any sense he wouldn't bother saving Frikki, he would save Magda *from* Frikki.

Frikki closed his eyes again. 'Please, God, don't take Magda away from me.'

Frikki thought he would be bored, but he wasn't. It was a peaceful building with its smooth blue columns. Although he didn't feel a part of the congregation of earnest worshippers, most of whom were foreign, they did give the place a sense of calm. No one stared at him, although Frikki was sure everyone must know he was the only Protestant in a Catholic church.

He could sort of see why Magda liked coming to places like this every week. He could understand why religion made sense for her. But not for him.

He didn't really believe in God. And he was quite sure that if there was a God, He didn't believe in Frikki.

Had he killed the banker? He had no way of knowing whether the man was already dead before Frikki had kicked him. Sometimes, in his better moods, Frikki was convinced he was. At other times, like now, Frikki was pretty sure he wasn't.

The worst thing was, for those few moments back in January, Frikki had actually *wanted* to kill him.

Those few seconds would stay with him for the rest of his life. He would always be a murderer, even when he was an old man. And now Magda knew.

But not only did she know, she understood. She said that she would forgive him, and that God would forgive him.

They were all standing up and walking up to the priest to kneel down and take the bread and the wine. The choir sang. Magda bobbed down on one knee, made the sign of the cross, and followed them. There was no way Frikki was going to do that.

Suddenly it came to him. For Magda truly to forgive Frikki, she had to believe God had forgiven him.

He knelt down to pray.

When he got back to Reykjavík, Magnus dropped Ingileif off at her apartment, and drove back to his own place in Njálsgata. He poured himself a beer and flopped into his armchair.

Seeing his grandfather again after all those years had shaken him. He knew he had been wrong to take it out on Ingileif, but she should have realized that it was time to back off.

He sipped his beer and tried to make sense of it all. His father's affair with Unnur. The series of deaths spanning fifty years. His father's own death.

He was very tempted just to ignore everything, focus on today, on Óskar and Gabríel Örn.

But Ingileif was right: he, of all people, couldn't step back now he was beginning to discover so much.

He needed to do two things. Find out whether his grandfather had been in America when his father had been murdered, and look at the file on Benedikt Jóhannesson's death in 1985.

His phone beeped. He checked it. A voicemail. He called the number and heard his brother's voice.

'Hey, Magnus, it's Ollie. Just checking in. Call me back when you have a moment.' The message had been left an hour before, probably when Magnus was out of reception somewhere on the way back from Stykkishólmur.

Ollie. Poor Ollie. Unlike Magnus, who had always been drawn by his Icelandic roots, Ollie had denied them. He was an American through and through: America still provided that service it had offered to immigrants throughout its history, the opportunity to stop being who they were and start being who they wanted to be. Ollie had taken up the offer with enthusiasm.

And given the miserable time he had had in Iceland, who could blame him?

Magnus considered calling Ollie back there and then and telling him where he had been. Perhaps it would give Ollie a chance to exorcize some old ghosts.

Or perhaps not. Magnus couldn't face talking to him that evening. He'd call back tomorrow. Or the day after.

He finished the beer, and turned on his small TV as he went to the fridge for another one.

It was the news on RÚV, the public broadcasting station. There was a story about Julian Lister, the former British Chancellor of the Exchequer. It seemed to Magnus the Icelanders should let that one go. Sure, they had been treated badly, but Lister wasn't the cause of their problems, nor was he the solution, especially after he had been dumped by his own Prime Minister.

But there was something about the newsreader's tone that was not quite right. Magnus glanced at the pictures. An ambulance. A hospital in France.

He sat down and watched.

Julian Lister had been shot twice by an unknown gunman at his holiday home in Normandy. He was in a critical condition at a hospital in Rouen. No arrests had yet been made. Speculation focused on a terrorist assassination attempt with Al-Qaeda the first-choice suspects and Irish Republicans second, but the French police were making no comment.

There are going to be some Icelanders that will be happy to hear that, thought Magnus.

Then he thought a little harder.

No. There couldn't be a link between Gabríel Örn, Óskar and Julian Lister, that was too far-fetched. Besides, Magnus had seen Björn and Harpa in Iceland that weekend, so there was no chance that they had shot anyone in France. He was letting his desire to get involved in an interesting murder case get the better of him.

And yet.

CHAPTER TWENTY-ONE

February 1985

Benedikt Jóhannesson sat on a rock and stared across the black causeway towards the Grótta lighthouse on its own little island. Behind it, swirls of grey cloud shifted and jostled as a strong cold breeze blew in from the Atlantic and the breakers crashed against the volcanic sand. He was alone.

Good.

Hunched into his parka, he opened the pack of cigarettes he had just bought and tried to light one. It took him a while in the wind, he was out of practice. Eventually it caught and he took a deep drag, suppressing the urge to cough.

That tasted good.

Sixteen hours after stumbling out of the hospital, he had taken his first positive decision: to start smoking again. It was nearly eight years since he had given up, and he had missed it. Now there was no point in protecting his lungs.

The nicotine made his head buzz, denting the pain lurking there from all the brandy he had drunk the night before. His brain was mush: he wouldn't be able to write that day. Would he be able to write again?

He wouldn't tell anyone. Not the kids, not his friends. He would have had to tell Lilja of course, but she had left him two years before. A sudden heart attack. No warning, a result of undiagnosed heart disease. He was glad he didn't have to tell Lilja.

There. Two decisions.

What about the writing? The moment he had asked himself the question whether he could write again, his subconscious had screamed yes, yes he could. But what? What could he write in six months that would make a difference? Two years, maybe he could force himself to come up with the great Icelandic novel, something to rival Halldór Laxness, something to ensure his name was remembered.

But who was he kidding? If he could write that book, he would have done so already.

The cigarette was fast disappearing. His cheeks stung in the cold air. But the wind brought clarity to his confusion.

Moor and the Man wasn't a bad book. It might even be his best. He would have time to finish that. And maybe a short story or two. But what, in the last few months of his life, could he tell the world?

Suddenly it came to him. He would tell the truth. After forty years he would finally tell the truth.

He stubbed out the cigarette, stood up and scrambled back towards his car. He needed to get back to his desk. There was no time to lose.

Monday 21 September 2009

'Did you see the news about Julian Lister?' Vigdís asked Magnus as she arrived for work, dumping her bag by her desk.

'Yes, poor bastard.'

'They say they don't think he'll make it.'

'Yeah.' Magnus had listened to the morning news as well. Lister had been operated on overnight at a hospital in Rouen. The doctors rated his chances as slim.

'Do you think there's a connection?'

'With Óskar?' Magnus looked at her sharply. 'I wondered about that.'

'Some Icelanders would be very happy to see him dead,' Vigdís said. 'Not the majority, not even a minority, but it would only take one.'

'Or two, or three.'

'You mean Björn and Harpa?'

'And Ísak, possibly.'

Vigdís raised her eyebrows. 'We don't have any concrete link between him and the other two.'

'OK, if not Ísak, maybe somebody else.'

'So we're saying there is a bunch of nutters out there who want to shoot bankers and politicians?'

'Who they think are responsible for the *kreppa*.'

Magnus and Vigdís looked at each other. 'If we raise this, the shit really will hit the fan,' Vigdís said.

'I know,' said Magnus.

'And I mean not just with Baldur. With Thorkell. And the Big Salmon himself.'

'I know.'

'We haven't got any evidence, have we? I mean, none at all.'

'I know.'

'So what do we do?'

Magnus had been thinking. 'Let's just keep an open mind for now. Baldur told me to go back to the police college today, and I have a lecture to give there at eleven o'clock. But I have an idea.'

'Yes?'

'Did the police take surveillance videos during the demonstrations in January?'

'Sure.'

'Dig them out for the day Gabríel Örn was killed. See if you can see Harpa. And Björn. See what they did. See who they talked to. Maybe you'll be able to figure out whether they really did meet then for the first time.'

'I'll do that,' said Vigdís.

'Let me know what you find. In the meantime, how do I get hold of the file on a murder from 1985?'

'Which case?'

'Benedikt Jóhannesson.'

'The writer?'

'Yes. Do you know anything about it?'

'I was only a kid at the time. But we studied it at police college. Stabbed in his home, I think. The crime was never solved.'

'That's the one.'

'Has this got a connection to Óskar?'

'Not really.'

Vigdís frowned. Magnus remained impassive. Vigdís decided not to push it. 'It won't be scanned on to the system, but Records will have the original file buried away somewhere. It will probably take them a while to locate it.'

'Thanks, Vigdís.'

While Vigdís made some calls to rustle up the surveillance video, Magnus composed an e-mail to one of his buddies in the Homicide Unit in Boston, asking to check with the US Citizenship and Immigration Services for immigration information for July 1996. Then he called Records.

Árni breezed in. 'Morning, Magnús. Good weekend? All quiet here?'

'Talk to Vigdís,' Magnus said. 'You've got some work to do.'

Ísak popped the toast out of the toaster, and spread on butter and marmalade. It was an English habit that was growing on him. The house off the Mile End Road which he shared with four other students ran on toast. And instant coffee. The kettle boiled and Ísak made himself a cup.

'Hey.'

He turned to see his girlfriend Sophie slope into the small kitchen in pyjama bottoms and an old *Save Darfur* T-shirt.

'I thought you didn't have any lectures until twelve?'

'I decided I really have to go to the library,' she said. 'I can't put it off any longer.' She perched herself on his lap and kissed him quickly on the lips. 'Good morning,' she said, and kissed him again, deeper.

Ísak smiled and let his hand brush over her breast. She wasn't wearing a bra.

She left it there for a moment, but then she extricated herself and stood up. 'No. Discipline. I need discipline.' She opened the cupboard and started rummaging around, looking for bread. Ísak had finished off the loaf. 'Do you want another slice of toast, Zak?'

'Yeah, OK. Thanks.'

The doorbell rang.

'I'll get it,' said Sophie. The bell rang again. 'All right, all right. You'll wake everyone up,' she complained, but in a voice too quiet for whoever was outside to hear.

Ísak heard the door open.

'Police,' an authoritative female voice said. 'Detective Sergeant Piper from Kensington CID. Is Ísak Samúelsson here?'

Ísak tensed.

'Er. I don't know,' said Sophie, taken aback.

'It's OK, Sophie,' Ísak said, moving into the hallway. 'Come in.' He led the detective into the kitchen. 'Sit down. Can I make you some coffee?'

'No thanks,' Sergeant Piper said, taking the chair Sophie had been occupying.

Sophie sat down next to her and scowled.

'What is this about?' Ísak asked, as coolly as he could.

'Do you mind if I talk to Ísak alone?' Piper said to Sophie.

'I bloody well do,' said Sophie, suddenly waking up. 'Like, where do you get off? This is our kitchen.'

Piper sighed.

'It's OK, Soph,' said Ísak. 'I don't know what this is about, but I'm sure it won't take long.'

'All right,' said Sophie, grumpily. 'But I want my toast.'

After she had left the room, Ísak smiled. 'Sorry about that. We're doing a course on European Human Rights at the moment.

And Sophie is a member of Amnesty. She gets excited about that kind of thing.'

'Breakfast is important,' said Piper with a smile. 'I'd like to ask you about last week.'

'I was in Reykjavík,' said Ísak.

'We know.'

'This is about Óskar Gunnarsson, isn't it?' said Ísak. 'My mother told me the police in Iceland had been asking about me.'

Piper asked Ísak a series of questions about what he had done the previous week. Ísak answered clearly and calmly. He had been out with some old friends from high school on Wednesday night, otherwise not much. Piper took down flight times, names and addresses.

'Did you know Óskar Gunnarsson?' she asked.

'No,' said Ísak. 'I mean I know who he was. But I've never met him.'

'Are you sure?' said Piper, leaning forward.

'I guess I saw him at the annual Thorrablót of the Icelandic Society here in London,' Ísak said. 'But I didn't talk to him.'

'Thorrablót?'

'It's a winter festival. A big feast – lots of traditional food. You know, sheep's heads, whale blubber, rams' testicles, rotted shark. It's a big deal for Icelanders.'

'Sounds revolting.'

'It's an acquired taste. Actually, the food is usually pretty good at the London one.'

Piper seemed to be examining Ísak closely. 'You didn't try to deliver something to him a couple of weeks ago? The Friday before last?'

'Deliver something?'

'Yes. A witness saw someone matching your description going from house to house in Onslow Gardens looking for Gunnarsson's address?'

'That wasn't me.'

'Are you sure?'

Ísak nodded. 'I'm absolutely sure.'

Piper waited. Neither she nor Ísak said anything for a long moment. Then she stood up. 'OK, that's all for now. Thank you for answering my questions.'

Ísak stood up. 'No problem.'

'Are you going in to college today?'

'I've got a lecture in an hour or so. I'll have to leave soon.'

Piper handed Ísak a card. 'Well, if you do remember anything about Óskar Gunnarsson, give me a call.'

Magnus had just turned off the main road out of Reykjavík into Árbaer where the National Police College was located, when his phone rang. He picked it up.

'Magnus, it's Sharon.'

'Hi. How are you doing?'

'I just spoke to your friend Ísak.'

'And?'

'And he was in Reykjavík last week. He gave me some names and numbers of who he saw there. Basically he stayed at home most of the time, but went out on Wednesday night.'

'E-mail the names to me, we'll check them out,' said Magnus. 'Did he say why he came home?'

'He said things were getting on top of him at uni, he needed to chill.'

'That sounds like bullshit to me,' said Magnus. 'It's too convenient. Almost as if he was giving himself an alibi.'

'Possibly,' Sharon said. 'There is something else.'

'Oh, yeah?'

'He fits the description we have of the courier who was looking for Gunnarsson's house. Early twenties, five nine, broad face, blue eyes, dimple on his chin.'

'Interesting,' Magnus said. 'Can you get a firm ID?'

'I'm outside his house now. He's got to go to a lecture pretty soon, so I'll get a photo. Show it to our witness. She's on the ball; if it's him she'll tell us.'

'Excellent. Um... Sharon?'

'Yes?'

Magnus took a deep breath. 'Is there any chance you can talk to him again?'

'I suppose so. I can grab him after he comes out, once I've got his photo.'

'Could you ask him where he was yesterday? Check that he was in London.'

'Why?' Then the penny dropped. 'You mean Julian Lister?'

'Maybe,' said Magnus

'You think he might have shot Lister?'

'Not really. It's an outside possibility. You heard how unpopular Lister is in Iceland when you were over here.'

'Have you got any evidence?'

'No. None at all. It's only a hunch, not even that. Please don't mention it to anyone else. It's just that if it turned out our student friend went to France for the weekend, that would be interesting.'

'I'll say.' Sharon paused. 'Look, if there is any chance there is an Icelandic angle, I'm going to have to tell someone.'

'Don't do that, Sharon. We're not at that stage yet. Once the Icelanders start thinking the British believe they are terrorists, there will be a new cod war, believe me.'

'I don't know...'

'Look, there's no evidence, no suspicion, even.'

'But you would like me to talk to Ísak?'

'Yes.'

There was a pause on the phone and Magnus could hear Sharon sigh. 'OK. I'll let you know what he says. Oh, by the way. Turns out the Metropolitan Police had thirty million quid invested in an Icelandic bank.'

'Oops.'

Magnus hung up and drove into the parking lot of the police college on Krókháls. It was on an industrial estate and shared the car park with a software company and a sports shop. As he turned off the engine his phone rang again. It was Vigdís.

'Magnús, can you get back to the station?'

'When?'

'Now. There's something you should see.'

CHAPTER TWENTY-TWO

MAGNUS, ÁRNI AND Vigdís were crowded around Vigdís's desk, watching her monitor. The sound was off: they didn't want to attract Baldur's attention unnecessarily.

Magnus had seen snatches of the protests on the news, but never more than a few seconds at a time. Austurvöllur, the square outside Parliament, was full of a seething mass of people, young and old, male and female, shouting and banging. The pots and pans were very much in evidence, as were wooden spoons, tambourines, flags and placards. The camera panned from face to face, each one flushed with varying combinations of anger, excitement and cold. Apart, that is, from those that were hidden by scarves and balaclavas.

'Look, there's Harpa,' Vigdís said. Sure enough, Magnus saw her banging diligently at her saucepan. 'And there's Björn.'

The fisherman was only a few yards away from Harpa, yelling his head off and shaking his fist. For a second the camera focused on his face. Björn had seemed a cool customer to Magnus, but at that moment his face was contorted into a fury that verged on hatred.

'See, they pass within a metre of each other, and they don't recognize one another,' said Vigdís.

It was true. Harpa moved in front of Björn, banged her saucepan and then moved on.

'So this really was when they met?'

'Hold on, I'll show you.' Vigdís fast-forwarded. In jerky movements the crowd surged, missiles were thrown at the police lines and pepper spray canisters were raised.

'Is that you, Árni?' Magnus asked.

'Yes.' Vigdís paused, and they admired Árni in his black uniform, a look of determination on his face as he raised his yoghurt-splattered shield.

'That can't have been fun,' Magnus said.

'Especially not since I knew the kid who threw that *skyr*,' Árni said. 'An old girlfriend's younger brother. I swear he recognized me.'

'OK, we start spraying the pepper,' Vigdís said, providing a commentary, 'Harpa falls over and there! Björn picks her up. From here on they stick together.'

Even from the poor image it was clear from the way Harpa looked at Björn that she was taken with him.

'All right, this is from maybe quarter of an hour later. See. There they are.'

'Who's that guy they are with?' Magnus asked. Harpa and Björn were moving about together with a tall man with a grey ponytail sticking out underneath a broad-brimmed hat. The man was chatting to all around him, laughing and then shouting slogans. Magnus thought he looked vaguely familiar.

'That is Sindri Pálsson.'

'OK, I've heard of him somewhere haven't I?'

'He's famous here in Iceland,' Vigdís said.

'Everyone's famous in Iceland.'

'He was lead singer of the punk rock group Devastation in the early eighties. Then he became an all-round troublemaker. Serial protester. Anarchist. Wrote a book about the evils of capitalism. Heavily involved in the protests against the Kárahnjúkar dam. You know, they dammed up a valley to provide hydroelectricity for an aluminium smelter.'

'I know,' said Magnus, although that was barely true. He had heard of the controversial project but knew nothing of the details. Once again he felt his ignorance about his own country.

'He tried to turn the protests violent, but the organizers wouldn't have anything to do with it. Threw him out.'

'Criminal record?'

'Only drugs offences.'

'But you have a file on him?'

'Oh, yes. He's one of the people we identified as capable of trying to turn the protests into a revolution. A violent revolution.'

'And here he is making friends with Harpa and Björn,' said Magnus.

Vigdís took Magnus through the rest of the demonstration. As light fell, so did the quality of the images. But there was no doubt that the three kept together.

Then came the tear gas. 'This is the last image of them we have,' said Vigdís. Björn, Harpa and Sindri were standing next to the statue of Ingólfur Arnarson. Then they turned and headed off up Hverfisgata. It was only possible to identify them by the shape of their bodies, but they were quite distinctive.

'Wait a moment, who's that guy?' said Magnus. A younger man seemed to be trailing along a short distance behind.

'No idea,' said Vigdís. 'We can't really see his face. But I can look at other images, see if I can narrow him down.'

'I bet it's Ísak,' Magnus said. 'Sharon is taking a photograph of him in London now. I'll get her to send it over.'

'There will be one on the drivers' licence registry,' said Árni. 'I'll check.' This database contained images of every Icelander who had a driver's licence, and the police had access to it. Useful.

Magnus stood up straight. 'I take it we have an address for this Sindri?'

'Hverfisgata,' said Vigdís. 'Right by the Shadow District.'

'Come on, Vigdís,' Magnus said. 'Let's go talk to him. Árni, get working on those images.'

As they were leaving the office they passed Baldur. 'Magnús? I thought you were at the police college?'

'Just come from there,' Magnus said, with a smile. 'Got to go.' And he and Vigdís hurried out of the building.

*

It was quiet in the bakery. Harpa looked up when the door opened. She recognized the couple who came in.

'Hi, Frikki,' she said warily.

'Hello, Harpa,' Frikki said. They examined the selection at the counter. Frikki took a *kleina* and his chubby girlfriend an éclair.

Frikki paid. Harpa gave him change.

Frikki hesitated. His girlfriend stared at him. 'Did you see the news?' Frikki said.

'About the British Chancellor?'

'Yes.'

'I did.'

'Can we talk about it?'

Harpa glanced around. There were no customers in the shop. Dísa was in the back icing a birthday cake. 'OK,' she said. They moved over to the table in the corner.

'Harpa, this is Magda, my girlfriend,' Frikki said.

'Good morning,' the woman said with a foreign accent, Polish probably. She smiled. Harpa nodded.

'What do you think?' Frikki asked. 'About Lister?'

'However big a bully he is, he doesn't deserve to die,' Harpa said.

'No. No, course not. But, well...' Frikki flinched as his girlfriend jerked slightly. An under-the-table kick. 'When we saw it on the news last night it made me think. About that night in January. And...'

'And what?'

'Well, perhaps *they* did it?'

'By *they* you mean...?'

'You know who I mean. The others. Björn. Sindri. The student guy. Them. What if they all got back together and decided to kill Julian Lister? And Óskar?'

'No,' said Harpa. 'Why should they?'

'Why should they? Well, they were talking about it, weren't they? I mean, weren't we? About what we would like to do to the bankers. To Julian Lister.'

'That was just talk,' said Harpa.

'But it wasn't, was it? I mean what we did to your boyfriend. I mean we...' Frikki's voice was wavering.

'You mean *I*,' said Harpa.

'No. No, Harpa. *We.* I've thought about it a lot. We don't know which of the two of us actually killed him, do we? Maybe it was you, maybe it was me. I kicked him in the head, after all.'

Harpa's eyes widened. She had held herself solely responsible for Gabríel Örn's death. She felt a surge of sympathy for the kid sitting opposite her. She knew what it was like to feel that guilty.

'Well, I don't know about the others, but I know Björn didn't kill them,' Harpa said. 'I've got to know him very well. He's a good man.'

'But what about Sindri? You remember what he was saying. About how the Icelandic people aren't violent enough. About how they should take physical action.'

'He was just talking big,' said Harpa. 'He was half-drunk. We all were. In fact you were talking loudest of the lot.'

'I know,' said Frikki.

'And anyway, those people were shot abroad, weren't they? England, France.'

'It wouldn't take long to fly there and back,' Magda said. 'A fisherman could do it when he said he was out at sea. Go to Keflavík. London or Paris. No problem.'

'That's absurd. I *know* Björn didn't do that.'

Magda shrugged. There was silence for a moment.

Frikki flinched as he received another kick under the table. Harpa glanced at the Polish girl. She had an open, honest face. Harpa didn't trust her.

Frikki spoke. 'The thing is, Harpa. I'm thinking about going to the police.'

'What! Why would you do that?'

'Well. Anonymously perhaps. But if all these people are being killed, then who's to say it will stop now?'

'No one. But it's got nothing to do with us.'

'It has. Believe me, I feel guilty already. If I don't do something to stop them...'

'You're making a massive assumption here,' Harpa said. 'It would be one thing if we knew that Sindri or one of the others had killed these people, but we don't. All we know is that you and I killed someone. And I feel quite strongly we should keep quiet about that.'

Frikki took a deep breath. 'I wanted to warn you first.'

Harpa turned to the Polish woman.

'Magda, is it?'

Magda nodded.

'Listen. I know you think you are Frikki's conscience, but this isn't up to you. He's a good kid. He doesn't deserve to go to prison for years, which he will do. Maybe I do deserve to be locked up, but I have a three-year-old son. And the others helped us, me and Frikki, cover everything up. Björn in particular helped us. He shouldn't go to jail.'

'But we have a duty to stop any more people being murdered,' Magda said.

'We don't know why these people were murdered! We don't know there is a connection. Óskar and Lister weren't even in Iceland. We just keep quiet, Frikki, do you understand me?' Harpa was surprised by the authority she heard in her own voice. 'And we don't become friends. We keep well clear of each other. Otherwise we both wind up in jail and achieve nothing. Do you agree? Frikki, do you agree?'

Frikki glanced at Magda who was frowning. Harpa could see how torn she was, between doing what she thought was the right thing, and sending the boy she loved to jail. But it wasn't up to her. It was up to Harpa and Frikki.

'Frikki, you'll never forget what happened,' Harpa said. 'But you are still young. You're not a murderer, you didn't mean to kill Gabríel Örn. You can still turn your life around. Focus on that.'

Frikki glanced at Magda. She closed her eyes and nodded. 'OK,' Frikki said. 'OK.'

*

The moment Magnus saw Sindri he remembered where he recognized him from.

Oh, shit.

He wished he had brought Árni along, rather than Vigdís. This could get embarrassing, and Árni was an easier person to be embarrassed in front of.

But Sindri didn't recognize him. He was full of indignation at being harassed by police in his own home. Magnus could tell that Sindri wasn't surprised by the visit. On the other hand Sindri was probably used to unannounced visits by the police.

The flat was a dump, and smelled faintly of marijuana, stale tobacco and rotten food. Sindri reluctantly led them into the living room. There was a pile of dirty plates by the sink in the kitchen alcove. A computer in one corner was surrounded by paper on the desk and on the floor. Sindri was obviously working on something which involved a lot of pages.

Sindri sat down at the dining table and folded his arms. 'All right, what do you want?' he said. His deep voice was defiant, but there was something friendly about his puffy eyes that he couldn't quite hide.

Magnus glanced up at the big painting on the wall by the table. 'Did you do that?' he asked.

'I did.'

'Is it Bjartur of Summerhouses?'

'Amazing. A cop who reads.'

'*Independent People* is a good book.'

'It's a great book. Everyone in Iceland should be forced to read it now. In fact they should have read it five years ago. If there were more Bjarturs around and fewer Ólafur Tómassons, this country would be one of the great survivors of the credit crunch.'

'There's something in that,' said Magnus.

Sindri grunted. He obviously didn't like policemen agreeing with him.

'We want to ask you about the protests over the winter,' Magnus said.

'Oh, yes? It's a bit late to round up the usual suspects, isn't it? But there will be more of them, you know,' Sindri said. 'The people won't put up with this Icesave agreement. Why should our grand-children and great-grandchildren have to repay debts that were incurred by a bunch of crooks we had no knowledge of?'

'Why indeed?' said Magnus.

Sindri was off. 'The government are just bending over back-wards for the British and the Dutch. What is all this crap? "The Icelandic nation will always stand by its obligations." Why the fuck should we? That's what I want to know. We should tell the British to get their money off the bankers themselves and leave the rest of us out of it.'

Sindri nodded, encouraging himself. 'I knew this would happen. We have a socialist government now, but what's the point? They are just like the last lot, but weaker. They haven't actually *done* anything. It's nearly a year since the banks went bust and they still haven't brought a banker to justice. Not one single one. Yet you guys raided the squat around the corner and threw ordinary people out on to the streets.'

Magnus had heard of the raid, although it took place just before he arrived in Iceland. Drug-dealers, he had heard, and some of them dangerous at that. But he didn't defend his colleagues.

'I get it,' said Sindri. 'You're trying to take me out before the new protests start.'

'Actually, no,' said Magnus. 'We want to ask you about one protest in particular. Tuesday the twentieth of January. The day Parliament came back from its recess.'

'Oh, I remember that one. Or at least the beginning of it. I missed some of the fun later on that night. Left too early. I went out the next day, the Wednesday, though.'

'Do you know Harpa Einarsdóttir and Björn Helgason?' Vigdís asked.

'No.'

'You were seen with both of them at the demonstration that day. They stuck with you most of the afternoon.'

'Have you been looking at your surveillance videos?' Sindri asked. 'I've often wondered what you did with them.'

'You are seen with Harpa and Björn.'

'And lots of other people,' Sindri said. 'I like to talk to people at these things. You've seen the video footage. You know.'

'So you don't remember these two?' Magnus asked.

Sindri paused. 'Wait a minute. I think I remember Harpa. Dark curly hair? Cute?'

'That's right. Have you seen her since then?'

'No, unfortunately. And I've got no idea who this Björn guy is. I went to all the protests. They all merge into one after a while.'

'Did you go anywhere with them afterwards?' Magnus asked.

'No. I was a bit pissed. I came back here, had a bit more to drink. Went to sleep. As I said, it was a shame. Things got a bit more exciting later on, apparently.'

'Did you come back here alone?'

'Quite alone.'

'Harpa and Björn didn't come with you?'

'No.'

'They were seen following you. Where did they leave you?'

'I really can't remember,' said Sindri. He smiled.

A dead end. Sindri knew it. And Magnus knew it.

'Have you been abroad recently?' Magnus asked.

'No,' said Sindri. 'Can't afford it. No one can afford it these days. I went to Germany at the end of last year to publicize my book, but nothing since then.'

'And where were you on last Tuesday evening?'

'Um. Let me think.' Sindri made a show of struggling to remember. But Magnus had the impression that he had an answer already prepared and he was just delaying for effect. That was interesting.

'I was in a bookshop. Eymundsson's. A friend of mine was launching his book there. They'll remember. Why? What am I supposed to have done?'

'What about yesterday?'

'Did nothing. Went to the Grand Rokk at lunchtime. Spent most of the day there.'

'The Grand Rokk?' said Vigdís. 'You mean the bar?'

'Yes. It's just around the corner.' Then Sindri's eyes widened. 'Wait a minute!' He jabbed a finger at Magnus. 'That's where I've seen you. The Grand Rokk.'

'Possibly,' said Magnus.

'Not possibly. Certainly. You're the guy who lived in America, aren't you?' He laughed. 'Last time I saw you, you were pissed out of your head.'

Vigdís's eyes darted to Magnus and then back at Sindri.

'Did anyone see you there yesterday?' she asked.

Sindri ignored her. 'I thought you had a bit of an American accent.' He smiled. '"Who loves ya baby?" Isn't that what Kojak says?' He raised his thumb and index finger in the sign of a revolver being cocked. '"Make my day."'

Magnus leaped to his feet, kicking back his chair. With two strides he was on Sindri, grabbing him around the collar. Sindri was heavy but Magnus was strong. He wrenched the big man out of his chair and shoved him against the wall.

'Listen, asshole,' he said in English. 'You know what happened to Óskar Gunnarsson and Gabríel Örn Bergsson. And probably Julian Lister as well. Now it seems to me you've got a choice to make. Whether you spend the rest of your life in a French jail or a British one. It's just a shame I can't find a space for you in Cedar Junction back home. You'd enjoy that.'

Magnus saw the fear in Sindri's eyes.

He let him go. 'We'll be back,' he said.

It was a short distance from Sindri's flat to police headquarters, which was at the eastern end of Hverfisgata opposite the bus station. Magnus was driving.

'That's not normally the way we conduct interviews here in Iceland,' Vigdís said.

'Maybe you should,' said Magnus.

'The Grand Rokk is a bit of a dive, isn't it?'

'I don't go there often.'

They drove on in silence.

'If you have a problem, I know people you can talk to,' Vigdís said.

'Why is it that if a guy has a drink on a Tuesday night, he's an alcoholic, but if he gets totally shit-faced on a Friday, he's just being sociable?'

'I'm just saying,' said Vigdís.

And that was all either of them said until they were back in the station.

Harpa served Klara, who was a regular customer, and partial to Dísa's *vínarbraud*. She was well into her seventies, and came in at about the same time every day for a slice. She liked to take her time over the purchase and usually Harpa was happy to chat, but this time she was distracted, only half listening.

She was pleased with how firm she had been with Frikki. But the more she thought about it, the more she worried that the kid might have a point. She was sure that Björn wasn't involved in any way with Óskar's death, or with Lister's. She had no idea about Ísak. But Sindri?

For years the man had publicly espoused violence to defeat capitalism. But then for years he had done nothing about it, as far as Harpa had heard. Icelanders loved to talk politics, to complain, to demand change, but they didn't resort to violence, even the anarchists. Harpa guessed that the big man was all talk.

But perhaps having been involved in one killing it became easier to kill again? There was no doubt that there was a possible link between Óskar and Julian Lister, and Gabríel Örn for that matter, and that was responsibility for the *kreppa*. And maybe there would be another death soon.

No. It was nothing to do with her. She should do what she had told Frikki to do, keep quiet and forget it.

Klara finally left and Harpa busied herself with rearranging the pastries under the counter. Forget it? She couldn't forget it. She felt guilty enough about the death of Gabríel Örn. Frikki was right, she wouldn't be able to face the guilt if someone else was murdered and it turned out that the murderer was Sindri.

Perhaps she should speak to Björn. But she already knew what he would say. He would discourage her, urge her to keep quiet, keep a low profile, just as she had urged Frikki.

At least she could trust him. There was no chance that he had shot Óskar or Julian Lister. The Polish woman was being ridiculous. What did she think, that he had left her house the previous week and gone straight to the airport instead of back to Grundarfjördur? Ridiculous. He'd need passport, tickets, money for a start.

Suddenly she couldn't breathe. Her ears begin to sing. She felt faint and slipped back against the wall, dropping the tray of pastries she was carrying with a clatter.

No. No, no, no, no, no! She couldn't believe it. She simply couldn't believe it.

'What is it Harpa? Are you OK?'

She scarcely felt Dísa's hand on her shoulder, or heard her concerned voice.

She was thinking about what she had noticed sticking out of the pocket of Björn's light blue coat when he had stayed with her that night.

An electric-blue Icelandic passport.

CHAPTER TWENTY-THREE

MAGNUS HAD JUST got back to his desk when his phone rang.
'Magnus, it's Sharon.'

'Did you get the photo?'

'Yeah. I got a good shot. I'm on my way to the station to print off a copy to show to Gunnarsson's neighbour.'

Magnus's pulse quickened. Matching a description was one thing, but a positive ID would be the first real evidence of a link between Óskar's murder and Gabríel Örn's death.

'If you don't get a good print, we've probably got a mugshot in our database here. Did you ask Ísak where he was yesterday?'

'That's why I am calling. I'm at the chaplain's office in the Icelandic Embassy, checking out Ísak's story. He said he was at the Icelandic Church service in the morning. The chaplain confirms it.'

'Damn.'

'Yes. Although it was the first time Ísak has attended. Made a point of coming up and talking to the chaplain. Which makes me think—'

'He was setting up an alibi?'

'Maybe.'

Magnus thought about it. He knew they were in danger of manipulating the facts to fit the theory. 'That's stretching it a bit.'

'Yeah. Perhaps. We'll see what the neighbour says.'

'Do you know anything about the investigation in Normandy?'

'Only what I've seen on the news. I've kept my nose well out of that one, like you asked me to.'

'Thanks, Sharon.'

'No problem.'

But Magnus couldn't help noticing the lack of enthusiasm in her voice. She did have a problem with his request: there was no doubt about it. Tough.

'Explain to me why you aren't at the police college?' Baldur demanded, glaring at Magnus.

Magnus exhaled. 'Vigdís found some new evidence on the video of the January protest the day Gabríel Örn was killed.'

'I thought I told you that case was closed?'

'Yes, I know. But listen to what we've got.' Magnus described the identification of Sindri on the video and most of his interview, missing Sindri's reference to Magnus's own presence at the Grand Rokk.

He summed up. 'So Harpa, Björn, Sindri, Ísak, they are all linked. Harpa, Björn and Sindri all met on the day Gabríel Örn was killed. Ísak started a fight with Harpa that evening in a bar at about the time Gabríel Örn died. And he fits the description of the Icelandic courier who was looking for Óskar's address in London a few days before the murder. Harpa is connected to Óskar – Óskar was her son's father and we know she met him in London in July. Björn and Harpa are in a relationship. And Sindri, well Sindri is an anarchist who believes in using violence to overthrow capitalism.'

'None of that is hard evidence,' Baldur said. 'The only real link between all these people is that you are suspicious of them.'

'That's right,' said Magnus. 'We need to go in and get the hard evidence.'

'What are you suggesting?'

'Set up a tail on Sindri. And Björn. Get warrants to search their apartments and their computers. Take a look at the phone company records – see if they've been talking to each other. Get a positive ID on Ísak and get the British police to arrest him.'

Baldur shook his head. 'We're not doing that.'

'Why not?' said Magnus.

'Because that will turn this case into a full-blown hunt for an Icelandic terrorist cell.'

'Which maybe it should be,' said Magnus.

'No!' said Baldur, slapping his hand on his desk. 'No. Not without evidence.'

'But what if I'm right? What if another banker is killed tomorrow?'

Baldur cupped his hands over his face and closed his eyes. Magnus let him think. 'So, what's the motive?' the inspector asked eventually.

'For Harpa, she had something personal against Gabríel Örn and against Óskar. All of them are victims of the *kreppa*, they could be getting their revenge against the people they blame for it. Bankers. The British government.'

'But half the country has suffered from the *kreppa*. And they don't want to kill anybody. Icelanders don't do that.'

'Half the country might not do that. But we're talking about three or four individuals. We know Sindri believes in violence. Maybe the others do too. Ísak is a politics student: his mother said he was a radical.'

Baldur shook his head. 'I don't buy that. Let's think about alibis. If you are right, and some or all of these people are responsible for Óskar and Lister's shooting, then at least one of them must have been in London last week and France yesterday? Now take me through them.'

Magnus knew that Baldur had found the hole in his theory. 'Óskar was shot last Tuesday night. Harpa was working at the bakery in Seltjarnarnes, Björn was fishing on a boat from Grundarfjördur, Sindri was at a book launch, although we'll have to check that.'

'And Ísak?'

'Was in Iceland, staying with his parents.'

'All right,' said Baldur. 'And yesterday? Were any of them in Normandy?'

'Harpa we interviewed late on Saturday afternoon – it would have been very hard for her to get to France in time, Björn I saw myself on Sunday, Sindri was in the Grand Rokk and Ísak was in church in London.'

'So how did they shoot the two victims?'

'The alibis are too pat, especially Ísak's,' Magnus said. 'There is no good reason why he came back to Reykjavík last week. And the going to church seems like a deliberate attempt to set up an alibi.'

'You're struggling here, Magnús.'

Baldur was right, damn him. 'Maybe there was someone else?' Magnus said. 'A fifth conspirator. The guy who pulled the trigger. The assassin.'

Baldur smiled thinly. 'That's my point, Magnús. Maybe someone else pulled the trigger. Two different someone elses, one in London and one in Normandy. And maybe neither of them had anything at all to do with Iceland.'

'All right,' Magnus said. 'I may be wrong. But there is a chance, just a small chance, I may be right. I *know* there are more connections here: we just haven't found them yet. I don't know what these connections add up to. But let us keep on digging. Because if I am right, someone else is going to get shot very soon.'

Baldur sat back in his chair. Magnus knew Baldur didn't like him, and this would be a chance for him to slap him down and send him back to college. Magnus had worked for bosses in Boston who would have done just that. But Baldur was an old-fashioned cop, a cop who respected gut instinct. The question was whether he respected Magnus.

'Here's what you do. Keep digging for a couple more days, the three of you. But dig *quietly*, do you understand? Keep this to the three of you, don't talk about it even around the station. I don't want to find myself defending a terrorist scare to the

Commissioner. And if you don't find hard evidence, we drop the case. Understand?'

'I understand,' said Magnus.

Sophie turned off the radio in the kitchen and rinsed out her coffee cup. She was in full procrastination mode, and she knew it. She should have been in the library hours ago. She had an essay on the rise of social inequality under socialist governments to write, and there was a ton of reading she still hadn't done.

She didn't know where her motivation had gone. It was the beginning of her final year and she really had to crank things up. Maybe living with Zak wasn't such a good idea after all. He had no trouble with the work, he was very smart and had a genuine passion for politics, especially the old Marxist thinkers that were going out of fashion. His tutors loved him; he reminded them of the good old days when LSE was a hothouse of radical politics, and not just a passport into investment banking. He had iron discipline, but she just liked to hang around him wasting time.

She wondered what the police wanted with him. When she had asked he hadn't answered. But she thought she knew what it was: Zak did some small-time drug dealing, just supplying his friends, but it helped him make ends meet. After the credit crunch the previous year the grants and loans from the Icelandic government didn't go nearly as far as they used to.

After the detective had left, Zak had seemed tense. Sophie should probably tell their house mates about the visit: make sure the house was clean of anything incriminating if the police decided to come back and search the place.

Now, to work. Fortified with new resolve, she headed for the front door, only to see it open.

'Zak? What are you doing back here?'

He looked worried. 'I thought you were going to the library,' he said.

'I am. What's up?'

He pushed past her on his way to his room. 'It's Mum. I just got a call from Dad. She's getting worse.'

'Oh, no!' said Sophie, following him. She knew all about his mother's cancer. 'I'm so sorry.'

'I'm going back to Iceland,' Zak said, pulling a bag out of his wardrobe.

'When? Now?'

'Yeah. I might get a flight today if I hurry.'

'Is it that bad? I mean, is this, like...' Sophie couldn't bring herself to say 'the end'.

'I don't know, Soph, I really don't know. It might be. I've got to get home.'

He was looking away from her as he said this.

'Come here,' said Sophie, holding out her arms. He ignored her. 'Come on.'

Slowly, reluctantly, he stood up and let her hug him. Sophie was mildly offended as he pushed her away. Sometimes he just put up barriers and she didn't like it. But how could she know what it was like to have your mother die?

She watched him pack. The silence was awkward. She was aware that he really didn't want to talk about his mother. 'They reckon there's a chance Lister's going to make it after all,' she said. 'I just heard it on the radio.'

'Pity,' said Zak.

'You don't really mean that!' said Sophie, shocked. 'I know he called you all a bunch of terrorists, but he's not a bad man.'

'So you say,' said Zak. 'There's a whole country that he bankrupted that might disagree.'

Sophie took a deep breath. She had never seen Zak so tense. She wanted so badly to reach out and comfort him.

The policewoman's visit troubled her. She considered asking him about it again, but rejected the idea. It would only upset him more. She watched helplessly as he finished his packing. He was very quick. She felt an irrational dread overwhelm her, as though he were leaving her for good.

'How long will you be gone?' she asked.

'Don't know. I won't know until I see how bad she really is.'

'Well, let me know once you see her. Have you told the uni?'

'Oh, I'll do that later. Actually, could you tell McGregor for me? I'll talk to him myself in the next day or two.'

Dr McGregor was head of the Politics Faculty.

'Yeah. Sure.'

Ten minutes later Zak was gone. Sophie sat at the kitchen table and burst into tears.

CHAPTER TWENTY-FOUR

DÍSA SENT HARPA home. The fresh air invigorated her as she hurried along the shore of the bay. To her right a small dark cloud was rolling over the Hallgrímskirkja and unloading its contents on the city centre. An easterly breeze was blowing the cloud towards Seltjarnarnes.

She played over what she would say to Björn. She had to call him. It was a conversation she wasn't looking forward to.

She beat the cloud home by a couple of minutes, made herself a cup of coffee and dialled Björn's number. She hoped he wasn't out at sea, she needed to get this over and done with.

He answered on the second ring.

'Hi, it's me,' she said.

'Oh, hi.' He sounded distracted.

'Björn, I... I need to talk to you.'

'OK?'

'You remember the kid who was with us that night in Sindri's flat? A boy named Frikki?'

'Yes, of course I remember him.'

'Well he came into the bakery the other day, with his girlfriend. And then they came back again today. He seems to think that Sindri is behind Óskar's death. And the shooting of the British Chancellor of the Exchequer.'

'That doesn't make any sense. Why?'

'He says that Sindri was talking about taking real action against the bankers and against the people who caused the *kreppa*.'

'Yes, but he was drunk. We all were.'

Harpa swallowed. 'And he said that you might be involved.'

'Me? How? They were shot abroad, weren't they?'

'Yeah,' said Harpa. 'But he said, or rather his girlfriend said, that you might have flown over to London and France when you told me you were going out on a fishing boat.'

'Oh, Harpa, that's just ridiculous!'

And Harpa agreed. When she said it out loud it did sound ridiculous. 'That's what I told them.'

'Good. They're not going to go to the police or anything, are they?'

'No, I don't think so. But...'

'But what?'

Harpa took a deep breath. Until now she hadn't voiced aloud her own distrust of Björn. She had never shown any mistrust of him. Ever. But now she had to.

'Björn. Why did you have your passport with you when you came down to see me last week?'

'What?'

'Why did you have your passport? I saw it. In your jacket pocket.'

'You're not telling me you believe them?'

'No. I just want to know about your passport.'

'Well. Um. I needed it.'

'To go abroad?'

'No. For identification purposes. The following morning I had an appointment to see a bank in Reykjavík about a loan to buy a boat.' His voice was speeding up and gaining in confidence.

Just as if he had stumbled on a good story made up on the spot.

'Which bank?'

'Um. Kaupthing.'

'But they don't ask for passport ID, do they?'

'No, I thought it was strange. New rules, probably. Tightening up.'

This sounded all wrong to Harpa. 'So then you went out on a boat for the next few days?'

'Yes. I told you.'

'Whose boat?'

'Hey, Harpa, I don't need to justify myself to you. Surely you don't believe this kid, do you? Do you?'

'I don't know. I don't know, Björn.'

'What is this, Harpa?' Anger was rising in his voice.

'OK,' said Harpa. 'OK. I'll ask you this question once and then I'll shut up. Were you involved in the shooting of Óskar? And Julian Lister?'

Silence.

'Björn?'

'No. No Harpa, I was not. I didn't shoot either of them. Don't you believe me?'

Harpa hung up.

Her phone rang. She didn't answer it. She had slumped to the floor of the kitchen, her back against a cupboard and she was sobbing.

No. She didn't believe him.

She was still sitting there ten minutes later when the door opened.

'Harpa?'

'Mummy?'

She looked up to see her father and her son staring at her, both of them full of concern.

'Mummy, did you fall over?'

Harpa began to pull herself to her feet. Einar gave her his hand. Markús ran to her and gave her a hug. It felt good.

Einar gently suggested the boy go into the living room to watch TV.

'Harpa, what's wrong?' he said.

'Oh, Dad. Dad, I'm in such trouble.'

'Come here.' He enveloped her in his strong fisherman's arms. His chest was broad and he smelled of tobacco. Usually she hated the smell of cigarettes, but on him it reminded her of her childhood, the joy of meeting him back from the sea. Then the tobacco had been mixed with fish. 'Sit down and tell me about it.' He smiled. 'On a chair, not the floor.'

Harpa sat at the kitchen table. She wanted to talk, she was desperate to talk. And now she no longer had Björn to talk to. What the hell? So she told him.

She started with the demonstration and meeting up in Sindri's flat. She told him about Frikki's suspicions that Sindri and Björn were responsible for the shooting of Óskar and Julian Lister. She told him about Björn's denial and how she didn't believe it.

And then, because otherwise the whole story didn't make sense, and because it was such a relief to unburden herself, she told him about luring out Gabríel Örn that night, and about how he died. She told him everything, except the relationship between her and Óskar and between his grandson and the banker.

'Oh, my poor love,' he said, clasping her hand in his. 'I thought something had happened last January. I had no idea it was this bad.'

'I know. Can you forgive me?' She looked deep into those strong hard blue eyes. It was a lot to ask her father. He had always loved her, she knew that, but he had high standards for his daughter and he had always been quick to chastise her if she failed him. That was one of the reasons for her success at school and university and then as a banker, the main reason: she didn't want to disappoint him.

And now she was telling him she had killed someone.

The blue eyes crinkled. 'Forgive you for what? It was an accident. You didn't mean to kill him, did you? And the bastard deserved a good thrashing – I should have done it myself.'

'But he died, Dad, he died!'

'Yes, well. I won't say he deserved it. But I will say it was not your fault. It was a horrible accident. You must remember that.' He gripped her hand.

'Thanks,' she said smiling, the relief running through her. She knew it was only temporary, but it did feel very good to have the support of her father. 'But what should I do now?'

'Well. I wouldn't tell your mother.'

'No,' said Harpa. Her mother was a much stricter moralist than her father. That really would be pushing it. 'But I'm worried, Dad. What if Frikki is right? What if there is another banker about to be shot? I could never live with myself.'

'Oh, I don't know,' Einar muttered. 'Perhaps the bastards do deserve it. And anyway, you're not responsible.'

'If I don't say anything, I am,' Harpa said.

'So what are you thinking of doing? Going to the police?'

'Yes.'

'Don't do that, Harpa. They'll find out about the whole Gabríel Örn business. You'll end up in jail. I don't want my only daughter going to jail, especially for something that isn't her fault. And what about Markús? I mean we would look after him, but he needs his mother.'

'I know,' said Harpa. A tear leaked out of her eye again. And another one.

They sat in silence for a moment. Then Einar spoke. 'I have an idea,' he said.

'What's that?'

'You could just be imagining all this. Björn might be telling the truth. About being out fishing when those men were shot.'

'But what about the passport? I'm convinced he was lying about that.'

Einar shrugged. 'Maybe. But we can check up on the fishing boat easily enough. I know the harbourmaster at Grundarfjördur. He would know whether Björn was out, or he would know who to ask to find out.'

Harpa brightened. Maybe, just maybe, Björn was telling the truth. Suddenly the prospect, which had seemed so distant a moment ago, seemed possible. 'Could you go up there and talk to him?'

'No need to do that. I can phone him. Now what precise days are we talking about?'

'OK,' Harpa said. She stood up to look at the calendar on the wall. 'Óskar was shot on the night of Tuesday the fifteenth. And Julian Lister was yesterday, of course.'

'Did you speak to Björn yesterday?'

'No. Until this evening, the last time I spoke to him was when he was down here last week. That was last Thursday. I thought he had been out at sea since then.'

'OK. I'll check. And once we have found out whether Björn is telling the truth, then we can figure out what to do.'

'Thank you, Dad. Thank you *so* much.'

Sindri lit another cigarette and stared again at the blank screen of his computer. There were sheets of paper covered with words all around the rickety table he used as a desk, but the words were not new.

He hadn't written anything in a week. Which was hardly surprising. He desperately wanted to put himself out of his misery and go to the Grand Rokk. But now more than ever he had to keep a clear head.

The doorbell rang. He took a quick puff of his cigarette and braced himself. The police again, most likely. He knew they would be coming back.

But when he opened the door, it was his sister-in-law who was standing there.

Sindri grinned. 'Freyja! Come in, come in!'

He kissed her on the cheek and led her into his flat.

'Sorry about the mess. I'm in the middle of working. Can I get you some coffee?'

'I'd love some.'

Freyja was dressed as a city girl in a black trouser suit, and her blonde curly hair was pulled back fiercely in a ponytail. But her cheeks had the pink bloom of the fells.

'You didn't tell me you were coming. What brings you to Reykjavík?'

'We got an offer for the farm over the weekend,' said Freyja. 'A good one. It's from the cousin of a neighbour. He's a farmer's son, and he wants to own his own place. Remarkably, he seems to have enough cash to buy it.'

Sindri frowned. 'I suppose that's good news. Are you going to take it?'

'I think we'll have to,' said Freyja. 'It's the only serious offer we've received. And it's also the only way we have of paying off the debt.'

'You could tell the bank to stuff it,' said Sindri. 'Stay on the farm. Let them try to evict you. You know how difficult the government is making it for banks to take possession of property these days.'

'Those are just temporary measures,' Freyja said. 'The debt isn't going to go away until I pay it off. This way I pay it off and we all get on with our lives.'

They sat in silence for a moment staring at their coffee. Sindri puffed at his cigarette. It was the farm of his childhood they were talking about, a property that had first been bought by his great-grandfather a century before. But that wasn't what got to him. It was Freyja and her children. His brother Matti's broken family.

'So you're moving to Reykjavík?' he asked.

'We'll have to,' said Freyja. 'I need to work.'

'Have you been to see your brother?' Sindri asked, remembering that he had offered Freyja a job.

'Yes. But nothing doing. Apparently he had to fire three people last week, so he can't be seen to be taking someone new on. Like me.'

'So what are you going to do?'

'Ask around. That's why I'm here. Do you know anyone who might be looking to hire someone?'

'Sorry,' said Sindri. He didn't have to think very hard. A number of his friends who survived from casual temporary jobs were looking. He was lucky he still had some of the royalties from his book left, and the authors' stipend that the Ministry of Education, Science and Culture in Iceland was still paying out to writers.

'I know I don't have any direct qualifications,' Freyja said. 'But I can work hard. I'm strong. I'm good with figures. I'm honest.'

'Oh, yes,' said Sindri, smiling. 'I don't doubt that for a moment. But I just don't think there is anything out there.'

'I could be a waitress. Shop assistant. Cleaner, even.'

'Sorry.' Sindri shrugged. 'I'm not exactly the kind of guy you need to talk to about the world of work.'

'No,' said Freyja, and Sindri thought he caught a touch of contempt in the glance she gave him.

'Where will you live?'

Freyja sighed. 'I don't know.'

'You can sleep on my floor if you like. All of you.'

Freyja laughed as she glanced around the mess and grime of the flat. 'I hope it won't come to that.'

The laughter died. They both knew it might.

'Hey, I'm sorry I couldn't buy the farm,' Sindri said. And he meant it. He would have done if he could, it would have been the least he could do to make up for his brother's actions. 'I just don't have the money.'

'Of course you don't,' said Freyja. 'Not that I'd expect you to do anything like that. But I sometimes wonder...'

'Wonder what?'

'What people like you *do* all day.'

'I'm writing a novel,' Sindri said. 'It's a reworking of *Independent People* by Halldór Laxness for the twenty-first century. I'm finding it kind of tough.'

'You call *that* kind of tough?' said Freyja, her eyes alight. 'Some of us have worked all our lives. Some of us have other people to feed. I sometimes wish people like you would get up off your fat arses and *do* something.'

Sindri's cheeks burned. He felt like he had been slapped. Anger fought with shame and shame won.

Freyja put her face in her hands. Sindri kept quiet. She looked up. Smiled thinly. 'Hey, I'm sorry, Sindri. I just try so hard not to let all this get on top of me. And I succeed, really I do. I never shout at anyone, not the bank, not my kids, not even the stupid sheep. Of course the person I would really like to shout at is Matti. But I can't do that.'

She looked Sindri straight in the eye. 'So I shout at you. I'm sorry.'

'I probably deserve it,' said Sindri. He reached over and touched her hand. 'I'll keep my ears open. There's a chance I might hear something about somewhere cheap to live.'

'Thanks,' said Freyja. 'Anyway, I must go. I'm talking to everyone I know in Reykjavík. *Something* will turn up.'

'I'm sure it will,' said Sindri. But he wasn't.

Long after Freyja had left, Sindri sat at the small dining table staring up at his painting of Bjartur carrying his sick daughter across the moor.

He would do what he could do.

Sharon Piper was frustrated as she returned to CID in Kensington police station on Earl's Court Road. Virginie Rogeon was out. And her mobile phone was switched off. Sharon had knocked on doors until she finally found someone, another French woman, who thought that Virginie had just left on holiday for India. The husband, Alain, worked for an American investment bank.

Piper thought her best bet was to try to get to Virginie through her husband's BlackBerry. Which meant she needed to call around the American investment banks in London to find him.

'How's it going, Sharon? Anything from Iceland?'

Piper looked up to see a short bald man hovering around her desk. DI Middleton, her boss. He looked worried.

She sighed. 'I don't know. Maybe. We might have a lead on the courier who was asking for Gunnarsson's address. An Icelandic student at the LSE named Ísak Samúelsson. He fits the description, but without a firm ID we can't be sure. I'm trying to locate the French neighbour who saw him, but she seems to have gone on holiday. To India.'

'Well do what you can. We're getting nowhere with Tanya and her Russian friends. Have the Icelandic police got anything on this kid?'

'I'm not sure,' said Piper. 'Not really.'

'If you want any help, just ask,' Middleton said. 'We need a breakthrough here.'

Piper watched her boss go into his small glass-encased office, and stare out of his window. It was all very well for Magnus to plead for her to keep his suspicions to herself. And he was right, they were no more than suspicions. But her loyalty to her boss must be stronger than her loyalty to the Yank, or Icelander or whoever he was. Besides which, Julian Lister was an important man. It was her duty to pass on any ideas or leads, however far fetched. It might stir up a hornet's nest: MI5, SO15. Or they might just ignore her. But she had to do it.

She opened the door to his office.

'Guv'nor. There is one thing.'

CHAPTER TWENTY-FIVE

MAGNUS GRABBED A beer and turned on the TV. The investigation was swirling around his brain. He was frustrated. He *knew* there were connections out there but he just didn't know where to find them. He had had Árni tracking down every bit of video footage of the January protests that he could. He needed to get a better picture of the younger man who seemed to be following Harpa, Björn and Sindri as they walked away from the demo.

He and Vigdís had been going through the police files on some of the so-called anarchists who had been involved in the protests. They had seen some of them on the video in balaclavas throwing flagstones at the police. Most were just troublemakers looking for an excuse to have fun. Some seemed to be following an ideology, but it wasn't well expressed. One or two were friends of Sindri.

Possible leads to follow up, but Magnus doubted they would come to anything. Unless one of them had been with Sindri, Harpa and Björn that evening. *That* would be interesting.

He had been hopeful that Sharon would get an ID of Ísak as the courier in Onslow Gardens. She had called explaining that the neighbour had gone on holiday, and how she was trying to get in touch with her.

All they could do was wait. Once the witness's husband checked in it would be easy for Piper to send the photograph she had taken of Ísak electronically. Once he checked in.

There was a discussion on TV about Julian Lister. The doctors were now saying there was a chance he might pull through. And

238

all the Icelanders were falling over themselves to pass on their good wishes. The nation had been struck by a huge dollop of guilt.

There was no getting away from it, the Icelanders were essentially a peaceful, non-violent people, terrified by the thought that they should appear to be otherwise. Magnus could understand why the authorities would not want the slightest hint of a terrorist investigation. Because if Magnus was right, and there was a little group of Icelanders who had a list of powerful people they wanted to kill, that was what it was.

Terrorism.

His phone rang. 'Magnús.'

'Hey, Magnus, you've gone all Icelandic.'

'Ollie! How the hell are you? I got your call yesterday. Sorry I didn't get back to you.'

'No problem. How is the land of our ancestors? Still bubbling away?'

'I guess so. I've yet to see my first volcanic eruption. But the hot tubs are nice.'

'How's the course going?'

'OK,' said Magnus. 'Although I'm working on a real live case at the moment.'

'Someone jerked off in the *skyr*?'

'Nice.'

'Sorry. Hey, you know it was Dad's birthday yesterday?'

'Huh?' Magnus sat up. 'Was it? Yeah, I guess it was.' He felt a twinge of guilt. He'd forgotten.

'Yeah. He'd be sixty. I can't imagine him at sixty, can you?'

'I can, actually,' said Magnus, smiling. His father had been in his mid-forties when he died. His fair hair had been turning quietly grey. The smile lines around his eyes had been deepening. 'Yeah, I can.'

'I've been thinking about him a lot recently.'

'So have I,' said Magnus. He took a deep breath. Ollie had a right to know, or as much of a right as Magnus.

Magnus talked for twenty minutes, telling his brother about Sibba and Unnur. And then about their grandfather's reaction to

Ragnar leaving their mother. And then about the deaths of the families of Bjarnarhöfn and Hraun over the years: Benedikt's father, their great-grandfather Gunnar, Benedikt himself.

'Christ!' said Ollie. 'So you think Grandpa might have had something to do with Dad's murder?'

'I don't know yet. Unnur says definitely not. I need to do some more digging.'

'Don't,' said Ollie.

'What do you mean, don't?'

'I just don't want you to.'

'But I have to know! *We* have to know.'

There was silence on the phone.

'Ollie?'

'Magnus.' Magnus heard his brother's voice crack. 'I'm asking you, man. I'm pleading with you. Just don't go there.'

'Why not?'

'Look, you're obsessed, Magnus. And that was cool when you were asking questions in America. But I can't handle you dredging up all that shit in Bjarnarhöfn again. That's buried and it's buried for a reason.'

'Ollie?'

'I've spent most of my life, over twenty years, trying to forget that place, and you know what? I've just about done it. So as far as I am concerned it should stay forgotten.'

'But Ollie—'

'And if you do find stuff out, just don't tell me about it, OK?'

'Look, Ollie—'

'Bye, Magnus.'

Five minutes later, the phone rang again. It was Ingileif, asking him round to her place. She would cook dinner.

'Are you OK?' she asked when he got to her flat. 'Something's wrong.'

'Just got a phone call from my brother.'

'What's up with him?'

'I told him what we found out over the weekend. About our father. And grandfather.'

'And?'

'And he wants to think about it even less than I do.'

Magnus could see Ingileif about to say something and thinking the better of it. 'Yes?' he said.

'Sorry,' Ingileif said. 'I can see it's a sensitive subject for you. And your brother. I can live with that.'

'Good.'

Ingileif was frying some fish. 'I got an offer today,' she said.

'What kind of offer?'

'You remember Svala? From the gallery?'

'Yes. Didn't you say she has moved to Hamburg?'

'That's right. She's teamed up with some German guy. They are selling Scandinavian stuff. Their gallery has only been open a couple of months, but she thinks it will do well.'

'Even in the recession?'

'Apparently. And Germany isn't as badly screwed as Iceland is. They are coming out of it there.'

'Lucky them.'

'Yes. Anyway, she wants me to join them. As a partner. She's told this German guy that I am just what they need for the business to take off.'

'Hmm.' Ingileif had her back to Magnus. 'Sounds like a good opportunity. But what about the gallery here?'

'I'd miss it. But the prospects have to be much better in Germany.'

'Do you speak any German?'

'A bit. Enough to get me started. I could pick it up pretty quickly if I'm living there.'

Magnus felt his body tense. 'So are you going?'

Ingileif didn't answer as she scooped the fish on to plates, and placed them on the table. They sat down.

'No,' she said.

'No? Why not?'

She leant over and kissed him. Deeply. 'Because of you, stupid.'

There wasn't much Magnus could say to that. He smiled.

'How's the case going?' she asked. 'Any new suspects?'

'A couple,' Magnus said. 'Do you know Sindri Pálsson?'

'That old windbag? Yes, I do.'

'Why am I not surprised? But he can't be a client.'

'Oh, no. He's part of Iceland's version of a liberal intelligentsia. He shows up to book launches. Exhibitions. He's a nice guy, despite all the "world-is-ending" crap.'

'He seems to believe that violence is the only way to destroy capitalism.'

'He's all talk. He's a big pussy cat. You don't think he killed Óskar, do you?'

'We think he might be involved.'

'No,' Ingileif said. She paused, thinking. 'No. He'd never kill anyone. I can always ask him.'

'I already have,' said Magnus.

'Yes, but he might tell me.' Ingileif chewed her fish. 'I'm serious. I'm pretty sure he fancies me. In fact I'd say he fancies anyone under the age of thirty – and Magnús, as you know, I am still under the age of thirty.' Ingileif was twenty-nine and three-quarters. 'He'd tell me if I asked him in the right way.'

'And I'm serious,' Magnus said. 'It would screw up the investigation.'

'Oh, don't be so bureaucratic. It would be kind of fun. I could solve your case for you.'

'No, Ingileif,' Magnus said. 'No.'

Several hours later, they were lying in Ingileif's bed. Magnus couldn't sleep. He was facing away from her. He could sense she was awake also.

He felt her touch his shoulder.

'Magnús?'

'Yes?'

'Are you thinking about Bjarnarhöfn?'

'Yes.'

She tugged at his shoulder so he rolled over on to his back. She kissed his lips gently. 'Tell me. If you want to.'

'OK.' Magnus swallowed. 'OK. I will.'

And so he told her.

CHAPTER TWENTY-SIX

January 1986

Magnus slipped out of the farmhouse into the cold fresh air, and stumbled through the snow towards the sea. He had to be alone.

It was night. They had just eaten and Grandpa was giving Óli a lecture about wetting his bed.

Christmas hadn't been so bad. The boys' uncle, aunt and cousins had visited from Canada to the delight of their grandfather. Grandpa had entered one of his phases of exuberant high spirits. There was Christmas cheer everywhere. The Yule Lads had come, placing little gifts in Magnus and Óli's shoes.

Christmas Eve dinner was a feast to remember: ptarmigan, browned potatoes fried in butter and sugar, which were Magnus's favourite, followed by leafbread and ice cream. Magnus received an American police car with sirens and flashing lights from his Canadian uncle and aunt. A touch babyish perhaps, but he liked it. Óli, for the first time for months, seemed to be actually enjoying himself.

Then, as Magnus knew it would, things had soured. Óli got scared again and had started wetting his bed. Just after New Year the relatives had left, leaving the boys alone in the farmhouse with their grandparents.

And Grandpa was in an evil mood.

Magnus trudged past the little church down to the sea and sat on a stone. He scanned the familiar isolated lights, which burned nearly all day at this time of year, when dusk and dawn brushed in the gloom of midday. The bright lights of the farmhouse behind him. The lights at Hraun on the other side of the lava field. The lighthouse on one of the islands in the fjord. The bobbing winks of fishing boats returning to Stykkishólmur.

It was a clear night. The reflection from the half moon glimmered on the snow, and shimmered in the waterfall streaming off the fell looming behind the farmhouse. The tall triangular racks for drying stockfish were silhouetted against the gleaming swell of the sea, which rustled gently against the shore. Twisted stone reared up out of the white Berserkjahraun. A gleam of green hovered behind the mountains away to the north of the fjord. The aurora. And high above all this, the stars, pricking the cold clear night in their thousands. He remembered his mother telling him when they still lived in Reykjavík that there were two things in the world that could not be counted: the stars in the night sky and the islands in Breidafjördur.

Magnus hunched into his coat. He was cold, really cold, but the cold felt good compared to the angry heat inside the farmhouse.

Two years before, Magnus, Óli and his mother and father had all been living happily together in their little house in Thingholt with the blue corrugated iron roof and the whitebeam tree in the garden. Then things fell apart. There was arguing, anger, his father's departure, his mother sleeping all the time, forgetting to get them dinner, not being able to speak properly. Within six months Magnus's father was in Boston, his mother was in Reykjavík and Magnus and his little brother were at their grandparents' farm at Bjarnarhöfn.

Magnus had never much liked his grandmother. She was a small woman, cool, detached, with a permanent look of mild disapproval on her face. His grandfather was scary but had a certain gruff charm. He would throw himself into playing games with his grandsons, and once they moved up to Bjarnarhöfn, took great pleasure in showing them the farm, the fells, the islands in the fjord. What Magnus and Óli enjoyed most was helping him collect the valuable feathers from the eider ducks' nests among the dwarf willows by the stream.

And of course there was the Berserkjahraun. Hallgrímur led his grandsons through the fantastic twisted lava sculptures, telling them tales of the berserkers who had lived at their farm and at Hraun, and of the kind of games he used to play there as a kid. Óli was scared, but Magnus was fascinated.

But Grandpa liked to drink. And when he drank he became angry. And he became a bully.

Hallgrímur liked Magnus, at least at first. But Óli was weak and Hallgrímur detested weakness. Óli scared easily and Hallgrímur liked to scare him. He told him stories about the Kerlingin troll who took the babies of Stykkishólmur away with her, and might take Óli as well if he didn't shape up. Of the berserkers who still tramped around the lava field at night. Of a man named Thórólfur Lame Foot who had been murdered centuries before, but roamed the fells terrorizing shepherds and their sheep. And of the *fjörulalli*, a sea monster with shells hanging from its fur, that cruised around the fjord just offshore, waiting to eat up small children who got too close to the sea.

Magnus stood up for his little brother. His grandfather didn't like that. Scaring Magnus didn't work, so Hallgrímur beat him instead. Hence the occasional visits to St Francis's Hospital in Stykkishólmur, with lies about complicated farmyard accidents.

Then Hallgrímur would sober up, the sun would shine, and he would try to play with his grandchildren again. But Óli was too scared and Magnus too proud.

Throughout all this, their grandmother kept an aloof detachment, as though she didn't care what happened to her grandchildren. As he got older, Magnus realized that she was beaten too.

The farm was isolated, cut off from the rest of civilization by the lava field. It became a kind of hell. Magnus thought of escape. Sometimes their mother would come to visit and for a while everything would be better, although by this stage Magnus had realized she was drunk, not sleepy. When he tried to explain what was happening to them, his mother just told them that 'Grandpa was a little stricter than Daddy.'

Sounds drifted across the snow towards Magnus from the farm-house, his grandfather's deep roar, the high pitched scream of his little brother. Poor Óli. Even though there was nothing much he could do, Magnus stood up and ran back towards the house, hoping that his presence might distract his grandfather.

When he reached the kitchen, his grandmother was scouring a large pan over the sink. The shouting seemed to have stopped.

'Where's Óli?'

'In the cellar, I think,' Grandma said, without turning around.

'What's he doing there?'

'He is being punished.'

'What's he being punished for?'

'Don't be so impertinent,' Grandma said. But she said it without force. She often said those words. It was her code for 'I don't know and I don't want to know, so don't ask me about it.'

Magnus ran down the stone steps to the cellar. It was cold with cement walls lit by a single bulb. It was used for storage, there were a couple of individual rooms, one filled with animal feed supple-ments and one with potatoes, most of which had rotted. The door to this last one was shut. Behind it he could hear Óli sobbing.

Magnus tried the door. It was locked. The key was upstairs on the door of the broom cupboard outside the kitchen, in plain view of their grandmother. 'Óli! Óli, are you OK?'

'No,' said Óli between sobs. 'It's dark and its cold and the pota-toes are slimy and I'm scared.'

'Can't you turn on the light?'

'He's taken away the bulb.'

Rage boiled up inside Magnus and he pulled at the door, hoping somehow to shake the lock loose. It didn't work of course, so he began kicking at it.

'Stop, Magnús, stop! He'll hear you.'

'I don't care,' shouted Magnus. He stood back and took a run at the door, throwing the entire weight of his nine-year-old body at it. He bounced off and fell on to the floor. He stood up, rubbing his shoulder.

'Magnús.'

The growl was familiar. Magnus turned to see his grandfather. A fit sixty-year-old with a strong granite jaw, steel grey hair and hard blue eyes. A tough, angry man. Magnus's nostrils caught the faint whiff of alcohol layered on top of the aroma of snuff which perpetually surrounded Hallgrímur.

'Magnús, go back upstairs.'

'Why have you done this, Grandpa? Is it because Óli wet himself? Óli can't help that. It's just because he is scared all the time. Let him out.'

'I said, get back upstairs.'

'And I said, let him out!' Magnus's voice was shrill.

His grandfather's nostrils flared, a sure early sign of an explosion. Magnus braced himself but held his grandfather's eyes.

'Let him out.'

Hallgrímur looked around him for the nearest weapon. His eyes alighted on an old blunt axe. He picked it up and took a step towards Magnus.

Magnus wanted to run, but he stood firm outside the door to the potato storage room, feet apart, as if guarding his brother. His eyes were fixed on the blade of the axe.

Hallgrímur jabbed the blunt end of the axe handle into Magnus's ribs. It wasn't especially hard, but Magnus was only a small boy. Winded, he doubled up. Hallgrímur swung the axe and hit Magnus on the side of his thigh with the flat of the head.

Magnus fell. He looked up and saw his grandfather raising the axe above his head, his eyes burning with anger. Magnus started to cry. He couldn't help it. As he lay there on the cold stone, he could hear Óli's sobs through the door.

'Up to bed! Now!'

Magnus limped up to bed. What else could he do?

*

He lay there for hours, his eyes wet with tears and anger, staring at his little brother's empty bed. Although his thigh hurt, there was nothing broken, so no humiliating trips to the hospital this time.

How could his grandfather leave a seven-year-old boy in the cold and dark all night? If Óli had wet his bed occasionally before, he would definitely wet it every evening now.

Magnus waited until he heard the sounds of his grandfather going to bed. Then he waited some more. Finally, after what seemed to him to be hours, but was probably much less, he slipped out of bed, pulled on a jersey, and crept downstairs.

He knew where the key would be, hanging on the door to the broom cupboard. He could see it in the moonlight reflected off the snow which seeped into the kitchen. He had to stand on his tip-toes to reach it. He crept down the stairs into the dark cellar, felt his way to the door to the potato storage room, and unlocked it.

The room smelled of rotten potatoes and little boy's urine.

'Óli? Óli? It's Magnús.'

'Magnús?' The voice was small, faint.

'Come out.'

'No.'

'Come on, Óli.'

'No. Don't make me do that. He'll find me and be angry.'

Magnus hesitated. He couldn't actually see Óli. He moved towards the direction of his voice, hands outstretched, bending down, until he felt an arm. He felt small hands clasping his. He grabbed hold of his little brother and held him tight.

'Why did he do this to you, Óli?'

'I can't tell you.'

'Yes, you can. I won't tell anyone else.'

Then Óli began to sob. 'I can't tell you, Magnús. I won't tell you. Please don't make me tell you.'

'OK, Óli. OK. I won't make you tell me anything. And I won't make you leave this room. I'll just sit with you.'

And Magnus sat with his brother, who soon fell asleep, until he guessed it was close to morning and he crept back to his own bed.

Tuesday 22 September 2009

Magnus fell silent, lying on his back in Ingileif's bed.

'God. That's dreadful,' she said. 'How did you cope?'

'I was a tough little kid, I suppose,' Magnus said. 'I used to think about my father. I knew he would want me to stand up for Ollie, so I did. And I knew that one day he would come over from America to rescue us. And one day he did. But only after my mother had driven her car into a rock.'

'It's amazing you are not totally screwed up.'

'No one goes through that kind of thing unscathed,' said Magnus. 'Like my mother and my grandfather I have tendencies to drink, which worries me. And sometimes I get so angry I just want to beat the shit out of people. Bad people.' He paused. 'I have got myself in trouble for that a couple times. It's not the kind of thing you should do if you're a cop. I scare myself sometimes.'

'Ollie must have been a mess. He must still be a mess.'

'He was pretty bad when he came to the States. My father did his best. Took him to see a shrink – that helped a lot. But Ollie's had problems all through his life, with relationships, with jobs, with drugs. I think he still sees a shrink.'

'Did you?' Ingileif asked.

'See a psychiatrist? No. No need.'

'Uh huh.'

'I know what you're thinking,' Magnus said. 'That I should get help with my issues. But frankly I'm quite happy burying all this stuff. I managed very well for twenty years without thinking about it.'

'Sure. You obsessed about your father instead.'

'Maybe,' said Magnus. 'I set him up as my saviour. He was my saviour. And then some bastard killed him.'

For the first time, Magnus's voice faltered.

'Come here,' said Ingileif. 'Come here.' He rolled over into her arms and she held him tight.

CHAPTER TWENTY-SEVEN

MAGNUS, VIGDÍS AND Árni were crowded around Árni's computer. With some difficulty, Árni had managed to get hold of footage from RÚV, the national TV company, of the demonstration.

They were looking at a segment taken in the dark. Faces were indistinct.

'OK, that's the three of them there,' said Árni. 'You can see Sindri's ponytail silhouetted against the flare.'

Magnus squinted at the figures – a big man, a thinner man and a woman. 'Yes, you can see the curls on Harpa's hair. And that must be Björn.'

'And you see there's a guy next to them, with no shirt on, talking to Sindri?'

'Yes, but you can't make anything out of his features. It's not Ísak, though, is it? Too tall.'

'No, it's not Ísak,' said Árni. 'But let's go back a bit.'

'OK.' Árni played the footage in reverse. Harpa and Björn walked backwards away from Sindri and the tall newcomer, who plunged his head into a bucket of water and put on his football shirt. Then he stretched himself out on the ground in front of the camera. A nurse was treating his eyes. The TV crew's lights picked up the features here. The man was not much more than a kid, eighteen or nineteen perhaps. He had spiky red hair. The nurse treating him had a round face, pink cheeks and a button nose. You could just make out Sindri in the crowd surrounding them. He seemed to be shouting encouragement to the kid.

251

'I see,' said Magnus. 'But we know Sindri spoke to lots of people at the demo. He says he always does. What's so special about this guy?'

'Hang on a minute,' said Árni. 'And you will see.' He tapped away at his keyboard and called up the police surveillance video. 'OK. Here are the three of them leaving the demonstration, and I think that's Ísak with them.'

'You can't really see, can you?'

'No, but the build and the hairstyle is right when you compare it with the picture Sharon took.' Árni held up a print of the photograph she had taken of Ísak outside his house in London.

'OK, it's possibly Ísak,' said Magnus.

'Probably,' said Árni. 'But look just a couple of feet behind him. There's the kid with the spiky hair. He's taken his shirt off and he's waving it around his head.'

'Are you sure he's with them?' Magnus asked. 'And not just walking along near them.'

'Not absolutely sure. He pauses here and shouts something to someone. The others get away from him, which is why we didn't notice they were together before. But then he turns back, realizes that they are moving off, and jogs after them.'

'Show me that again,' said Magnus.

It wasn't conclusive. Indeed, without the earlier footage of the kid talking to Sindri and walking off with him, it wouldn't arouse suspicions at all.

'OK, so who is this kid?'

'I don't know,' said Árni.

'I don't recognize him from those anarchist files,' said Magnus. 'Do you, Vigdís?'

'No. But I can go back and look again.'

'We might have more luck with the nurse. Get the best still you can from that, Árni, and go off to the National Hospital. See if you can track her down. Maybe she got the kid's name.' Magnus smiled. 'Well done, Árni. Good work.'

As Vigdís returned to her desk, Magnus thought of something. 'Aren't you supposed to be in New York?'

'I cancelled,' said Vigdís.

'Why?' Magnus asked.

'This.'

'Oh, I'm sorry. There was no need to follow me on my wild goose chase.'

'This is no wild goose chase.'

'What about the poor guy in New York?'

Vigdís shrugged. 'That's what you get for dating a cop.'

Magnus went back to his desk, feeling guilty. Vigdís could have gone on her vacation, they would have coped. But he was pleased that she didn't seem to think it was all a wild goose chase. And they were making progress. If they could find another conspirator, everything would begin to slip into place, although the kid looked a little too immature to be an international assassin.

The more he thought about it, the more Magnus was convinced there *was* another conspirator. The other alibis were just too convenient. Supposing Ísak was the man the French woman had seen in Kensington, asking for Óskar's precise address. He must have been preparing the ground. Ísak lived in London, he knew the city, he could do the necessary reconnaissance, perhaps watch Óskar, confirm his habits, his routine, perhaps get hold of the gun and the getaway motorbike. Get everything ready for someone else. Someone who flew in from Iceland just to do the job.

The man who actually pulled the trigger. The assassin.

And who the hell was that? The kid with the spiky hair? Or someone else.

Magnus remembered Björn's brother, Gulli.

'Árni! Before you go!'

Árni paused on his way out. 'Yes?' Vigdís looked up from her files.

'Do you remember much about Björn's brother Gulli from when you interviewed him?'

'No,' said Árni. 'Just that everything he said about Björn and Harpa staying with him that night seemed to stack up. Why?'

'I tried to see him on Saturday. He wasn't in. A neighbour said he was away on holiday and had been for a while.'

'You think he might have gone to London?' Vigdís asked.

'Or Normandy?' said Árni.

'Or both,' said Magnus.

'Do you want me to see if he is back?' said Vigdís.

'Yes.' He checked his notebook and gave Vigdís the phone number from Gulli's van. 'And if he is back, find out where he has been. If he isn't, have a word with all his neighbours. See if any of them have a better idea of where he went.'

Magnus scanned his computer. There was an e-mail from Boston. His buddy in the Homicide Unit had been in touch with the USCIS and the State Department. There was no trace of an Icelandic citizen named Hallgrímur Gunnarsson entering the United States in June or July 1996.

Magnus was surprised to feel a surge of relief. On the one hand he desperately wanted to find who had killed his father. On the other, especially after his conversation with Ollie, he was relieved it wasn't his grandfather. Too much pain.

'Sergeant Magnús?' He looked up. A solid woman of about forty was holding a sheaf of old dusty files. Quite thick. 'You asked for this? The Benedikt Jóhannesson murder, 1985?'

'That's right, thanks for bringing them up.'

She gave him a form to sign, and left the files with him.

He knew he should wait, but he couldn't help leafing through the pile of paper.

As was his habit, he looked for the pathologist's report first. It was missing, with a note that it had been signed out to an inspector whom Magnus recognized as a fellow lecturer at the police college.

He debated whether to call the inspector, whom he knew vaguely, to ask him for the file, but decided it would raise less attention if he went through Records. He made a quick call; they said they would track the report down and get back to him.

He had just begun to leaf through the rest of the file when his phone rang.

*

The moment Magnus entered the National Police Commissioner's office he could tell he was in trouble.

Baldur, Thorkell and the Commissioner himself all looked at him with undisguised hostility.

'Take a seat, Magnús,' ordered the Commissioner.

Magnus sat. Outside, over the bay, Mount Esja was bathed in soft morning sunshine. Not a cloud in sight. Inside the Commissioner's office the mood was distinctly grimmer.

'I have just had a call from a Chief Superintendent Trevor Watts. He's with the Counter Terrorism Command of Scotland Yard.'

'Oh,' said Magnus.

'He was curious to know what leads we had regarding Icelanders who had been planning the assassination of Julian Lister. I said we had none. He said that one of my detectives was pursuing that line of inquiry. I said I would get back to him. When I asked Baldur which was the most likely detective Watts was referring to, he suggested you. Was he right?'

'Yes, Commissioner.' Magnus reverted to using his superior's title. Calling him 'Snorri', as was the Icelandic convention, no matter how important he was, seemed all wrong.

'We thought so. Now Baldur informs me that while he did give you permission to investigate possible connections between Gabríel Örn Bergsson, Óskar Gunnarsson and Julian Lister, he made very clear that you were to do it *quietly*. Is that correct?'

'Yes it is.' Magnus glanced at Baldur. To be fair to the man he looked more angry than gloating. Magnus didn't know a chief who wouldn't be angry in those circumstances.

'All right. Now, do you understand that alerting a foreign government to the possibility that this country's nationals were trying to kill one of its leading politicians does not constitute "quietly"?'

Magnus sighed. 'Yes, I do. I'm sorry.'

'What were you thinking?' Snorri said, the anger rising in his voice.

'It was just a hunch. Sergeant Piper was about to interview a possible Icelandic suspect in London, and I wanted her to check if the suspect was in France when Lister was shot.'

'A hunch! You started an international incident over a hunch!' Snorri's face was going red. His bright blue eyes, which normally twinkled, glinted. He looked dangerous. 'And was he in France?'

'No,' Magnus admitted. 'But I did ask Piper not to tell anyone else.'

'Well at least she had some loyalty,' Snorri said. 'She told her superiors.'

'It's hardly an international incident, is it?' Magnus said. 'There's no proof, no evidence, no firm line of inquiry.'

'Exactly!' Snorri slammed his hand down on the desk. 'And if you were a real Icelander you would know that this is precisely the last thing we want to raise with the British government. You know about the Icesave negotiations that have been going on all summer. We're talking about billions of euros of debt that every one of us owes to the British. And what you've done is throw a hand grenade into the discussion. How do you think the British will react when they think they are dealing with a bunch of real terrorists? This country has been humiliated enough without *this* getting out.'

'I said it was a hunch, but it is a hunch with merit,' Magnus said. 'We can't turn a blind eye to any links just because it is politically difficult. What if there *are* a bunch of Icelanders who wanted to kill Óskar and Lister? What if they have their eyes on someone else as we speak? We have a duty to check that possibility out.'

'Don't lecture me on duty!' The Commissioner was shouting now. 'Baldur did the right thing. He told you to keep digging, but do it quietly. You disobeyed him. You are now off the case. I want you back at the college today. And...' he paused. 'When this has all settled down I will review whether we need you in this country at all.'

Magnus swallowed. 'I understand,' he said. 'And I'm sorry.'

'Sorry doesn't cut it, Magnús.' The Commissioner glared at him. Magnus took that as an invitation to leave the room.

There was a queue of three people at the bakery when Harpa saw her father come in. Immediately, her heart started racing. What had he discovered? Had Björn really gone to London and France as Frikki's Polish girlfriend had suggested?

She glanced at him. He smiled reassuringly and stood in the queue. That was a good sign, wasn't it?

The three customers seemed to take for ever. Then a fourth came in, and Einar let her go in front of him. Fortunately Dísa was serving as well.

Finally Einar reached the counter.

'Well?' Harpa asked, her eyes wide.

'I'll have a *kleina*,' Einar said, a smile cracking his rocky face.

'I meant, did you ask about Björn?'

'I did. And he was out with Gústi on the *Kría* last Tuesday. And on Sunday he spent the morning with Siggi in Grundarfjördur harbour helping him install his navigation software.'

Harpa smiled broadly as the relief surged through her. 'Thanks, Dad. There's no doubt about it is there?'

'No. I spoke to the harbourmaster and to Gústi. I couldn't get hold of Siggi, but the harbourmaster sounded confident. Apparently Björn had a visit from the police on Sunday as well.'

'I'm not surprised,' said Harpa. 'Thank you *so* much, Dad.'

Einar leaned forward so that Dísa couldn't hear. 'So no need to go to the police then, eh?'

'I don't know. Maybe I still should?'

'Oh, come on, Harpa. You'll just get yourself in trouble.'

'OK,' she said, nodding.

'Good girl. See you later.'

'Nice to see you smiling for once,' said Dísa after the door closed behind Einar.

'Yes,' said Harpa. The relief was making her giddy. How could she ever have suspected Björn?

'That your Dad?'

'Yes.'

'Good. Because he didn't pay for his *kleina*.'

'Oh, sorry,' said Harpa. 'I'll pay. We were a little distracted.'

'I could see that.'

Harpa smiled to herself. Her father had come through for her. Again. To the outside world, to some of his crew for instance, she knew he came across as a tough irascible bastard. But she had always known he was a good man. And it was so comforting to know that that toughness and strength was on her side.

He would do anything for her, and for his wife and for little Markús.

But within a few minutes the euphoria wore off, elbowed aside by a nagging worry. Yes, it was good that Björn wasn't involved in a plot to murder Óskar and Julian Lister, but that didn't mean that Sindri wasn't. Harpa was beginning to regret the promise she had made to her father. He was right, it was none of her business, but if Sindri had killed two people he could kill three. She had to let the police know about her suspicions.

But they were just that, suspicions. What if the police checked them out, discovered Sindri was totally innocent, and also decided to ask more questions about Gabríel Örn? Then she would have achieved nothing and still end up in jail.

But what if she was right? And perhaps jail was where she should be. She had committed a crime, she should pay for it.

Whatever she had told her father, she knew the right thing to do. Tell the police. But first she should speak to Björn. At least now that she knew he was innocent she could talk to him properly about it.

The bakery was quiet. She told Dísa she was going outside to make a phone call.

It was a lovely morning. Above the city the light grey concrete of the Hallgrímskirkja gleamed almost white through its sheath of scaffolding. The bay sparkled. She took a deep breath, dialled Björn and told him what she had decided. He wasn't happy.

'Do you still think I flew off to London?' he asked.

'No,' said Harpa. 'I'm sorry I suggested that. I believe you. But I am worried that Sindri is responsible in some way.'

'You know if you speak to the police they'll reopen the Gabríel Örn business?'

'Yes, I know, I've thought of that.'

'OK, so when they do, are you going to tell them what really happened that night?'

'No. I'll say that we all went back to Sindri's apartment. And then I'll say I called Gabríel Örn and he didn't show up.'

'They'll be all over you,' said Björn. 'Once you admit you lied to them, they won't give up until they break you.'

'Well, then I just won't answer their questions,' said Harpa.

'They'll charge you.' Björn said. 'You'll go to prison.'

'I didn't intend to kill Gabríel Örn,' Harpa said. 'Maybe the judge will understand that. Perhaps I should be in prison.'

'But, Harpa, there are two crimes here. There's Gabríel Örn's death. We know that was accidental and maybe a judge would agree. And then there's the cover-up. We did that on purpose, you, me, Sindri, the student guy, the cook. They'll get us for that. All of us.'

Harpa sighed. 'Maybe I'll try to tip them off anonymously. But I must find a way of warning them.'

'Look,' said Björn. 'I'll come right down to Reykjavík now and we can discuss how you do this.'

'You won't be able to talk me out of it.'

'I understand. But don't do anything till I get there.'

CHAPTER TWENTY-EIGHT

THE SHOP WAS one of several with *Til Leigu* signs displayed on Laugavegur, meaning 'For Rent'. Vigdís remembered the location: it had been the site of a high-end boutique, way beyond Vigdís's pocket. And everyone else's in Iceland nowadays, she suspected.

She had spotted the blue VW Transporter outside with Gulli Helgason's name and number on it, parked on a side street a few metres away, the front wheel half a metre outside the marked parking bay. She walked in to the shop. Three men were stripping the walls of bright orange paint. A radio was playing Jay-Z loudly.

'Gulli?'

One of the three men turned towards her. He was older than the other two, probably in his early thirties, with dark hair cut very short and strong tattooed arms. He would have been quite attractive, if it wasn't for his belly thrusting out aggressively beneath his painters' overalls.

The man raised his eyebrows in surprise. 'Yes?'

'I'm Detective Vigdís from the Metropolitan Police. I called earlier. I'd like to ask you a couple of questions.'

The man laughed.

'What's so funny?'

'You're not a cop.'

'And why not?' said Vigdís.

'It's obvious. You're black. You can't be a black policewoman. So who the hell are you?'

Vigdís fought to control herself. She was used to people doubting her identity, but rarely so blatantly. She pulled out her ID, and thrust it in his face. 'See that? A black face. My face.'

Gulli raised his hands in mock surrender and then held out his wrists as if he was about to be handcuffed. 'OK, OK. I'll come quietly.'

'Very funny.' Vigdís turned to the other two younger painters who were watching with grins on their faces. 'You two, outside. And turn the radio off as you go.'

'Hey! They've got work to do,' Gulli protested.

'I said, outside.'

The men looked at their boss and then at Vigdís. They shrugged, turned Jay-Z off, and sauntered out into the street.

Vigdís scanned the room. It had been cleared of everything except dustsheets, brushes and tins of paint, as yet unopened. There was nowhere to sit, so they remained standing. 'Now, where have you been this past week?'

'Away. On holiday.'

'Oh, yes? Alone?'

'No. With my girlfriend.'

'And where did you go?'

'Tenerife. In the Canary Islands.'

'I see. When did you get back?'

'Yesterday. We started in here this morning.'

Vigdís pulled out her notebook. 'All right. I want your girl-friend's name and address, and details of your flights and which hotel you stayed at.'

Gulli shrugged and gave them to her. 'What's all this about?'

'We're taking another look at the death of Gabríel Örn Bergsson last January.'

'But why do you want to know where I was last week?'

Vigdís ignored the question. 'So, on the twentieth of January your brother Björn stayed with you in Reykjavík?'

'That's right. He came down about lunchtime. He wanted to go to the demonstration outside Parliament, so I said he could crash at my place.'

'Did you go to the demo?'

'No.' Gulli snorted. 'I have no interest in that stuff. A waste of time. And look what happened. We got rid of one lot of politicians and now we have another lot who are just as bad.'

'Did you see your brother that day?'

'Yes. I had no work on, it's hard getting work these days. I let him in the flat. We had lunch together. I gave him a key and he went off to the demo.'

'And you?'

'I stayed in my flat. Watched TV. Then I met my girlfriend. I was out all night, didn't get back till the following morning.'

Vigdís jotted it all down. 'And then you saw Björn?'

'Yes. And Harpa. She had spent the night with him. I saw her as she was leaving.'

'Had you ever seen Harpa before?'

'No. Never. But I've seen her since, of course. Not often, but Björn and she are pretty much an item these days.'

'And what about Björn? What did he do?'

'Went back to Grundarfjördur that morning, I think. I went out, looking for work. I don't remember whether I actually found anything. Probably didn't. But I told all this to the police at the time.'

Vigdís nodded. He had. And what he had told her just now tallied pretty closely with Árni's notes.

'Did Björn say anything about the demonstration that morning?'

'Yes, he did. He told me all about it.'

'Did he seem preoccupied? Worried?'

Gulli frowned and shook his head. 'Nah. I don't know. I didn't notice anything, and if I did I can't remember. Now can I get my lads back to work?'

Vigdís could tell she wouldn't get much of use out of Gulli without a thorough interview at the police station, and probably not even then. The main thing was to confirm his story about his holiday.

'Thank you for your help, Gulli, and for giving me so much of your valuable time,' she said, with exaggerated politeness.

She hurried back to the station to call Iceland Express and check Gulli's flights. On the street outside she passed a traffic warden, and told her about the front wheel of Gulli's van. Got to keep the thoroughfares clear.

Magnus tramped along the cycle path by the shore of the bay. The Benedikt Jóhannesson files were stuffed in a briefcase at his side. A gentle breeze coming in from the water tingled his cheeks. The sky was a soft pale blue, and the giant rampart of rock that was Mount Esja glowed softly. There was a smattering of snow along the ridge of its summit, the first of the year.

Magnus needed the air. After leaving the Commissioner's office, he had gone straight back across the road to police headquarters. He explained to Vigdís what had happened, and extracted a promise from her to keep him informed of what she and Árni turned up. The news that Magnus had been taken off the case seemed to make her even more determined to break it. Magnus was impressed.

As long as they kept their heads down, he thought there was a good chance that she and Árni would make progress. If Baldur didn't stop them.

Magnus was angry: angry at the Commissioner, angry at Sharon Piper, and what was worse for his emotional equilibrium, angry at himself.

He kept walking as he pulled out his phone and called her.

'Piper.'

'It's Magnus.'

'No news on Virginie Rogeon, I'm afraid. Her husband still hasn't checked in with his employer.'

'Damn! I really needed something firm to tie Ísak into this case.'

'We'll get there.'

'It might be too late.'

'What do you mean?'

'The National Police Commissioner here got a call from your anti-terrorist unit.'

'Oh.'

'Yes, oh.'

'Was he upset?'

'You could say that. I'm off the case.'

'You're what? Oh, Magnus, I'm sorry. Did he give you a bollocking?'

'I don't know what a bollocking is, exactly, but he was pretty pissed. Sharon, why did you do that when I specifically asked you not to? I *knew* what would happen. I thought I could trust you.'

'Oh, come on, Magnus, think about it. I had to do it. If there was any chance at all that you were on to something, I'd look like a right idiot if I hadn't told people back here. Don't worry, they're not taking it too seriously, or else there would be a plane load of them on the way to Reykjavík. They are focusing on the Dutch angle.'

'Dutch angle?'

'Yes. A farmer saw a guy the day before the shooting. He was nosing around in the woods from where the shots were fired. The farmer thought he had gone for a pee. They found a hole in the earth big enough to contain a rifle; they assume the man must have been burying it. The man's motorbike had Dutch number plates.'

'Did he give a description?'

'Not much. Just that the guy was wearing a light blue jacket.'

'What have the Dutch got against your Chancellor?' Magnus asked.

'There is a Muslim community in Holland. Although it could just as easily be someone passing through.'

'Al-Qaeda?'

'That's their favourite theory so far. Although Al-Qaeda tends to prefer blowing people up to shooting them.'

'Interesting.'

'I am *really* sorry, Magnus. I appreciate you taking me into your confidence.'

'Don't give me that bullshit, Sharon! I trusted you and you screwed me. It's that simple.'

'I did what I thought I had to do.'

'Yeah, right. Well, keep me in the loop. And talk to Vigdís; she's still on the case at our end. Especially if you do get a firm ID on Ísak. I'm thinking maybe he was preparing the ground in London for someone else. The guy who pulled the trigger.'

'I see what you mean,' said Sharon. 'I'll bear it in mind. Sorry, Magnus.'

'Yeah.' Magnus hung up.

Sharon's contrition took some of the sting off Magnus's anger. He liked her. What was that word she had used? Bollocking? He'd never heard that one before.

For some reason what rankled most about the Commissioner's 'bollocking' was the crack about Magnus not being a real Icelander. That was because it was partially true. But he knew that even if he had spent his whole life in the country he would still have alerted Sharon to the possibility that Ísak might have been in Normandy. He would always put finding the truth before political niceties, whether he was in Boston or in Iceland.

That was just the way he was.

What was the Commissioner thinking of anyway? Magnus hated it when his bosses talked about the 'bigger picture', the 'political angle'. Justice wasn't like that. The law wasn't like that. If someone broke the law, especially if that someone had murdered someone else, then it was Magnus's duty to bring him to justice. Not just Magnus's duty, everyone else's.

Simple. Once politics took precedence over the law, things fell apart. He'd seen it in Boston and now he was watching it in Iceland.

He wondered whether the Commissioner would follow through on his threat to send him back to America. Perhaps that would be a good thing. Perhaps the Commissioner was right, Magnus wasn't a true Icelander at all. This wasn't where he belonged: he belonged on the streets of Boston, processing the dead bodies with holes in them.

He could go back to Boston, and Ingileif could go to Germany. That would be good for her. But it would be a shame. He still didn't know what kind of relationship he had with her. Her explanation that it was because of him that she wanted to stay in Iceland surprised him. And pleased him.

He walked on towards Borgartún, the avenue lined with the gleaming new bank headquarters. Just in front of it, in its own green island surrounded by roads and modern offices, was the Höfdi House. It was an elegant white wooden mansion built at the beginning of the twentieth century, and famous as the meeting place of Reagan and Gorbachev in 1986. It was also the place where Ingileif had asked him to meet her to talk about the case he was working on when he had arrived in Iceland the previous spring. The place where Ingileif changed in his eyes from being another witness to something more.

He realized that in his mind the Höfdi House would always be connected with her.

He crossed the road and sat on the wall outside the house. He pulled out his phone again and called up her number.

'Hi, it's me.'

'Oh, hi, Magnús, I'm with a customer.'

'OK. Do you want to go out to dinner tonight?'

'I'd love to, but I can't. I'm going to the public Icesave meeting in the Austurvöllur square.'

'You are?'

'Yes. Don't sound so surprised. I'll come to your place when I get back. It might be late. Very late. Got to go.'

That was strange. Typically strange. An exhibition at a gallery or a party for the beautiful people, Magnus could understand. But a political meeting? Although Ingileif shared the average Icelander's anger at the Icesave bail-out loan, until that moment, she had shown no interest in getting actively involved. And what was that about being late?

Magnus shook his head. What was she really doing? He never really knew where he was with Ingileif. It unsettled him.

He wondered what to do next. He should probably put in an appearance at the police college some time during the day. They wouldn't be expecting him, but the Commissioner might check up. He had cancelled his teaching for the week, but he had a law class after lunch which he was supposed to attend: he probably ought to show up for that. That was several hours away.

But he couldn't just walk away from the Óskar Gunnarsson case. And he was intensely curious to read that thick file on the Benedikt Jóhannesson murder. The café on Borgartún where he had met Sibba was close by. He decided to get himself a cup of coffee and look at it more carefully.

Benedikt was murdered between Christmas and New Year 1985, on 28 December, to be precise. He lived on Bárugata, a street in Vesturbaer just to the west of downtown Reykjavík. It was five o'clock in the evening, it had already been dark for an hour and a half, and it was snowing.

Benedikt's adult son, Jóhannes, had stopped by the house later that evening, and found his father lying in the hallway, dead.

Unsurprisingly, a major investigation was launched, led by one Inspector Snorri Gudmundsson, the current Big Salmon himself. It was thorough, boy was it thorough. Because of the snow, very few people were out and about, and those that were couldn't see anything. The only person identified near the house at the time acting suspiciously was a fourteen-year-old schoolboy. He claimed he was trying to find shelter to light a cigarette. Nothing Snorri could do would shake him from this story.

Forensics produced nothing, although since the case was twenty-five years old the report was much less detailed than Magnus was used to. There were no signs of a break-in, implying perhaps that Benedikt knew his attacker. There were a couple of footprints in the hallway, which was slightly unusual. In Iceland guests would always take off their shoes when they entered a house. Size forty-three. Which was about nine in the US system,

Magnus guessed. About average for a man. If, of course, they belonged to the murderer.

The investigation got nowhere, but that wasn't for want of trying. Snorri was an energetic investigator, and Magnus could guess the pressure he was under. The file was bursting with interviews, including one with the famous writer Halldór Laxness, Magnus noticed. Benedikt had no real enemies, but any rivals were interviewed and alibis checked. There was one notoriously sensitive fellow writer whose most recent book Benedikt had reviewed with heavy irony. The writer claimed he was at home alone reading all evening. Despite his lack of an alibi, and all Snorri's efforts, there was no proof linking him to the murder.

It turned out Benedikt had had a brain tumour. There was an interview with a doctor at the hospital who had told Benedikt in February of that year that he had only six months to live. Timing a little out, thought Magnus, but not by much. Questions had been asked, but none of Benedikt's friends or children seemed to know anything about it. He had kept the knowledge to himself.

The tumour must have been quite advanced when he died. Magnus wished he had the pathologist's report. It was pretty clear from the file that Benedikt had been stabbed, but the search for a knife with a three-inch blade had turned up nothing. With any luck the report would show up on Magnus's desk in the next day or two.

Snorri had then begun to interview every burglar who had ever been arrested in Reykjavík; a major undertaking that had taken weeks. Magnus was amused to see that Baldur Jakobsson's name appeared on the bottom of many of the reports of these interviews. There was no mention of any interviews with anyone at Bjarnarhöfn. Why should there be? It was decades since Benedikt had lived at Hraun.

Snorri could not find a single hard lead. No suspects, nothing. Twenty-five years on, the murder of Benedikt Jóhannesson was still a complete mystery.

Magnus tucked the file away in his briefcase, and left the café. There was one more thing he wanted to check about his grandfather.

The National Registry was right on Borgartún. As befitted the very heart of the national bureaucracy, it was the scruffiest building on the street. Magnus had some difficulties with the clerk, who regarded his Boston Police Department badge with scepticism. He still hadn't got himself an official Reykjavík Metropolitan Police badge, and he wouldn't until he graduated from the police college. However, the clerk smiled when he mentioned that he was working with Vigdís Audarsdóttir, whom she clearly knew, gave Vigdís a quick call at police headquarters, and then asked Magnus what he wanted.

It took her only a moment to confirm what Magnus had suspected. Although Hallgrímur Gunnarsson of Bjarnarhöfn in Helgafellssveit had a *kennitala,* or national identity number, he had never been issued with a passport.

Björn ordered himself a second cup of coffee from the counter. This place was expensive. You'd never pay that much for a cup of coffee in Grundarfjördur.

He took it back to the table he had been occupying for the last twenty minutes. He was in the café in the upper reaches of the Pearl, a grey bulbous building squatting on top of Reykjavík's hot-water storage tanks. It was situated at the summit of a small hill overlooking the whole city. It had been chosen because the approach road up to the building from the main thoroughfare was open and empty. Impossible not to spot a car following you.

It had taken him a little longer to reach Reykjavík in the pickup than on his motorbike, but Björn had driven fast. He tended to drive fast when he was tense. And there was no doubt he was tense. He would soon be face-to-face with Harpa. He hoped he had the courage to see his plan through.

Through the broad expanse of glass he looked west out across to the sea, itself gleaming a pearly grey in the sunshine. In the foreground was the irregular crossed triangle of the runways of the Reykjavík City Airfield. And the spot where Björn had dumped Gabríel Örn's body nine months before.

But before he faced Harpa, Björn had some people to see. Where the hell were they?

'Björn! How's it going?'

Björn felt a heavy pat on his shoulder, and turned to see Sindri and behind him the neat figure of Ísak.

'Let me get some coffee,' said Sindri. 'We have a lot to talk about.'

CHAPTER TWENTY-NINE

'WERE YOU FOLLOWED?' Sindri asked Björn as he sat down with his coffee.

'No. You were right, this is a good place.'

'We've got to make sure the cops don't see us together,' said Sindri.

'I don't understand what Ísak's doing here,' said Björn, frowning.

'He just arrived back in Iceland yesterday,' said Sindri.

'Why?'

'The British police might be on to me,' Ísak said. 'One of them came to my house to interview me. Wanted to know whether it was me who had been asking Óskar's neighbours where he lived. She didn't push it, but she's suspicious. So I thought I'd come back here. Make it that bit more difficult for her.'

'The cops here are asking awkward questions too,' Sindri said. 'There's a big red-haired bastard called Magnús who won't leave us alone. Some kind of American.'

'I told my mother things were getting on top of me and I needed to get away for a few days,' Ísak said. 'Go camping in the hills. Sort myself out. I borrowed her car, she's too ill to drive it these days.'

'Did she believe you?'

'She knew I was acting a bit weird, but she didn't know why and I didn't tell her. That's the best way to deal with parents. Never explain. Keep them guessing.' Ísak sipped his coffee and glanced at Björn. 'So, Sindri tells me there's a problem with Harpa?'

Björn didn't like Ísak, never had. He was too cool. Too self-possessed for a student. Sindri wore his passion on his sleeve. Ísak's was in there, it had to be to do the things they were doing, but it was a cool, calculated determination to follow a carefully worked out plan. It was as if Ísak was trying to win an intellectual argument and willing to go to any lengths to prove himself right. Björn wasn't trying to prove anything: he was just bringing justice upon those people who had destroyed his life and the lives of so many other Icelanders.

'Yes,' he said, turning to Sindri. 'She's got this idea that we, or rather you, Sindri, are behind the shooting of Óskar and Lister. She spoke to the kid Frikki the other day; he was the one who put the idea in her head. She suspected me as well, but she seems to believe my innocence now. Anyway, she wants to go to the police.'

'You have to tell her not to,' said Sindri. 'She'll just get herself locked up.'

'She thinks there might be another victim,' said Björn. 'She wants to stop us before we get to one.'

'She *thinks*, she doesn't *know*,' said Sindri.

'Yes. But she's going to talk to them. I know she is.'

'So what are you going to do?' asked Ísak quietly.

Björn took a deep breath. 'I'm going to take her away for a couple of days. There's a hut I know in one of the mountain passes near Grundarfjördur. It's totally isolated. If I can keep her there for tomorrow and the day after, that will be long enough.'

'Until we've dealt with Ingólfur Arnarson you mean?' said Sindri.

Björn nodded.

'How are you going to persuade her to go there?' Ísak asked.

Björn winced. 'Charm. Persuasiveness. And if that doesn't work, Rohypnol.'

'Rohypnol? Where did you get that?' asked Sindri.

'A mate in Reykjavík. A fisherman.'

'You have dodgy mates.'

Björn shrugged. 'Don't we all?'

'OK,' said Ísak. 'That's fine for the next couple of days. But what happens after that?'

The student was really irritating Björn. But that was the key question. 'Ingólfur Arnarson is our last target, right? The climax. Once he has been dealt with I can persuade Harpa there is no point in going to the police. There will be no one left at risk. All she will be doing is putting herself and the rest of us in jail.'

'Do you think she'll go with that?' asked Sindri.

'She might.'

'And if she doesn't?' Ísak asked.

Björn shrugged. 'I don't know. It seems to me the police are going to catch us anyway. They are getting closer. They've started asking questions about Ísak. Once we've got Ingólfur Arnarson maybe we should just accept what's coming to us.'

'No!' said Ísak. 'When we started this we never intended to give ourselves up at the end. That's why we chose to operate abroad. The aim was always to walk away once we were finished.'

'Maybe we'll start something,' said Sindri. 'You know, a real revolution, not a pots-and-pans one.'

'I think it will take more time,' said Ísak. 'It seems to me that the people are too busy apologizing to the British.'

'How do you know?' said Sindri. 'You've been in London.'

'I can read the Icelandic news sites on the Internet.'

'Yeah, well, there's other stuff on the web. Some people are getting really angry. There's an Icesave meeting this afternoon. We'll see what happens there.'

'Are you going?' said Ísak.

'Of course I'm going,' said Sindri. 'I want to be there when it happens.'

Ísak leaned forward. 'Look, Sindri. I believe that capitalism is dead as much as you do. But whereas Marx and Engels thought it would die through oppressing the workers, it turns out that it is strangling itself through debt. And it's here in Iceland where there is way too much debt. We've OD'd, we're the first to go. But it's going to take time for the people to realize that. Which is why we mustn't be caught. We need to be around for the next few years to see the revolution through.'

Björn watched the two of them argue. He had no views on a revolution. The idea had appealed briefly at first, but all he had really wanted to do was to make sure that the bastards who had ruined his country were brought to justice. Not all of them, that was impossible, but enough of them to make the point.

'Which brings me back to Harpa,' Ísak said. 'We need a better plan.'

'Like what?' said Björn. 'You're not suggesting we kill her, are you?'

Ísak held Björn's eyes.

'Of course Ísak isn't suggesting that we kill her,' Sindri said. 'Are you, Ísak?'

'No,' said Ísak, without conviction.

'Because she's a totally innocent bystander,' Björn said. 'I mean Julian Lister deserves it. Óskar deserved it. Even Gabríel Örn deserved it. But not Harpa.'

'Of course not,' said Sindri. 'Let's figure it out once Ingólfur Arnarson has been dealt with, eh?'

They agreed to leave the Pearl one at a time. Björn went first, he had things to do.

Sindri and Ísak stared out over the airfield and the Atlantic beyond.

'You know we *are* going to have to do something about Harpa,' Ísak said. 'Once he drugs her and drags her off somewhere, she's not going to keep quiet.'

'She might,' said Sindri.

'She won't,' said Ísak. 'You know she won't.'

'We can't kill her, Ísak. Björn's right. She's innocent. I can convince myself that killing Óskar or Julian Lister is necessary, that they deserve to die. But not Harpa. She was just the wrong person at the wrong time.'

'Sindri, it would be nice if the world worked like that, but you know it doesn't. If a revolution is to be successful, its leaders must be ruthless. You *know* that. You've read your history. Lenin, Trotsky, Mao, Che Guevara, Fidel Castro, even the Africa National Congress in South Africa. There are times when innocent people have to die for the revolution to succeed. Sure, you keep those deaths to a minimum. But you don't back away from them. Because if you do, you are letting down the people.'

'Yeah, but this is Iceland, not Russia.'

'Sindri, I've read your book. Three times. It's good, it's very good. My father is a member of the Independence Party. He was a Minister. I've seen the complacency of the establishment in Iceland, the way they have been seduced by the capitalists, the way that what was one of the most decent, egalitarian societies in Europe has changed into one of the most unequal. My father and his mates were responsible for that. Capitalism is a sickness, and our country has got that sickness very bad. We're close to death.'

Sindri frowned.

'You can't be squeamish, Sindri. You of all people should know that. You taught me that. From the moment that banker Gabríel Örn died, we crossed a line. We can't go back over it now, not after Óskar Gunnarsson. We're committed. But at least we are doing it all for a purpose. Don't sabotage that purpose now. Otherwise everything else we have done becomes a waste of time. Then we really will have been murderers.'

Sindri shook his head and folded his arms. 'I won't be a part of killing anybody.' He corrected himself. 'Anybody who's innocent.'

Ísak smiled. 'Fair enough. I'll take care of it. I've got to disappear anyway, I may as well go up to Grundarfjördur. If I don't do it there will be no revolution. Capitalism will crush Iceland. And it will be our fault. *We* will be responsible. Are you going to stop me?'

Sindri didn't say anything. He avoided Ísak's eyes.

'I'm going now,' said Ísak. 'You leave in another ten minutes.'

CHAPTER THIRTY

IDENTIFYING THE NURSE was easy. Árni showed the photograph to the woman at reception in the National Hospital. 'Oh, that's Íris,' she said. Within a couple of minutes Árni was in a quiet corner of one of the endless corridors, talking to the woman with the round face and the snub nose.

'I remember him,' the nurse said. 'He'd got tear gas in his eye. He was in quite a lot of pain, that stuff is no joke. He had this idiotic idea that I should get two raw steaks and place them on his eyes. He said he knew where to get some. He was quite insistent.'

'Did you do it?' asked Árni.

'Of course not,' said the nurse, glancing at Árni as if he was an idiot.

Árni smiled encouragingly. That happened to him quite a lot. Smile and move on, was his motto.

'I gave him a solution of water and sodium bisulphate. Tear gas wears off of its own accord in a few minutes.'

'Did the boy say what his name was?' Árni asked.

'He may have done. I don't remember it if he did.'

'You didn't keep a record anywhere? Notes?'

'No. Just treat one and move on to the next one.'

Pity, Árni thought. 'Do you recognize any of these people?' Árni asked, showing the nurse photos of Harpa, Björn and Sindri.

'No,' said Íris, studying them. 'Actually, I think I recognize the big guy with the ponytail. I saw him wandering around in some of those protests.'

'But you didn't see him talking to the boy?'

'No.' The woman shook her head.

Árni pulled out another photograph, a still from the RÚV video showing Sindri standing behind the nurse as she tended the boy.

'I see him now, but I didn't notice him then,' she said. 'Or hear what he said.'

Árni replaced the photographs. 'Thank you for your help.' As he walked away from the nurse, he considered the next step. He wasn't actually any closer to identifying the boy.

Suddenly he had a brainwave.

He turned. The nurse was just disappearing around a corner of the corridor.

'Íris?' He ran after her.

'Yes?'

'One last question. Where did the boy think he could get the steak?'

'Oh, I remember that. The 101 Hotel. He said he used to work there as a chef.'

Björn drove the pickup to the bakery on Nordurströnd. He knew that what he was about to do would change his relationship with Harpa for ever.

But he had no choice.

Of course Ísak was right. Once Ingólfur Arnarson had been dealt with, there would be the problem of what to do with Harpa. But Björn had a plan for that. It was probably wishful thinking, but he would give it a try.

He loved Harpa, and he was sure that she loved him. They shared similar values. She hated the credit crunch and the people who had caused it as much as he did. She would understand what he had done. Perhaps she would join him.

In the hut where he was taking her there would be a lot of time to talk. Perhaps he could persuade her. Yes, he *could* persuade her. He had to.

He remembered the chance meeting with Sindri in the Grand Rokk three months before. Things would have been very different if he had just walked away then. But he didn't regret what he and the others had done over the last couple of weeks. Someone had to bring the bastards to justice.

Björn and Gulli were having a beer in the tent outside the Grand Rokk, so Gulli could smoke. Although it was eleven o'clock it was June, and so still light. The drinkers were full of the midsummer hyperactivity that strikes Iceland at that time of year: a nation running faster and faster without sleep.

'Björn? Is that Björn?'

Björn turned to see a large figure with a broad leather hat and a ponytail. 'Sindri!' He stood up and shook the big man's hand.

Sindri glanced at his companion and Björn introduced his brother. Sindri was a little drunk, Björn was a little drunk, Gulli was very drunk. Sindri and Björn talked about this and that, but not about January. They did exchange rants about the bankers. Gulli watched them, knocking the beer back steadily, not really paying much attention.

'Do you remember I told you my brother was in danger of losing his farm?' Sindri said.

Björn nodded. 'Did he lose it?'

'He couldn't wait. Topped himself. Three months ago.'

'I'm sorry,' Björn said.

'Yeah. A wife. Two daughters. They will still lose the farm. How are you doing? Have you kept hold of your boat?'

'Had to sell it,' said Björn. 'Not much hope of ever getting another one.'

The two men sat in silence staring at each other. Gulli lit another cigarette.

'We weren't wrong, were we?' said Sindri.

Björn hesitated. Swallowed. 'No, we weren't.'

'Look. I'm having breakfast with an old friend of ours tomorrow. At the Grey Cat. Ten o'clock. Do you want to join us?'

'Old friend?' said Björn.

Sindri shrugged. Not in front of Gulli.

'OK,' said Björn. 'See you then.'

The Grey Cat was a cosy book-lined café down some steps on Hverfisgata. It lay opposite the Central Bank, also known as 'The Black Fort', built in brutalist bunker style, the most hated building in Iceland. Just outside, Ingólfur Arnarson leaned on his shield staring out towards the harbour.

Björn saw Sindri's broad leather hat as soon as he walked in. He was sitting in a booth at the back, the bulk of his body wedged between the orange table and the red leather bench. Opposite him was a smaller, trimmer figure. It took Björn a moment to recognize Ísak, the student.

Björn took a chair next to Ísak and asked the waitress for a cup of coffee. Sindri ordered a large American breakfast of pancakes and bacon, the Grey Cat's speciality, served all day. Ísak ordered a bagel.

'Have you two kept in contact?' Björn asked. 'I thought we decided to stay away from each other?'

'No, at least not until last week,' Sindri said. 'Ísak dropped by my flat. We had a talk.'

'About what we did last January?' Björn said.

'More about what we are going to do this autumn,' Ísak said.

Björn raised his eyebrows. 'We?'

'Ísak and me,' said Sindri. 'And you. If you want to join us.'

Björn parked the pickup outside the bakery. He hesitated, glancing across the bay towards the Hallgrímskirkja above downtown Reykjavík. There was no going back now. He took a deep breath and opened the door.

The place was empty. Harpa's face lit up when she saw him. She skipped around the counter and fell into his arms.

'Oh, Björn. I'm so sorry I doubted you. Will you forgive me?'

'There's nothing to forgive. I need a cup of coffee. Do you want one?'

'OK.'

'I'll get it,' Björn said. There were a couple of urns containing coffee along one wall. Björn poured himself and Harpa a cup. They sat down at a table.

'So you've decided you are going to the police?' Björn asked.

Harpa nodded her head.

'Are you absolutely sure? No matter what the consequences?'

'I have to,' said Harpa. 'If someone else were to die, I couldn't bear it.'

'I understand.' Björn relaxed. There was no point in trying to talk her out of it. He was committed now. He sipped his coffee. Harpa didn't touch hers.

She smiled at Björn. 'I'm so glad you do. What I feel worst about is that I might get you in trouble.'

'And Sindri and Ísak. And the kid Frikki.'

'I don't care about them. Well maybe I care about the boy. I certainly don't care about me. But I do care about you.'

Björn smiled. He was touched. He was beginning to think he really could persuade her. Later.

'Can you help me think how to do it? I mean, if there is a way I could warn the police without getting you thrown in jail? I've been thinking about an anonymous tip-off, but I'm not sure how I can do that without giving them details that would incriminate you.'

'That's why I came down here,' said Björn. 'To come up with a plan. But first there is someone I want you to meet.'

He gulped down his coffee. Harpa still hadn't touched hers. What was wrong with the woman? She always drank her coffee. Especially when she was wound up.

'Who?'

'You'll see.'

Harpa sipped some of her coffee. Björn took her hand. 'We'll figure this out, Harpa. I know we will.'

Harpa looked up and smiled. 'God, I hope so.'

'Come on, finish your coffee and let's go.'

Harpa hastily emptied her cup. 'OK. Wait a second. I just need to make sure it's OK with Dísa to leave early.'

Björn waited for Harpa as she had a quick word with her boss. 'All right, let's go,' she said. They went outside. Harpa saw Björn's pickup. 'No motorbike?'

'It's being serviced,' Björn said.

They climbed in and Björn headed off towards the ring road. He headed east. He didn't have any specific destination in mind. Just drive. Rohypnol was a sedative and one of the most popular date-rape drugs because it was tasteless and could induce amnesia, especially when mixed with alcohol. The guy who had given it to him had said it was supposed to take effect within twenty minutes to half an hour, but that could only be an approximation. And of course Harpa hadn't drunk any alcohol. Björn didn't trust the guy at all. He hoped he'd got the dosage right.

Björn slipped a CD into his player and turned the music up. Nirvana. He wanted to keep small talk with Harpa to a minimum.

After fifteen minutes, she yawned. 'God, I feel sleepy. How far are we going?'

As far as it takes, Björn thought. 'Probably another half hour.'

'Why won't you tell me where we are going?'

'You'll see.'

Ten minutes later, Harpa was leaning against the side of the door of the pickup. Five more minutes and she was asleep.

Magnus sat at the back of the class, listening to the lecturer, a police superintendent, talk about fraud and the Penal Code. Magnus was wearing the uniform of a sergeant in the Boston Police Department. Everyone at the National Police College wore uniform, lecturers and students, unless they were civilians, of course. The superintendent in charge of the college had thought it appropriate for Magnus to wear a BPD uniform rather than that of a police cadet, so Magnus had brought one back with him after his brief trip to the States for a few days back in May to pack up his life and move it to Iceland. Hadn't taken long.

He knew he should focus; the last thing he wanted to do was to fail his exam and have to retake. Except now it looked like he would be on a plane back to the States before he even had a chance to take the damn exam.

Part of him wanted to forget about Harpa and Björn and Sindri. If Snorri didn't want to listen to him that was his problem.

Except Magnus couldn't think like that. If he was right, and he was damn sure he was right, then the people who had shot Julian Lister and killed Óskar and probably Gabríel Örn would go free. And worse, there was a chance some other poor bastard, with a family, perhaps with kids, would end up dead, probably in the next few days.

The phone vibrated next to his hip. Magnus surreptitiously slipped it out of his pocket to check it. He felt like a schoolboy. Vigdís.

It was strictly forbidden to take cell phone calls in class, or to leave the class to take them. Magnus quietly headed for the door.

The superintendent paused. 'Magnús?'

'I'll be back in a moment,' Magnus said with a smile. He was out in the corridor before the lecturer could reprimand him.

'Yeah, Vigdís, what is it?'

'We've identified the kid who was being treated for tear gas. Fridrik Eiríksson, known as "Frikki". He used to be an assistant chef at the Hotel 101. Got laid off back in December. We've got an address in Breidholt. Shall we pick him up?'

Magnus appreciated Vigdís asking him. 'Yes. But check with Baldur first. And let me know how the interview goes.'

'Speak to you later,' said Vigdís.

Magnus smiled apologetically as he took his seat in the classroom.

He was in his car heading back home when he got a text from Vigdís. Frikki was out somewhere with his girlfriend, his mother didn't know where. They would let Magnus know when they picked him up.

He bent down to look at the magnified image on the screen of the camera resting on its tripod. The long lens was pointing out across the Tjörnin, the large lake in the centre of Reykjavík and a hub for international bird travel in the North Atlantic. In its pale blue waters, reflecting the pale blue sky, swans, geese, many species of duck, terns, coots and a host of other birds, paddled, glided and swooped, busy, busy, busy.

There was a particularly noisy cluster down at the far end of the lake, behind the parliament building and the futuristic glass, steel and chrome box that was the City Hall. This was where locals and tourists gathered to feed the birds. Beyond that, the murmur of the crowd gathering in the Austurvöllur square for the Icesave public meeting drifted towards him.

But despite the appearance he was eager to give, he wasn't watching the waterfowl. He was examining one of the large white houses on the far shore of the Tjörnin.

He had been observing the house for a couple of hours already. He was convinced there was no protection, no police cars loitering outside, no men in uniform or out of it patrolling the garden. He was pleased to see that the target's car, a black Mercedes SUV, was parked up by the side of the house, almost out of sight of the road. Behind it was a hedge and some small trees. A possible entry point. Worth checking out later.

As he watched and waited a plan settled in his mind.

The target emerged from the front door of the house and walked around to his car, climbed in, and drove off.

He unfastened the camera, took down his tripod and left.

He knew what he was going to do.

Ingileif pushed through the crowd in the square outside the Parliament building, searching for the large frame of Sindri. There were a few hundred people there. The atmosphere was different to that of the demonstrations Ingileif had attended over the winter. The crowd was more serious. The anger was there, but it was more muted. There were no pots and pans, no foghorns, no anarchists in balaclavas, and very few police. Less excitement, more quiet determination.

Ingileif soon spotted Sindri's brown leather hat and grey pony-tail and pushed herself into a space beside him. Sindri was chatting randomly to those around him when he noticed her.

'Ingileif?'

She turned and gave him a big smile. 'Sindri! I'm not surprised to see you here.'

'It's an important issue,' Sindri said.

'Very,' said Ingileif. 'Do you know who the speakers are?'

'Old windbags,' Sindri said. 'I don't know why I bothered to come. They'll talk about refusing to pay the British, but that's all it will be, talk.' He gestured at the crowd. 'Take a look around you. I was hoping for some revolutionary spirit. People who are prepared to *do* something. This lot look like they're at church listening to a sermon.'

'I know what you mean,' said Ingileif. 'We need to scare them.'

Sindri focused on her with interest.

'Scare who?'

'The British, of course,' Ingileif said. 'Make them believe that unless they give us a better deal the people will revolt. We've done it before. We can do it again.'

'Dead right,' said Sindri. Ingileif could see he was looking at her with a mixture of admiration and, well, lust. That was OK.

A woman, one of the organizers, picked up a loudspeaker and made a little speech about how she was speaking for everyone there when she noted the horror the Icelandic people felt about the shooting of Julian Lister.

'We are not terrorists, Mr Lister!' Sindri bellowed in Ingileif's ear. The refrain was familiar to the crowd from the previous autumn, but no one took it up. Those standing around him turned to frown. A few people hushed him.

'Pathetic,' Sindri muttered. Ingileif muttered too.

There was a series of speeches, some of them inspiring to Ingileif's ear, but Sindri didn't like them. He grumbled louder and louder, until finally he said, 'I can't stand this any longer.'

'Neither can I,' said Ingileif.

'This country is so spineless,' said Sindri.

'You wrote a book about all this, didn't you?' said Ingileif. 'Can you tell me about it?'

Sindri smiled. 'With pleasure. Let's get a coffee.'

CHAPTER THIRTY-ONE

THE HUT STOOD alone in the lonely valley. Björn coaxed his pickup truck down towards it, rattling and jolting over the potholes. The road was appalling, and Björn was amazed that Harpa hadn't been wakened by the lurching.

This road had always been bad. For years, no, centuries, it had been the most direct route from Stykkishólmur south to Borgarnes. It wound around twisted volcanic rocks, including the famous Kerlingin troll with her haul of stone babies over her shoulder. But then the government had built a new road in a parallel pass just a few kilometres to the west. There was now no reason for anyone to come this way. The road had deteriorated rapidly.

The hut was old, perhaps a hundred years old, and had been built to provide shelter for travellers stranded in the pass. Björn had stayed there a couple of times with his uncle and aunt when he was a kid, just for fun. It had been built on a knoll, to remain above snowdrifts, a short distance from what remained of the road. Rocky walls rose up on either side of the valley, down which streams and waterfalls tumbled before accumulating in a larger stream that ran beside the road. There were patches of grass and some moss, but the valley was mostly grit, stone and bare rock. Although there had been clear skies during the drive up from Reykjavík, here in the mountains moisture ruled. Mist swirled around the rocks, the air was full of the muffled tinkle of running water.

The door to the hut was open; it was never locked in case travellers needed its shelter. Inside it was surprisingly clean. There were signs of recent habitation: a gum wrapper on the floor, an empty half-bottle of vodka on a window sill. Drovers, no doubt: Björn was pretty sure the *réttir* had taken place the week before around Helgafellssveit. There was a stove, and a ladder led up to a sleeping loft. Björn had driven from Reykjavík straight to his home in Grundarfjördur and loaded the pickup with supplies. He had sleeping bags, bed rolls, wood for the stove, food and other camping equipment. Enough to keep them both going for three days.

He had also brought plenty of rope.

He settled the still slumbering Harpa in a sleeping bag in the loft, and lit a fire in the stove. He put some water on to boil for coffee.

He checked his phone. No signal: hardly surprising. That could be a problem. He would need to communicate with the others in the coming couple of days, and that would involve driving back down the pass towards Stykkishólmur until he got a signal.

He made the coffee and took it outside. He sat on the step of the hut watching the light seep out of the moist valley as dusk fell. A raven flapped down the valley on the far side of the stream, its croak sinking into the mist.

The place was eerie. Björn smiled as he remembered the night he and his cousins had slept in the hut when they were kids. The frisson of fear. There was not just the Kerlingin troll waiting for them. There was a story, well known among the kids in the area, of an empty bus being driven through the pass. The driver had felt the presence of something behind him and turned to see the bus full of people.

Ghosts.

But Björn felt safe here. More importantly, he felt Harpa was safe. He wished that the two of them could stay here for always, away from the world outside, the world of the *kreppa* and bankers and corrupt politicians. The world he had decided to stand up and fight against.

Could he make Harpa understand what he and the others had done? He could try.

There was no sound from her. In theory the drug was supposed to wear off in eight hours. In practice, Björn thought Harpa would be out all night.

The pub in Shoreditch was crowded and there was barely enough room for the eight students squashed around two tables pushed together. Sophie hardly knew most of the others, but when her friend Tori had asked her out for a drink she had agreed to come. She had spent an unproductive afternoon in the library.

She was worried about Zak. The only response to her texts she had received so far was one line: *It doesn't look good.* She wished he would talk to her more instead of clamming up.

There were three other girls and four guys around the table. She didn't know the guys very well, although they all studied politics with her. The conversation had moved on from *Big Brother* to Julian Lister. She was barely listening.

'So is he going to make it?'

'They say he's going to be fine.'

'I heard he was still critical.'

'No, it was on the radio this evening. They now think he's going to make a full recovery.'

'So who did it then?'

'Al-Qaeda.'

'But they use bombs not bullets.'

'Al-Qaeda. Operating out of Holland.'

'Holland?'

'Yeah, they saw a motorbike with Dutch number plates hanging about right where he was shot.'

'It's the Icelanders.'

That caught Sophie's attention. The guy talking was tall with longish curly hair. She thought his name was Jeff.

'The Icelanders! Don't be stupid, Josh. Why not the Greenlanders?' Not Jeff, Josh.

'No, I'm serious.' Josh was leaning forward, his eyes alight. 'I've got it all figured out. The Icelanders hate Julian Lister. Ever since the credit crunch. He confiscated all their assets and called them a bunch of terrorists.'

'Yeah, well, loads of people hate Julian Lister. So what does that prove?'

Josh lowered his voice. 'You know I was working in the House of Commons as a research assistant over the summer? I was working for Anita Norris who was a junior treasury minister. Well, Zak Samuelsson, you know, the Icelander, asked me where Julian Lister was going on holiday this summer. I mean what kind of question is that?'

'So what are you suggesting? That Zak shot him?'

'Or told one of his mates back in Iceland.'

Sophie felt her ears redden. Everyone around the table was looking at her, apart from Josh, who clearly was the only one who didn't know she was going out with Zak.

'What?' Josh said, aware that something was wrong.

'You're such an arsehole, Josh,' said Tori.

'What do you think, Sophie?' It was one of the other guys, Eddie. The question was well meant, he was trying to give Sophie a chance to defend her boyfriend.

'That doesn't make any sense,' said Sophie. 'Icelanders don't do that sort of thing.'

'I bet Zak was pleased about what happened to Lister,' said Josh, still not quite getting it.

'He wasn't,' said Sophie. 'I know him, you don't, and he had nothing to do with it.'

'Yeah, Josh,' said Tori. 'You talk a lot of shit. Don't mouth off about stuff you know nothing about.'

The penny dropped. Josh glanced around the group. 'Sorry. I didn't know he was a friend of yours,' he said to Sophie.

She smiled weakly. 'That's OK,' she said.

But as soon as the conversation moved on she finished her drink and slipped away. She was desperate to get out of there.

Magnus paced up and down in his tiny room. He felt imprisoned. Árni had been waiting for Frikki, and when Frikki eventually returned home with his girlfriend, Árni had whisked him back to the station. He and Vigdís were interviewing the boy at that very moment. Magnus wanted to be there too. And if that wasn't possible, he wanted to know what Frikki was saying. But he couldn't disturb them; he just had to wait.

He had called Sharon Piper to find out if there was any news on the French couple holidaying in India. Nothing yet. Magnus swore as he hung up. Matching a verbal description was not conclusive. Magnus really needed a positive ID on Ísak if he was to get himself back on the case. Without it, any attempt to link Óskar's death to Iceland was just speculation. As Snorri and Baldur would make very clear. Having called Sharon once, Magnus couldn't very well call her again.

It was getting dark and he was hungry. He grabbed his coat and headed outside. Around the corner and up the hill towards the church was Vitabar, the nearest thing the neighbourhood had to a diner. Magnus ordered a burger and a beer. He wolfed the burger down too quickly.

Rather than go back to his apartment he wandered the streets. Any call would come through to his cell phone. He found himself in the square in front of the Hallgrímskirkja. The church rose tall above him, illuminated against the night sky. Beneath it the statue of Leifur Eiríksson, the first European to discover America, stared out over the city to the west.

Sending Magnus home, perhaps.

His phone rang. It was Vigdís.

'Hi. Did he talk?' Magnus asked her.

'No,' Vigdís said.

'What do you mean, no? Didn't he say anything at all?'

'Nothing. Nothing at all.'

'What, has he got a lawyer or something?'

'He doesn't want one. It's weird. He just sits there looking miserable. Not arrogant or cocky, you know the way they sometimes are when they think they can keep quiet and you can't touch them. It looks like he's just about to cry.'

'So? Didn't you make him cry?'

'Hey, Magnús, cool it,' said Vigdís.

'All right.' Magnus realized Vigdís had a point. He knew she was a good detective. He had to trust her. And there was no harder suspect to interview than one who said nothing at all. 'Sorry, Vigdís. What's your gut telling you?'

'He's guilty as hell. He knows what we are talking about. I asked him about Gabríel Örn and Óskar and Julian Lister and he showed no surprise at any of it. He knows the names of Harpa and Sindri and Björn. And it seems like he knows he is going to jail.'

'Then why isn't he talking?'

'I don't know. I think the softly-softly approach will work best. And if that doesn't do it, we can always try keeping him in overnight.'

'Is Baldur OK with that?'

'I've squared it with him.'

'A night in the cells can work wonders,' Magnus said. 'I wish I could be there too. Call me if you get anywhere, will you?'

Magnus returned to his apartment, waiting for Vigdís to call again. None came. Nor did he hear from Ingileif. That was strange. The Icesave meeting had taken place in the late afternoon. What was she doing afterwards?

In the end he found solace in a saga, the tried and tested medicine from his adolescence. He picked the *Saga of the People of Eyri*. Within a few minutes he was lost in the world of the Norse settlers, of Ketill Flat Nose, Björn the Easterner, who had built the first farmhouse at Bjarnarhöfn, Arnkell, Snorri Godi, and Thórólfur Lame Foot. The countryside around Bjarnarhöfn seemed closer and more real in the saga than in his own memory.

At about eleven o'clock his doorbell rang. It was Ingileif.

'Hi,' she kissed him as he answered the door. 'Hi, Katrín.' She waved at Magnus's landlady as she climbed the stairs to his room. She tripped on a step. 'Whoops-a-daisy.'

When they got into his room, she kissed him again. 'Sorry I'm so late,' she said.

'That's OK.'

'I'm *so* drunk.'

Magnus had guessed. 'Where were you?' he asked, trying to keep any hint of accusation out of his voice.

'Solving your case.'

'What do you mean?'

Ingileif began to unbutton his shirt. 'I'll tell you afterwards.'

'What do you mean, solving my case? Did you see Sindri at the Icesave meeting?'

'Yup.' Ingileif smiled. Magnus's shirt was undone now. Her hands moved down to his pants.

'You planned to see him all along?'

'Yup.'

Magnus felt the anger rise. He had specifically told Ingileif not to do that. He backed away.

'What's wrong with that?' Ingileif said. 'You'd have been so proud of me. He told me everything.'

'What? What did he tell you?'

Ingileif sat on Magnus's bed. 'Everything. How he shot Óskar. And the British Chancellor. Everything.'

'*He* shot the chancellor?'

'Well, not him, exactly. Him and his friends.'

Magnus sat down next to her on the bed. Angry though he was with Ingileif, he was desperate to know what she had found out. 'Who are his friends?'

'I don't know. I didn't ask him. But there's a group of them.

He's the leader. They think capitalism is all wrong. I can tell you *all* about what's wrong with capitalism, I listened to hours of it.'

She swayed on the bed, and seemed about to keel over, when she straightened herself up. 'I placed myself next to him at the Icesave meeting in Austurvöllur. He started talking to me. We went for some coffee. Had some more coffee. Went to his place. Had something to drink. Had some more to drink. Had some *more* to drink. Then he started to take my clothes off.'

'And then?'

Ingileif giggled. 'And then I came home to you, what do you think? He was a little upset. I think he thought I had taken advantage of him.'

'He might have been right,' said Magnus.

'Hey! He admitted that they planned to kill the people they thought were responsible for the *kreppa*. The chairman of a bank. The British ex-Chancellor of the Exchequer. And other people.'

'Other people? Like who? Did you find out?'

'Oh, yes,' said Ingileif. She giggled. 'I got him to tell me. Ingólfur Arnarson.'

'Who's he? Apart from the guy who discovered Iceland.'

'I don't know. I suggest you look him up in the phone book and tell him to lock his door. And then you arrest Sindri.'

'I can't arrest Sindri,' Magnus said.

'Why not?' Ingileif said. 'He confessed, didn't he? I can stand up in court and tell them what he told me.'

'As evidence that's useless,' Magnus said harshly.

'What do you mean, useless? You're just jealous.'

'Jealous? Why would I be jealous?'

'Yes, jealous. Because I found out more in one night than you've been able to find out in a whole week.'

'That's ridiculous!' said Magnus. What really riled him was that there was a germ of truth in what Ingileif said. He *was* jealous. And she had used illegal methods: she had cheated, not just the law but him. 'We can't use any of that evidence. And if the defence attorneys discover there is a link between you and me, which they will, then there is a good chance that the case would be thrown out for entrapment.'

Actually Magnus had no idea whether that would apply in Iceland. But it would certainly have been one hell of a problem in America.

'How can you be angry with me when I helped you like that?' said Ingileif. 'Can you imagine how creepy it is to talk to that lecherous old man for hours, have his hands all over me, when all I'm trying to do is help you?'

'His hands all over you?' Magnus asked.

'You see you *are* jealous.'

'Yes, I damn well am jealous!' Magnus shouted. 'I didn't ask you to do all that. I didn't ask you to seduce Sindri.'

'I didn't exactly seduce him. And anyway, I can talk to whoever I want.'

'Talk, yes. But everything else?'

'Are you accusing me of sleeping with other men?'

'I don't know,' said Magnus. But it was a question that always nagged at the back of his mind with Ingileif. 'Maybe. Do you?'

Ingileif stared at him. 'Do up your shirt. I'm off.'

For a moment Magnus thought of asking her to stay, but only for a moment. Under her rules she could come and go as she pleased. Then so be it.

She went, banging the door behind her.

CHAPTER THIRTY-TWO

Wednesday, 23 September 2009

HARPA SMELLED THE coffee. She opened her eyes. Blinked. Her head was heavy with sleep and she was confused. Above her, not very far above her, were wooden beams and a roof. She was lying in a sleeping bag. Next to her was another sleeping bag, empty.

But it had the familiar smell of Björn: male sweat and a hint of fish.

She leaned on her elbow. The coffee smelled good.

She was in a hut. Grey early morning light slipped in through the top of a window. She could hear someone moving about below.

'Björn?'

'Good morning.'

She slid over to the top of a ladder. She realized she was in a raised sleeping loft in some kind of hut. Panic overtook her, but disappeared when she saw Björn's reassuring smile. 'Here. Come down and have a cup of coffee. Do you want some breakfast?'

Carefully she climbed down the ladder. She was wearing a T-shirt and underpants, but the hut was warm. Wood was burning in a stove.

Her head was still muzzy. She felt as if she had just woken up from a dream, except she was waking up *into* a dream.

'Björn, where are we?' she asked.

He kissed her quickly on the lips. 'In a mountain hut. I thought we could get away for a few days.'

Harpa blinked. 'You know, I don't remember coming here at all.'

'You were very tired. You slept in the car.'

'Did I?' Harpa scrambled to make sense of it. She could remember Björn coming to meet her in the bakery, and then nothing. Very strange.

'Where's Markús?'

'With your parents. We left them a note.'

'I don't remember that.'

'Well, I left them a note.'

Harpa sat on a chair by the table and sipped her coffee. Her brain cleared a little. 'Where is this hut, Björn?'

'Near Grundarfjördur. It's on the old road from Stykkishólmur to Borgarnes. But no one comes here any more. It's very peaceful.'

'I don't understand,' said Harpa.

Björn took her hand over the table. 'You've been under a lot of pressure recently. You need a rest.' He squeezed it. Smiled. For a moment she was comforted by that smile.

Then she withdrew her hand. 'Wait a minute. We didn't talk about this, did we? We were going to the police. To tell them about Sindri and the student. Isn't that where we were driving?'

Björn swallowed. 'No.'

'Björn. What's going on here?' Then Harpa's eyes widened. 'You've kidnapped me, haven't you?'

'No,' said Björn.

'OK. In that case let me find my phone and I'll ring the police.' She grabbed her handbag which was lying by the door and rummaged inside it.

'There's no reception here,' said Björn.

'Where's my phone, Björn?'

'You don't need it. There's no reception.'

Harpa looked up from the bag. 'You've taken it, haven't you. My God, you *have* kidnapped me. Björn, what the hell is going on?'

'I think we should spend some time...'

'That's bullshit.' A look of panic overwhelmed Harpa's features. 'You *did* shoot Óskar and Lister, didn't you? You want to stop me going to the police!'

'I didn't kill anyone.'

'Then what the hell are we doing here?' Harpa shouted.

'Sit down,' Björn said. 'And I'll explain.'

'You had better,' said Harpa. But she sat down. She sipped her coffee.

'To start with, I haven't killed anyone,' Björn said. 'I promise.'

'But you know who has?'

Björn nodded his head. 'I know who has.'

'And you did go to France?'

Björn nodded again. 'Yes. I flew to Amsterdam and then rode down to Normandy to prepare the ground for someone else.'

'Who?'

Björn shook his head.

'Sindri? Ísak?'

'Sindri and Ísak are involved, yes.'

'So Frikki was right?'

Björn nodded. 'But we did it for a good reason.'

'Oh, come on, how can killing anyone be for a good reason?'

'You killed someone, Harpa.'

'Yes, and I've regretted it ever since!'

'I haven't,' said Björn quietly.

Harpa looked at him closely. His blue eyes were steady, strong.

'I mean the more I thought about it, the more I thought Gabríel Örn deserved to die. He was a nasty man. He treated you like shit.'

'That's not a good enough reason to murder him,' Harpa said.

'Maybe not, but ruining our country is. People like Gabríel Örn have destroyed Iceland and the people in it. The strong, hard-working honest Icelanders like me, and the thousands like me. You know how hard I worked to build up my fishing business. Why should I lose it all? Why should thousands like me lose it all? Farmers losing their farms, shopkeepers losing their shops, and yes, fishermen losing their boats. Young families losing their houses. You remember Sindri talking about his brother that night after the demo?'

Harpa shook his head.

'Well, his brother lost his farm to the bank in the end. And killed himself. And now the brother's wife and kids will have no home and no job. These people have worked hard all their lives. It's not their fault! And it hasn't even really started yet. They say unemployment will go up. We're going to be a nation of paupers for decades. Because of people like Gabríel Örn.'

'But it's not just Gabríel Örn's fault, is it?' said Harpa.

'Precisely!' said Björn, and he struck the table with the flat of his hand. 'What do they say, there are thirty people who destroyed Iceland?'

'People like Óskar?'

'Yes.'

'And Julian Lister?'

'Yes.'

Harpa frowned. 'You're crazy. You're all crazy.'

'Are we? Sure, the Icelanders protest, but they don't actually *do* anything. When the Americans start a war on terror, they take out a couple of countries and kill tens of thousands of people. We should be waging war against these guys. And we're only talking about four people.'

'Four?' Harpa counted them off on her fingers. 'Gabríel Örn, Óskar, Julian Lister... who's the other?'

Björn shook his head.

'So Frikki was right. One more to go?'

Björn didn't answer.

A tear leaked from Harpa's eye. 'I don't understand you, Björn. I mean Sindri, I do understand. He has always said he believes in violence. He's deluded himself into practising what he preaches. But you? You are one of the most practical men I know.'

'That's what I thought,' said Björn. 'But I've learned a lot over the last year.'

'Such as?'

'Such as that people like my father and Sindri are right. They always said that capitalism hurts real people, people who work and save. It's a tool for the rich to screw the rest of us. I can see now how that is blindingly obvious. But I never listened to my father. I thought he was a dinosaur from the wrong side in the Cold War. I believed in the Independence Party, that capitalism meant people like me could work hard to build a business. Boy was I wrong. But at least I realize it now. At least I am going to do something about it.'

'Like kill some people?'

'Harpa.' Björn reached across the table for Harpa's hand. She drew back from him. 'Harpa, you've suffered almost as badly. You lost your job. Your father lost his savings. Gabríel Örn treated you badly, as did Óskar. Don't you see we're the good guys here?'

'You are a murderer, Björn. OK, you didn't pull the trigger yourself, but you are a murderer.' Her eyes widened. 'Wait a minute! Did you pick Óskar because of me? Did you know he was Markús's father?'

'The police only told me that on Sunday. But yes, when we were talking about which bank boss to go for, Óðinsbanki seemed a good choice to me.'

'So you killed him on my account?'

'Yours, mine and every other ordinary person in Iceland.'

Harpa pursed her lips. Anger flared through the couple of tears that had gathered in tiny pools around her eyes. 'So what are you doing with me? Holding me prisoner?'

'I'd like you to stay here for the next twenty-four hours.'

'Until the next guy on the list is shot?'

Björn shrugged.

'And what happens after that?'

Björn sighed. 'I think it's inevitable they catch us. The others think there's going to be a revolution, but I don't know. It's just not the way the Icelanders do things. So I guess I'm going to jail.'

For a moment Harpa almost felt sorry for him. But only for a moment. 'You deserve to,' she said.

'Maybe. Perhaps I should pay for what I've done; I knew the consequences when I did it. I will just have to accept them.' His voice was calm.

'Perhaps you should.'

'One more day, and then it won't matter. The others think they've still got a chance. I'd like you to keep quiet for a couple of days, until the police have caught us. Then you can say what you like. I'll make sure you aren't implicated in any of this.'

'You're mad if you think I would go along with that.'

'Please, Harpa,' Björn said. 'For my sake.'

Harpa glared at him. 'You make me sick,' she said. 'Now give me my phone and let me make a call.'

'No,' said Björn.

'In that case, I'm leaving now,' Harpa said, pulling herself to her feet.

'You have to stay in the hut,' said Björn.

'No, I don't,' said Harpa. 'Are you going to stop me?'

She walked a couple of paces towards the door. Björn leapt to his feet, grabbed her from behind, twisted her around and pinned her to the floor. Harpa screamed and kicked. Björn stretched out and grabbed the length of rope that was lying on a chair.

He wrapped it around her body, pinning her arms to her sides, and tied a firm knot. Harpa screamed louder as she writhed against the rope. Björn left her on the floor and stood by the cooker watching her.

'I hate you, Björn!' Harpa yelled. 'I hate you!'

The screams were muffled by the walls of the hut and the mist outside, so by the time they reached the rocky slopes of the valley they were scarcely powerful enough to create an echo.

CHAPTER THIRTY-THREE

MAGNUS WOKE UP thinking about Ingileif. Or rather he didn't know *what* to think about Ingileif.

Her accusation that he was jealous of her, that he suspected her of seeing other men, was ironic. In Magnus's previous relationship, with Colby, the lawyer in Boston, he was always the one who was being controlled. Colby wanted to regularize the relationship, to get married, to send Magnus off to law school. He was relieved to get away from that, and indeed that was one of the many things that attracted him to Ingileif. She was independent, she did what she wanted, and she allowed him to be the same way.

So if she went off to parties with her beautiful friends, what business was that of his?

Except he didn't like the idea of her sleeping with other men. And he wasn't even sure whether her anger with him was because she did occasionally do that and she thought it none of his business, or because he didn't know her well enough to trust her to stay away from other men.

Which all showed she had a point. He didn't really know her.

She wanted to go to Germany. He was likely to be sent back to the States. It was fun while it lasted, but it was over. Face it. Move on.

But rather than be braced by this thought, it depressed him.

Ingileif was part of the life he was building in Iceland. Unpredictable, beautiful, untameable.

Mind you, he had been right to be angry at her. A defence lawyer in the States would run rings around a prosecution if they ever found out what she had done. Iceland had a less adversarial system, it would be a judge who would question the evidence and how it had been obtained. But if the whole case collapsed because of Ingileif's activities, Magnus would be buying a one-way ticket back to Boston.

Yet she had found out something. There was to be another victim: Ingólfur Arnarson.

There was a slight chance that this might be the target's real name, a very slight chance. Much more likely it was a codename.

Ingólfur Arnarson was famous as the first settler in Iceland. He had sailed there from Norway in 874, and as he approached the island he had cast his wooden 'home pillars' into the sea, vowing to settle wherever they washed up. It took three years for his slaves to find them, but eventually they were discovered in a smoky bay, Reykjavík: *reykur* meaning smoke and *vík* bay. A fine statue of the Viking stood on a mound downtown.

The question was, who did the name Ingólfur Arnarson represent in the twenty-first century?

There were a number of obvious candidates. The young men who had built up business empires overseas in the previous decade were known in Iceland as *útrásarvíkingar* – literally 'Outvasion Vikings'. They recalled the great Vikings who had set forth from Norway a thousand years before to use their youth, vitality and aggression to make their fortunes. Men like Ingólfur Arnarson.

And like Óskar Gunnarsson. As he himself had recognized by commissioning the sculpture of a Viking riding a Harley Davidson in the lobby of his family office.

The trouble was there were several other candidates for Ingólfur. But which one did Sindri have in mind?

People would have to be warned, which meant that Magnus was going to have to admit how he came upon the information. He could imagine Baldur's ridicule, quite justified, of Magnus's investigative techniques. For a moment Magnus thought about claiming that the information came from a confidential informant. But that wouldn't wash.

He made himself a cup of coffee and called Vigdís at the station. She had just got in. He told her what Ingileif had been up to the previous night.

'Impressive work,' said Vigdís. 'Unconventional.'

'Damn stupid, if you ask me,' said Magnus.

'And probably if you ask Baldur,' said Vigdís. 'But at least we know for sure Sindri is involved.'

'Any ideas who Ingólfur Arnarson might be?' Magnus asked. He outlined his own view that it might be one of the Outvaders.

'I think you are right,' said Vigdís. 'I don't know whether one of them is more like Ingólfur than any of the others. I don't know them well enough, they all seem like a bunch of greedy fat cats to me. The Special Prosecutor might have an idea.'

'Yes, I remember him talking to me about them. Or there's Óskar's sister Emilía,' said Magnus. 'She probably knows them all personally. Find out what she thinks.'

'OK. We should also go through the phone book, just in case. There are bound to be some people whose real name is Ingólfur Arnarson.'

'Worth checking. And you could ask Frikki when you speak to him again this morning. Let's hope he's more talkative after his night in the cells.'

'We're going to have to tell Baldur,' said Vigdís. 'These people are in danger. Or at least one of them is. And we don't know which one.'

'Leave it with me,' said Magnus.

'Before you go, I saw Björn's brother yesterday. He was in Tenerife for a week with his girlfriend, came back Monday. Iceland Express confirms it. They both flew out, they both flew back.'

'Well, that pretty much rules him out,' said Magnus. 'Speak to you later.'

He took a deep breath and called Baldur. He told him about Ingileif, Sindri and Ingólfur Arnarson. He got the ridicule he expected, but not for the reason he expected it.

'Do you really think I'm going to take any notice of this information?' Baldur asked.

'Well, yes,' said Magnus. 'We need to warn all the Outvaders we can find. Their lives might be in danger.'

'These are still some of the most important people in the country. And you want me to put them on high alert on the basis of the ravings of a drunken fantasist trying to get a woman into bed?'

'He's not necessarily a fantasist,' said Magnus.

'Oh yes he is,' said Baldur. 'We've been watching Sindri on and off for at least a decade. He talks big, but he doesn't *do* anything. People like Sindri never *do* anything. And when they get drunk they just talk bigger.'

'So you think that Sindri was just boasting?'

'Show me evidence that he wasn't.'

'We saw him with Björn and Harpa at the demonstrations in January.'

'Which proves nothing.'

'All right,' said Magnus. He had been reluctant to make the phone call in the first place. If Baldur didn't want to respond to it, there was nothing much more Magnus could do.

Perhaps Vigdís would get something out of the kid.

Sophie sat at the back of the small lecture theatre. European Human Rights. She had no idea what the lecturer was saying, her concentration had wandered within the first minute.

The seat next to her was empty. It was usually where Zak sat, but Zak was... Zak was where, exactly? She had no idea.

She had scarcely slept all night. She had called his mobile and texted him at regular intervals without reply, and then, first thing in the morning, she had called his home number.

His mother had answered. To the polite question 'how are you?' the woman had answered, 'fine'. She wasn't supposed to be fine, she was supposed to be dying, but maybe she was just being polite in return. But when Sophie had asked to speak to Ísak, she was told he had disappeared on a camping trip.

Then his mother had asked whether there was anything wrong with Ísak, and Sophie had answered, truthfully, 'I don't know.'

Sophie was worried about what Josh had said the night before about Zak asking about Julian Lister's holiday arrangements. That was very strange: she could think of no plausible explanation. She knew that Zak hadn't actually shot the ex-Chancellor himself, he was at home in London on Sunday. Although he *had* gone to church that day. And Sophie knew for a fact that Zak didn't believe in God.

Something was up. All her instincts were screaming at her that something was up.

But what? Sophie couldn't really believe that Zak was a terrorist, or part of a conspiracy of terrorists. In which case why not call the police with her suspicions? Let them clear him. She had the card that the policewoman had left Zak in her jeans pocket.

Because it would be disloyal, that was why. She would never be able to look Zak in the eye again.

Josh was sitting at the front of the lecture theatre, typing away on his laptop. Really taking notes, probably, he didn't look like a Facebook surfing type.

He was a bright guy, if a little overenthusiastic. Sophie scarcely knew him – she remembered some perceptive questions he had asked in that class, and some that were a little out there.

She had an idea.

When, finally, the lecture finished, Sophie was one of the first through the exit, which was at the back of the theatre by her seat. She loitered, waiting to pounce. Josh was the third to last out.

'Josh!'

'Oh, hi. Sophie, isn't it?' He shrank back a little.

'Can I have a quick chat about something?'

'If it's about what I said about your boyfriend last night, I'm sorry. I didn't realize. I'm sure I was wrong.'

'It is about that,' said Sophie. 'And quite frankly I don't know whether you are wrong or right. But, well, if Zak really did ask you the questions you say he did about Lister, then I think you should tell the police.'

'I'm sure he didn't mean anything,' said Josh.

'Listen to me, Josh,' Sophie said, looking straight into his eyes. 'I'm not at all sure of that. Do you understand me? You might be right, I just don't know. Here's the number of a policewoman who interviewed Zak a couple of days ago. If you're still suspicious, call her. OK?'

'OK,' said Josh, staring at the card Sophie had handed him.

He let her go first, and then ambled into Clare Market in the heart of the tight cluster of buildings that made up the London School of Economics, pulled out his phone and dialled the number. Detective Sergeant Piper didn't answer, but he left a message.

Josh was always having outlandish theories but none of them ever turned out to be true. Could that really be about to change?

Magnus walked the short distance to Ingileif's gallery. It was on Skólavördustígur, a short road that led up the hill from Laugavegur directly to the scaffolding-clad sweeping spire of the Hallgrímskirkja. The street was lined with galleries and art shops, although since the arrival of the *kreppa* quite a few had closed. Ingileif's gallery had survived, just. She owned it with five partners, all female artists of one kind or another. They sold paintings, jewellery, some furniture, fish-skin bags designed by Ingileif herself, lava candle-holders and some small items of furniture. All high-end expensive stuff.

As Magnus walked past the window, he saw her staring outside, an empty expression on her face. Even though she was looking straight at him, she didn't seem to see him. It was only when he walked through the door that she noticed him.

She smiled quickly and briefly. He held her. After a few seconds they broke apart. She turned away from him, moving towards the back of the gallery, putting a little distance between them.

'I'm sorry I stormed out on you last night,' Ingileif said. 'I was pretty drunk.'

'I could tell.'

'But why don't you *trust* me, Magnús?'

'I do.'

'No, you don't,' Ingileif said. Pink spots appeared on her pale cheeks, a sure sign that she was either angry or embarrassed. Magnus guessed angry. 'Admit it, you don't trust me.'

'I do,' Magnus said. 'I didn't last night, but I do now.'

'Why now? What's changed? Magnús, I did it all for you, don't you see that? Do you think I enjoyed listening to that fat old man droning on for hours on end? Do you think I actually wanted to sleep with him? I was trying to help you out. I thought you'd be pleased with me, instead of which you are upset because I didn't stick to the rules and you think I enjoy seducing old men. I'm sorry, but if you think that, there isn't much of a future for us.'

Magnus sighed. 'I don't think that, Ingileif. You're right, I got the wrong end of the stick. I didn't understand what you were doing. And it's true I don't completely understand you. That's one of the reasons why I love you.'

Ingileif's grey eyes searched Magnus's. He didn't know whether they found what they were looking for.

'I think I'm going to go to Germany, Magnús.'

Magnus was about to say, 'don't do that,' when he stopped himself. He couldn't stop her: she could do what she wanted. 'That would be a shame.'

'You said there's a good chance you'll be going back to the States. Why should I stay for you if you won't stay for me?'

Magnus nodded. 'That's true.'

'Well, then?' Ingileif's expression softened. 'It's not just you, Magnús. I should go. It would be a good opportunity for me. And it would be good to get away from this country for a bit. That stuff earlier this year with Agnar's murder, all the things I learned about my father, my brother, I need to put that behind me.'

'I thought I helped you with that,' Magnus said.

'I thought so too. But part of me holds you responsible for it. It's not fair, but it's true. I need to leave, Magnús.'

Magnus looked at Ingileif. The familiar grey eyes, the little nick above her left eyebrow, the smaller scar on her cheek. He had been lucky to know her, to love her even. But he couldn't control her. He couldn't keep her, he shouldn't keep her. Why should someone like her stay just for him?

'Do what you have to do,' he said. And he turned and left the gallery.

Ísak walked out of the small shop with a plastic bag full of half a dozen items: bits and pieces of fishing tackle and a sharp knife that one could use for gutting a fish.

Or for something else.

The other items were just cover: to make it less likely that the shopkeeper would take note of a stranger coming into town to buy a knife, and just a knife.

His phone beeped. He pulled it out. A text message from Sophie asking where he was. He had no intention of replying. A shame about Sophie. She was cute but that relationship had no future. She would figure out eventually what he was up to, and she was too much of a good girl not to tell someone.

The back of his mother's Honda was filled with his parents' camping equipment. Ísak had parked it under the rocky outcrop upon which the church at Borgarnes stood. The town was about a third of the way between Reykjavík and Grundarfjördur. He pulled out a map and examined it.

Björn had talked about a hut on a mountain pass behind Grundarfjördur. Grundarfjördur was on the north coast of the Snaefells Peninsula, the backbone of which was a range of mountains. There was no pass directly to the south of Grundarfjördur, but there were two candidates a little further away, one to the east and one to the west. Ísak would check these first.

He felt tense and strangely excited. Gabríel Örn's death had genuinely shocked him. But over time he had got used to the idea, and his anger with the Icelandic establishment, including his father, had grown. When he, Björn and Sindri had met that summer to talk about taking things further, intellectually he had been all for it. But, like the other two, he hadn't been ready to pull the trigger himself. They had found someone else to do that.

But now, after Óskar and Julian Lister, Ísak was ready to do the deed himself.

And there was no doubt in his mind Harpa had to be killed.

He had spent so long reading and arguing about ideas such as 'the end justifies the means', and 'the vanguard of the people', it was exciting to find himself actually living by those precepts. Lenin, Trotsky, Castro, Che Guevara, they had all begun their careers like him, young intellectuals with ideas and enthusiasm but no experience of violence. And then at some point ideas had become action. That point for him was now.

He knew Björn had given up hope of getting away with it, and he suspected that Sindri had too, but he still thought there was a good chance that they might escape prosecution. None of the three of them had actually killed anyone and there was no evidence suggesting they had. Conspiracy would be much harder to prove, especially if the police had no idea who had actually been pulling the trigger. Which Ísak was pretty sure they didn't.

Sindri was naïve hoping that the time of revolution was now. It would come, it might take years, but civil society would eventually break down under the weight of the contradictions of capitalism. And when it did, Ísak would be ready for it. He would spend the coming years building up an elite cadre of revolutionaries, a true vanguard of the proletariat who would be able to lead people like Björn to a better world.

It would come. He was young. He could be patient.

Everything would be fine as long as they all stayed quiet. He thought he could trust Björn and Sindri to do that. But not Harpa. Harpa would talk.

He would have to be careful. Killing Harpa would of course lead to its own inquiry and he would be a prime suspect. He would have to be sure not to leave any forensic evidence in the Honda. It would be important to dispose of the body miles away from Grundarfjördur, or anywhere he had been seen.

He wouldn't be able to set up a perfect alibi, but he had spent the previous night in a small campsite just outside Reykjavík on the road to the south-east, taking care to give the owner his name. He had got up early that morning and doubled back, driving north. Once Harpa was out of the way, he planned to drive across Iceland, through the night if necessary. If he was seen camping in Thórsmörk, well to the east of Reykjavík, the morning after Harpa's death, the police might believe that he had spent the whole time in the area.

Ísak trusted his own intelligence. He would be able to figure it out.

CHAPTER THIRTY-FOUR

VIGDÍS LOOKED AT the nineteen-year-old boy opposite her. His eyes were rimmed with red and he looked miserable.

He hadn't talked after his night in the cells, and Vigdís was surprised. She had done her best to coax something out of him, to make him feel good about confessing to whatever he wanted to confess to. She had mentioned Gabríel Örn, Sindri, Björn and Harpa. Nothing.

Ingólfur Arnarson. Nothing.

Then Árni had tried. His histrionics, including a bit of shouting at Frikki and banging on the table had been, quite frankly, embarrassing. For a moment Vigdís thought that she had exchanged a half-smile of amusement with Frikki, but then it was gone. She fervently hoped that they wouldn't have to play back the videotape. There was no doubt about it: Árni watched too much TV.

There was a knock at the door and one of the duty constables from the front desk appeared. 'Vigdís? There's someone to see you.'

Vigdís left Árni to it and followed the constable into an adjoining interview room. There sat a dark-haired woman of about twenty.

'I am Magda, Frikki's girlfriend,' she said in English.

Vigdís remembered that Árni had mentioned a girlfriend when he had picked Frikki up from his mother's house. 'Do you speak Icelandic?' Vigdís asked.

'A little. Can I talk to him?'

311

'I'm afraid not. We are interviewing him in relation to a very serious incident.'

'Please. Just for five minutes.'

Vigdís shook her head. 'I'm sorry. But perhaps you can help. Do you know anything about the death of Gabríel Örn in January this year?'

Magda shook her head. 'I was in Poland then.'

'Has Frikki spoken to you about it?'

Magda hesitated. There was silence in the small interview room. Vigdís waited. She could almost see the wheels turning in Magda's head as she tried to come to a decision.

'Yes,' she said. 'Yes, he has. But it is better if he talks to you directly about it.'

'I agree,' said Vigdís. 'But he won't.'

'Let me talk to him, then,' said Magda. 'Alone.'

Vigdís considered it. As a rule, it was best to keep witnesses separate, pin down the differences in stories, prevent them from conferring. But this case was different. She nodded.

Ten minutes later Magda knocked on the door of the interview room. Vigdís opened it.

'Frikki wants to talk,' Magda said.

Vigdís was sitting at a table at the back of the coffee shop on Hverfisgata, just a few metres from the police station. At moments like this, outside the police station, Magnus had trouble remembering she was Icelandic and not American. An attractive black woman in jeans and a fleece, she could easily be one of the detectives from the Boston Police Department.

After seeing Ingileif he had walked the streets aimlessly. He had nowhere to go: he couldn't face the classroom at the police college, and it was clear Baldur wouldn't welcome him at the station. His thoughts bounced between Ingileif and the Óskar Gunnarsson case. Both depressed him. He came up with no great ideas about either problem.

There seemed an inevitability about Ingileif's decision. The case involving her father's death in the 1990s had been very painful for her. Although it had brought Magnus and her together, he could see how she associated him with it. He could understand how she might want to run away. Start again somewhere new. She was doing what she felt she had to do.

But the Óskar Gunnarsson case was different. Although he had been sidelined, he was confident that he was right.

And he could never let a case go.

So when Vigdís had called him on his cell phone, he had hurried to the café.

'What have you got?' he asked her.

'Frikki talked.'

'The night in the cells did its stuff?'

'More his girlfriend. She persuaded him.'

'And?'

'And you were right. Gabríel Örn's death wasn't suicide.'

'Who killed him? Björn?'

'Possibly Frikki. Probably Harpa.' Vigdís explained everything that Frikki had told her. About the night in January. The drinking at Sindri's flat. Harpa calling Gabríel Örn, tempting him out. The scuffle, Harpa hitting him over the head. And the plan to cover everything up, a plan which Frikki had little directly to do with.

'Got them!' said Magnus in triumph. 'What about Óskar? And Lister?'

'Frikki didn't know anything about them,' Vigdís said. 'He suspects something, much as we do, but he has no evidence.'

'Any clue about the identity of Ingólfur Arnarson?'

'He has never heard of him. We checked the phone directory, by the way. There are a dozen real Ingólfur Arnarsons listed. Róbert is checking them out now.' Róbert was another detective in the Violent Crimes Unit.

'Has Frikki seen any of the others since Gabríel Örn's death?'

'Only Harpa. He bumped into her in the bakery in Seltjarnarnes.

He told her his theory that Sindri and Björn might have shot Óskar and the British Chancellor. She wasn't impressed.'

'Meaning she's involved?'

'Frikki didn't think so. Neither did his girlfriend, for what it's worth.'

'So are you arresting them now?'

'Baldur's dithering. He's in with Thorkell discussing it.'

'But surely there's a case for murder here? Or manslaughter at the very least. Baldur can't hide from that.'

'Yes, the Gabríel Örn case will definitely have to be reopened. But there's also the question of whether you were right all along. Whether there is a link with the Óskar investigation.'

'We can't prove that until we get the ID on Ísak from London,' said Magnus. 'But we should get these people in custody right away. Before anyone else gets killed.'

'Maybe,' said Vigdís. 'Look, I've got to get back. If they do take a decision to make some arrests, they'll be looking for me.'

'Yes, of course,' Magnus said. 'Well done, Vigdís. And thanks for keeping me in the loop.'

Magnus finished his coffee as Vigdís left the café, leaving hers untouched. He smiled to himself. It felt good to be vindicated, there was no denying it. And he was absolutely sure now that there was a link between this little group and the recent shootings.

His phone rang. Sharon Piper.

He picked it up. 'Hey, Sharon. Ísak's ID come through?'

'Soon,' said Sharon. 'The witness's husband has been in touch with his office and we've just e-mailed the photo to him. We haven't heard back from his wife yet.'

'Why the hell not? Tell her to pull her finger out. It's important.'

'Steady on, Magnus, hold your horses. There is some news from Normandy.'

'Oh, yes?'

'A girl in a bakery in a village a few kilometres from where Lister was shot served a customer the morning before the shooting.

He was wearing a light blue jacket and he drove a motorbike with Dutch licence plates.'

'The same guy the farmer saw?'

'Sounds like it.'

'Did she give a better description?'

'Yes. But the really interesting thing is the coin the man gave her for change. At first she thought it was twenty cents, but then it turned out to be something else.'

'Let me guess. Icelandic krónur?'

'You're right. A fifty-krónur piece.'

'Jesus. So what's the description?'

'Good-looking guy. Dark hair, unshaven. Blue eyes. Slim but strong. About thirty, thirty-five. Fairly tall, maybe one metre eighty-five. That's about six-foot one.'

'I know.'

'It's not Ísak,' said Sharon. 'But is it Harpa's boyfriend, Björn?'

'Could well be,' said Magnus. 'The description fits.'

'OK, I'll tell SO15 that.'

'SO15?'

'The Counter Terrorism Command. There's a lot of people getting very excited over here. I think your guys are going to hear from our people pretty soon. Or from the French. Can you send over a photo of Björn?'

'Yeah. Maybe.' Magnus thought it through. 'I'm technically off the case and out of the police station. The Icelanders are going to be real sensitive about this. You know what cross-border co-operation can be like once things get political.'

A year before, in Boston, Magnus had been investigating a case involving a Canadian citizen in Montreal. The RCMP had been much less helpful than usual. The Canadians had taken exception to their informal help in another case leading to a terrorist suspect being arrested and taken to Guantánamo Bay. Since then everything had had to go through official channels. A pain, but Magnus could see their point.

'Your guy can expect to hear from someone shortly,' said Sharon.

'Thanks, Sharon.'

So it was Björn who went to Normandy. Via Amsterdam, probably. Hired a motorcycle there, or stole one. Or borrowed one. Got hold of a rifle. Drove to Normandy and buried it.

And it had been Ísak who had done similar legwork in London. Located Óskar's address. Perhaps got hold of the gun, the motorbike.

But for whom? Neither of them had shot anybody. Nor had Sindri: he was in Iceland the whole time. There was someone else. Someone who could use a gun, who wasn't afraid of killing, but who wasn't able to make his own preparations. Perhaps wasn't well travelled enough. Perhaps didn't speak English.

Who could it be? Magnus had no idea.

It should be straightforward to check whether Björn flew to Amsterdam the previous week, though.

Magnus had to see Baldur right away. He hurried out of the café and into the police headquarters.

'Where's Baldur?' he asked Vigdís.

'With the Commissioner. I think Thorkell is in there too. They are discussing whether to arrest Björn and Sindri.'

'I've got to see him.'

'I don't know how long he'll be.'

'Then I'll interrupt him. Árni, check and see whether Björn was on any flight to Amsterdam last Thursday and Friday, and if he came back to Reykjavík on Saturday.'

'What's happened?'

'He's the guy the farmer saw the day before Lister was shot. The Dutch guy. Except he wasn't Dutch, he had Icelandic coins in his pocket. Vigdís, come with me. I may need your help.'

Magnus noticed a thin file on his desk. He glanced at it. The pathologist's report on Benedikt Jóhannesson's murder. He left it there and headed for the door.

The Commissioner's office was only a couple of hundred metres away, over a busy intersection in a modern building on the road that overlooked the bay. On the way, Magnus told Vigdís more about Sharon's call.

They were dodging through the traffic when Magnus felt his phone vibrate. He took a quick look. Sharon Piper.

'Hi, Sharon.'

'Things are really hotting up. Just got a call from a student at the LSE, a friend of Ísak's. This student was a research assistant for a junior treasury minister over the summer. Anyway, Ísak asked him over the summer if he knew where Julian Lister went on holiday. The student thought it a little strange at the time, but he told him about the place in Normandy.'

'Jeez. Are you arresting Ísak?'

'I expect so. Haven't told SO15 yet, I thought I'd give you a heads-up first. They are going to go crazy over there. Oh, and we finally got the ID through from the French woman in India. It *was* Ísak she saw asking for Óskar's address.'

'Big surprise. Thanks, Sharon. Before you go, I've been thinking. Seems to me that Ísak and Björn were both acting as point men for someone else. The guy who actually pulled the trigger. Ísak in Kensington and Björn in Normandy.'

'Who's the guy?'

'No idea. But I bet he's an Icelander. And I'd guess one who doesn't speak English.'

'Worth a thought. I've got to go now, Magnus.'

Magnus hung up and ran into the Commissioner's office building. The Commissioner's office itself was guarded by a secretary. As she picked up the phone to tell her boss about Magnus, he pushed past her and burst in, Vigdís trailing behind.

There were four people in the office: Baldur, Thorkell, the Police Commissioner and a silver-haired man whom Magnus recognized as the Prosecutor, the senior lawyer within the Police Department.

Snorri Gudmundsson glared at Magnus as he entered. 'What the hell do you think you are doing?'

'I've had a call from London. Björn Helgason has been identified in Normandy the day before Julian Lister was shot. And Ísak Samúelsson asked an intern who worked in the British treasury about Lister's vacation plans. I'm sorry to barge in, but

I thought you ought to know before the British police call. Or the French.'

Snorri breathed in. Thought for a moment. 'Is it a firm ID of Björn?'

'Not yet. But it will be once we send a photograph.'

'You can't be sure of that,' said Baldur.

Snorri raised his hand to quieten his inspector. 'This changes things. Baldur, I want Björn and Sindri arrested immediately. And Harpa Einarsdóttir.'

'On what charge?' said Baldur.

'Gabríel Örn's murder for now,' said Snorri. 'Once they are in custody we'll see if we can expand it to the other two cases. I need to be up to speed for when the British call. Magnús, you stay here.'

Magnus stayed as Baldur left with Vigdís. He took Baldur's chair. Thorkell and the Prosecutor were listening closely.

'OK, Magnús. If there was a conspiracy to shoot Óskar and Lister, and I emphasize the word *if*, what does it look like?'

'Assuming Frikki's story is correct, a group of five of them all met at the demonstration in January. That's Sindri, Björn, Harpa, Ísak and Frikki. At that stage they were all strangers and they were all fired up over the *kreppa* and who caused it. They drank a lot, Harpa lured out her ex-boyfriend Gabríel Örn, they beat him up and killed him. Probably accidentally, but we need to establish that. They planned a cover-up to dress up the death as suicide. That worked.'

Snorri was listening closely.

'Now, later, we don't know when, some of them got together and decided to take things further. Having killed once, they wanted to kill again, once again people they thought were responsible. Óskar Gunnarsson. And Julian Lister.'

'So who was involved at this stage?'

'Of the original five, probably just Björn, Sindri and Ísak, who was in London. But I'm convinced that another conspirator joined them. The guy who actually pulled the trigger.'

'And who is that?'

'We have no idea. My bet is that he's an Icelander who doesn't speak any foreign languages, but that's just a guess. Ísak speaks English, I wouldn't be surprised if Björn does too, and I think they prepared both hits.'

'And is it just the two targets?'

'I think there's another. A, um, contact of mine spoke to Sindri.'

'By contact you mean girlfriend?' said Snorri. 'Baldur told me.'

'Yes,' Magnus admitted. 'They were both drunk, but Sindri suggested that there is another target, someone he called Ingólfur Arnarson.'

'The first settler?'

'I thought one of the Viking Outvaders.'

'I see what you mean.'

'And even if we pick up Björn and Sindri, the assassin, whoever he is, will still be at large. So they are in danger.'

'You think we should warn the Outvaders?'

'I do.'

'Which ones?'

'All of them. Or at least the highest profile ones.'

Snorri blew through his cheeks as he thought through the consequences of all this. 'These men are terrorists. Icelandic terrorists.'

Magnus could see the impending national shame. 'Seems to me they are criminals,' he said. 'A bunch of three or four individuals, not a political movement. We're talking nutters here, not terrorists.'

Snorri gave him half a smile. 'Maybe. But if we are not very careful this is going to get caught up in the Icesave negotiations.'

'We don't have to cooperate with the British,' said the Prosecutor. 'We could force them to make a formal application for assistance. And of course the Lister shooting is in French jurisdiction.'

'We should cooperate,' said the Commissioner. 'Magnús, leave the politics to me, I'm going to have to speak to the minister. For now help Baldur arrest these people and find out who their accomplice is. The man who pulls the trigger.'

Snorri's phone rang. He answered it. It was his secretary. 'Put him through,' he said. He switched to English. 'Good morning, Chief Superintendent Watts. How can I help you?'

CHAPTER THIRTY-FIVE

WHEN MAGNUS GOT back to the Violent Crimes Unit, Baldur had the whole team in a meeting. Magnus strode into the conference room and took a seat. Baldur acknowledged his presence with a quick flick of his eyes.

'Árni, I want you to arrest Harpa,' the inspector commanded. 'Do you know where to find her?'

'She'll be at the bakery, I expect. Or her home. I have both addresses.'

'Vigdís. Take a couple of uniformed police officers and arrest Sindri. Magnús, you've been in touch with the Grundarfjördur police?'

Magnus nodded.

'Get them to arrest Björn right away. And bring him down to the station here.'

'I got a result from Icelandair,' Árni interrupted.

'And?'

'Björn was on a flight from Reykjavík to Amsterdam on Friday. Returned on a flight Saturday evening.'

'In time to get back to Grundarfjördur for Sunday when I saw him,' said Magnus.

'And when Julian Lister was shot,' said Baldur. 'Sounds like he *was* preparing the ground for someone else.'

'What about Ísak?' Magnus asked.

'Aren't the British arresting him now?'

'Probably,' said Magnus. 'Shall I call them to make sure?'

Baldur thought a moment. 'No. Better to leave all communications with the British police to the Commissioner from now on. This could get delicate.'

Magnus understood that.

'OK, everyone move,' Baldur said. 'And when you get them all back here, we'll start asking them questions. Like who is Ingólfur Arnarson?'

'We need to warn the Outvaders,' Magnus said.

'I'll talk to the Commissioner and Thorkell about that,' said Baldur.

'Do you mind if I interview Sindri?' Magnus asked Baldur after everyone else had left the conference room.

'I'll do that with Vigdís. I'd like you to be available, though.'

'Be available?' Magnus was frustrated. He knew Baldur was the boss, but Magnus was the one who had the case clearest in his mind.

'Look, Magnús. We all have a lot to do. You can start by getting in touch with Grundarfjördur.'

Magnus went back to his desk and called Constable Páll, telling him to arrest Björn for the murder of Gabríel Örn Bergsson and bring him to police headquarters in Reykjavík as soon as he could. Magnus got the impression that Páll had been expecting his call. He was a good man: Magnus was sure he could trust him to arrest his friend.

Magnus struggled to control his impatience. Vigdís called in to say that they had found Sindri at his home and he was coming quietly. Then Baldur appeared at Magnus's desk.

'Árni called. Harpa wasn't at the bakery. She left with Björn yesterday afternoon and didn't show up for work today. No one answered at home and her mobile is switched off.'

'How did she seem when she was with Björn?'

'I don't know,' said Baldur. 'Árni is checking her house now.'

'She's got a small kid,' said Magnus. 'Three years old, I think. Árni should look for the kid. Whoever has the kid may know where Harpa is.'

Baldur bit back his frustration. It was obvious he didn't like taking instructions from Magnus. But it was a good point.

Magnus called Páll back.

'Páll, it's Magnús. Apparently Björn was with Harpa in Reykjavík yesterday afternoon. They left together.'

'Right,' said Páll. 'He's not at his house, I've just checked. But I'm talking to the next-door neighbour now. I think she saw something. I'll call you right back.'

Magnus drummed his fingers. The Benedikt Jóhannesson pathologist's report caught his eye. He would look at that later, when he could concentrate on it.

It was only five minutes before Páll called back but it seemed much longer.

'The neighbour saw Björn come back home yesterday evening. About six o'clock. He was driving his pickup. She saw him as she was getting out of her own car. She remembers it because she saw his girlfriend fast asleep in the front seat.'

'Asleep?'

'That's what she said.'

'And she recognized Harpa?'

'Yes. Dark curly hair. She's seen her around a couple of times. Her kitchen looks out over Björn's driveway and she saw Björn putting stuff in the pickup. He drove off about a quarter of an hour later.'

'What sort of stuff?'

'Food. A sleeping bag. She assumed they were going off on a camping trip together. She didn't actually see a tent, but then she wasn't watching Björn's every move.'

'She was pretty close,' said Magnus. 'Thank God for nosy neighbours.' He thought quickly. 'OK, see if you can find him. Your regional HQ is Stykkishólmur, right?'

'Yes.'

'I'll get people here to talk to your superintendent.'

Magnus considered what to do. The inactivity here was killing him. He'd love to have a go at Sindri himself, but he knew it would be very frustrating to be second fiddle to Baldur. Or third fiddle. He might not even be allowed into the interview room.

And if Sindri had any sense he wouldn't say anything, especially if there was another target. Harpa was the only one who would talk. And she was with Björn.

All Magnus's instincts told him to go to Grundarfjördur.

'Páll, I'll be with you in a couple of hours.'

He hesitated a moment, grabbed the Benedikt Jóhannesson file, and headed for the door.

Árni drove up the narrow street of Bakkavör, one of Reykjavík's most exclusive, leading up from the western shore of Seltjarnarnes. The houses were much less grand than the rich people's homes he had seen in America, and indeed to an American eye they were nothing special, but in Reykjavík, a city of small, unpretentious, wind-battered dwellings, they were something.

The street was split into two. On one side, the houses were bigger, the sea views slightly better. Many of these properties belonged to the newly wealthy, including the owners of a multi-national food company which they had named 'Bakkavör'. On the other side of the street were slightly more modest homes, with the view of the sea partially hidden. Many of these were owned by the quota kings.

Árni stopped outside one of these and rang the bell.

The door was answered by an older and plumper version of Harpa.

'Good morning,' Árni said. 'My name is Árni and I am with the Metropolitan Police. I am looking for Harpa.'

'Oh, hello. Come in,' the woman said frowning. As Árni took off his shoes he saw Harpa's son staring at him. There was an unmistakeable resemblance to the late Óskar Gunnarsson.

Harpa's mother, whose name was Gudný, led Árni into the kitchen. Her grandson disappeared into a living room.

'Has something happened to her?' Gudný asked.

'No,' said Árni. He almost added, 'at least we don't think so,' but thought better of it. 'Do you know where she is?'

'She's gone off with Björn, her boyfriend.'

'Oh, I see. And do you know *where* she has gone?'

'Is she in trouble?'

'We just need her help with an inquiry. The death of Gabríel Örn Bergsson.'

'Oh, that.' The frowned deepened. 'No, I don't know where she is. My husband went to drop off Markús at her house around the corner and found a note. It just said she had gone off with Björn for a few days.'

'It didn't say where?'

'No.'

'Have you been in touch with her?'

'No,' said Gudný, still frowning.

'What about Markús?' Árni asked. 'Hasn't she wanted to talk to him? Say good night last night?'

'No. I tried to call her on her mobile, but it was switched off.'

'Do you think that's strange?' Árni asked.

Gudný sighed. 'Yes. A little. I mean, she always gets in touch when she is away with Björn. To speak to Markús as much as anything else. Is she all right?'

'We don't know,' said Árni. He watched as Gudný's eyes widened. 'We believe she is in Grundarfjördur with Björn. Or she was. Björn was seen loading his truck with supplies. Where do you think they might have gone?'

'I don't know. Camping perhaps? Perhaps he has taken her out on a boat? I don't know.'

Árni considered the woman's replies. They seemed to reflect genuine ignorance of where her daughter was.

'Has she had a row with Björn, do you think?'

'No,' said Gudný. 'At least not that I know of. I don't think they ever row.'

Árni raised his eyebrows. Couples always rowed, in his experience.

'Harpa looks up to Björn,' Gudný said. 'She relies on him. She has had a very bad year. First losing her job, then her boyfriend killing himself. Björn has been a rock the whole time.'

Árni was pretty sure he wouldn't get anything more out of Harpa's mother. It was clear that Harpa had kept her in the dark about what was really worrying her. 'You say your husband found the note?'

'Yes.'

'Is he around somewhere?'

'Oh, yes, he's fiddling about in the garage.'

'Can I speak to him?'

Gudný led Árni out of the kitchen towards the back of the house. 'He's tying flies,' she said. 'He's a very keen fly-fisherman. He can't go sea-fishing any more, so fly-fishing is the next best thing. He just came back from a few days in the north.'

Einar, Harpa's father, looked very little like her. A squat strong man with grey hair, blue flinty eyes and the familiar weather-beaten face of one who had spent decades on the North Atlantic waves.

There was something about the man's body language when they were introduced that suggested to Árni that he knew more than his wife about Harpa. This wasn't a surprise visit. He knew his daughter was in trouble.

'Do you mind if I speak to your husband alone?' Árni said.

Gudný hesitated and then left them to it.

Árni looked over Einar's shoulder, where there were indeed signs of fly tying – he saw something in a vice and a magnifying glass. Árni examined it: a few drab feathers wrapped around a hook.

'Doesn't look much like a fly to me,' he said.

'You're not a salmon,' said Einar.

'That's true.'

'Have you ever been fly-fishing?' Einar asked.

'No. It always seemed a bit expensive for me,' Árni said.

'It's got cheaper in the last year or two, with the *kreppa*. But then people have less money to throw around. I can't afford the good rivers any more.'

'Your wife said you had just come back from a trip. Any luck?'

'Some. It's more of a challenge when there are fewer fish to catch, and that's fun in its own way. As long as you catch some. Which I did this time. Have a seat.'

Árni sat on a plastic chair, while Einar removed a small coil of wire from another one and sat opposite him. Árni scanned the garage. There was no room for a car: it was full of tools and other clutter, including a set of golf clubs in a corner – a bolthole for a practical man in retirement who needed things to do with his hands.

'How much do you know?' Árni asked the man in question.

'About what?'

'About the trouble Harpa is in.'

'What trouble?' The question was more of a challenge than the response of a worried parent on hearing bad news. Einar's face was rock hard. Impassive.

'I think you know that Harpa is in trouble,' Árni said. 'I think you know more than your wife. We can discuss this with her. Or you can tell me. How much do you know?'

Einar sighed. He smiled grimly. 'Quite a bit. I went to drop off Markús the other day and I found Harpa collapsed on the floor, weeping. She told me everything.'

'What did she tell you?'

Einar looked uncomfortable. 'I can't say. It's up to her to talk to you.'

'You don't want to incriminate her?'

Einar shrugged. His square shoulders stiffened. An immovable object.

'Did she tell you about Gabríel Örn? About what really happened to him?'

Einar didn't reply.

'Look. Einar. We need to locate Harpa urgently. We know she is with Björn. Do you have any idea where they might be?'

Einar shook his head.

'We know that Gabríel Örn's death wasn't suicide. We know your daughter struck him, and he fell and hit his head. I don't want to ask you about that, at least not now. We can discuss it later. But we believe that some of the people she was with that night were involved in the shooting of Óskar Gunnarsson and Julian Lister, the British government minister.'

Now Árni did get a reaction. 'That's ridiculous! I know Björn. He's a good man. In fact...' Einar hesitated.

Árni waited.

'In fact Harpa asked me to check where Björn was when those two people were shot. I did that. He was out at sea the first time, and in Grundarfjördur harbour the second.'

Árni decided not to point out that Björn had actually been to France the day before the ex-Chancellor was shot. But it was interesting that Harpa herself had been suspicious enough to get her father to check out her boyfriend.

'Einar, although we know that Björn did not carry out the shootings himself, we believe he was involved,' Árni said. 'In which case your daughter might be in some danger. Wherever she is. Now do you have any idea where that might be?'

'I can't believe it of Björn,' Einar said.

'I'm sorry, but it's true. Now, where is Harpa?'

'I don't know,' Einar said. 'The note just said they were going away for a couple of days. It didn't say where.'

'Who signed the note?' Árni asked. 'Was it Harpa?'

'No,' said Einar. 'It was Björn.'

CHAPTER THIRTY-SIX

MAGNUS WAS MAKING good time. The road beyond Borgarnes was virtually empty, and there were long straight stretches where he could put his foot down.

To his left, in the distance, the sea glinted in rays of sunshine filtering through the clouds. To his right, a lava field rolled all the way up to the road. Beyond that, through partings in the grey curtain of mist, he could see the flanks of mountains, grey battlements with moist green valleys in the gaps between their turrets.

In front of him, growing steadily larger as he approached it, was the Eldborg crater, a perfect circle of raised grey stone thrusting up out of the plain.

It wasn't just the urgency of arresting Björn that was propelling Magnus forward at such speed. It was Ingileif. His grandfather. Benedikt's murder. His own father's murder. Ollie's distress. Thoughts all crowding in on him, requiring his attention.

But he needed to focus. On Björn. On Harpa. And on Ingólfur Arnarson, whoever he was.

He wished he had a gun; he felt naked without it. He doubted Björn was armed, but he could be. They had used a handgun in London, a rifle in Normandy, why shouldn't he have a firearm in Iceland? A cop without a gun wasn't a real cop, as far as Magnus was concerned.

After a couple of kilometres of straight road, a bend rushed towards him faster than he expected, and the Range Rover nearly overturned as he took the corner.

He eased his foot off the accelerator a touch.

His phone rang. He glanced at the display before he answered.

'Hi, Sharon.'

'Ísak's gone.'

'What?'

'We went to pick him up. His girlfriend said he left the country yesterday. Had to go back to Iceland to see his sick mother. She's getting worse apparently, or at least that's what he told her.'

'Yeah, right.'

'The girlfriend called his mother in Iceland, who said she was fine.'

'Had his mother seen Ísak?'

'Briefly. He arrived home and then he went off again. Apparently he's gone on a camping trip alone. To sort himself out.'

'Where?'

'His mother didn't tell the girlfriend. I suggest you get someone to ask her.'

'We'll do that. Thanks, Sharon.'

Ísak was in a bit of a quandary. He had checked both passes leading towards Grundarfjördur, and had seen no sign of Björn's pickup. It had been a lot of driving and he returned to Grundarfjördur unsure what to do next. The map didn't show any other passes with roads through them directly to the south of the town. Indeed Grundarfjördur itself sat in a horseshoe-shaped cove, with green slopes rising smoothly to cliffs the whole way around. Lots of waterfalls, but nothing remotely resembling a pass. There were other possibilities further away, but which to try?

He cruised slowly through the little fishing port. Although his fuel gauge still showed half full, he pulled into a petrol station.

The guy at the counter was reading a book. He was about Ísak's age, maybe a year or two younger. He was a little flabby, with long wispy fair hair and pasty skin. Ísak didn't know how people like him survived stuck in the middle of nowhere all their lives. It would drive him mad: he would be out of there as soon as he could afford the bus ticket to Reykjavík.

He paid for his petrol. 'Can you help me?' he asked the guy. 'I'm looking for a mountain pass near here. A friend of mine said there is an old hut that is worth looking at.'

'There are no passes here in Grundarfjördur,' the guy said. 'You have to go to Ólafsvík or over towards Stykkishólmur.'

'I've tried those,' said Ísak. 'I couldn't see any old huts.'

'Sorry.' The man went back to his book. *The Grapes of Wrath*, Ísak saw.

Ísak headed towards the exit.

'Wait a minute,' the man said. 'There is the Kerlingin Pass. Where the troll is.'

'Troll?'

'Yes, haven't you heard of the Kerlingin troll?' The man tutted, amazed at the ignorance of these people from Reykjavík. 'It's just to the east of the new road to Stykkishólmur. There is an old hut there, I am pretty sure.'

Björn sat outside the hut, listening to Harpa inside. The screams turned to sobs, and eventually to silence.

He had been shocked by her response. He had hoped she would at least understand his point of view. Perhaps she still would, given time. He knew how important he was to her, how much she trusted him.

After about forty minutes he went back in.

Harpa had pushed herself over against the wall of the hut, and was slumped against it.

Björn untied her. 'Sit down on the chair,' he said. It was more of a suggestion than a command.

Harpa ignored him. So he sat down next to her against the wall.

'Can I leave you untied?' Björn asked. 'There's nowhere you can really go. It's several kilometres to the main road.'

Harpa nodded.

In the end she spoke, as he knew she would. 'So what happened? Did you all get together right after Gabríel Örn died? I thought we agreed we would keep away from each other. So the police wouldn't be able to make a link.'

'Not right after. I think it was in June. I went to a bar with my brother one evening, the Grand Rokk. I bumped into Sindri there. I met him with Ísak the following day.

'We all felt the same way. That what had happened to Gabríel Örn wasn't actually that bad. That he deserved it. That others deserved it too.'

'So you went to France. But if you didn't shoot Julian Lister, what were you doing there?'

'Preparing the way. Sindri's drug-dealing friends had contacts in Amsterdam who could get hold of a rifle and a motorbike. I needed to talk to them and pay them. Then I checked out Julian Lister's home in Normandy and buried the gun. Ísak had done the same kind of thing in London.'

'Pay them? Where did you get the money?'

'Most of it from Ísak. I don't know where he gets it. Parents maybe?'

'And you won't tell me who pulled the trigger?'

'No.'

Silence. 'But don't you realize it is murder, what you've done? What you've all done.'

Björn sighed. 'I don't think it is, Harpa. Not really.'

'How can it not be?'

'People have always died in Iceland. It's a dangerous place. Farmers die in snowdrifts looking for their sheep. Fishermen drown at sea.'

'Not any more, they don't,' Harpa said. 'It's years since a farmer died of exposure. And my father never lost anyone on his boat.'

'He was lucky,' said Björn. 'I lost my elder brother and my cousin on my uncle's boat when it sank. He survived with two others.'

Harpa raised her eyebrows. 'I didn't know that.'

'I was fourteen,' said Björn. 'I should have been on the boat too, but our football team had an important cup match. I have felt guilty ever since.'

'You never told me.' Björn saw a flicker of sympathy in Harpa's eyes and then it died. 'But these people weren't murdered.'

'Not directly. But they died trying to put food on their families' tables. Unlike the bankers who never ran any risks at all.'

'That's no justification, Björn.'

'My point is, people die, Harpa. And Gabríel Örn and Óskar died for a better cause than my brother.'

'I don't see that.'

Björn's patience snapped. 'These people destroyed our country! They have put us and our children and our children's children into debt for a century. And they are getting away with it! Not a single one is in jail. Someone had to do something.' He fought to control himself. He wanted to win Harpa over, not shout at her. 'It turned out that was us.'

Björn took a deep breath. There was more he could tell her, something that would persuade her, but now wasn't the time. Not yet. Not until Ingólfur Arnarson had been dealt with.

'I have to make a phone call,' he said. He took hold of the rope. 'I'm going to tie your hands together, and your feet. I'm sorry, I won't be long.'

He tied two complicated knots around Harpa's wrists and ankles. He made them tight, confident that she wouldn't be able to untie them herself. And even if she did, where could she go?

He grabbed his phone, her phone and the knife he had brought with him, and went out to the pickup truck. He drove up to the top of the pass, and down the other side. In front of him, bathed in sunshine, stretched a magnificent view: the whole of Breidafjördur dotted with its islands, the holy bump of Helgafell and beyond that the town of Stykkishólmur to his right, the mountains of the West Fjords in the distance, and in the foreground the Berserkjahraun tumbling down towards the sea.

On the ridge above him stood the lonely figure of the stone troll herself, her head only a couple of metres below heavy cloud.

He got out of the truck and checked for a signal. There was one.

He made his call and was about to return to the hut, when he paused. He could hear the sound of a car. He looked down and saw a small hatchback climbing the potholed road towards him. A car like that was not robust enough to make the cratered track down to the hut. Probably a tourist wanting to check out the troll.

Björn decided to wait and watch.

The road was a nightmare. Ísak was amazed that this could ever have been the main route in to Stykkishólmur. He did his best to navigate around the craters as the Honda heaved and jolted its way up the pass, but it was impossible to avoid them entirely.

He was only a couple of hundred metres away when he spotted Björn's red pickup, and Björn himself leaning next to it, watching him.

Think.

Ísak slowed. There would be no way that Björn would be able to recognize him as the driver yet.

He stopped. Executed a jarring three-point turn, and slowly headed down the hill, as though he had given up in the face of the bad road.

He drove slowly, his eyes flicking constantly up to the mirror where he could see the pickup behind him. Sure enough, after a minute or so, Björn climbed in and turned around, heading back over the pass. Another minute and Björn's vehicle was out of sight.

Ísak waited a couple of minutes more, turned his car around yet again, and followed his co-conspirator.

He made his way carefully, getting out of his vehicle before each bend to peer around it on foot: he didn't want Björn to see his car suddenly appear in the open. After half an hour or so of very slow progress, Ísak put his head around a boulder and saw the hut, standing alone on a knoll in the valley of stone, rock, moss and water, with Björn's truck parked outside it.

Harpa had spent much of her childhood untangling fishing nets. She had strong nimble fingers and knew how fishermen tied knots.

She had watched closely as Björn tied the rope around her wrists and ankles. He knew what he was doing. She couldn't reach the knot on her wrists, and the one on her ankles would be extremely difficult. In fact she suspected that Björn himself would have to use a knife to cut it.

But she could only try. She tugged, pulled, pushed and puzzled. Eventually, she made progress and she could feel the whole knot loosen. But just as she was about to pull it apart, she heard the sound of Björn's vehicle approaching.

She hesitated, and then tightened the knot again.

Next time.

CHAPTER THIRTY-SEVEN

A NNA ÖSK SET her little pony off at a canter around her bedroom. She had had the pony for three weeks now, since her birthday, and she still liked to play with it all the time.

Her mother said she could have a real one when she was nine. Her daddy wasn't so sure. He was worried about money. He was always worried about money. Silly man. Mummy had told her that they were rich. It was obvious: they had a really big house right in the middle of Reykjavík by the lake.

But when she got her pony they couldn't keep it at home. Apparently their garden wasn't big enough. Which was also silly. Their garden was *really* big, much bigger than the one belonging to Anna Ösk's best friend Sara Rós.

Anna Ösk lifted up her pony to the window to look at the garden. Her bedroom was on the second floor, high up, and she had a good view. She could see exactly where you could put a stable, right in the corner where the little tree was. Easy-peasy.

As she was planning the exact positioning of the structure, Anna Ösk noticed some movement in the next-door garden. Someone was crawling through the bushes at the back. It was a man. He was really difficult to see, but Anna Ösk could tell it wasn't the man who lived in the house next door. She wondered if he was playing hide-and-seek.

He must have been because he crawled right up to the neighbour's car, which was parked at the top of the driveway, and then slid until he was halfway underneath.

Anna Ösk looked around for a child. As a rule, grown-ups didn't play hide-and-seek by themselves. She couldn't see one, but she was sure there must be one somewhere. Probably at the front of the house, the man was well hidden from the front or the road.

Very strange. She would tell her mummy what she had seen.

'Anna Ösk!' Her mother's voice crashed up the stairs. This didn't sound good.

'Anna Ösk, come downstairs this minute! How many times have I told you to pick up your toys from the kitchen floor when you have finished playing? I've had enough! No TV this afternoon, do you hear me?'

Anna Ösk began to cry.

Magnus pulled up outside the wooden police station in Grundarfjördur and stepped out of the Range Rover.

'Magnús!'

He turned to see the burly figure of Páll in his black uniform walking rapidly towards him from the direction of the harbour.

'That was quick,' Páll said.

'Not much traffic.'

Páll smiled.

'Any trace of Björn?' Magnus asked.

'None so far. No one has seen him for a couple of days in the harbour. It's unlikely he took a boat out: certainly no one saw him if he did. The harbourmaster said he would check whether any small boats were missing that hadn't been reported. I stopped in quickly to talk to his parents and his sister. They say they haven't heard anything from him either. Same at the café the fishermen often use. The police in Stykkishólmur and Ólafsvík are looking for him too. They've set up road blocks on every route out of the peninsula.'

That at least was possible: there were no more than a couple of routes out of the Snaefells Peninsula. But the peninsula itself was big, perhaps eighty kilometres long and fifteen wide, and full of mountains. Impossible to search thoroughly.

Magnus wondered about a helicopter. But although sun shone along the shoreline, the mountains themselves were enveloped in cloud.

Of course if Björn had left the area the night before he could be over the other side of Iceland by now. But if he was planning to hide Harpa he might choose somewhere he knew. Somewhere close to home.

'So what's next?'

'I thought shops and petrol stations,' said Páll. 'He may have stocked up with supplies or fuel. There aren't many of them in town: do you want to split up or come with me?'

'Let's do it together,' Magnus said. 'You know the town and the people. I'll just waste time.'

'Good,' said Páll moving towards his white police car. 'Jump in. And you can tell me what's really going on.'

Ísak drove his mother's poor Honda off what was left of the track, and round the back of a large conical rock. Miraculously the axle didn't break. He scuffed the tyre marks in the dirt with his foot. He didn't want Björn to notice the car should he decide to drive back up the pass.

He took the knife he had bought in Borgarnes out of the plastic bag and thrust it into the pocket of his coat. Then he crept back to the boulder. The hut was about two hundred metres from where the road emerged into the open. There was virtually no cover, but only one of the windows in the hut faced that way, and that was high up, probably a little higher than eye level.

He noticed that the cloud was thickening and creeping down the walls of the valley.

On the other side of the building was a cliff about thirty metres high, with a waterfall cascading down it. There seemed to be a vertical crevice in the rock there big enough for a man to squeeze and still have a view of the hut.

Ísak gave it a try. He ran, crouching, around the hut, keeping himself out of the field of vision of the bigger windows at the side of the building. He pressed himself into the crevice. His view of the hut was indeed clear, and he was pretty sure that Björn wouldn't be able to see him. The only problem was that water from the cascade was constantly splashing on to him, and it was cold. Very cold.

He would wait until Björn left the hut again. Then he would slip inside and deal with Harpa. Wait until Björn came back and as he discovered her body, slash a tyre of Björn's truck and run up the road to his own car.

Leave it to Björn to dispose of Harpa's body.

But then, if Björn was subsequently caught, which he probably would be, he would talk.

No. Ísak would just have to kill Björn as well as Harpa. Either wait until Björn left the hut and surprise him when he returned, or if Björn didn't leave, creep into the hut after night fell and they were both asleep. If Ísak wasn't frozen to death by then.

It wasn't ideal, but he was committed now.

Magnus waited in the car as Páll went into Samkaup, the main supermarket in town. He called Baldur and told him that there was no sign of Björn. He had already passed on Sharon's message about Ísak's disappearance.

Baldur was businesslike. Sindri wasn't talking. Not a word. Wasn't even bothering with a lawyer. Magnus wasn't surprised. If there was one more hit still to come, Sindri would be happy to bide his time.

Árni had checked with Ísak's parents. Ísak had left home at nine o'clock the previous evening in his mother's car, a small Honda, loaded with camping stuff. She said that the family had been on a number of camping trips to Thórsmörk, a hundred and fifty kilometres to the east of Reykjavík.

They had struck lucky. Calling around campsites, they had discovered that Ísak had been spotted at a site near Hveragerdi, to the south-east of Reykjavík, on the way to Thórsmörk. Although

Baldur and Magnus agreed that Ísak wasn't going on a little holiday jaunt, it was possible that if he was looking for wilderness to hide in, he might choose an area with which he was familiar.

Or he might be in the Snaefells Peninsula with Björn and Harpa.

Magnus suggested that they pull Gulli in. Perhaps somehow he had travelled from Tenerife to London and Paris and then back to Tenerife. Unlikely, but they didn't want to take any chances: if he was in custody he couldn't assassinate anyone. Baldur agreed. He had given up condemning Magnus's wilder ideas. The stakes were too high.

Páll returned to the car. 'Nothing. Let's go on.'

Grundarfjördur was a small, compact town and it didn't take long for Páll to get from place to place. They checked Vínbúd, the state liquor store, and then went on to the petrol station.

The kid behind the counter knew Björn Helgason but hadn't seen him since he had filled up his red pickup the morning of the day before.

'That was probably to get down to Reykjavík,' Magnus said. As an afterthought, just as he was leaving, he paused.

'You haven't seen a young guy in here have you? A student, twenty-two years old, neatly dressed, about one seventy-five tall, fair hair, little dimple on his chin? Driving a small blue Honda?'

'Yes,' said the kid. 'A guy like that was in here about an hour ago. Asked me where a mountain pass was with a hut. I told him about the Kerlingin Pass. He'd never even heard of the troll. Can you believe it? These guys from Reykjavík don't know anything.'

CHAPTER THIRTY-EIGHT

HARPA SAT ON the floor examining the man who, until a couple of hours before, she had loved more than any other. She knew her stare was discomfiting him, but she didn't care. She didn't care about him at all.

Because suddenly, for the first time in a year, she felt strong again. The confusion, the mistrust, the guilt, the self-doubt, all those destructive feelings that had swirled around inside her head for a year now, were gone.

She knew what was right and what was wrong. And she knew what she had to do.

Compared to the agonies that she had gone through about her own role in Gabríel Örn's death, and in the cover-up, what Björn had done was much simpler. He had conspired to murder someone. That was unequivocally wrong. It was her duty to do all she could to right that wrong.

She couldn't bring Óskar back to life, but maybe, just maybe, she could save whoever the next target was, and then perhaps bring Björn and Sindri and Ísak to justice. And whoever else was their accomplice.

She knew what she had to do and she was determined to do it.

Escape.

When Björn next left the hut, it would take her less than a minute to untie the rope around her ankles. She would have to cope with her wrists tied together, but she would be able to run. She had tried to recall the geography of the Snaefells Peninsula. She was pretty

341

sure she knew where they were, and that a modern road ran through a parallel pass not far away. What she couldn't quite remember was whether it was to the west or the east. She guessed the west.

Her plan was to clamber up the side of the valley and over the top to the road on the other side and then flag down the first car that came past. Anyone would stop immediately for a woman standing in the middle of the road with her hands tied.

But first Björn had to leave the hut again. She had no idea when that would be, and she was afraid to ask him in case he suspected something.

She thought about what she would tell the police. It would be good to give them the names of the next victim and the assassin. Björn had been reluctant to tell her: she would see what she could do about that.

'So when you have dealt with the next name on your list, will you let me go?'

'I don't know,' said Björn. He looked as if he was pleased with the question. 'It depends. On you.'

'Hmm.' Harpa let the silence hang there. She knew that Björn wanted to believe that she could be persuaded to agree to keep quiet for a few days. 'And when will that be?' she asked him.

'I can't say.'

'Today? Tonight? Tomorrow? Next week?'

'This afternoon, possibly. Probably this evening. Almost definitely tomorrow morning.'

'How will you know?'

'A text.'

'Which is why you need to go and make your phone calls?'

'Once I have heard everything is ready, then all I will have to do is wait for the text.'

'From?'

Björn shook his head. ' I can't tell you, Harpa.'

'OK. At least tell me who the target is.'

Björn shook his head. Harpa could see that his earlier pleasure in her talking to him was waning.

'I don't see why you won't. After all there's nothing I can do about it, is there? You may as well tell me now.'

'I'll tell you when it's done.' Björn's voice was firm.

Harpa didn't want to push him any more in case he realized what she was planning. 'Suit yourself,' she said.

They were silent for five, maybe ten minutes. Through the window, Harpa watched as the clouds swirled across the valley, bringing thick fog one moment and sunshine the next.

Fog would be good for evading Björn. But it would make it very easy to get lost on the mountain. She would just have to seize her opportunity whenever it came.

Björn checked his watch. 'I'm going to go and check for that text.'

Harpa grunted.

Björn glanced at Harpa's ankles and wrists and left the hut. A few seconds later Harpa heard the engine of his pickup starting up and the sound of the vehicle bumping down towards the track.

She bent down and attacked the knot. It wasn't coming, damn it! And she was sure she had nearly untied it.

Slow down, Harpa. She stopped, took a couple of breaths, examined the knot, thought about it, tugged the rope here, pushed there.

She was free!

She scanned the room for her phone, or a knife, but couldn't see either. No time to mess about. She pulled open the door with her bound hands and ran outside.

Ísak saw Björn leave the hut. His heart rate quickened as he watched the pickup clatter its way down to the track, and then up the pass. A patch of cloud drifted down the valley, fingers of moisture stretching ahead of it as it clutched at the rocks and the boulders, silently hauling itself forward. The head of the pass was obscured. Excellent. He would wait until Björn's pickup disappeared into the mist before making his move.

The vehicle was swallowed up by the cloud. Ísak hesitated. Gripped the knife in his gloved hand and set off towards the hut. He had barely gone five metres when he heard the door open again, and a moment later he saw Harpa rushing down the knoll towards the stream at the floor of the valley.

She was escaping! He broke into a run. She hadn't seen him yet. He tried to run softly so as not to scare her. The closer he could get the better. Then one final sprint.

But Harpa was running as fast as she could already. She tore down the side of the knoll, crossed the track and forded the stream, slipping once and falling in, uttering a small yelp as she did so. She clambered out, turned and saw Ísak.

Ísak hesitated. Perhaps if he didn't scare her she would mistake him for a rescuer. They had only met once, in January, and she might not recognize him from a distance.

He slowed to a walk. 'Are you all right?' he shouted.

Harpa hesitated. 'Who are you?'

'I was hiking through the pass and I saw you run,' Ísak called. 'Are you OK?'

Harpa approached him gingerly. Ísak was close to the stream now. He gripped the knife in the pocket of his coat.

'Ísak! You're Ísak aren't you?' Harpa shouted. She took a couple of steps back and then ran up the slope.

Ísak leaped into the stream. The water was freezing and more powerful than he expected. He slipped on a rock and rolled over once, his head striking another stone. The shock of the cold water seemed to squeeze the air out of his lungs. For a moment he panicked. Fast flowing mountain streams in Iceland were much more dangerous than they appeared. He fought for air and grabbed a stone, pulling himself to his feet.

He could see Harpa scampering up the rocky side of the valley a few metres ahead, hurrying towards the base of the cloud.

Then he heard the sound of a vehicle behind him.

*

Björn was thinking about Harpa as he drove up into the mist towards the head of the pass. Her calm unnerved him. He was used to her confused, panicky. This sense of purpose was new. It didn't bode well for her changing her mind and keeping quiet once he let her go.

In which case, what was he to do with her?

He glanced down at his phone. A couple of bars flickered. Maybe he could get reception here without going all the way over the head of the pass. He stopped the car. He was right at the point where the road disappeared behind a boulder, but he couldn't see back to the hut because of the fog. The two bars flickered and died. He stepped out and moved around the black volcanic dirt at the side of the track, trying to get reception, but there was nothing.

He was surrounded on three sides by thick moisture, but above him, through a thin patina of white, he could see the blue of the sky.

He trotted back to the truck.

Then he saw it. A footprint in the dust, a couple of metres from where he had walked himself. He put his own feet by the print. Smaller, definitely not his.

He followed the prints back into the mist. The dirt had been scuffed. There was part of a tyre mark.

A small conical rock lay about twenty metres back from the track. He checked behind it: a car. The same car he had seen struggling up the pass earlier.

Who the hell's was it? A strange walker, who for an unknowable reason had wanted to hide his car before setting out? He doubted it.

Could it be the police? The small Honda didn't look like a police car, and he could see various bits of camping equipment in the back.

It could be Ísak. After Harpa.

Björn ran back to his truck, spun it around and hurtled down the hill to the valley.

He burst through the cloud, and the valley floor opened before him. He noticed the door to the hut hanging open. He scanned the valley as he drove and saw a figure clambering out of the stream and up the hill on the other side. Ísak.

Further up the hill he could see Harpa, only a few metres below the cloud base.

He swerved off the track and drove down towards the stream. Within a few seconds the truck came to a halt as a front wheel slid into a hole with a clang. Björn flung open the door and leaped out. He saw Ísak turn towards him and then keep climbing.

Björn bounded from stone to stone in the stream, and was soon on the other side. He could no longer see Harpa. And the cloud was descending further. In a moment it had swallowed up Ísak.

Björn kept his eyes on where he had last seen Ísak and kept his legs pumping. He was a fit man, fitter than Ísak he would bet.

He scrambled upwards past a rock. A snipe darted up to his right with a whirr of wings. He saw a flash of steel, and twisted, raising his arm to parry the blow. There was the sound of tearing as a knife ripped the upper arm of his jacket. He stepped backwards, ready to face his assailant, but one of his feet slipped from under him.

Ísak was quick and surprisingly strong. As Björn fell backwards and hit the ground the blade of the knife penetrated his coat, his fleece, his shirt and his skin, and lodged between his ribs.

Björn felt the blow, but no pain. He reached up and grabbed Ísak around the throat. Ísak's eyes opened in surprise. He tried to wriggle free, but Björn would not let go. The two men rolled down the slope, Björn's fingers clamped to the student's throat. They came to a halt against a rock, Björn on top.

He increased the pressure. Ísak made choking noises as he gasped for breath. Björn's vision began to go. He forced himself to focus on Ísak, to keep those fingers tight just for a few seconds longer. But he could feel the strength flowing from his body, from his arms.

Ísak saw it too. He bucked and Björn's fingers came loose, another buck and Björn was tossed sideways. He lay panting on his back in the moss. Beside him Ísak gulped for breath in great choking spasms. But with each second that passed, Ísak was getting stronger and Björn weaker.

Björn glanced downwards at the handle of the knife protruding from his chest. Strangely, it still didn't hurt.

Ísak bent over him and yanked it out.

Björn yelled. That hurt. That hurt like hell. But the yell was little more than a croak.

He tried to pull himself to his feet. He couldn't do it.

He moved his lips, tried to force air through his vocal cords. 'Come here, you bastard!' But it was just a whisper.

Sindri wished they would offer him a cigarette. It would be easier to zone out with a cigarette. There was a red no-smoking sign on the wall of the interview room, but there was also a cigarette butt in a white plastic cup on the window sill. The bastards could give him a cigarette if they wanted to. But he wasn't going to ask.

Since they had brought him in, he hadn't said a word. Hadn't asked for a lawyer, he didn't need anyone to tell him not to say anything. It wasn't long now, only a few hours, and then he could talk. But it should be easy to keep quiet until then.

The black one was talking now. The bald one was staring at him. He tried not to focus on what she was saying, but couldn't avoid hearing the words 'Ingólfur Arnarson'. If they were smart, they would have figured out who that was by now. If Sindri had been smart, he would have chosen an irrelevant codename. The others thought the whole notion of a codename was ridiculous, but it had turned out to be a good idea. He wondered how the police had got hold of the name. Someone wrote it down somewhere, perhaps? Or they were overheard.

Sindri knew he was going to jail. But the more he thought about it, the more he grew to like the idea. Litla Hraun could hardly be worse than his squat. There would be company, they would probably allow him to write, and he would be famous. Finally people would notice him.

That morning, despite the hangover, he had posted his manifesto on his blog. It had come out surprisingly well. It was both a call to arms and the distillation of ten years of his ideas. And once he went on trial, people would read it all over the world.

He had been bitterly disappointed at the Icesave meeting the day before. That was why he had got so drunk. It was clear that Ísak was right, the Icelandic people were just too nice, too polite to take to the streets to fight. At least Ingileif had listened to him. She was gorgeous. And smart. He had really thought he was going to get lucky there, but it had turned out that it was his mind she was impressed with, not his body. Perhaps, in time. When she heard about his trial on national TV.

That was one problem with prison. No sex. Who was he kidding? It was at least a year since he had last had sex. And he used to find it so easy.

Maybe Ingileif?

No. He would have to reconcile himself to several years in jail. But he would be a hero to some people. And over time the number of people who believed in his cause would grow, he was sure of it. He'd be a kind of Icelandic Nelson Mandela.

'What's so funny?' the bald one snapped.

Sindri didn't answer, but let the smile fade from his lips. No need to provoke them.

'Where's Harpa?'

Not telling you, buddy.

'And Ísak?' asked the black woman. 'Where is Ísak? Are they together?'

Not telling you that either.

But Sindri answered the question in his own head. Ísak was looking for Harpa with the intention of killing her.

That didn't fit into Sindri's self-image of a hero of the people. He should have stopped Ísak somehow, called Björn and warned him. Harpa's death would be a waste. And Björn was right, she was entirely innocent.

Sindri could look anyone in the eye and tell him he was proud of what they had done to Óskar Gunnarsson, or Julian Lister, or what they would do to Ingólfur Arnarson. Even Gabríel Örn's death could be justified.

But not Harpa. Killing Harpa would be wrong. And he would be implicated in that as well, with some justice. It wasn't the law that worried him, he knew he was a murderer anyway according to the law, but it was the people. He couldn't justify Harpa's death to the people. Or to himself.

'What is it, Sindri?' the bald one said. 'You look worried. We know Björn is with Harpa. Is Ísak with them? Or is he somewhere else?'

Sindri took a deep breath.

'Tell us,' said the bald one, gently. He and the woman leaned back, patiently.

Sindri thought about it. Then thought about it some more. Then he spoke.

Páll could drive fast, Magnus would give him that. He had the lights flashing, although there were only a few sheep and a couple of horses to admire them. They seemed interested, though.

There was a good chance they would be the first to the Kerlingin Pass. The small complement of police based at Stykkishólmur were spread far and wide, some of them manning roadblocks into and out of the peninsula.

Páll belted through the Berserkjahraun, past the new road up over to Borgarnes, and turned right up the old Kerlingin Pass track. Over to their left towards Helgafell on the way to Stykkishólmur Magnus could see the flashing blue light of another police car on its way.

'I don't suppose you happen to have a rifle in the back of this car?' Magnus asked.

'No, of course not,' Páll said. 'You know Icelandic policemen don't carry guns.'

'What if Björn is armed?'

'Why should he be? He's only a fisherman. And I know for a fact he doesn't have a gun licence.'

'These guys had guns in London. And Normandy.'

'He won't have a gun.'

'But he could have a knife,' Magnus said.

Páll didn't answer for a moment. 'He will probably have a knife,' he admitted.

'Oh, great.' The car was bucking like a demented stallion as it leapt over the potholes in the track.

'What do you use for shooting the polar bears, then?' Magnus asked. Three times in the previous couple of years polar bears had made the long journey to Iceland on drifting icebergs, only to be blasted as soon as they hit dry land by trigger-happy policemen.

'That's different,' said the constable. 'Jesus!' He fought to retain control as his car nearly went spinning over the edge.

Magnus decided to let Páll concentrate on the road.

His phone rang.

'Magnús, it's Baldur. Have you found Ísak yet?'

'We're on our way to the pass.'

'Sindri just talked. He says Ísak is planning to kill Harpa. Keep her quiet.'

'Does Björn know about that?'

'No. And Sindri says he won't like that idea at all.'

'Interesting. Did he say who Ingólfur Arnarson is? Or the assassin?'

'No. Nothing.'

'Did you get hold of Björn's brother?'

'Yeah, we brought him in to the station as well. He just looked surprised. And he's been painting the shop on Laugavegur since eight this morning. Not exactly preparing an assassination attempt.'

The car plunged into fog. Baldur was beginning to break up as the reception deteriorated. 'Tell me when you locate Ísak,' he said and rang off.

The car followed the track around bare volcanic rock and soon they were descending. It was impossible to make out the Kerlingin troll, although Magnus knew it was above them somewhere.

Suddenly the cloud seemed to lift and they were in a valley of rock and moss. There, on the left, was the hut, its door wide open. And on the right was a pickup truck, its nose pointing down towards the stream, one of its front wheels wedged in a hole, and one of its back wheels raised off the ground. The driver's door was hanging open.

'Slow down! You take the hut, I'll take the truck!' said Magnus. He jumped out of the car before it had come to a halt, ran to the truck and looked inside. Nothing. He scanned the hill. A short distance up the far wall of the valley he saw a body splayed out on the ground.

He forded the freezing stream and ran uphill. It was Björn. Stab wound to the chest. It didn't look good unless they could get rapid medical attention.

At least he was conscious. His eyes flickered up at Magnus.

Magnus asked the key question. 'Who did this?'

Björn tried to speak, but was finding it difficult. Magnus lowered his ear towards Björn's mouth. He heard one word. 'Ísak.'

'Where's Harpa?' he asked.

Björn couldn't answer, but he flicked his eyes upwards.

'She's gone up the hill?' Magnus asked.

Björn nodded, just a brief downward movement of the chin.

'And Ísak's after her?'

Another nod.

Magnus tried for one more question. 'And who is Ingólfur Arnarson?'

Björn closed his eyes and moved his head to the side.

Magnus waved at Páll who was trotting heavily towards the stream. 'Get an ambulance!' he shouted.

Páll raised an arm in acknowledgement and ran back to his car and the radio.

Magnus turned and looked up the hill. The cloud seemed to be lifting, moving off to his left down the valley. But he couldn't see either Ísak or Harpa. He closed his eyes and listened. He could hear running water, the croak of a raven, Björn's laboured breathing, and somewhere above, the clatter of falling stones.

He set off up the hill into the fog.

CHAPTER THIRTY-NINE

HARPA RAN AS fast as she could, which wasn't nearly fast enough. Her wrists were a real problem; because they were tied together she couldn't use her arms to help her balance. And she was wearing the wrong shoes, they kept slipping on the scree, sending torrents of stones falling down behind her. She fell every few seconds, it would only be a matter of time before she twisted something. Her heart felt like it was going to explode.

The fog was dense around her. Above the crescendo of the blood in her ears and her own panting, she could hear the rattle of stones below as Ísak caught up on her.

Then suddenly the mist lifted. Above her was blue sky. To her left and right was rock. And behind and in front was a thick carpet of grey. She was at the top, on the ridge between one valley and the next.

She stopped for a second. She could hear Ísak close behind. Summoning up a renewed burst of energy she sprinted downhill towards the cloud. She slipped and fell, twisting one knee and grazing the other. She couldn't stop herself emitting a cry of pain. The fog was only a few metres away. She limped towards it.

She felt an enormous sense of relief as once again she was enveloped by the blanket of moisture. Although the slope was broadly downhill, her knee was giving out.

The fog was thick now. She spotted a cluster of boulders to the left. If she just lay down there and kept quiet, Ísak would never find her.

She changed direction and headed for the rocks.

Suddenly she heard the regular thump of Ísak's feet hitting the ground. She couldn't see him, but it sounded as if they were going to collide. She took the decision to keep going for the rocks.

She threw herself at them and lay still, huddled between two boulders. Except she wasn't exactly still, her chest was heaving and her heart pounding.

Seconds later she heard Ísak lope past. She could see his legs. He was barely five metres away from her as he stopped to listen. She tried to hold her breath, but she could only do it for a few seconds. Her lungs needed the air. The sound as she exhaled seemed loud to her, but Ísak appeared not to notice. He walked cautiously forward into the mist.

She stood up, and made her way as quietly as she could laterally along the slope of the hill, putting distance between her and Ísak.

But then the fog rolled away, revealing a valley glistening in the pale sunshine.

Ísak was a hundred metres away to the left, slightly below her. He stopped, scanned the hillside below, to his right. He turned towards her.

She ran downhill as fast as her jellied knee would let her.

Magnus plunged into the fog. The slope was tricky, rocks that were sharp in places, slick in others, moss, dirt and the odd patches of grass. Occasionally he would pause to listen out for the sounds of dislodged stones. He couldn't hear any.

The fog was good. Provided Harpa kept quiet it would be impossible for Ísak to find her. In fact, if she had any sense, she would just lie low and wait.

Magnus's situation was different. He was a big lumbering target making a lot of noise, whose adversary had a knife and had just used it. And he was unarmed. If only he had a firearm. According to the manual he should hold off and wait for back-up.

Screw that. Apart from anything else the back-up wouldn't be armed either.

He pressed on.

His heart pounding, he found himself in a shallow dip between two wind-eroded rocks. He had the impression that he was on the ridge between the two valleys.

He heard the sound of someone falling and a cry. It sounded as if it was coming from ahead and to the right but lower down, not too far away.

Magnus altered direction towards it. He was going downhill. A few seconds later he emerged from the clouds. Below him was a new valley, grassier than the bleak one they had just left, with a road of pristine black asphalt running up the centre of it.

And a couple of hundred metres down the slope of the valley, he saw Harpa sliding down the hill, Ísak close behind her. She was finding it hard to keep her balance with her hands tied in front of her.

Magnus hurried after them. In dismay he could see Harpa heading for the top of a rocky outcrop perhaps fifty feet high. She obviously couldn't see the drop. 'To the left!' he shouted. 'Run to the left!'

But she ignored him. It looked for a second as if she was going to propel herself off the cliff, but she stopped just in time. Turned. Saw Ísak close behind her and slid down a crevice.

She came to rest on a narrow ledge and began to work her way awkwardly along the rock face, her back to the cliff, hands in front of her.

Ísak hesitated at the top of the outcrop. He turned to see Magnus approaching down the hill.

'Wait, Ísak!' Magnus shouted.

Ísak looked down, and slid down the crevice as well.

It took Magnus a minute to get to the rock. Below him, Harpa had run out of ledge. Ísak was inching towards her, knife outstretched. There was still some of Björn's blood on the blade.

'Put the knife down, Ísak!' Magnus shouted. 'There's no point in killing Harpa now!'

Ísak hesitated. He was listening.

'Sindri has talked. We know you stabbed Björn. It doesn't matter what Harpa tells us now. So let her go!'

For a moment Magnus thought Ísak would do the rational thing. But then he seemed to come to a decision. 'No!' he shouted. 'You back off! Back off or I will kill her!' He continued making his way carefully along the ledge.

A hostage situation. It was some progress. At least Ísak wouldn't kill Harpa right away.

But hostage situations were inherently uncertain. Magnus had been involved in a couple back in Boston where people had died when they shouldn't.

Although Ísak was desperate, he wasn't high and he wasn't a psycho. And yet, you never knew what might happen with hostage situations.

There were still a few seconds before Ísak reached Harpa. Magnus weighed the options. Ísak and Harpa were probably twenty feet below him. Below them was a further twenty to thirty feet to a steep grassy slope.

If Magnus slid down the rock face he could take Ísak with him in a tumble all the way to the bottom. A dumb thing to do. Magnus would probably break something, possibly his neck. And Ísak might easily stick him with the knife.

Whereas if Ísak reached Harpa the situation might resolve itself with nobody getting hurt.

Or not.

Ísak closed on Harpa. She had nowhere to go. She screamed.

What the hell. Magnus jumped.

He slid down the near-vertical smooth rock on his ass. Ísak turned and raised his knife, jabbing upwards. Magnus twisted. The knife caught his arm, but Magnus's legs knocked into Ísak's and the two of them rolled and bumped their way to the bottom of the slope.

Magnus hit his back, his chest and then his head on a rock.

Everything went black.

He had no idea how long he was out. It must only have been a few seconds, because when he opened his eyes, he saw Ísak scrambling towards him, clutching the knife, blood running down one of his cheeks.

Magnus tried to heave himself on to his elbow, but his head swam. His body was receiving mixed signals, his confused brain was unable to make use of the adrenalin flooding his system.

Ísak reached him. Swayed. Two Ísaks.

Magnus tried to force his brain to tell his legs and arms to co-operate, but they wouldn't.

Ísak raised the knife. Magnus couldn't even cry out.

Then he saw a grey stone come crashing down on the back of Ísak's skull and the kid crumpled.

Two Harpas came into Magnus's vision and slowly merged into one.

Finally he managed to pull himself onto his elbows.

'Thanks,' he said.

'What shall I do?' said Harpa, looking down at the prone body of Ísak. A stone a bit bigger than a baseball still in her bound hands.

'If he moves, hit him again with that,' said Magnus.

'Do you think I've killed him?'

'I hope so.' Just then a police car came roaring up the road, its lights flashing. 'Give them a wave, will you?'

Magnus's head hurt, and his forearm stung where Ísak's knife had grazed it. He was leaning against the police car which had pulled over on the verge of the road up through the pass. There had been two officers in it. One was watching over Ísak who was still unconscious, the other one was summoning an ambulance from the hospital in Stykkishólmur.

'I've killed him, haven't I?' Harpa said.

'Not yet, unfortunately,' said Magnus. 'He's still breathing.'

'After Gabríel Örn, I couldn't handle knowing I had killed someone else.'

'Harpa?'

'Yes.'

'A bit of advice. From now on, don't talk to anyone, especially a policeman, about what happened to Gabríel Örn. Not unless you have a lawyer present.'

'It doesn't matter,' said Harpa. 'I don't care.' She winced, and bent down to rub her knee. 'That hurts.'

'Trust me,' said Magnus. 'For Markús's sake.'

She smiled quickly. 'OK. But I thought you were trying to get me to confess?'

'Yeah. But that was before you saved my life. Don't worry, we'll figure out what happened. I just don't want you to screw up your defence.'

She smiled. 'Thanks. And thanks for coming after me.'

Magnus's brain was beginning to clear. 'There are a load of questions we need to ask you, but I guess the most important is, do you know if they have another target?'

'Yes,' said Harpa. 'Yes, they do.'

'Do you know who?'

'I asked Björn, but he wouldn't say.'

'Ingólfur Arnarson? Did he mention the name Ingólfur Arnarson?'

'The first settler? No. He did say there's someone else out there. Someone who actually does the killing. But I don't know who that is.'

'Do you have any clue? Think, Harpa.'

'No. I tried to make him tell me, but he wouldn't.'

'Did he say when it's going to happen?'

'Yes. Kind of. What did he say?' Harpa frowned, trying to remember. 'How did he put it? "This afternoon maybe. Maybe this evening. Certainly by tomorrow morning." Something like that. That's where he was going. To receive a text from the killer on his phone. He couldn't get reception in the hut so he went back up the pass. Have you found him? Have you arrested him?'

Magnus realized that Harpa didn't know what had happened to

her boyfriend. She had to know; he may as well be the one to tell her.

'Yeah, I found him. He had been stabbed. By Ísak.'

'Oh, my God!' Harpa put her hand to her mouth. 'Is he all right?'

'He was in a bad way when I left him to go after you. A chest wound.'

'You left him?'

'Yes. With another police officer. He was going to call an ambulance.'

'Do you know how he is?'

Magnus raised an eyebrow at the uniformed policeman who had finished on the radio. 'I'll check,' the constable said.

He left the car door open as he called Páll on the radio. Magnus considered asking Harpa to step back, but there wasn't much point. She would want to know.

'Do you have Björn Helgason there?' the officer asked.

'Yes.' Magnus heard Páll's voice. From his tone, he knew what was coming next. 'But he's dead at the scene.'

Magnus heard a short gasp from Harpa. He took the radio mike from the constable. 'Páll, it's Magnús. Did you get a chance to ask him any questions?'

'No. He lost consciousness as soon as I got to him.'

'Damn!' Magnus was focused on the next victim. Ingólfur Arnarson, whoever that was, did not have long to live, unless they figured something out. He had an idea. 'Páll?'

'Yes?'

'See if you can find Björn's phone. Then check "last number called".'

'Roger.'

Magnus straightened up as he waited for Páll to get back to him. The colour had drained from Harpa's face, but her eyes were dry.

'I'm sorry,' Magnus said.

'I'm OK,' Harpa said. 'It will probably hit me soon. But in the hut back there I realized what Björn was doing was wrong. He killed other people. He brought this on himself.'

The radio crackled into life. 'Magnús?'

'Yes?'

'I tried redial. It didn't just have the number it had the name of the contact.'

'And who was it?'

'Einar.'

Behind Magnus, Harpa let out a cry. 'No! No, no, no, no, no!' There was pain and desperation in her voice. 'Don't believe him, Magnús. He must have made a mistake!'

But Magnus knew Páll had got it right. And so, he thought, did Harpa.

CHAPTER FORTY

Á RNI WAS DRIVING back to Reykjavík from Hafnarfjördur, having spoken to both of Ísak's parents and learned nothing. They were as mystified as the police as to their son's whereabouts. The mother especially had sensed that something was seriously wrong, but Ísak had been totally uncommunicative.

Árni was almost back at police headquarters on Hverfisgata when his phone rang. It was Baldur. 'Árni, get over to Seltjarnarnes right away. We know who the assassin is. Harpa's father. Einar.'

'I'm on my way.'

'OK. Don't make an arrest until the uniformed back-up is there.'

'What am I arresting him for?'

'The murder of Óskar Gunnarsson. We'll start with that and work up from there.'

Blue-light time. It took Árni longer than he would have liked to fix it to the roof of his unmarked Skoda, but then he was off. He put his foot down and sped through the Reykjavík traffic, a tense grin on his face. He swerved as he almost caught a motorbike he hadn't seen in the oncoming lane. He checked the mirror. The guy had come to a stop but hadn't actually fallen off.

He slowed down as he approached the Bakkavör turn-off. It was lucky he did, because he caught sight of Einar stepping out of his Freelander and going into his house.

Árni slowed to a stop, just as two patrol cars swerved into the road behind him, sirens off, fortunately. Árni waved them down.

'The suspect has just gone into his house! Come on!'

'Hold on a moment.' One of the officers was on the radio. 'They want us to hold off. They think he's armed. We wait for the Viking Squad.'

So Árni waited in his car fifty metres along from Einar's house. He had the front door covered: there was no way Einar could leave without Árni spotting him. The two patrol cars were joined by another one, and they retreated around the corner to lurk.

Everyone was waiting for the Viking Squad, Reykjavík's SWAT team made up of volunteer officers from across the Metropolitan Police. Árni was disappointed not to make the arrest himself, but it would be cool to see the SWAT team in action.

Then his phone rang. It was Baldur. 'Árni? I want you back at the station.'

'But Einar—'

'The Viking Squad will arrest him as soon as they get there. I want you back here now. We need to figure out who the next target is. Róbert will relieve you.'

Árni saw his colleague approaching in another unmarked Skoda. Reluctantly, Árni turned his own car around and headed back to the station.

They had almost reached Helgafell when Magnus's phone rang. Baldur.

'Árni has spotted Einar. He has just returned home.'

'Has he arrested him?'

'We're calling in the Viking Squad. Einar is probably armed.'

'Now you're talking,' said Magnus. 'I could have used some of their help an hour ago.'

'Any luck on the next victim?'

Magnus glanced at the woman next to him. She was staring out of the window at the little hill of Helgafell coming ever closer, her hand to her mouth, her face stricken with anguish.

'Harpa doesn't know. Ísak is still unconscious so he hasn't talked.' Magnus was about to add that they wouldn't hear anything more from Björn, but with Harpa listening he decided not to.

'Is Ísak going to make it?'

'You never know with head injuries, do you?'

'Well, at least we know where Einar is. He's unlikely to do much damage while he is at home, and we'll grab him as soon as he tries to leave.'

'If he's the only other conspirator,' said Magnus.

'Do you think there's another one?' said Baldur.

'I don't know. We mustn't assume that there isn't. Let me know when you have arrested Einar.'

Magnus thought through the possibility. Had it been Einar who had shot Óskar and Julian Lister? Or someone else?

'Harpa?'

'Yes?'

'Does your father speak English?'

'Not really. Just a few words. Why?'

So that meant he wouldn't be able to make his own preparations for the shootings in France or England.

'Has he been away over the last couple of weeks?' Magnus asked, as gently as he could.

Harpa stared away from him, out of the car window, at the new little houses on the outskirts of Stykkishólmur. 'Yes,' she said, barely audibly. 'He went fly-fishing. Twice.'

'Does he go hunting as well as fly-fishing?'

She nodded, still not meeting his eye. 'He used to go reindeer hunting in the highlands when he was a bit younger and he could afford it.'

Reindeer were not indigenous to Iceland, but they had been introduced in the eighteenth century and now roamed wild over parts of the interior. Where they were hunted. With rifles.

'Does he have a gun at home?' Magnus asked.

Harpa nodded. 'I'm sure he has a licence.'

Magnus called Baldur back and told him. The Viking Squad was a good precaution.

'I can't believe Dad is doing this,' Harpa said. 'I mean, I know he hates the bankers. He lost all his savings in Óðinsbanki. And he likes to bear grudges. But the worst thing is I think he did it for me.'

'What do you mean?'

'He thought the bankers had ruined my life. Gabríel Örn. Óskar. He should have blamed me for suggesting that he put his savings into Óðinsbanki shares, but he seems to have blamed them for deceiving me.'

'But that's true, isn't it?' Magnus said. 'They did.'

'Yes, but I didn't ask him to do it, did I?' Tears were running down her cheeks now. 'Björn must have suggested it. Dad and Björn. I knew they liked each other; they used to meet up at the Kaffivagninn sometimes. But I had no idea what they were talking about. None.'

Magnus tried to give her a comforting smile. He did feel sorry for her. The two people she loved most in the world had turned out to be murderers. And she had had no warning.

She tried to smile back. 'You know,' she said, wiping her cheeks, 'from what Björn was saying, I'm not sure my father, or whoever, is going to shoot someone.'

'What do you mean?' Magnus asked.

'Björn was vague about the timing. Yet he was expecting a text when everything was ready. What did he mean by "ready"?'

'I get you,' said Magnus. He followed Harpa's idea through. It could be that there was someone else. Unlikely but possible. Or Einar could have found a spot where he was watching a target and waiting for the ideal time to shoot. In which case, why would he go back home?

What threat was there that would apply while a killer was safe and sound in his own living room?

Poison? No. A bomb?

A bomb.

If there was a bomb primed and ready somewhere in Reykjavík they really were in trouble. They had no clue which of the Outvaders was the intended victim.

Magnus had an idea. He called Páll, but no reply. Which meant he must still be by the hut, out of reception. With the help of one of the uniformed constables he got hold of him on the police radio.

'Páll, where are you?'

'Securing the scene.'

That made sense. The hillside was the scene of a murder, after all.

'Can you check the hut? See if there's a notebook or anything.'

'Shouldn't I wait for forensics?'

'No, do it now. We know who killed Björn. We need to know who the next target is.'

Páll hesitated. 'OK.'

'Let me know what you find.'

The car pulled into the car park outside the police station on the edge of Stykkishólmur. Magnus let the others go ahead and waited in the car for the call back. Four minutes, maybe five. He was feeling nauseous. It was a sensation he remembered from football games in high school. The after-effects of concussion.

His phone rang.

'OK. I checked the hut. There are no notes anywhere.'

'Nothing? Not a laptop?'

'No. There's a book, that's all. Looks like he was reading it.'

Magnus was disappointed. 'OK. What's the book?'

'*Independent People* by Halldór Laxness.'

'That figures,' said Magnus. He sighed. 'All right, Páll. Can you do one more thing? Einar might have sent Björn a text, in which case he probably hasn't received it yet. Can you get his phone and go back up the pass until you get reception?'

'Roger.'

Independent People. Magnus remembered the painting of Bjartur in Sindri's apartment. Sindri had obviously encouraged Björn to read the book too. It was a shame that such a good book could be used to justify such twisted ideas.

Magnus had read it when he was about eighteen. He probably hadn't appreciated it then, he should reread it.

His phone rang. It was Árni, not Páll.

'What's up? Have they got Einar yet?' Magnus asked.

'Not yet. They're waiting for the Viking Squad.'

'How long will that take?'

'Don't know,' said Árni. 'I've been ordered back to headquarters. Did you find Björn?'

'I did. I'll explain later,' he said. 'I've got to go now, I'm expecting a call.' He cut Árni off.

Páll came back on the radio.

'Got the text. It was from Einar. One word. "Ready."'

'Thanks,' said Magnus. He got out of the police car, his brain racing. So Einar was ready. But ready for who? Who the hell was the next victim?

Wait a moment.

Independent People. Wasn't one of the characters in the book called Ingólfur Arnarson? Yes, that was right.

Who was he? The son of the local landowner Bjartur had worked for? Something like that. Magnus strained to remember. The boy had been named after the first settler of Iceland by his mother, who was a nationalist and a bit of an intellectual snob.

Sindri was talking about the character in Halldór Laxness's book, not the man who had landed in Reykjavík a thousand years ago.

OK, so which of the Outvaders was he? Magnus couldn't remember much about Laxness's Ingólfur Arnarson, except that he became rich.

He needed to find out quickly. Who would know?

Ingileif. It was one of her favourite books.

He took a deep breath and dialled her number.

She answered quickly. 'Hi, Magnús.' Her voice was flat. Not pleased to hear from him.

'Ingólfur Arnarson,' Magnus said. 'I know who he is. Or at least which character. He's the man in *Independent People.* The landowner's son.'

'Oh, yes,' said Ingileif. 'That makes sense, I suppose.'

'I don't remember the book well. How can we figure out which one of the businessmen he represents?'

'Well, I'm not sure he represents any of them,' Ingileif said.

'What do you mean? He must do. He was very rich, wasn't he? Didn't he buy a new car or something? The first in the region?'

'Yes, he was rich. But he was involved with the Cooperative movement. That's where he got all his influence. Hardly a greedy capitalist, in fact the merchants were his rivals. He put them out of business. Then he went off to Reykjavík.' There was silence on the phone.

'Ingileif?'

'Oh, my God. I know who they mean!'

'Who?'

'In Reykjavík Ingólfur Arnarson became a director of the National Bank, and then its governor. And then Prime Minister.'

'Ólafur Tómasson!' The Prime Minister until the pots-and-pans revolution. The former leader of the Independence Party. And one-time governor of the Central Bank.

'That's right,' said Ingileif. 'But, Magnús?'

'Yes?'

'Can you wait a moment? Just a minute. I need to talk to you. I think I *will* go to Hamburg. I'm just about to call Svala now.'

'Look, I'm sorry, Ingileif, we'll have to discuss this later,' said Magnus. 'I've got to go.'

For a second he wondered whether he had made a mistake cutting her off like that.

Then he called Baldur.

He outlined his fear. That the next victim was Ólafur Tómasson and the means could be a bomb.

'Are you sure?' Baldur asked.

'Of course I'm not sure,' said Magnus. 'But you need to tell him to be careful. Does he have protection?'

'He did until two months ago. Then we pulled it. Cost savings.'

'Well, you had better get it back, pronto,' said Magnus and hung up.

He was standing alone in the car park. The Stykkishólmur police station was a more substantial building than its Grundarfjördur counterpart, as befitted a regional headquarters. A small white concrete office block, shared with the district court.

He hesitated before entering. There was nothing more he could do, was there? He would have to rely on Baldur to get the message out. That might take several minutes, even longer if there were approvals to go through, people to talk to, decisions to be dithered over. Maybe they would decide once again that Magnus was operating on no more than a hunch.

Magnus remembered that the former Prime Minister lived in one of the houses on the shore of the Tjörnin, the bird-strewn lake right in the heart of Reykjavík. If Árni was driving from Seltjarnarnes to police HQ, he was right there.

Magnus called him.

'Árni, where are you right now?'

'On the Hringbraut, just coming up to the university.'

That was just a few hundred metres from the Tjörnin.

'OK. Listen closely and do exactly as I say.'

'Go ahead.'

'You know where Ólafur Tómasson lives?'

'Yes.'

'All right. We believe he is the next victim. Probably from a bomb. I want you to go to his house and get him and his family out of there. Don't let him touch any packages and above all don't let him get in his car. You got that?'

'Are you sure about this, Magnús? He's an important guy.'

'Which is why they want to blow him up.'

'I'm on my way,' said Árni.

Good man, thought Magnus. Ólafur was famously irascible, especially since he had been forced out of office, and he wouldn't take kindly to being pushed around by a skinny detective.

Tough.

*

Blue light again.

Árni put his foot down on the accelerator, swerved round the roundabout in front of the university and in less than a minute was speeding along the road on the edge of the Tjörnin. The houses along the lake were some of Reykjavík's most majestic, and Ólafur Tómasson's was at the northern end near the City Hall.

As he neared the house he could see the familiar tall, gaunt figure of the man himself. He was standing by the door of his Mercedes. Opening it. Getting in.

Árni leaned on his horn. But that might not be enough to prevent Ólafur from turning on the ignition.

Ólafur's car was parked in the driveway outside his house, facing downhill towards the road and the lake. Árni had to do something in the next couple of seconds that would persuade Ólafur not to insert his keys in the ignition, but to get out of his car.

There was a blonde woman pushing a buggy along the pavement by the lake, pointing at the ducks. Blaring the horn all the while, Árni swerved and aimed straight at her. He saw, rather than heard her scream. At the last second he changed direction and hit a tree. The airbag exploded and smashed into his face.

He heard the mother's screams and the sound of shouting and running feet.

He opened his car door, extricated himself from the airbag and staggered out on to the pavement.

'What the hell do you think you were doing driving that fast?'

Árni turned to see the angry face of the former Prime Minister of Iceland yelling at him.

He smiled.

CHAPTER FORTY-ONE

THERE WAS A bomb under Ólafur's car. Árni checked it himself, crawling under the chassis. Probably a dumb move, but he had to do something to shut up his former Prime Minister. The Explosive Ordnance Disposal Unit from the coastguard was called in. More used to dealing with unexploded mines from the Second World War, it took them a while to locate their two experts who were trained to deal with car bombs. One was on holiday, and the other one turned out to be in one of the hot tubs at the Laugardalur pool.

In the end the expert played it safe and went for a controlled explosion. Wrought havoc with the ex-Prime Minister's garden, and scared the wits out of the little girl next door.

The Viking Squad, when it eventually assembled, burst into Harpa's parents' house and arrested Einar watching the golf on TV. A forensics team was poring over his garage looking for signs of bomb-making, and finding them.

In Stykkishólmur police station, Magnus prepared to drive back to Reykjavík. Before he left he brought a cup of coffee in to the interview room where Harpa was waiting. The plan was to drive her down to Reykjavík where she would be formally interviewed at police headquarters. Uniformed officers would escort her.

'Thanks,' Harpa said, accepting the coffee.

'And thank you for stopping Ísak. I meant to ask you, how did you get down there so fast?'

'Jumped. Just like you.' She smiled. 'I seemed to do myself less damage, though. How is Ísak? Is he going to live?'

'He's in intensive care in hospital. They are keeping him unconscious and giving him drugs to prevent the brain swelling, apparently. They can't be sure, but the chances are good that he will make a full recovery. Unfortunately.'

'You say that, Magnús, but I'm glad. I don't want to have anyone else's death on my conscience.'

Magnus was going to argue with her, but stopped himself. He sipped his coffee.

'What happens now?' Harpa asked. 'Do I go to jail?'

'Probably,' said Magnus. 'You may be lucky, with a good lawyer. This is Iceland, not Texas.'

'I'm not sure I can face it.'

'You've had a tough time,' said Magnus. 'A really tough time. Most other people would have cracked long ago.'

Harpa smiled, weakly. 'I think I'm not far off it.'

'I'm sure you're not. Just think of Markús. Keep on thinking of Markús. Hold it together for his sake.'

'Yeah,' said Harpa. 'Yeah.'

Magnus drained his cup. 'Despite everything, he's lucky to have you as his mother. If you hold it together, he'll grow up into a fine boy. I'm sure he will.'

Harpa struggled to control her tears. 'Thanks,' she mouthed so quietly Magnus could barely hear it.

The sun was sinking slowly towards the western ocean, brushing the broad shoulder of Bjarnarhöfn Fell as it dropped. Magnus was glad to be alone as he started the drive back to Reykjavík, savouring the two hour interlude between the hubbub of Stykkishólmur police station and police headquarters.

His phone rang. Magnus didn't recognize the number, and almost didn't answer. After the third ring he decided he had better pick it up.

'Magnús.'

'Hello, Magnús, it's Snorri here.'

Magnus felt himself straightening in the driver's seat. The Big Salmon himself.

'Hello, Snorri.'

'I'm calling to apologize. You were right all along. We should have listened to you.'

'It was a difficult call,' Magnus said. 'I never had the evidence.'

'It was a good call. I guess that's why we have you here. And why we want you to stay.'

'Thank you,' said Magnus. 'And Snorri?'

'Yes.'

'Remember these guys are criminals, not terrorists.'

Snorri laughed. 'I'll remember that. I'll just have to convince everyone else of it.'

Magnus smiled as he disconnected the phone. The apology was appreciated. Policemen didn't like to apologize, in his experience, especially important ones.

He was staying in Iceland. So be it.

But what about Ingileif? She would have called Svala by now. Taken her decision. Perhaps he should have stayed on the phone with her just a minute longer. Told her to wait, at least until he had warned Ólafur Tómasson.

But he hadn't.

Too late.

Or was it? He didn't want her to go. Sure, it was up to her what she did with her life. Sure, Germany was a good opportunity. Perhaps she really did need to get away from him and from Iceland. But he didn't want her to go.

He picked up his phone. Selected her number. And waited.

She didn't answer. She could probably see it was him calling, but she chose not to pick up.

Her message kicked in. It was good to hear her voice. The pause for him to leave his message was long. Profound. Unbreakable.

He hung up.

The fell at Bjarnarhöfn was coming closer, as was the Berserkjahraun. He felt a wave of nausea sweep over him. The damned concussion.

He pulled over to the side of the road and got out of the car. He stood up straight and took some deep breaths. The fresh air in Iceland is really fresh. The breeze thrust oxygen into his lungs and tingled his pale cheeks.

After a couple of minutes he felt much better. As he climbed back into the car, he noticed the pathologist's report into the Benedikt Jóhannesson case lying on the back seat.

He left the driver's door open and began to leaf through it. He was confident there would be nothing there that hadn't been referred to in the rest of the file, but you never knew.

You never knew.

It was right there, up front, under *Cause of Death*. Something that he, and only he, would find significant.

Benedikt had been stabbed once in the back and twice in the chest, by a killer who was probably right handed.

On a July day eleven years later, Magnus's father had answered the door of the house he was renting for the summer in Duxbury. Let someone in. Turned away from him. Had been stabbed in the back, and then stabbed again twice in the chest. And died. The killer was right-handed.

Same MO. Same killer. No doubt about it.

It never ceased to amaze Magnus how criminals stuck to the same modus operandi, whether they be small-time car thieves, or the most cunning serial killers. There was something about the routine, the familiarity of doing things exactly the same way they had been done before, which seemed to help them deal with situations of maximum stress.

He could imagine the killer, whoever he was, ringing the bell at the house in Duxbury, wearing gloves, greeting his father and entering the hallway. Perhaps he always planned to wait until his father turned his back on him, just as Benedikt had done ten years before. Then he would stab him once, and finish him off with two more stabs to the heart. It had worked before. It would work again.

There was only one man Magnus could think of who was linked to both Benedikt and to Ragnar.

Hallgrímur. Magnus's grandfather, Ragnar's father-in-law and Benedikt's childhood playmate. And the man who lived at the farm just across the lava field in front of him.

Magnus knew that the police investigation hadn't touched his grandfather. Why should it, when Benedikt had moved to Reykjavík decades before his death?

Magnus tried to remember if his grandfather was right- or left-handed. He couldn't visualize him writing, but he could remember being hit. The old man had favoured his left fist, he was pretty sure. But there was a more obvious problem. The USCIS had confirmed that Hallgrímur had not visited the States in the summer of 1996. More importantly, Hallgrímur didn't even have a passport.

So where was Hallgrímur on 28 December 1985, the afternoon Benedikt was murdered?

That would have been Magnus's second Christmas at Bjarnarhöfn. The time when Sibba and his uncle and aunt had visited from Canada. But Magnus couldn't possibly remember his grandfather's every movement that December.

There was a definite pattern. A family feud, fit for the *Saga of the People of Eyri*, starting with the death of Jóhannes, Benedikt's father in the 1930s, moving on to Gunnar plunging off a cliff in the 1940s, and then to the stabbing of Benedikt in the 1980s. Could Ragnar's death in the 1990s somehow be connected to this feud? Magnus couldn't see how. Yet.

He looked up from the report, over the lava field to the white buildings around the farm, and the darker dot of the church.

If he was going to stay in Iceland, what would he do about Bjarnarhöfn? Would he continue to run away from it? Or would he face up to it?

Anger swept through him. The tension of the previous few days overwhelmed him. Ingileif, his grandfather, the hunt for the killers of Óskar Gunnarsson, the stabbing of Björn, his own escape from death.

He took a decision. He didn't want to think about it: it was something he had to do while he had the anger to see it through.

He put his foot down and sped through the lava field, turning off on the road to the farm.

He passed the hollow where the two berserkers were buried and in a moment he was approaching the familiar cluster of buildings. It should have been a beautiful spot, the imposing fell with the waterfall pouring down its flanks, the little wooden church, the sun setting in pink streaks on the ocean.

But Magnus could feel a heavy blanket of dread descending upon him.

He didn't want to run into his uncle Kolbeinn. He remembered Sibba saying that their grandfather no longer lived in the main farmhouse, so Magnus drew up outside one of the two smaller houses.

He got up out of the car. Through the window he could see a man bent over a newspaper in a sitting room. His face was obscured as he worked at the crossword, but Magnus could see it was an old man. And he could see he was holding his pen in his left hand.

He rang on the bell. Then he knocked. Loudly.

'All right, all right!' He heard the familiar voice, gruff but perhaps a touch frailer than he remembered. 'Give a man a chance. Patience! Patience!'

Magnus knocked louder.

The door was opened by an old man in a green shirt. His face was wrinkled with the erosion of a thousand gales. The corners of his mouth pointed downwards. His small blue eyes burned angrily.

'Magnús?'

'That's right.'

'Didn't I see you here a couple of days ago?'

'You did.'

'Well, what are you doing here?'

'I've come to give you a message.'

'And what makes you think I wish to hear it?'

The man might be in his eighties, but Magnus felt his power. He was struggling to control the situation, the conversation, Magnus himself. Magnus could almost feel himself shrinking, back to the proud but scared twelve-year-old he used to be.

'I don't know how my father died. And I don't know how Benedikt Jóhannesson died. But I do know you had something to do with both their deaths. And I am going to find out what.'

'Is that your message?'

'No, my message is don't die before I do find out. Because you are going to pay, old man. I am going to make sure you pay.'

Hallgrímur's face reddened as he puffed out his chest. 'Who the devil do you think you are?'

Magnus wasn't listening. He spun on his heel, jumped into his Range Rover and turned it around to face Reykjavík.

He *would* be back.

AUTHOR'S NOTE

Icelanders like to say that the people who bankrupted their country number no more than thirty. Óskar Gunnarsson is intended to represent one of these thirty, but not any specific individual.

Similarly, the characters in the book who held prominent political positions, such as Prime Minister of Iceland or the British Chancellor of the Exchequer during the crisis, do not represent the individuals who held those positions in reality. And indeed any similarity between other characters and real people is coincidental.

I should like to thank a number of people for their help. Nic Cheetham and Pétur Már Ólafsson my British and Icelandic editors, Oliver Munson my agent, Richenda Todd, Liz Hatherell, Tom Bernard, Toby Wyles, Karl Steinar Valsson, Anna Margrét Gudjónsdóttir, Sigrún Lilja Gudbjartsdóttir, Ármann Thorvaldsson, Ída Margrét Jósepsdóttir, Alda Sigmundsdóttir, and Lara Gillies. It is a challenge, but an enjoyable one, to write about a country which is not your own. If there are any errors, they are all mine.

Lastly, I should like to thank my wife Barbara and my children for their patience, support and encouragement.